Jackie Collins

Dangerous kiss

PAN BOOKS

First published 1999 by Macmillan

First published in paperback 2000 by Pan Books

This edition published 2007 by Pan Books
an imprint of Pan Macmillan Ltd
Pan Macmillan, 20 New Wharf Road, London N1 9RR
Basingstoke and Oxford
Associated companies throughout the world
www.panmacmillan.com

ISBN 978-0-330-51851-2

A CIP catalogue record for this book is available from
the British Library.

Typeset by SetSystems Ltd, Saffron Walden, Essex
Printed and bound in the UK by
CPI Mackays, Chatham ME5 8TD

Dangerous Kiss

Books by Jackie Collins

Acknowledgements

I would like to thank the wonderful team at Macmillan for their dedication and enthusiasm every time they publish one of my books. I would particularly like to thank all the sales force and the great group of people I get to work with:

Ian S. Chapman, Arabella Stein, Clare Harington, Elizabeth Bond, Katie Roberts, Nadya Kooznetzoff, Morven Knowles, Jacqui Graham, Chris Gibson, Annie Griffiths, Mark Richmond, Liz Davis, Tess Tattersall, Matt Smith, Neil Lang, Annika Roojun, Fiona Carpenter, Lucy Hale, Vivienne Nelson, Michael Halden, Julie Wright, Dan Ruffino, Jeannine Fowler, Andrew Wright, David Adamson, Fiona Killeen, Gabrielle Dawwas, John Lee, John Neild, John Talbot, Kate Hales, Keith Southgate, Keren Western, Norman Taylor, Phil Trump, Robert Ferrari, Sally Ferrari, Steve Shrubsole, William Taylor Gill, Kay Charlton, Ray Theobald, Alison Muirden, Karen Schoenemann and Ray Fidler.

I would also like to thank Andrew Nurnberg and everyone at Andrew Nurnberg Associates for selling my books worldwide with such class and style:

Beryl Cutayar, Paola Marchese, Vicky Mark and Christine Regan.

Jackie
xx

P.S. And a big thank-you to my loyal and dedicated readers.

BOOK ONE

Los Angeles

1

'**Take it!**' *the young white girl urged, thrusting the gun at the sixteen-year-old black youth, who immediately backed away.*

'No!' *he said fervently.* 'My old man would bust my ass.'

The girl, clad in a mini-skirt and tight tank top, had long legs, a big bosom, a pointed face, hazel eyes heavily outlined in black, and unevenly cropped dark hair. She stared at the boy scornfully. 'Chicken!' *she jeered, in a scathing voice.* 'Daddy's little baby chickee boy.'

'No way!' *he grumbled, pissed that she would talk to him that way. He was tall and gangly with large ears that stuck out, and big brown eyes.*

'Oh, yes,' *she taunted.* 'Way!'

On impulse he snatched the gun out of her hands, sticking it down the front of his pants with a macho grunt. 'Satisfied?'

The girl nodded, hazel eyes gleaming. She was eighteen, but looked older. 'Let's go,' *she said authoritatively. It was obvious who was in charge.*

'Go like where?' *he asked, wishing she could be a bit nicer. She was always so short with him.*

'To have a blast,' *she answered airily.* 'Y'know, cruise around, get shit-faced. We'll take your car.'

His father had recently bought him a black jeep for his sixteenth birthday. It was also a present to celebrate their return to LA after a year and a half of living in New York.

'I dunno . . .' *he said hesitantly, remembering that tonight he was supposed to have an early dinner with his dad, but thinking that the idea of getting shit-faced with her seemed much more appealing.* 'An' why we need a gun?' *he added.*

The girl didn't answer, she simply made chicken noises as she sauntered towards the door.

The boy followed, his eyes glued to her legs. He had a hard-on, and he knew that if he played it right, tonight might be the night he scored.

2

Lucky Santangelo Golden stood up behind her enormous art-deco desk in her office at Panther Studios, then she stretched and yawned. It had been a long hard day, and she was beyond tired. However, the day was not over yet because tonight she was being honoured at the Beverly Hilton Hotel for her work towards raising money for AIDS research.

As owner and head of Panther Studios, Lucky was in an extremely high-profile position, so she had no choice but to accept the limelight gracefully.

The problem was that she was not looking forward to being the centre of attention. It wasn't as if she'd *asked* to be honoured – the evening had been thrust upon her, making it impossible to refuse.

She reached for a candy bar, nibbled hungrily on the sweet chocolate. *Nothing like a sugar rush to get me through the next few hours*, she thought ruefully. Michael Caine's famous Holly-wood quote kept running through her head: 'In a town with no honour, how come everyone's always being honoured?' *Yeah, right on, Michael!* she thought, with a wry grin. *But how does one avoid it?*

Lucky was a slender, long-limbed woman with an abundance of shoulder-length jet curls, dangerous black-opal eyes, full, sensual lips and a deep olive skin. Hers was an exotic beauty mixed with a fierce intelligence. A brilliant business-woman, she'd been running Panther Studios for eight years, making it one of the most respected and successful studios in Hollywood. Lucky had a knack for greenlighting all the right movies and picking up others for distribution, which always did well. 'You're Lucky in more ways than one,' Lennie was forever telling her. 'You can do anything.'

Lennie Golden, her husband. Whenever she thought about him her face brightened. Lennie was the love of her life. Tall, sexy, funny – yet, most of all, he was her soulmate, and she planned on staying with him for ever, because they were truly destined to be together and after two previous marriages she was finally totally happy. Lennie and their children – seven-year-old Gino, named after her father, and adorable eight-year-old Maria – satisfied her completely.

And then there was her fifteen-year-old son Bobby from her marriage to the late shipping magnate Dimitri Stanislopoulos. Bobby was so handsome and adult-looking – over six feet tall and extremely athletic. And there was Bobby's niece, Brigette, whom Lucky considered her godchild. Brigette lived in New York where she was a supermodel. Not that she needed the money because she was one of the richest young women in the world, having inherited a Greek shipping fortune from her grandfather, Dimitri, and her mother, Olympia, who'd died tragically of a drug overdose.

Tonight, Steven Berkeley, Lucky's half-brother, was picking Lucky up, because Lennie was on location downtown, directing Steven's wife, Mary Lou, in a romantic comedy. Lennie had once been an extremely successful comedian and movie star, but since his kidnapping ordeal several years ago he'd given up performing in front of the camera. Now he concentrated solely on writing and directing.

The movie he was shooting with Mary Lou – a talented and successful actress – was not for Panther. Both he and Lucky had decided not to provide any opportunity for snide rumours of nepotism. 'If I'm doing this, I'll do it on my own,' he'd said. And, of course, he'd succeeded, just as she'd known he would.

Tonight she was going to make an announcement at the end of her speech – an announcement that would blow everyone away. She hadn't even told Lennie about it – he would be as surprised as everyone else and, she hoped, pleased. Only her father, Gino, knew what she was planning to say. Feisty old Gino, eighty-seven now, but still a man to be looked up to and admired.

Lucky adored Gino with a fierce passion; they'd been through so much together – including many years when they hadn't spoken at all. Now their closeness was legendary, and Lucky always went to him first when it came to making decisions. Gino was the smartest man she knew, although she hadn't always felt that way about him.

Oh, God! What a checkered past they shared – from the time he'd married her off to a senator's son when she was barely sixteen, to the years they hadn't spoken while he was out of America as a tax exile and she'd taken over his Las Vegas hotel empire.

Gino Santangelo was a self-made man who had power, charisma, and quite a way with women. Women adored Gino, they always had. Even now he still knew how to charm and flatter. Lucky remembered her adopted uncle, Costa, telling her all about the infamous Gino when he was a young man. 'His nickname was Gino the Ram,' Costa had confided, with an envious chuckle. 'That's 'cause he could have any woman he wanted, an' did. That is, until he met your dear mother, God rest her soul.'

Maria. Her mother. So beautiful and pure. Taken from her when she was a child. Brutally murdered by the Bonnatti family.

Lucky would never forget the day she'd run downstairs to find her mother floating on a raft in the family swimming-pool. She was five years old, and the memory had stayed with her for ever – as vivid as the day it happened. She'd sat by the side of the pool staring at her exquisite mother, spread-eagled on the raft in the centre of the pool. 'Mama,' she'd murmured quietly. And then her voice had risen to a scream, as she'd realized her mother was no longer with her. 'MAMA! MAMA! MAMA!'

Discovering her mother's body at such a young age had coloured her entire life. After the tragedy, Gino had become so protective of her and her brother, Dario, that living at home in Bel Air was like being shut away in a maximum security prison. When she'd finally been sent abroad to a boarding-school in Switzerland, she'd immediately rebelled and turned into a wild child, running away with her best friend, Olympia Stanislopoulos, to a villa in the South of France where they'd wreaked havoc and partied non-stop. Oh, yes, those were crazy times. Her first taste of freedom, and she'd lived every minute of it, until a sour-faced Gino had tracked her down. Shortly after that he'd decided she would be better off married than careening around on the loose. So he'd made a deal with Senator Peter Richmond to marry her off to his son, the extraordinarily unsexy Craven. What a trap *that* had turned out to be.

When she thought about it, Lucky realized that her life had

been a series of incredible highs and lows. The highs were so utterly amazing: her three beautiful, healthy children; her marriage to Lennie; the success of running a major Hollywood studio; not to mention her earlier achievements in Vegas and Atlantic City where she'd built hotels.

The lows were too dreadful to contemplate. First, the murder of her mother, then the brutal killing of her brother, Dario, and her beloved Marco getting shot in Las Vegas. Three devastating tragedies, for which she'd extracted her own form of revenge.

But she had survived. Gino had taught her that survival was everything, and she'd learned the lesson well.

The intercom on her desk buzzed, and her assistant informed her that Venus Maria was on the line. She hurried to pick up. Not only was Venus Maria an adored and controversial superstar, she was also Lucky's best girlfriend.

'What's up?' Lucky asked, flopping down in the leather chair behind her desk.

'Good question,' Venus replied. 'Here's the major problem – I have nothing to wear tonight.'

'*Boring.*'

'I know you're not into fashion like I am, but I'll be photographed from here to Puerto Rico, and you *know* I can't look ordinary.'

Lucky laughed: Venus was such a drama queen. 'You? Ordinary? *Never!*'

'Nobody understands,' Venus grumbled. 'The expectations are enormous.'

'*What* expectations?' Lucky asked, picking up a pen and doodling on a pad.

'I'm a superstar, dear,' Venus announced, tongue in cheek. 'A superstar who's supposed to alter her look daily. I mean – for Chrissake – how many times can I change the colour of my hair?'

'What colour is it now?'

'Platinum.'

'Then wear a black wig. Clone me – we can go as twins.'

'You're no help,' Venus wailed. 'I need assistance.'

The *last* thing Venus needed was assistance. She was one of the most together and talented women Lucky had ever met. At thirty-three, Venus was not only a major movie star, she was also a video and recording superstar, with legions of fans who worshipped her every move. Everything she did still made headlines, even though she'd been doing it for over a decade.

Several years ago she'd married Cooper Turner, the ageing but still extremely attractive movie star. After a shaky start, their marriage had taken, and they now had a five-year-old daughter named Chyna. In addition to the joy of a daughter, Venus Maria's career was going great. Ever since being Oscar-nominated for her cameo role in Alex Woods's *Gangsters*, she'd been able to pick and choose her roles.

'It's not that simple,' Lucky had replied. 'You have to keep trying. Pick a goal and go for it.'

'I guess that's what *you* did,' Venus had said. 'I mean, considering you started off with a father who hated you and—'

'Gino *never* hated me,' Lucky had interrupted.

'Well, you told me he always put you down 'cause you were a woman and he wanted his son to run his empire, right?'

'Ah, yes,' Lucky had said. 'But I soon changed his mind.'

'That's it,' Venus had said. 'You *got* what you wanted. Now I'm going for what *I* want.'

Lucky listened as Venus carried on about what her look for the evening ahead should be. She knew that her friend already had her entire outfit planned, but Venus liked affirmation.

'And what are *you* wearing?' Venus asked, when she finally stopped talking about herself.

'Valentino,' Lucky said. 'Red. It's Lennie's favourite colour on me.'

'Hmm . . .' Venus said. 'Sounds sexy.' A pause. Then – 'Is Alex coming?'

'Of course,' Lucky said matter-of-factly. 'We're all sitting together.'

Venus couldn't keep the purr out of her voice. 'How does Lennie feel about *that*?'

'Will you get off it?' Lucky said, irritated that Venus was always trying to make a big deal out of her and Alex when there was absolutely nothing going on. 'You *know* Alex and Lennie are good friends.'

'Yes, but—'

'No buts,' Lucky interrupted briskly. 'Take your fertile imagination and go write another song!'

As soon as she hung up, she opened her desk drawer and took out the scribbled speech she planned on giving. She studied it for a few minutes, changing a word or two.

One final read-through and she was satisfied.

Tonight she was going to shock the socks off everyone in Hollywood.

But, hey – shocking people – wasn't that what her life was all about?

3

'**Fantastic! Unbelievable!** More! More! Give me the lips! Those delectable lips!' Fredo Carbanado crooned encouragement, his expressive Italian eyes flashing signals of deep lust as they appeared above his camera. 'I get off on those luscious lips. More! *Bellissima!* More!'

Brigette moved her body sensuously in front of the camera, giving him the exact poses he wanted. She was blonde and curvaceous, with luminous peaches-and-cream skin, enormous blue eyes fringed with the longest lashes, and full pouty lips. Devastatingly pretty and sexy in a child-woman way, her huge appeal had to do with a distinct air of vulnerability.

'Can it, Fredo,' she scolded, adjusting the top of her revealing coffee-coloured lace slip. 'How many times must I tell you? I do *not* need to hear the riff. Save it for some new little bimbette who'll get off on your phoney bullshit.'

Fredo frowned, forever puzzled that Brigette didn't fall for him like all the other models.

'Brigette!' he said sadly, lowering his camera and pulling a disappointed face. 'Why you always so *mean*?'

'I'm not mean,' she retorted. 'Merely honest.'

'No, you *mean*,' Fredo said, scowling. 'Mean and ornery.'

'Thanks!' she said tartly.

'But, Fredo, he knows what you need,' the Italian photographer said, nodding knowingly.

'And what might that be?'

'A man!' Fredo announced triumphantly.

'Ha!' Brigette said, shifting her provocative pose. 'What makes you think I'm into *men*? Maybe *women* do it for me.'

'Hallelujah!' exclaimed Fanny, her black lesbian makeup artist, stepping forward. 'I'm here! All ya gotta do is *say* the word!'

Brigette giggled. 'Just f–ing with Mr Charm,' she said sweetly.

'As if I didn't know,' Fanny retorted, touching up Brigette's full lips with a sable brush. 'You have *no* idea *what* you are missin'. Women got it goin', girl!'

'Can we turn up the music,' Brigette requested. 'I so *love* Montell Jordan.'

'Who doesn't?' said Fanny. 'If I was ever considering changin' tracks, *that*'d be the man who'd do it for me!'

'And if *I* made a switch,' Brigette retorted, toying with all of them, 'I'd definitely go for k.d. lang. Saw her at a benefit last week, she has, like, this *insane* sexual aura. It's almost as if she's Elvis or something.'

'Dyke alert!' screeched Masters, her hair stylist, a skeletal man dressed in a one-piece yellow jumpsuit with spiked hair to match.

'Get *out*!' said Brigette, giggling again.

She loved the camaraderie of working on a shoot. These people were her family – even if Fredo *was* the lech of all time. He was a star photographer, and for that reason she would never dream of succumbing to his somewhat suspect charms, because Fredo could have anyone – and usually did. He went through models at an alarming rate, loving and leaving them like a regular Don Juan.

Brigette watched him as he danced around behind his camera. Fredo missed being handsome on account of an exceptionally large nose, small eyes and alarmingly bushy eyebrows. He was also very short, which didn't seem to faze him because most of his conquests towered over him. Her best friend, Lina, had given her a strong warning. 'Stay away from Fredo,' Lina had said, rolling her saffron-coloured eyes in a knowing fashion. 'That boy fucks an' tells. *And* in spite of all 'is boastin', 'e's got a tiny little dick! So, girlfriend, you do *not* wanna go there.'

Lina was an incredibly exotic-looking black girl from the East End of London. At twenty-six she was a year older than

Brigette, but in spite of their very different backgrounds, over the last eighteen months they had become good friends. Brigette had recently purchased an apartment in Lina's building, so now they were neighbours on Central Park South.

The fashion industry regarded them as supermodels. The very word 'supermodel' sent them both into paroxysms of uncontrollable laughter.

'Supermodel, my arse!' Lina would exclaim. 'They should catch me in the mornin' with me curlers in! *Not* a pretty sight!'

'I can vouch for that,' Brigette would reply.

Lina's turn. 'An' 'ow about *you* with no makeup? You look like a bloody albino caught in some bloke's headlights!'

Unlike Brigette, Lina went through men at an alarming rate. Rock stars were her favourites, but she wasn't averse to any man as long as he was extremely rich and bought her lavish presents. Lina *loved* receiving presents.

The other thing she loved was trying to fix Brigette up, but Brigette shied away from all involvements. She had a checkered history with men – as far as she was concerned they were all trouble. First boyfriend, young actor Tim Wealth. She'd been an innocent teenager with a crush; he'd been an ambitious man with an agenda. And he'd gotten himself beaten up and murdered – all because of his connection to her.

Next there was the frightening encounter with the Santangelos' arch enemy, Santino Bonnatti, who'd tried to sexually molest both her and her uncle, Bobby, when they were both kids. She'd shot Santino with his own gun. Lucky had tried to take the blame, but Brigette had made sure the truth came out. The judge had pronounced it a clear case of self-defence, and ordered her to check in with a probation officer once a month for a year. After that it was over.

Then there was Paul Webster. She'd had a crush on Paul for a long time, right up until she got engaged to the wealthy son of one of her grandfather's business rivals. When Paul finally came running, she'd decided a career was more important than any man, so she'd broken her engagement and concentrated on making it as a model. Unfortunately, one of the first people she'd hooked up with in the modelling world was Michel Guy, a top agent who'd turned out to be a sick pervert, forcing her to perform scenes with other girls, then blackmailing her with the photos. Once again Lucky had come to her rescue. Brigette loved and admired Lucky. She was her self-appointed godmother and a true friend.

Since her disastrous experience with Michel Guy, Brigette had put men on the back burner, suspicious of their intent. And, apart from a brief affair with fellow model Isaac, that was it as far as involvements were concerned.

'Doncha miss *sex*?' Lina was forever demanding, after another night of passion with one of her retinue of ardent – sometimes married – rock stars.

'Not at all,' was Brigette's airy reply. 'I'm waiting for the right guy, *then* I'll make up for it.'

Truth was she was wary of any serious involvement. To her, men spelled disaster and danger.

Occasionally she dated. Not that she enjoyed the dating game – it was always the same dance. Dinner at a hot new restaurant; drinks at a happening new club; the inevitable grope; and then, as soon as they moved in for the kill, *she* moved on.

Safe and never sorry, Brigette had found it was the only way to go.

'What you and Lina do tonight?' Fredo asked, snapping away.

'Why?' Brigette retorted, changing poses as fast as he clicked his shutter.

' 'Cause I got a cousin—' he began.

'No!' she interrupted firmly.

'From England.'

She raised an eyebrow. 'An *English* cousin?'

'Carlo's Italian, like me. He work in London.'

'And *you* promised to fix him up with a couple of hot young models, right?'

'It's not like that, *cara*.'

'I bet!'

'Carlo is engaged.'

'Even better,' Brigette said, shaking her head vigorously. 'Last fling before the wedding. I think not.'

'So suspicious,' Fredo grumbled. 'I thought we could have nice dinner, the four of us. Just friends.'

'The only thing *you*'re just friends with is your cat,' Brigette said tartly. 'And there's been rumours about *that* . . .'

Fanny and Masters, listening on the sidelines, shrieked

with laughter. They loved seeing Fredo rejected, it was *so* unusual.

Later, when the photo session was finished and Brigette was on her way out of his studio, Fredo stopped her by the door. 'Please!' he wailed. 'I *must* impress my cousin. He's what you Americans call a prick.'

'Wonderful!' Brigette said crisply. 'Now you want us to have dinner with a *nasty* guy. This is getting better every minute.'

'Brigette,' Fredo pleaded, 'for me. It make me look good. One big favour.'

She sighed. Suddenly Fredo the ladykiller appeared needy, and since she was a sucker for anyone in trouble, she immediately felt sorry for him. 'Okay, I'll ask Lina,' she said, sure that Lina had a date with bigger and better, while *she* had a date with a double cheese pizza and an *Absolutely Fabulous* marathon on the Comedy channel.

Fredo kissed her hand. He was still so Italian, in spite of having lived in America for many years. 'You are special woman,' he crooned. 'My little American rose.'

'I'm not *your* anything,' she retorted crisply, and quickly skipped out of the studio.

☆

'Don't!' commanded Lina.

'What?' said Flick Fonda, a married rock star with a penchant for gorgeous black women.

'Don't touch me feet!' Lina warned, rolling away from her latest victim.

'Why?' he asked, crawling across the bed after her. 'You ticklish?'

'No,' she said crossly. 'Me feet are very sensitive – stay away!'

'As long as that's *all* I gotta stay away from,' Flick said, with a ribald laugh.

Lina tossed back her long straight black hair, inherited from her half-Spanish mother, and turned onto her stomach. She had hoped for Superman. What she'd got was an ageing rock star with no technique. She was bored with Flick. He was just another conquest and not that exciting between the sheets.

The trouble with rock stars was that they were sated with

women – all they really wanted to do was lie back and get their dicks sucked. Not that she was averse to such activity, but she did expect it to be reciprocal, and rock stars *never* cared to return the favour.

She stretched languorously. 'Gotta go,' she said.

'Why?' he said, lecherously eyeing her smooth black skin. 'I have all night. My wife thinks I'm in Cleveland.'

'Then she's an idiot,' Lina said, jumping off the bed in his sumptuous hotel suite. She'd met Flick's wife once at a fashion show. Pamela Fonda was an ex-model who'd given him three kids in a pathetic attempt to keep him home. Trouble was, there was no one who could keep Flick home. The man craved constant action. He was a Hall of Fame rocker with a wandering cock and macho attitude.

'Where you goin'?' Flick whined, not used to women leaving unless he ordered them to.

'Meeting my girlfriend,' Lina said, plucking her skimpy Azzedine Alaïa dress off the floor and shimmying her slender body into it.

'Whyn't I take you both to dinner?' Flick suggested, watching her as she dressed.

'Sorry,' Lina said, stepping into her scarlet Diego Della Valle exceptionally high heels. 'We already got arrangements.'

Flick stretched his sinewy body across the bed. He was naked, very white and quite hairless, apart from a full pubic bush of fuzzy orange. He was also hard again. Quite impressive for an almost-fifty non-stop raver, Lina thought. Shame he didn't know what to do with it.

He caught Lina looking. 'See anything you might wanna hang around for?' he asked, with a self-satisfied smirk.

'Nope,' she said. 'Can't be late for me best friend.' And before he could stop her she beat a hasty retreat.

She stood in the elevator on her way down to the lobby trying to ignore an elderly couple who were blatantly staring at her. The woman began nudging her husband to make sure he recognized the famous supermodel.

Lina was used to the scrutiny; in fact, there were times she got off on it. Tonight wasn't one of them, however. She began staring back at the man, licking her full lips suggestively, poking out her extra long tongue. He blushed a dull red.

Oh, yes, this was slightly different from the life she'd led in England where she'd been a hairdresser's apprentice and treated like crap because she was young and had no money and lived in a one-room dump with her waitress mother, her Jamaican father having taken off shortly after she was born. What a bastard *he* was. Not that she'd ever met him, although one of these days – if he ever realized she was his daughter – he'd probably come crawling back to bask in the fame and glory.

Fuck him if he did. She didn't need a dad: she'd done very nicely without one.

Everything changed when she was discovered by the aunt of a modelling agent who insisted she go see her niece. Even though Lina was only seventeen at the time, the niece, recognizing enormous potential, had signed her on the spot.

After that it was all go, a dizzying ride to the top with plenty of adventures along the way.

She'd moved to America permanently five years ago, although most of her time was spent travelling the world. From Paris to Milan to the Bahamas, Lina was always in demand, always the centre of attention.

Downstairs she slipped the doorman ten bucks to get her a cab and fished a small cellphone from her oversized Prada purse. 'Brig,' she said, when her friend answered, 'what we doin' tonight? It just so 'appens I'm free.'

4

Hanging out in his trailer during a late lunchbreak, Lennie Golden leaned over and grabbed a bottle of beer from his portable fridge, swigging heartily until the bottle was almost empty. Lennie was tall and lanky with dirty-blond hair and ocean-green eyes. He was extremely attractive in an edgy, offhand way, with a dark humour and sometimes acerbic wit. Age agreed with him: at forty-five, women found him more attractive than ever.

Lennie liked being alone in his trailer where he could concentrate on his work, especially as he was writing an original script and was well into it. His laptop was laid out ready for action, so it was annoying that soon it would be time to put on black tie – which he hated – and get his ass in gear. He wasn't into big-time Hollywood events, but since tonight it was Lucky who was being honoured, there was no getting out of it.

Lucky Santangelo Golden, his wife – the most beautiful woman in the world *and* the smartest. He often thought how fortunate he was to have her, especially a few years ago when he'd spent several soul-destroying months as the victim of a horrible kidnapping plot, trapped and manacled in an underground cave in Sicily. He'd sat out those interminable months dreaming of his escape and of returning to Lucky and his children. Thank God his prayers had been answered. Now he was safe and settled and things had never been better.

Looking back on his nightmare, it all seemed surreal – as if it had happened to someone else. If it hadn't been for Claudia, the Sicilian girl who'd answered his prayers and helped him escape . . .

A second assistant hammered on his trailer door, interrupting his thoughts. 'Ready on the set, Mr G.'

'I'll be right there,' he responded, shutting down his laptop, banishing the vision of Claudia with her big, soulful eyes, long tanned legs and smooth skin.

Skin like silk . . .

He'd never told Lucky what really happened, how he'd managed to secure his escape from the underground prison he'd been trapped in. He'd never told her and he never would. It was the one thing he kept from his wife because he didn't want to hurt her.

Lucky would not believe he'd had no choice. It was his secret, and he planned on keeping it.

He turned off his laptop, left his trailer and headed for the street location nearby, greeting Buddy, his black cinematographer, with a friendly high five on the way.

'Whass up, man?' Buddy said, falling into step beside him. 'No food today?'

'Saving myself for the plastic chicken tonight,' he answered, with a wry grin.

'Yeah!' Buddy said forcefully. 'Bin there!'

They both laughed.

☆

Mary Lou Berkeley was feeling nostalgic. It was a week away from her ninth wedding anniversary and she couldn't help thinking about how she and Steven had first met. Of course, what she *should* be thinking about was her role in Lennie's movie, especially the upcoming scene. But reminiscing about Steven was irresistible. *He* was irresistible, and thankfully she still loved him as much as when they'd first gotten together. They were a perfect fit, and they always would be.

Mary Lou was a glowingly pretty curvaceous black woman of thirty-one, with huge brown eyes, shoulder-length black curls and a totally captivating smile.

The day she'd met Steven had been traumatic, to say the least. She'd been eighteen at the time, a TV star and full of her own importance. It had *not* been love at first sight. She'd walked into his office at the prestigious New York law firm of Myerson, Laker and Brandon, accompanied by her mother, her manager aunt, and her edgy white boyfriend. Some entourage.

But Steven had been pleasant and reassuring, managing to persuade everyone else to wait outside while she told him her story. And what a sorry story it was. Rashly she'd allowed her then boyfriend to take nude pictures of her when she was fifteen – nothing hard-core, simply some fun stuff they'd gotten into together while fooling around. Recently, cashing in on her TV fame in a family sitcom, the old boyfriend had sold the offending photos to a skin magazine, they'd been published, and now Mary Lou was determined to sue.

Steven warned her that suing a magazine was not easy: there would be depositions, endless questions and all the pressures of negative publicity. 'I can handle it,' she'd said, full of the confidence of youth. 'I want to see those scummy rats pay for what they've done to me.'

'Okay,' Steven had said. 'If that's what you want, we'll go for it.'

Finally, almost three years later, they'd gone to court. Her appearance went well. She was poised and articulate and the jury fell in love with her – especially when she smiled. They loved her so much that on the final day they awarded her sixteen million dollars in damages.

Mary Lou was elated and triumphant. So was Steven. They

went out to dinner to celebrate, and before long the innocent celebration turned into something more.

One thing about Mary Lou – when she wanted something, she was determined. And apart from suing the magazine, she had her big brown eyes firmly fixed on Steven – even though he was over twenty years her senior.

Later that night they ended up in bed. It was warm and exciting and it made Steven feel guilty as hell. She was too young. He was too old. As far as he was concerned it was a no-win situation.

'This relationship is not going to work,' he told her sternly.

'Sure,' she answered cheerfully. 'I have a *great* idea. Let's make it not work together.'

All she had to do was smile and he was lost. A week later she moved into his house.

Mary Lou gave him the personal happiness he'd been lacking for so long. His life had fallen apart for a while when his mother, Carrie, had revealed that she wasn't sure who his father was. Mary Lou helped him to get his head straight, and to stop obsessing about his past and concentrate on his work as a lawyer.

Then came the second magazine incident. The publisher of the magazine Mary Lou had sued published a ten-page spread of extremely explicit photos, claiming they were of Mary Lou. They weren't. They were clever fakes with *her* face superimposed on a porno star's body. Unfortunately, the magazine hit the stands before anyone could stop it.

When Mary Lou saw the magazine, she was so distraught that she attempted suicide. Fortunately Steven managed to rush her to the hospital in time.

Mary Lou was released a week later and Steven knew for sure that he couldn't live without her. They were married shortly after.

Marriage saved both of them. For Steven it was finding someone who cared about him above all else. And for Mary Lou it was the security and love she'd always craved.

Within a few months she was pregnant, eventually giving birth to a beautiful baby girl they named Carioca Jade. Carioca was now eight. Looks-wise she was the image of her mother. Smarts-wise she wanted to be a lawyer, exactly like Daddy.

Mary Lou was a sensational mother. In spite of a successful

career she always managed to put Steven and Carioca first, making them feel like the two most important human beings on the planet.

It had been Steven's idea to move to LA when they'd returned to the States after a two-year stay in England, where he'd studied English law, played golf and generally done nothing except enjoy spending time with his wife and daughter. 'Settling in LA will make it easier for you to get back into the business,' he'd told Mary Lou. Besides, he didn't want to live in New York again, and he had the urge to spend some time with his half-sister, Lucky, and his father, Gino. It had taken him a lifetime to find out that he had a family, and when he did it was a strange, overwhelming feeling. Lucky had accepted him immediately, but it had taken Gino a while to fully realize he had fathered a black son, the result of a long-ago one-night affair with Carrie, Steven's mother.

When Steven told his friend and partner, Jerry Myerson, that he wanted to settle in LA, Jerry had been understanding as usual. He'd suggested that they open a West Coast branch of Myerson, Laker and Brandon. Steven liked the idea, so did Mary Lou.

Fortunately Steven had been proven right: re-locating to LA was great for Mary Lou's career. She started getting the movie roles she'd been missing out on while living in Europe. And after taking on two junior partners, Steven's new law firm took off. It was an excellent move for both of them.

'They're ready for you on the set, Miz Berkeley,' said a second assistant director knocking on the open door of her trailer.

'Oh, right,' Mary Lou said, jumping back to the present. 'I'm on my way.'

5

Zipping along the Pacific Coast Highway in her red Ferrari, vintage Marvin Gaye blasting on her CD player, Lucky felt pretty good about everything. All she hoped was that she was making the right decision. Gino seemed to think she was.

'You gotta do what you feel in your gut,' he'd told her. 'So if you feel it, do it!'

Well, she'd find out soon enough when she got everyone's reaction to her announcement – especially Lennie's.

It was too late now, but it occurred to her that maybe she *should* have told him first. The problem was that Lennie had a way of analysing things, and she didn't want him analysing her decision, she simply wanted to do it.

At the beach-house everyone was assembled in the big, comfortable kitchen overlooking the ocean. There were little Gino and Maria with their cheerful black nanny, CeeCee, and Bobby – who was so damn good-looking, a taller version of his grandfather, Gino.

'Hi, Mom,' Bobby said. 'Wait'll you see my Armani tux. You're gonna freak.'

'I'm sure,' Lucky said drily. 'Who told you you could go to Armani?'

'Grandad,' Bobby said, chewing on a carrot stick.

'Gino spoils you,' Lucky said.

'Yeah,' Bobby said, laughing. 'And don't I love it!'

Lucky had agreed that Bobby could come to the event tonight. However, she did not want little Gino and Maria coming too, they were too young. She had no intention of raising them as Hollywood kids: she'd seen enough of those brats with no manners and a Porsche at sixteen.

CeeCee, who'd been with the family since Bobby was born, was busy serving the younger children rice and beans.

'Mmm . . .' Lucky said, hovering over the table. 'That looks yummy.'

'Where's Daddy?' Maria asked. 'He promised we could jog along the beach.' Maria was a pretty child, with enormous green eyes and wispy blonde hair. She looked a lot like Lennie, while little Gino favoured Lucky in the looks department.

'Daddy's working,' Lucky explained. 'He'll jog with you this weekend. How's that?'

'I'm going to my friend's this weekend,' Maria announced. 'She's having a big, big birthday party.'

'You're deserting us for a whole weekend?' Lucky said, pulling a sad face.

'You *told* me I could go, Mama,' Maria said seriously. 'You *promised*.'

Lucky smiled. 'I know,' she said, remembering how she

had been at eight. She'd had no mother to watch over her, only the gloomy walls of the Bel Air house, with Gino keeping guard. 'I'm going upstairs to get ready for tonight,' she said, 'and when I come down, I want to see all this food eaten up. *And* I want to see pyjamas on bodies, and two small people ready to give me big hugs and kisses.'

Little Gino giggled. She bent over and gave him a hug before hurrying upstairs to her bedroom, where Ned, her hair-stylist, was waiting patiently. She usually fixed her hair herself, but since tonight was such an important event, she'd decided that she'd better make a special effort.

Ned appeared quite agitated.

'What's up?' Lucky asked.

'You make me nervous,' he complained. 'You're always in such a rush.'

'Especially today,' she said, causing him to become even more agitated. 'I've got to be dressed, made up and in the limo by five thirty.'

'Okay, into the chair,' Ned said, clapping his hands together. 'How are we doing your hair?'

'Up. Something sophisticated.'

'You mean something that's completely not you?'

'Ha ha!' Lucky said. 'I can look like a grown-up for once, can't I?'

'Of course,' Ned said. 'Only do *not* nag. Nagging gives me heart palpitations.'

'You've got twenty minutes,' she said, glancing at her watch. 'I can't sit still for longer than that.'

'Oh, God,' he groaned. 'Give me a movie star any day. At least they'll stare at themselves in the mirror for hours and not utter a word.'

Ned fixed her hair in record time. She thanked him, paid him and hustled him out. As soon as he was gone, she raced into the shower, making sure to angle her head back so that she didn't ruin Ned's do. Then she quickly towelled herself dry and sprayed herself all over with Lennie's favourite scent. Next she applied her makeup, and slid into a long slinky red Valentino, with spaghetti straps, plunging neckline, and a slit to the top of her thigh. The dress was very revealing; fortunately she was slender enough to carry it off.

She stared at herself in the mirror. *I look like a real grown-up now*, she thought with a smile.

Lucky Santangelo. Little Lucky Saint, as they'd called her at school so that her real identity was never revealed, and it would not be known that she was connected to the notorious Gino Santangelo – the Las Vegas hotel tycoon with the somewhat shady past.

Gino. Daddy. What memories they shared. Nobody could ever break the bond between them. Not one single person.

She remembered how at nineteen she had pleaded with him to let her take over the family business. But no, Gino had never entertained the idea, until finally she'd proved to him that there was no stopping her.

'Girls gotta get married and have babies.' That's what he used to say to her.

'Not *this* girl,' she'd replied, full of steely determination. 'I'm a Santangelo – just like you. I can do anything.' And in the end she'd won.

She opened her safe, removing the diamond hoop earrings Lennie had given her on her fortieth birthday. Then she added a wide diamond and emerald bracelet, a present from Gino, and she was ready to go. It was exactly five twenty.

Downstairs Bobby was showing off his new tux to his siblings.

'Why can't we come, too?' Maria complained, adorable in Snoopy pyjamas.

'Because this is not a children's event,' Lucky explained. 'It's strictly for adults.'

'Then why's Bobby going?' little Gino asked.

'Because he's taller than all of us,' Lucky said, thinking this was rather a good answer. 'Is the limo here?' she asked Bobby.

'Yeah, Mom, it just arrived.'

'Then let's go,' she said, kissing Maria and little Gino.

☆

'Honey,' Steven said, frantically rummaging through his top drawer, the phone balanced precariously against his ear, 'I can't find my bow-tie.'

'Steven,' Mary Lou said, 'how can you call me when I'm on the set? You just blew a take.' She was speaking into her cellphone, trying to edge away from her co-star, who could not believe she'd left her phone on while they were in the middle of a scene.

'Sorry, sweetheart,' Steven said, 'but this is an emergency. Lucky's gonna be here any moment.'

'Your tie is on your dresser where I put it this morning. I *told* you where it was before I left.'

'Oh, yeah, right,' he said, suddenly remembering.

'You drive me crazy, Steven,' she said crossly.

'Good crazy?'

A quiet giggle. 'Well, *of course* good crazy.'

He put on his real low-down sexy-soul-singer voice. 'Later tonight, I'll *really* getcha outta your mind.'

'Oooh, baby, baby . . .'

Now they both giggled, secure in the knowledge that they were still crazy about each other, and that the sex got better as each year of marriage passed.

'Mary Lou,' Lennie yelled from behind the camera, 'we'd like to get out of here sometime this year. Is that okay with you?'

'Sorry, Lennie,' she said guiltily. And then into the phone. 'See you soon, lover. There's somethin' special I have to tell you.'

'What?' he asked, hoping she hadn't signed for another movie without telling him, because in his mind they both needed a nice long vacation.

'You'll see,' she said provocatively, and clicked off her phone.

'Can we get back to work now?' Lennie enquired.

'You got it,' Mary Lou said, smiled her captivating smile, and nobody could stay mad at her.

6

Cruising around getting shit-faced was not exactly what the boy had imagined they'd do. He'd kind of pictured sex in the back of his jeep, or at least a blow-job. But no: the girl – who was extremely bossy – had her own agenda.

She'd always pushed him around, ever since they were kids. It was do this, do that, and usually, because he was in awe of her, and she was two years older than he was, he obliged.

But he resented her big time.

He also lusted after her with a permanent hard-on.

He was sure that if he could have sex with her, just once, it would break the hold she had over him. Meanwhile, she kept on telling him what to do.

They drove to a supermarket, where she purchased a couple of six-packs of beer. She looked much older than her eighteen years and, besides, she knew the checkout clerk, so the dude didn't bother carding her; he was too busy staring at her tits.

In the parking lot she opened two cans of beer and thrust one at him. 'Last one to finish is a pussy,' she said, immediately lifting the can to her lips.

He was up to the challenge, conveniently forgetting his dad's words when he'd handed him the keys to the jeep: 'Now you gotta promise me, son – you will never drink and drive.'

'Yeah, Dad,' he'd said. 'You got my word on that.'

The beer was ice cold and tasted good. Not only that, but he beat her to emptying the can, a minor triumph.

'Not bad,' she said grudgingly.

'Where we goin' now?' he asked.

'Dunno,' she said.

'How about a movie?'

'Waste of time,' she said disdainfully, fiddling with one of several stud earrings attached to her left ear. 'Movies are for morons who got nothin' better t' do.' She knew he was crazy about her, and used it. 'Let's go steal something,' she suggested, as if it was the most normal thing in the world.

'Why'd we wanna do that?' he asked, pulling on his ear – a habit he had when he was nervous.

'Kind of an initiation,' she answered casually. 'If you wanna stay tight with me, you gotta do stuff that'll make me believe you're committed to our friendship.'

'Committed?' he said, wondering if committed meant an eventual blow-job.

'It's easy. All we gotta do is go by the CD store an' see how many you can score.'

'Why don't I pay?' he said logically. 'My dad picks up my credit-card bill.'

'What's the matter?' she jeered mockingly. 'Daddy's precious little boy don't wanna mess with trouble?'

'That's crap.'

'What did Daddy do?' she continued, in her mocking tone. 'Keep you locked in the house in New York? I would've thought living in the city would've given you balls.'

'I got balls,' he said, suddenly angry.

'Naw . . . you're a daddy's boy.'

'No way.' And as if to prove her wrong, he opened another can of beer and took a few hearty gulps.

'Oh,' she said. 'Mr Macho, huh?'

'You don't know anything about me really,' he said.

'I know everything about you,' she answered quickly. 'Bet you've never had sex.'

The fact that she knew he was still a virgin threw him. 'That's crap,' he said, quickly denying it.

'Good,' she said. 'I like a guy who can get it up an' keep it that way.'

He swigged more beer. Did that mean that later she'd allow him to prove it?

The first can of beer had made him more relaxed; the second one was helping with the job. 'Okay, let's do it,' he said, swallowing a burp. 'Bet I can score more CDs than you.'

'That's what I like to hear,' she said, pleased. 'Want me to drive?'

'No,' he said. 'I'm cool.'

And they set off.

7

Things were moving slower than Lennie had anticipated, and on top of everything else they would soon be losing light. He'd promised he would get to Lucky's event as soon as he could, but the way it was going, he and Mary Lou would definitely be late arrivals.

No good obsessing. Two more set-ups, and they could finally wrap this particular location. Especially as everyone was co-operating by working as fast as possible.

The good news was that Mary Lou was a pleasure to work with. Some actresses were divas, bitching and complaining about every little thing. Not Mary Lou. She had it down. She was pretty and talented, but above all she was nice, and the entire crew adored her.

Buddy had a major crush, which Lennie found amusing to

observe, because usually Buddy was Mr Stud, a true ladies' man with a happening wardrobe and an Eddie Murphy swagger.

'She's married, you know,' Lennie remarked, strolling over to Buddy while they were setting the lights for the second to last shot.

'Hey, man, I know that,' Buddy said, hardly able to take his eyes off Mary Lou, who was sitting in her chair chatting with one of the grips. 'And I also know if she wasn't—'

'Hey, hey,' Lennie interrupted. 'She's *married* to my brother-in-law.'

'Fortunate guy,' Buddy said.

'He sure is,' Lennie answered. 'Good fortune runs in the family. My wife . . . well, what can I tell you about my wife?'

'I've seen her,' Buddy said. 'You don't have to say a word. But, let me ask you, isn't it kinda difficult being married to a woman like Lucky?'

'Why difficult?'

''Cause she's running a studio, man, making all kinds of big decisions. The woman's a real power player in Hollywood, and, uh . . .'

Lennie shook his head and laughed. 'You think my wife running a studio threatens my ego?'

'Naw, didn't mean that.'

'Oh, c'mon, that's exactly what you meant.'

'No, man,' Buddy insisted. 'All I'm thinkin' is that *I* couldn't do it.'

'Do what?'

'Be with a woman who got all the attention.'

'I *had* the attention,' Lennie said. 'When I was acting in movies the attention never stopped. Hot and cold running women. Phone numbers stuffed in my pocket. Naked pictures in the mail. Believe me, I much prefer it this way.'

'That's cool,' Buddy said.

'Right,' Lennie agreed. 'Now, keep your eyes off Mrs Berkeley an' let's get it going here.'

☆

Gino Santangelo was dressed and ready to go. It didn't take much preparation to get ready when you were eighty-seven years old. Christ! He looked in the mirror and saw this old, grey-haired man, and he thought, *When the fuck did this happen?*

In his mind he still felt about forty. Forty and ready for action. Only the action wasn't so easy to come by when you were his age. There were aches and pains to contend with. A stiffness in his joints. Getting up to go to the john a thousand times a night. Growing old was a bitch, but it sure as hell beat out the alternative.

He went to the bar in his Wilshire apartment and poured himself a hefty slug of Jack Daniel's. *Two inches of Jack Daniel's a day keeps the doctor away* – that was his motto, and he was sticking to it.

He thought about Lucky, his crazy daughter – she was strong, smart, and knew all the right moves. In fact, she was him in a dress. What a girl!

He was *so* goddamn proud of her, which is why he'd flown from his home in Palm Springs to attend this special evening honouring her. His wife, Paige, had been planning on coming with him, only Paige had gotten the flu at the last minute and stayed in Palm Springs. Paige was a good woman. They'd been married several years and got along fine, even though she was over thirty years younger than he was. He liked her spirit, not to mention her sexy pocket-Venus body, which *still* turned him on. Not that he was as into sex as he once was. But at least he could still get it up on occasion – much to his doctor's amazement. 'You're eighty-seven, Gino,' his doctor had told him last week. 'When is it going to stop?'

'Never, Doc.' He'd laughed. 'That's the secret.'

Gino had never really gotten over his first wife and one true love, Maria. Her murder had shattered his life, and changed him for ever. Even now, all these years later, he still lived surrounded by high security. He often begged Lucky to do the same, but she ignored him. She didn't realize the Santangelos had enemies out there going back many years. Between them, he and Lucky had dealt with the Bonnatti family in a vendetta that had lasted several decades. Now, with the demise of Donatella Bonnatti, the last of the clan – that particular feud was over. But there were others who'd always harboured a grudge.

Gino worried about Lucky. Sure, she was independent and feisty, but she was still a woman, and no woman could ever be as strong as a man.

Not that he'd dare tell her that. Lucky would bust his chops if he ever voiced such a thought.

He grinned, downing the Jack Daniel's in one fell swoop. His daughter, Miss Balls of Fire, the original feminist. And tonight she was being honoured. Tonight she was the most important person in Hollywood. *His daughter*. It was some thrill.

The intercom buzzed and the doorman informed him there was a limo waiting downstairs.

'I'll be right there,' Gino said.

And he wished his precious Maria were alive to see this memorable day.

☆

Meanwhile, in his house on Sunset Plaza Drive, Steven found his tie, put it on, stared at himself in the mirror, decided he didn't look too bad for a guy in his fifties, and, with a smile on his face, thought about Mary Lou and their conversation.

Steven was extremely modest, having no idea that he gave handsome a whole new meaning. He was six feet three inches tall with a killer body. His skin was the colour of rich milk chocolate, his black curly hair only slightly touched with grey, and his eyes were an unfathomable deep green. Mary Lou spent hours telling him he was the most handsome man she'd ever seen. This from an actress who mixed with perfect specimens every day. 'You're just prejudiced,' he told her.

'You bet your ass I am,' she answered, with the sweetest smile in the world.

Steven figured he was a pretty lucky guy. He had a wife he adored, who adored him back; the cutest little daughter in the world, and a whole new family. Lucky was the greatest: she treated him as if they'd grown up together. 'When my brother, Dario, was murdered,' she'd told him, 'I never imagined anyone could replace him. Then *you* came along, and I'm so grateful to have you in my life, Steven.'

Gino had finally accepted him too. 'Gotta tell you,' he'd growled one day, 'never thought I'd have myself a black kid.'

'Yeah, well,' Steven had responded, 'never thought I'd have myself a white Italian father.'

'Guess we both got unlucky,' Gino had joked, and then he'd hugged Steven.

Sometimes the three of them went out for dinner. To Steven, those nights were the best of times, special evenings that he treasured.

He never thought about his past – the dark days when he was married to ZeeZee, a crazy, exotic dancer; or being raised by Carrie, his mother, who once worked in a whorehouse; and then there were the interminable years of never knowing who his real father was.

He had good friends too. Jerry Myerson had always come through for him, even when he was at his most miserable and a real pain in the ass.

Now he was content, he had everything he'd ever wanted and it was a satisfying feeling.

His eight-year-old daughter came into the room. She was the image of Mary Lou, with her sweet smile, light brown skin, and cascades of curly hair.

'Anyone ever told you you look *exactly* like your mom?' Steven said.

'Daddy, *you* look *sooo* handsome,' Carioca Jade said, peering up at him.

'Why, thank you.'

'You're welcome, Daddy.'

His daughter was growing up so fast. Surely it was about time they considered having another child? He'd been meaning to talk to Mary Lou about it. He wanted a son. A boy he could go to ball games with and teach many things – not that he didn't adore his daughter, she made every day worthwhile, but a son . . . Well, it was his dream.

'Where's Mommy?' Carioca Jade demanded, tilting her head on one side.

'On location, sweetheart,' he answered. 'She asked me to tell you to be a good girl and be sure and do your homework.'

Jennifer, their English au pair, appeared. 'Everything all right, Mr Berkeley?' she asked crisply, shades of Mary Poppins.

'Everything's fine, Jen,' he said. 'You've got the number of my cellphone if you need me. I guess we'll be home around midnight.'

'Don't worry about a thing, Mr Berkeley. Come along, Carrie, let's get into that homework.'

'Daddy, can't I watch TV and do my homework later?' Carioca pleaded, all big eyes and quivering lower lip.

'No way.'

'Why?'

''Cause education is everything. And don't you ever forget it.'

'*Okay*, Daddy,' Carioca said reluctantly. 'I get it.'

'I'll see you in the morning, sweetheart,' he said, giving her a hug and a kiss. Then he walked out the door just as the limo drew up in front of the house. The driver jumped out and opened the car door.

'Hey,' Steven said, ducking inside.

'Hey,' Lucky answered. And they grinned at each other.

'Evening, Steven,' Gino said.

'Hey – Gino, Bobby. Everyone's lookin' mighty good,' Steven said. 'This must be a special occasion.'

'Let's go,' Lucky said impatiently. 'This is going to be a big night, and now that I'm committed, I do not intend to miss one single moment.'

8

'**It's babe alert** big time!' Lina said.

'What?' Brigette said.

'*Look* at 'im,' Lina said admiringly, staring at Fredo's cousin as they headed to their table on their way back from the ladies' room where they'd gone to touch up their makeup and discuss the situation. 'He's definitely the shit!'

Brigette took another look. True. Carlo Vittorio Vitti *was* handsome in an arrogant way: he was tall, with dark blond hair, piercing ice-blue eyes, designer stubble and a slender body. He was wearing a grey pinstriped suit and casual black silk T-shirt. She figured him to be in his early thirties.

In spite of her afternoon session with Flick, Lina was in lust at first sight. '*And* 'e's got a title,' she said, fully impressed.

'Fredo told me 'e's a count. My mum would 'ave a fit if she knew I was out with a real live count!'

Brigette wasn't really listening. She was too busy regretting eschewing pizza and *Ab Fab* for a night on the town. This was not her idea of a good time. Fredo was all over her like a particularly annoying rash, and his arrogant cousin had barely said a word. What did she need this for?

Lina was definitely after the cousin. Brigette couldn't care less: she merely wanted to go home.

'I'm gonna fuck 'im tonight!' Lina announced, licking her full, glossy lips in a predatory way. '*Oh*, yeah!'

'He's engaged,' Brigette pointed out, idly wondering to whom.

'Ha!' Lina snorted. 'Engaged means *nothing*.'

Brigette nodded as if she agreed, although actually she didn't.

'Just lookin' at 'im makes me dead horny,' Lina continued. 'Know what I mean?'

Brigette nodded again, as if she knew exactly what Lina meant when, actually, she didn't get it at all. It had been several years since she'd slept with a man. Sometimes she thought her libido had died and drifted off to heaven. Now she felt no desire at all. *Nada.* None. It was quite obvious she was a freak of nature.

Sometimes she wondered how her friendship with Lina survived. Because of their great camaraderie, she tried not to let the fact that Lina was man hungry get in the way of their friendship. The truth was that she understood exactly where Lina was coming from. Both of them had grown up with no father around, so Lina was always chasing the strong masculine image, whereas Brigette did the opposite and shied away from men altogether. They were so different, yet they had fun together and plenty of laughs, especially when they travelled around the world on their various assignments. Location shoots were the best. Brigette was especially looking forward to flying to the Bahamas where they were doing a major shoot for *Sports World International* magazine. Last year she'd been on the cover. This year she knew that Lina was after the coveted spot and she was rooting for her to get it.

Back at the table Fredo had ordered a bottle of Cristal. He

was so delighted they'd agreed to have dinner with him that he hadn't stopped beaming all night. 'Well, my beauties,' he said enthusiastically, 'what club shall we visit next?'

'You choose,' Lina said, flashing a seductive smile at Carlo, who, much to her annoyance, failed to respond. Lina was used to men falling all over her and she did not appreciate indifference.

'I want to go home,' Brigette announced, causing both Lina and Fredo to glare at her.

'It's much too early,' Lina snapped, shaking her head in an exasperated fashion. 'It's time for dancin'.' She turned to Fredo. 'I should *never* 'ave warned 'er about you.'

'What you mean?' Fredo said, bushy eyebrows shooting up. 'You warn her about *me*?'

'Yeah,' Lina said, with a wicked grin. 'I told 'er you're a real fuck-an'-run merchant. *That*'s why you've never got any-where with 'er.'

'Thanks,' Fredo said huffily. 'Now I must show her my true personality.'

'She's seen your true personality all right,' Lina said slyly. 'An', believe me, *that*'s all she wants to see.'

While Lina and Fredo were bantering back and forth, Brigette took the polite route and leaned towards Carlo. 'Fredo told me you live in London,' she said. 'That must be inter-esting.'

He fixed her with his piercing blue eyes. 'You are very beautiful,' he said in a low voice – so low that neither of the other two heard.

'Excuse me?' Brigette said, taken aback.

'I think you understand me,' he said.

She glanced quickly at Lina. Her friend would not be happy if she thought Carlo was coming on to someone else. 'Well, uh ... thanks,' she said, slightly flustered. 'It's my job to look good in front of the camera.'

'I'm not talking about your photographs,' Carlo said smoothly.

For a moment she felt uncomfortable under the scrutiny of his probing eyes. 'Well,' she said, lifting her champagne glass and making a big show of including the others, 'I'd like to propose a toast. Here's to Carlo and his fiancée. What a pity she's not here.'

Lina shot her a deadly look for mentioning that her new object of lust was engaged.

'*What* fiancée?' Carlo asked, as if he had no idea what she was talking about.

'Fredo told us you were engaged,' Lina said, shooting Fredo a look that said, Well, is he or isn't he?

'Me? I think not,' Carlo said, with a fleeting smile. 'It is over.'

'You didn't mention it was over to me,' Fredo said accusingly.

'You did not ask,' Carlo replied, freezing him out.

Lina immediately moved in, snuggling close to Carlo. 'Not engaged, huh?' she said happily. 'Nor am I. That makes us a cosy couple, don't it?'

Carlo smiled politely, but his eyes remained on Brigette.

9

'**Where the hell** are they?' Lucky muttered, pulling on the sleeve of Steven's jacket so she could take a peek at his watch.

'It's only eight,' Steven said, calm as usual. 'They'll be here in time for your speech.'

'Yeah, honey,' Gino joined in. 'You gotta learn t' relax. Lookit me.'

'I guess it's easy when you're eighty-seven,' she murmured drily.

'My kid,' Gino said, with a wide smile. 'Always with the smart answers.'

'Wonder where I inherited *that* from,' she drawled.

They'd just sat down after a long cocktail hour. Bobby was hovering at the next table, desperately trying to make conversation with the perky young star of a TV sitcom as he strutted proudly in his first tux. He was certainly good-looking, with his mother's striking colouring and his deceased father's charisma. Dimitri had been a major charmer.

Lucky nudged Gino. 'Was that you at fifteen?' she asked, watching her son as he attempted to put a move on the eighteen-year-old sitcom star.

Gino checked out his grandson and roared with laughter.

'When *I* was his age,' he said, 'I was screwin' my way around the block.'

And so was I, Lucky wanted to say, but she didn't; Gino wasn't too fond of remembering his daughter in her wild days. He'd married her off at sixteen to curb her out-of-control behaviour. Big deal. She'd soon gotten out of *that* fiasco, and the moment Gino took off for Europe on an extended tax exile, she'd moved back to Vegas and taken over the family business with a vengeance.

'Is that how you got your nickname, Gino the Ram?' she asked innocently, pretending she didn't know he hated that tag from so long ago.

'I always knew how t' treat a woman,' Gino said indignantly. 'Treat a lady like a whore an' a whore like a lady. Works every time.'

'Now don't you be teaching my son sexist crap like that,' Lucky scolded sternly.

'Bullshit!' Gino spat. 'The sooner he learns, the better off he'll be. For his sixteenth birthday I'm takin' him to Vegas an' buyin' him the best-lookin' hooker in town.'

'No, you're not.'

'Yes, I am.'

'The last thing I need is my son getting your antiquated take on women.'

Gino roared with laughter. 'I never had no complaints, kiddo.'

'Shove it up your ass, Gino.'

They did not have the traditional father–daughter relationship.

Steven returned to the table. 'What are you two up to?' he asked.

'I'm listening to Gino blow wind,' Lucky said, feigning an exaggerated yawn.

'That's nice,' Steven said, shaking his head. 'When you two get together it's exactly like being back in high school.'

'I can't help it if he's stuck in a time warp,' Lucky said, laughing.

'Time warp, my ass,' Gino interjected. 'I'm tellin' you the way it is with men and women. It's about time you understood.'

'Hold that thought,' Steven said. 'Here comes Alex and his date.'

Lucky glanced up at the approaching couple. 'And what exotic little number is Alex with tonight?' she asked casually.

'What do you care?' Steven asked. 'It's you he wants.'

'Nonsense,' Lucky said, knowing that Steven, along with Venus, was absolutely correct. Alex Woods *did* have a thing about her, and she was strongly attracted to him, too, but not enough that she would ever betray Lennie – except, of course, that one time when Lennie had been gone for months and she'd thought he was dead. It was a secret she kept close to her heart, because it was better Lennie never knew. Instead of lovers, she and Alex had become best friends, a friendship they shared with Lennie, although he was not as close to Alex as she was.

Alex Woods. Writer. Director. A man who did everything his way and usually got away with it because he *was* Alex Woods, and in the great Hollywood tradition he was one of those characters who stood alone. Alex was shining brilliance in a sea of mediocrity, a true original talent like Martin Scorsese, Woody Allen and Oliver Stone.

'Lucky,' Alex said, bearing down on her. At fifty-one he was still a dangerous-looking man: darkly brooding, with compelling eyes, heavy eyebrows and a strong jawline. He was tall and fit, due to vigorous daily workouts. His hair was longish, curling just above the back of his collar, and he always wore black. Tonight he was in a black tuxedo with matching shirt and no tie. Alex enjoyed making statements.

His date was Asian. *Big surprise*, Lucky thought. The girl was petite and in her twenties. Lucky hadn't seen this one before. It was rare that any of them lasted longer than six weeks. She often joked with Alex that he had an assembly line that churned out Asian women on a regular basis.

'Hi, Alex,' she said warmly, standing up to greet him.

He let out an admiring whistle. 'Spectacular!' he said, checking out the floor-length red Valentino that skimmed her slender body, plunging at the back to reveal almost everything. 'Sometimes,' Alex said, 'I almost forget how dazzlingly beautiful you actually are.'

'Compliments,' she said, smiling. 'You must want something.'

'Oh, yeah,' he said, smiling back. 'That shouldn't surprise you.'

'Stop it, Alex,' she said sharply, not in the mood to deal with his heavy flirting, which he indulged in whenever Lennie wasn't around. 'Introduce me to your date.'

'Pia,' he said, pulling the girl forward.

'Hi, Pia,' Lucky said, checking her out.

'Hi, Lucky,' Pia said, not quite as submissive as his usual type.

Thank God! Lucky thought. Dealing with Alex's never-ending procession of girlfriends was exhausting. Recently she'd told him that she couldn't do it any more. 'Do what?' he'd asked innocently.

'Well,' she'd said, 'when the four of us go out to dinner, you and Lennie have a fine old time talking about everyone and everything, while *I*'m stuck making polite conversation with your date.'

'So?' he'd said.

'So,' she'd answered, '*you* get to fuck 'em. *I*'ve got to talk to them!'

Alex had roared with laughter.

Lucky smiled at the memory.

'Where's Lennie?' Alex asked, looking around.

'Working,' Lucky explained. 'He'll be here shortly.'

'Shame!' Alex said.

'Will you *stop*?' Lucky said.

'Never,' Alex said.

There was a sudden commotion and turning of heads as Venus Maria made her way to the table, accompanied by her extremely smart movie-star husband, Cooper Turner.

Venus was huffing and puffing, all platinum hair, luscious cleavage, and glossy lids and lips. 'Jesus!' she exclaimed, finally reaching the table. 'It took us twenty-five minutes to negotiate the press line. The things one does for friends!'

'What did they ask you?' Lucky said.

'What *didn't* they ask me?' Venus replied. 'Am I pregnant again? How's my marriage? Do I consider Madonna competition? If I was single would I date Brad Pitt? The usual crap.'

'No, I mean what did they ask you about *me*? This *is* my evening, remember?'

'I thought you hated publicity.'

'I do.'

'So I tried not to mention you – except to say that next to Sherry Lansing you're probably the smartest woman in Hollywood, and that under your amazing guidance Panther makes the best movies. Lucky Santangelo is the queen of equal sexuality, I said. How's *that* for a killer quote?'

Lucky grinned and kissed Cooper, who was his usual smooth self. Before marrying Venus he'd been the number-one playboy in Hollywood. Now he was Mr Married and revelling in it. Fatherhood suited him, and had certainly calmed him down. Chyna, their five-year-old daughter, was the pride of both their lives.

'Hi, Alex,' Venus said, kissing the director on both cheeks. 'When am I going to star in your next movie?'

It had become a joke between the two of them that since she'd been nominated for her small role in his film, *Gangsters*, he'd never asked her to work for him again.

'Dunno . . .' he said hesitantly. 'Can you play a flat-chested psycho with a penchant for cutting off men's balls?'

'My dream!' Venus squealed, her animated face lighting up. 'You won't find another actress more suited to the role!'

'Well . . .' Alex said thoughtfully. 'Would you be prepared to shoot a test?'

'Hmm . . .' she said, pretending to think about it. 'I guess it would depend on whose balls you wanted me to chop!'

Everyone laughed.

Lucky looked around. *At least I'm surrounded by friends*, she thought. *People who genuinely love me. And that's a good thing considering the announcement I'm about to make concerns all of them in one way or the other.*

She wished Lennie would hurry up and arrive. He was all she needed to make the evening complete.

10

Finally Lennie said the magic words: 'Cut. Print. That's a wrap, everyone.'

'Thank goodness,' Mary Lou said, rushing to her trailer, unbuttoning the suit she'd worn in the scene on her way.

Terri, one of the wardrobe assistants, ran behind her. 'Can

I help?' Terri asked. She was black, overweight and out of breath, but full of enthusiasm. Like everyone else on the set, she adored Mary Lou and would do anything for her.

'Yes!' Mary Lou said. 'I need to be ready, like, an hour ago!'

'You got it,' Terri said. 'I'm here to assist.'

'How's that little brother of yours?' Mary Lou asked, as they reached her trailer.

'Doin' okay, thanks,' Terri answered, marvelling that Mary Lou even remembered her confiding about her sixteen-year-old brother, who'd recently been arrested for vandalism. 'They gave him three months' probation.'

'That should teach him a lesson.'

'My *mama* taught him a lesson,' Terry said, rolling her eyes. 'She paddled his ass so fine he couldn't sit down for a week!'

'Good,' Mary Lou said. 'Now he'll think twice next time he plans on getting out of line.'

'Ain't *that* the truth,' Terri said, hanging up Mary Lou's skirt after she stepped out of it.

'Y' know,' Mary Lou said, opening the small fridge where she'd hidden her heart-shaped diamond earrings and necklace – anniversary gifts from Steven, 'if you like, I can arrange for my husband to see him, give him some advice about how *not* to get into trouble.'

Terri's expression perked up. 'Really?'

'Steven's great with kids. He occasionally talks to boys at a school in Compton – helps them with career tips, that kind of thing. They think he's the greatest.'

'I bet.'

'Sometimes we have a few of them over for a barbecue. Steven knows how to motivate. He makes them *want* to get an education and do well.'

'Sounds like exactly what my little brother needs,' Terri said, carefully removing Mary Lou's shimmering white evening gown from its protective plastic covering.

'I'll arrange it,' Mary Lou said, unhooking her bra and reaching for her dress.

'You're so slim,' Terri said enviously, watching as Mary Lou navigated her way into the slinky gown.

'It's called hardly ever eating!' Mary Lou said ruefully. 'In my job you *have* to be thin. I'd much sooner be pigging out on fried chicken and grits. But I figure one of these days – way, way in the future – that's what I'll do. Right now it's important I keep my figure.'

'Look at me,' Terri said, with a helpless shrug. 'I'm eighty pounds overweight.'

'Make a goal,' Mary Lou said. 'Promise yourself you'll lose four pounds a month. Take it slow and easy, and in less than two years you'll be down to the weight you want.'

Terri laughed at the thought. 'I can't do that.'

'Yes, you can,' Mary Lou said. 'We can do anything we set our minds to.'

'Gee, I wish *that* was true,' Terri said wistfully.

'Do I look all right?' Mary Lou asked.

'Fine as silk,' Terri said, with a sigh, zipping the back of her dress.

'Thanks,' Mary Lou said, quickly applying a thin coat of lip-gloss. 'Now, I promise I won't forget about your brother. I'll talk to Steven tonight.'

'You're the best,' Terri said.

'No, I'm not,' Mary Lou said. 'It's just that I understand when someone needs guidance. One day I'll tell you how Steven and I first met. Boy! Did I need guidance then! Actually, it's quite a story.'

'Tell me now,' Terri pleaded.

'No time now,' Mary Lou said, laughing. 'Sit with me at lunch tomorrow and I'll reveal everything. Oh, yes, and tomorrow you're starting your diet – right?'

'If you say so.'

There was a knock on the trailer door, followed by Lennie calling out, 'You ready?'

'Just about,' she said, quickly putting on her spike-heeled silver shoes as Terri opened the trailer door.

'Let's get going,' Lennie said. 'If I don't make it in time for her speech, Lucky will kill me.' He took her arm and helped her down the steps.

''Bye, Terri,' Mary Lou said, waving.

'Don't *you* look something?' Lennie remarked, as they made their way to his car.

'Like my dress?' Mary Lou asked, doing a little twirl for him.

'Love it,' he said. 'But you'd better prepare yourself – Steven'll have a heart-attack when he sees you. He's too old to have a wife who looks like you.'

'Great!' Mary Lou said. 'Don't tell *him* that, he's already experiencing a mid-life crisis.'

'Steven is?'

'He thinks he's getting fat and boring.'

'C'*mon*. Mr Handsome?'

Mary Lou giggled. 'I told him he can turn into the fattest, most boring man in the world, and I'll *still* love him.'

'What a woman!'

'He's the best.'

'So are you.'

'Thank you, Lennie. I appreciate that.'

'Hey,' Lennie said, as they trekked down the street. 'I'm afraid it didn't occur to me to hire a limo for tonight. I prefer driving myself. But what with you looking so outrageous, I realize I should've gotten us a car.'

'Don't be silly,' Mary Lou said. 'I'm happy as long as we get there. And the sooner the better.' She smiled softly. 'Y' know, it's so funny: Steven and I have been married almost nine years, yet when I'm away from him, I *still* miss him. Even if it's only for a day.'

'I know what you mean,' Lennie said. 'Sometimes I look around at all the miserable marriages in this town – people playing musical beds and getting divorced – and I think how happy I am with Lucky. She's my everything. Yes, I'm into working, but coming home to her at the end of the day makes it all worthwhile.'

'That's how I feel,' Mary Lou said, wide-eyed. 'We're exactly alike.'

'Yeah, except you're a *little* bit younger than me,' Lennie said.

'Just a tiny bit,' she said, smiling.

Buddy caught up with them on their way to Lennie's car. 'Baby, you look *hot*!' he said to Mary Lou, checking her out admiringly.

'Why, thank you, Buddy,' she said, well aware of his respectful crush. 'Coming from you that's a real compliment.'

'What's *that* mean, coming from me?' Buddy said, putting on the charm big time.

'Well,' Mary Lou said, 'everyone *knows* you're the campus superstud.'

'Yeah?' he said, preening. 'I got myself a reputation, have I?'

'Let me see, Buddy,' she said, pretending to think about it. 'Since we've been making this movie I've observed at least *three* different girls visiting you on the set.'

'My sisters,' Buddy said, grinning.

She grinned back. 'Your sisters, my ass!'

'And a fine ass it is, too, if I may say so.'

'C'*mon*,' Lennie said, opening the passenger door of his Porsche and hustling Mary Lou inside. 'You two can flirt tomorrow. Right now we gotta get going.'

She settled into the front seat, fastened her seatbelt, and gave a little wave to Buddy who hovered by the car.

'Does your husband know how lucky he is?' Buddy said as Lennie ran around and started the car.

'I hope so,' she said, blowing him a kiss.

'Baby,' Buddy sighed, 'if you *ever* decide you want bigger and better, I am *waiting*!'

'There's no such thing as bigger and better than my Steven,' Mary Lou said. 'Sorry to disappoint you.'

'Oh, baby, baby,' Buddy said, shaking his head. '*You* are something else.'

The Porsche took off. Mary Lou closed the window and grinned. 'I hope he makes me look good on screen.'

'Buddy's the best,' Lennie said. 'And, considering he has a thing about you, *you* will look sensational.'

'It's so much fun to be making a movie with you, Lennie,' she said. 'I never imagined we'd work together, and now it's even better than I thought it would be.'

'Hey – you're a pleasure to work with.'

'Coming from you that's a big compliment.'

'I'm bummed we had to run so late tonight,' Lennie said, adjusting his rear-view mirror. 'D'you think Lucky will be pissed?'

'Lucky *never* gets pissed at you.'

'Oh, yeah?' he said, knowing his wife. 'It's almost eight thirty. By the time we get there it'll be past nine. Trust me, *tonight* she will be pissed.'

11

The boy *threw himself into the jeep, adrenalin coursing through his veins, vision blurred. The girl wasn't far behind, giggling insanely.*

'How many didja get?' she asked, falling into the passenger seat.

'Four,' he said, heart pumping wildly.

'Chicken,' she said. 'I got six. We'd better get outta here before they send a guard after us.'

The boy didn't need to be told twice. He started the jeep and they roared out of the parking lot, practically colliding with a blue Toyota driven by an elderly man who shook his fist at them.

The girl reached for a beer, cracked one open and handed it to him. He was already drunk, but who cared? He felt like he could do anything. He wasn't stuck in the house, he was out and free. Freedom was a good thing. Freedom ruled!

The girl knew how to enjoy herself, she always had. When they'd been small and growing up together she'd always taken the initiative, shown him the way to go. Sometimes she'd even stood up for him.

'Let's see what you got,' the girl said, fumbling in his pockets.

'Didn't know I was supposed to choose. Grabbed anything I could.'

'Crap,' the girl said, disgusted. 'You're supposed to get stuff we want.' She pulled a CD out of his pocket. 'Celine Dion!' she exclaimed. 'Who listens to her?'

'I told you,' the boy said, embarrassed. 'Wasn't looking.'

'Dunce!' the girl said, reaching under her sweater and pulling out a CD of Ice T. 'Put this on.'

He slipped the disc into the player, and throbbing loud rap filled the jeep.

The girl began moving her body to the beat, then she reached in her pocket for a cigarette, lit up, took a drag and handed it to him.

'Don't smoke,' he mumbled.

'You're such a wuss,' she muttered. 'New York sure didn't wise you up.'

'I smoked grass there,' he boasted.

'Ooooh!' she said mockingly. 'What a bad motherfucker you are. How about coke – you ever done that?'

He shook his head. His dad was against drugs, having once been a major user of anything he could get his hands on.

'Wanna try?' she suggested. 'I got some, y'know.'

'Where'd you score coke?' he asked.

'Don't you worry 'bout that,' she said, with a sly smile. 'I can score anything I want. I got friends in all the wrong places.'

12

'Where's that husband of yours?' Gino asked.

'I wish I knew,' Lucky replied, tight-lipped as she wondered the same thing herself.

'Has he left the location yet?' Venus asked, leaning into their conversation.

'Yes,' Lucky said. 'I called the production trailer. He and Mary Lou took off ten minutes ago.'

'Where were they shooting?'

'Downtown. It'll take them at least half an hour to get here.'

'Not the way Lennie drives,' Steven interjected. 'I hope Mary Lou remembers to buckle her seatbelt.'

'Are you accusing Lennie of being a bad driver?' Lucky sniffed.

'He's a road warrior,' Steven said, sounding amused. 'Thinks he's the only one out there.'

'He's a defensive driver,' Lucky explained, 'and certainly better than you, Steven. *You* drive like an old lady, huddled over the wheel like it's gonna jump up and bite your ass!'

'*Whaaat?*'

'Seriously,' Lucky said. 'What shall I do? My speech is already half an hour late, but I refuse to give it without Lennie being here.'

'Why?' Steven asked.

'Because I can't, that's why.'

'He must've heard it? Didn't you rehearse?'

'No. It's a surprise. Okay?'

'Well, maybe you could read it to him later. Y' know, like when you're in bed.'

'Brilliant bad idea,' she drawled sarcastically.

'Don't get uptight. Go tell the organizers to delay it.'

'They're already on my case. My speech was supposed to be *before* dinner. After dinner there's entertainment.'

'Why don't you tell 'em to serve dinner, and by the time it's finished Lennie will be here and you can make your speech.'

'Oh, great!' Lucky said. 'When everyone's stuffed and complacent, *I* get up.'

'Hey, listen, it's your problem, not mine. If I were you, I'd give it now.'

'No, Steven. I'm going to wait, okay?'

'Whatever you want.'

Right, she thought. *The story of my life. I've always done whatever I want.*

She was mad at Lennie. Oh, sure, he was shooting a movie, but he *was* the director, so if he'd planned it right he could've wrapped early.

She got up and went to talk to the organizers, stopping at several tables along the way, greeting friends and acquaintances in the movie business. Oh, yes, they were all nice to her now because she owned and ran a movie studio. But when she wasn't in the movie business, would it be true what they said? That in Hollywood, if you didn't have a hit, people crossed the street to avoid you?

Maybe, maybe not. She couldn't care less, because she'd always walked her own road. Lucky was not conventional in any way. Perhaps that was why she and Venus were such good friends.

The organizers threw a fit when she told them her plan. She stood firm. They finally agreed. Since she was the star of the evening they had no choice.

Alex joined her as she made her way back to their table. 'Husband running late, huh?' he said, taking her arm in a proprietary fashion.

'Hey – nobody knows better than you what it's like when you're in production,' she said coolly.

'True,' he said. 'But if it was *me*, and I knew it was your evening, I would've wrapped early.'

Alex was voicing her thoughts, and it aggravated her. He had an uncanny way of tuning into what she was thinking. 'How's your mother?' she asked, knowing exactly how to set his teeth on edge. Alex had an extremely domineering mother, the French-born Dominique, who up until the last few years had ruled his life with an iron fist, or at least tried to.

'Fine,' he said noncommittally.

'Still interfering in your life?' Lucky asked.

'You've got it wrong,' Alex said calmly. 'She gave that up a while ago.'

'Hmm . . .' Lucky said disbelievingly. 'One of these days you'll admit it. You know you're always trying to please her.'

'I hardly ever see her any more,' he said.

'Have it your way,' she said. 'I've no desire to get into your personal business. And perhaps you'll do me the same favour.'

'I *like* Lennie,' he objected. 'Just because he's acting like a rude jerk tonight, I don't hold it against him.'

'He's *not* acting like a jerk,' Lucky countered, furious at his criticism. 'He'll be here any moment.'

'Okay, okay. In the meantime allow me to escort you back to the table so you don't have to stop and talk to every asshole who grabs you.'

'Thanks, Alex. I'm sure this will make the gossip columns very happy.'

'What do you mean?'

'Lucky Santangelo Golden being escorted across the ballroom by bad-boy director Alex Woods.'

Alex laughed. 'Big fucking deal.'

'Where's Pia?' Lucky enquired. 'And where exactly did you come up with this one?'

'You seem to be under the impression that I only date bimbos and actresses,' Alex said. 'Well, let me tell you, this one's a very capable lawyer.'

'She is?' Lucky said, trying to keep the amusement out of her voice.

'What's the matter with you?' Alex said irritably. 'Don't you think an attractive woman can function as a lawyer?'

'Sure I do. And if this one's so smart, maybe she'll last longer than five minutes.'

'You can be such a bitch.'

'I can be a good friend, too. Never forget that, Alex.'

'There *is* something I'll never forget.'

'What?' she said, before she could stop herself.

'Remember that one special night long ago and far away?'

'No, Alex, I do not remember it. We both promised we would forget it ever happened. And if you *ever* tell Lennie, I will personally slice your balls off with a blunt knife. Do you get the picture?'

'Yes, ma'am,' he said, thinking that only Lucky could come up with such a descriptive phrase.

'It's *not* funny,' she said sternly. 'I am quite serious, so quit with the shit-eating grin and let's go back to the table where I'll try to be nice to Mia or Pia, or whatever her name is.'

'If I didn't know you better,' Alex said, fixing her with a quizzical look, 'I'd think you were jealous of all my girl-friends.'

'I told you the problem, Alex. I've got to talk to them; *you* get to fuck 'em.'

'Hey,' he said, straight-faced. 'You think it's *fun* for me? One blow-job and they expect me to return the compliment.'

She shook her head. 'You're absolutely incorrigible.'

'Thanks,' he said, with a big crocodile grin. 'I love it when you talk dirty!'

13

The white girl took the black boy into a restroom at a gas station. *She locked the door and laid out the white powder next to the basin, then she snorted it with a rolled dollar bill, carefully showing him how to do the same.*

'I'm not gonna get sick, am I?' he asked, feeling like a dumb ass. 'Or maybe it'll turn me into an addict?'

'You're really whacked,' she said, running a hand through her short dark hair. 'Snort the coke for fuck's sake and shut up.'

He was drunk enough to do as she said. Drunk and horny. Tonight he was definitely getting lucky. After all, he'd done every-thing she'd told him to do – stolen the CDs, driven around with her in the jeep, played music and had a blast. Obviously she wanted to be with him. Why else would they be spending all this time together?

The coke tickled his nose. He began to sneeze.

'For Chrissakes, don't sneeze in this direction,' she said irritably. 'You'll blow it away.'

'Where'd you get it anyway?'

'Why do you keep on asking me that? I've got my suppliers.'

'You do this often?'

'Don't you worry about it,' she said secretively. 'I do what I do.'

After a few minutes he began to feel pretty damn good. Maybe it was because he was drunk, but the coke must be helping too, because as each moment passed he felt better and better. Shit! He could do anything. Anything she asked him to. He could jump off a fucking mountain if that's what was gonna get him laid.

Why did he have this fixation on her?

Because she'd always been there. Always in his face. Always challenging him. And when his dad was doing drugs and sliding into one of his manic rages, she'd been there to rescue him.

They left the restroom and got back into the jeep. 'I'll drive,' she said, shoving him over. 'You're too wasted.'

'No, I'm not,' he argued.

'Yes, you are,' she said, getting behind the wheel as he slumped back into the passenger seat. 'You're fuckin' out of it.'

Maybe she was right. Everything was rolling around in circles in front of his eyes. It was like being on a high-speed rollercoaster ride.

Zoomin' up.

Zoomin' down.

Zoomin' in a big wide old circle.

Shit! He didn't care about anything at all. He was one happy guy.

14

'**You know** what's nice?' Mary Lou said, gently touching Lennie's arm.

'No, what's nice?' Lennie said, staring straight ahead as he drove the Porsche fast, anxious to get to Lucky's event as soon as possible.

'The fact that you and I are brother-in-law and sister-in-law. Family.'

'Yep,' Lennie agreed. 'That *is* nice.'

'And the other thing,' Mary Lou continued, 'is Carioca and Maria being cousins and all, *and* the same age. The two of them are so cute together. Have you ever watched them? They play Barbie dolls for hours on end. And the thing I like about it is that Carioca is so politically correct. She's got the black Barbie, Maria's got the white Barbie, and they kind of share the Ken doll. It's so adorable. I love it that they're so close.'

'I know,' Lennie said. 'The thing I love is that they're growing up with no prejudices at all, because they understand that whatever colour your skin is, everyone's the same.'

'*Very* profound, Lennie.'

'Y' know,' he said thoughtfully, 'my mom was a total racist – only she didn't know it. She'd make all these rude comments when I was a kid, and I never really understood what she meant until I got smart enough to realize. Course, I never blamed her, she didn't know any better.'

'Your mother lives in Florida now, huh?'

'*Finally* she moved out of California. She met a ninety-year-old retired gangster who took her to Miami. I see her once a year when she comes out here to spend Christmas with the kids.'

'Is that an ordeal?' Mary Lou asked.

'Not really,' Lennie said. 'Alice has mellowed as she's gotten older. Years ago she used to be something else. My dad was a comedian in Vegas and Mom was a stripper – Alice the Swizzle. We were quite a family!'

'Wow!' Mary Lou exclaimed. 'Your mom was a stripper. Didn't that give you hang-ups with women?'

'Not really. I guess it could've, though. Never thought about it.'

'I love how you and Lucky first met,' Mary Lou said, sighing. 'It's *so* romantic, what with you both being married to other people and all.'

'Well, you know the story. Things worked themselves out. *She* left her husband and I split up with my wife. Then Lucky and I got together, and neither of us has ever looked back.'

'You're a great couple,' Mary Lou pronounced.

'Same goes for you and Steven.'

Mary Lou grinned, totally happy. 'I know.'

15

Instead of leaving as she wanted to, Brigette allowed Lina to talk her into making a round of the clubs. Lina insisted, although Brigette would have been much happier at home, in bed, watching TV.

Fredo continued to pay her plenty of attention, but she

tuned him out. She was too busy thinking about the men in her life and how dangerous they'd all turned out to be. Sometimes, when she was alone, her thoughts drifted to Tim Wealth and how he'd lost his life because of her. His gaunt face haunted her. Oh, sure, he'd taken advantage of her youth and treated her badly, but he hadn't deserved to die for it.

Tim Wealth was her recurring nightmare.

Lina kept on pleading with Carlo to dance with her. 'I do not dance,' he said politely, dismissing her with an elegant wave of his hand.

'Then I guess I'll 'ave to make do with you, Fredo,' Lina said, jumping up, her long lean body already moving to the beat. 'Let's go show 'em how it's done,' she said, dragging him on to the crowded dance floor.

Brigette stared straight ahead, her mind still on Tim.

'What are you thinking?' Carlo asked, sliding along the banquette, getting uncomfortably close.

She noticed that he had hardly any accent at all, and she wondered where he'd learned English. Lina was right, he *was* a babe, only she was totally uninterested.

'Oh . . . stuff,' she replied vaguely, sipping more champagne because he made her nervous.

'You are different from other girls,' he remarked.

'What "other girls" did you have in mind?' she asked flippantly.

'Every time I come to New York, Fredo attempts to impress me with his model friends. They are usually quite stupid. Beautiful but dumb.'

'Now that's a myth,' Brigette said, annoyed that he would lump every model into the same category. 'All models are *not* dumb.'

'I can see that now,' Carlo said, his probing ice blue eyes making her more and more uncomfortable.

She took another gulp of champagne. 'Uh . . . I'm quite tired,' she said. 'Would you mind if I took a cab home?'

'It's still early,' Carlo pointed out. 'Besides, I cannot allow you to go home alone. A gentleman would never do that.'

'Nobody minds,' she said, feeling suddenly hot and flustered.

'*I* do,' he said, putting his hand on her arm.

His touch made her even more nervous. She edged away.

'Y' know,' she said, struggling to stay sober, 'Lina really likes you.'

'I like her too,' he answered mildly. 'That doesn't mean I have to be with her, does it?'

And then his eyes were all over her again, and she didn't know what to do. For the first time in a long while she felt a slight flicker of something. Was it attraction? Fear? Too much champagne? She wasn't quite sure.

She stood up from the table, swaying slightly because she was not used to drinking so much. 'I absolutely have to go,' she said, feeling dizzy and light-headed. 'Please say good night to everyone for me.'

He stood also. He was much taller than she, and he had extremely broad shoulders. He smelled of some masculine scent that she found quite intoxicating.

'I will escort you home and come back,' he said.

'I told you, it's not necessary,' she said, panicking slightly as the room began to spin.

'I will be most insulted if you don't allow me to do this.'

Who cares? she wanted to scream. *Who cares if I insult you?*

'Come,' he said, taking her arm. 'I will have the maître d' inform our friends that I shall return shortly.'

What could she do? Lina and Fredo were on the dance floor, lost in a sea of gyrating bodies. And she knew if she didn't get out of there fast she might faint.

'Okay,' she said at last, knowing she should have said no, absolutely not, but somehow or other, Carlo had managed to penetrate her defences.

They got into a cab outside the club and rode in silence to her apartment. She closed her eyes and almost fell asleep. When they arrived she leaned across the seat and attempted to shake his hand. 'Thanks for bringing me home. Good night.'

'An Italian gentleman would *never* allow a lady to go up to her apartment alone,' he said. 'I will escort you to your door.'

'No, please,' she protested, getting out of the cab. 'I'm perfectly safe.'

But he was already right behind her.

They walked into the building together, past the night porter, into the elevator and up to her apartment. She fumbled in her purse for her key, found it, and couldn't fit it in the lock.

Very gently he removed the key from her trembling hands and inserted it himself. Before she knew it he was in the apartment with her.

Why are my hands shaking? she thought, furious with herself. *Why am I allowing him to cross the line?*

She hit a light switch. Her apartment was all pale beige and marble, with huge Moroccan pillows scattered across the floor, oversized coffee tables, Tiffany lamps and real art on the walls.

'You have a most interesting style, Brigette,' he said. 'May I fix us a drink?'

'I'm sorry,' she said quickly, feeling even more disoriented and dizzy. 'I can't let you stay. Lina's waiting for you, so's Fredo. You've got to get back to the club.'

And she turned away.

Her mistake. He grabbed her from behind, surprising her completely, turning her towards him, crushing his mouth down on hers so hard that she could barely breathe.

She struggled to get free, but as she did so a strange thing happened – her body reacted in such a way that she found herself unable to resist. It was almost as if she were powerless.

'Why are you doing this?' she managed.

'Because we both want me to,' he said, and immediately began kissing her again.

This was crazy. She'd held out all this time, and now suddenly here was this stranger, this Italian who lived in London, and he was kissing her, and she was incapable of fighting him off.

Too much Cristal. No more drinking for you, young lady.

'Carlo, you've got to go,' she said, finally summoning the strength to push him away.

'Why?' he said calmly. 'Are you married?'

'No, of course not.'

'Engaged?'

'No.'

'Do you have a boyfriend?'

'I don't.'

'Then what is stopping us? Are you a lesbian?'

'That's ridiculous . . .'

He thrust his strong hands into her long blonde hair and concentrated on her mouth.

She tried to pull back, but her body wouldn't let her. Besides, everything was spinning again . . .

'Brigette,' he murmured, between deep, soulful kisses. 'Ah, my sweet, adorable Brigette . . .'

16

It was past nine and dinner was finished.

'You've got to make your speech without Lennie here,' Steven urged. 'It's getting too late to wait any longer.'

'Where *are* they?' Lucky demanded, impatiently drumming her fingers on the table. 'They left the location an hour ago. It doesn't take *that* long at this time of night.'

'I don't know, Lucky, but you *have* to make your speech. You can't do it after the entertainment – half the people will have left by that time.'

'All right, Steven, don't nag,' she said irritably, signalling one of the organizers. 'I'm ready,' she said briskly. 'Let's get going.'

'Good,' said the man, relieved. 'I'll see if I can find Mr Dollar. He's making the introduction.'

'Charlie Dollar is introducing me?' she said, unable to conceal her amusement. 'Whose brilliant idea was *that*?'

'It was supposed to be a surprise, but uh . . . due to the delay we had to keep him in the back. I hope he's still here.'

'You mean you left old Charlie alone with a bottle of Scotch. *That* was daring!'

'If you'll wait a few moments I'll try to locate him.'

Charlie Dollar was one of Lucky's favourite people. He was a fifty-something movie star with stoned eyes, and an off-the-wall, irreverent attitude. Women loved him in spite of his generous gut, slightly receding hairline and penchant for eighteen-year-old beauty queens. He'd won an Oscar for his last movie, and kept it propped against the door of his guest toilet. Typical Charlie.

When they found him he was stoned and drunk – nothing unusual for Charlie. He swayed his way on to the podium with his usual shit-eating grin, trademark tinted shades, and a glass of Scotch in one hand, which nobody had managed to extract. He immediately began speaking.

Lucky listened with a smile as he extolled her virtues, ending up with, 'An' now ... I wanna introduce you to one of the greatest broads in this town. She's a friend. She's a beauty. An' I love her. May I present – Lucky Santangelo.'

The audience responded to his introduction with enthusiasm, leaping to their feet and applauding heartily. Charlie was a popular number.

Lucky took a deep breath as she made her way up to the podium. She'd learned her speech, doing away with any prompters. The only disappointment was that Lennie wasn't there to hear it.

The audience were quiet as she reached the microphone, patiently waiting to hear what she had to say. She took another deep breath and started off slowly, telling them how delighted she was to be there and how satisfying it was to have helped raise so much money for AIDS awareness and research. Then she related a story about two very young brothers she'd met who both had the AIDS virus, inherited from their mother who'd been infected by a blood transfusion. The two boys had convinced Lucky to become involved. 'Mark and Matthew are no longer with us,' she said quietly, 'but I do know they'd be happy to see the progress being made to find a cure.' The audience applauded. 'On a personal note,' Lucky continued, 'I have decided, after a great deal of thought, to step down as head of Panther Studios.'

This was a bombshell. The audience gasped.

'Many movies and a lot of fun later, I feel the time has come to move on and explore other things. And while I'll miss the non-stop action in Hollywood, I've decided to concentrate on my husband and family. Oh, yes, and maybe write a book about all of you.' Another gasp from the audience. 'Seriously,' Lucky continued, 'if I *do* decide I'm capable of writing a book, it'll be dedicated to women and how to make it in what is still mainly a man's world. I feel if *I* did it, anyone can. So ... I guess there's nothing else to say except keep up the good work for AIDS research. Good night and thank you. I leave you with good thoughts and may the best studio win.'

Charlie was waiting to escort her off the podium. 'You're freakin' unbelievable!' he muttered.

'I am?'

'Walkin' away from a studio when you're kickin' prime ass.'

'I'm bored.'

'Bored?'

'Movie stars are boring.'

He raised an incredulous eyebrow. 'You talkin' to me?'

'No. You, Venus and Cooper are the only exceptions.'

'*Sheeit!*'

'What?'

'You're crazier than me. An' that ain't easy.'

Then the press were coming at her, cameras and tape recorders on red alert; a babble of voices and questions.

She was cool and polite. 'I've said all that I'm going to say,' she murmured, moving forward, somehow making it back to her table where everyone wanted an explanation.

'Why?' Venus demanded.

'When?' Cooper questioned.

'Mom,' Bobby complained, thinking of all the benefits he'd miss out on, 'your decision sucks.'

'Thanks, Bobby,' she said evenly, 'but here's the thing of it, it's *my* decision, not yours.'

'Congratulations, kiddo,' Gino said, beaming. 'You make an old man proud.'

'Is Lennie here?' she asked anxiously.

'Not yet.'

'Then I guess he doesn't know,' she said, disappointed that he still hadn't shown up. She hoped nobody would tell him on his way in – that would really go down well.

Now she was regretting that she hadn't discussed it with him first because, knowing Lennie, if he heard it elsewhere, he'd be pissed – maybe even hurt.

She'd been thinking about doing it for months. Being the head of a studio took up too much time and energy. There were always decisions to be made, producers and agents on her case trying to sell her this movie, that star. Problems with back-end, development, giant egos, distribution. Since she'd taken over at Panther she'd turned the studio around, which is exactly what she'd planned on doing. She'd made several movies she was extremely proud of, movies that portrayed women as strong, independent, sexually equal beings who could achieve anything they set their minds to. And in this day of ageism and sexism, that was quite something.

Now all she wanted to do was nothing for a while.

Maybe she *would* write a book, it could be a challenge, and she *always* had relished challenges.

Perhaps Lennie would help her.

No. Bad idea. She didn't need any help.

She glanced across the table to see how Alex was taking the news. He appeared to be deep in conversation with Pia, which Lucky knew meant he was ignoring her on purpose, probably because he was pissed she hadn't confided in him.

Jeez! How many people did she have to check in with before she made a move?

She slid into her seat beside Gino, just as the David Foster-produced show commenced. The MC was the adorable and very funny Howie Mandel, who was set to introduce talented singer and producer, Baby Face, the scintillating Natalie Cole, and finally Price Washington, the superstar comedian. Quite a line-up.

Lucky settled back to enjoy the entertainment.

17

Fuck, she drove fast! The boy had a strong urge to throw up, his stomach couldn't take it. But he managed to control the feeling, because barfing all over her would not be a cool move, and tonight he was determined to make her realize he* was *cool – in spite of all her criticisms.*

He'd been away in New York for eighteen months, back for ten days, and this was the first time she'd taken any notice of him. Bitch! But he'd get her attention tonight. Oh, yeah! He'd get her attention big time.

'Where we goin' now?' he asked.

'Cruisin',' she replied vaguely. 'Lookin' for an opportunity.'

'An opportunity for what?'

'For whatever comes along, jerk,' she said, throwing him a disdainful look.

He had no clue what she was talking about. But who cared? This was good. He was with her. He'd forgotten all about his controlling father, who was more than likely pissed that he hadn't turned up for their early dinner. So what? He didn't have to do anything he didn't want to. And that included graduating high school and going on to college. His dad had never attended college, so why did he have to? His plan was to get out and enjoy himself, not be stuck in some boring classroom learning useless crap for several more years.

The girl raced the jeep towards a yellow light, trying to make it. Too late. The light turned red and she pulled up with a sharp jerk.

It occurred to him that maybe he should fasten his seatbelt. But no, she'd think he was stupid if he did that. Stupid and afraid.

'I gotta take a piss,' he mumbled, feeling the urge.

'What?' she said.

'Gotta go t' the john.'

'Jesus H,' the girl said excitedly. 'Take a look at the diamonds on that bitch in the car next to us.'

Now he knew for sure he had to take a leak immediately. There was no waiting.

'Take a look,' the girl repeated, speaking low and fast.

He leaned across her, peering into the neighbouring car. He saw a pretty black woman sitting in the passenger seat of a silver Porsche. She had on a low-cut dress, diamond necklace and sparkling earrings.

'So?' he said.

'So,' the girl said, looking around and observing they were the only two vehicles on the street. 'We're gonna take 'em.'

'Take 'em where?' he asked blankly.

'You're so fucking stupid,' she spat in disgust. 'We're gonna take her necklace and earrings an' make ourselves big bucks.'

'No way,' he scoffed, sure she was joking.

'Wanna get your dick sucked?' she said.

His eyes bugged. 'Huh?'

'You heard. 'Cause if you're chicken, I ain't doin' it.'

Jesus! She was serious. 'Sure,' he said quickly, before she changed her mind.

'Then all you gotta do is wave the gun at them, an' order the bitch to give you her stuff.'

'You're crazy,' he said, swallowing hard. 'I can't do that.'

'Okay, okay, we'll both do it,' she said. 'There's no one around, we're alone on the street. C'mon, asshole, if we don't act now we won't get another opportunity.'

He couldn't think straight. His mind was totally fogged out and *he wanted to pee more than anything else. But, still, the fact that she'd offered to suck his dick . . .*

Suddenly the girl hit the accelerator, swerving the jeep in front of the stationary Porsche, blocking it. 'Move!' she yelled, opening the door. 'Gimme the fucking gun.'

Blindly he groped for the gun stuck in his belt, and thrust it at her. She jumped out of the jeep and ran around to the passenger side of the Porsche, waving the gun in the air. He trailed behind her.

18

'Oh, sweet Jesus!' Mary Lou exclaimed. 'Lennie – look!'

He didn't have to look, he'd already seen. And before he could take any kind of action, a skinny girl with cropped dark hair had pulled open Mary Lou's door and was brandishing a gun in her face. Behind her hovered a black teenage boy who seemed to be having trouble keeping his balance.

'Gimme your fuckin' necklace!' shrieked the girl at Mary Lou. 'An' your earrings and rings. Give 'em to me *now*, bitch – or I'll blow your fuckin' head off!'

Jesus! Lennie could not believe this was happening to them. 'Hand her your jewellery,' he said to Mary Lou, speaking in a reasonable, calm voice, desperately trying to figure a way out.

'No!' Mary Lou said stubbornly. 'Steven gave me these things. I'm not giving them to her.'

'Take off the fuckin' jewellery, bitch!' the girl yelled.

'You don't want to do this,' Mary Lou said, exhibiting great bravery in the face of a dangerous situation.

The boy, stationed behind the girl, didn't move.

Lennie's mind was racing. He kept a gun in the glove compartment of his car, but there was no way he could reach across Mary Lou and grab it. The best thing to do was simply comply with their wishes.

The girl waving the gun was flushed and edgy. 'You'd better do it, cunt,' she said, in a low, angry voice. ' 'Cause I'm gettin' impatient.'

'For God's sake, give it to her *now*,' Lennie urged Mary Lou.

Reluctantly Mary Lou reached up, attempting to unclasp

her necklace. Her hands were shaking so much that she couldn't quite get it undone.

In the distance, Lennie heard the sound of a police siren.

The girl heard it too, which started to freak her out. 'Gimme the fucking shit!' she shouted excitedly, reaching over, grasping Mary Lou's necklace and yanking it off her neck. The boy standing behind her still hadn't moved. 'Take it, asshole!' the girl screamed, thrusting the necklace at him. He stuffed it in his pocket.

'Now the earrings,' the girl snarled, as the sound of the police siren grew nearer.

'No,' Mary Lou said. 'You've got my necklace. Take it and go.'

'You dumb bitch!' the girl shrieked, whacking Mary Lou across the face with her gun.

That was it for Lennie. He threw himself across Mary Lou, grappling to reach his own gun stashed in the glove compartment.

The girl saw what he was trying to do and completely lost it. 'Fuck you!' she bellowed. 'Fuck all of you!' And with that she raised her gun, took a step away and fired, hitting Mary Lou in the chest.

The explosion was so loud that the boy jumped back a couple of paces and pissed himself.

Lennie was in shock. It was like he was caught in the middle of a slow-motion nightmare. All he could think of was that at any moment he'd open his eyes and it would all be a bad dream.

But he saw Mary Lou's blood soaking the front of her gown, and he knew with a feeling of dread that this was no dream, this was the real thing.

'You've shot her,' the boy cried out in a panic. 'You've fucking shot her.'

'*We*'ve shot her,' the girl yelled back. 'An' the dumb cunt deserved it.' Then she reached forward, snatching the earrings from Mary Lou's ears and began going for her rings.

Lennie roared into action, struggling to grab the girl and stop her. Cold-bloodedly she fired again, the bullet catching him in the shoulder.

He fell back, groaning with a sudden onslaught of sharp pain.

'Let's get outta here,' yelled the girl, and the two of them began running back to the jeep.

Somehow or other Lennie managed to hoist himself up, frantically trying to catch a glimpse of their licence plate.

The numbers danced before his eyes. Then he slumped back in his seat and passed out.

19

Brigette stirred, almost awake, but not quite. She'd been dreaming – vivid sensual dreams about love and passion. She rolled over and opened her eyes with a start. The room was dark. Reaching for her bedside clock, she pressed the top button to illuminate the time. It was just before one a.m.

She tried to collect her thoughts because the last few hours were a complete blur. Dinner with Lina, Fredo and his cousin. A club or two, and after that – nothing.

Hmm . . . she thought. *Aren't I a bit young for short-term memory loss?*

She stepped out of bed and padded into the kitchen to get a glass of water, suddenly realizing she was completely naked.

She *never* slept naked. Had she been drinking?

She couldn't remember.

She poured a glass of water and drank it down in several large gulps, quenching a raging thirst. Then she started going over the events of the evening one more time. She remembered the restaurant where they'd had dinner, drinking champagne, dropping by a couple of clubs. She had a vague memory of Lina and Fredo heading for the dance floor, and Carlo talking to her. After that it was all one big blank.

Oh, God! Am I losing my mind?

She gulped down another glass of water, satiating her incredible thirst. Then she went back into her bedroom, put on a robe and sat on the edge of the bed desperately trying to recall at least something.

Had she gotten sick? Drunk? What the hell had happened?

This was ridiculous. She couldn't remember a thing. *Someone must have brought me home*, she thought. *Maybe Lina.*

She wondered if Lina was home. Probably not. When Lina

didn't have to work the next day she was into partying all night and sleeping until past noon the following day.

Brigette tried her number. No response. She kept trying until the service picked up. Then she left a message for Lina to call her.

She felt . . . different. Her breasts were tender, and when she parted her robe she discovered bruises on the insides of both her thighs.

If I didn't know better, I'd think I'd been making love, she thought. But that was impossible.

And yet . . . she felt as if she'd had sex.

Her mouth was so dry she needed more water. She ran back to the kitchen, panicking slightly. Something had happened and she wasn't sure what.

Fredo would know. She hurriedly dialled his number. He mumbled hello.

'This is Brigette,' she said urgently.

'I'm asleep.'

'Sorry, but I need to talk to you.'

'You and Carlo deserted us,' he said, between yawns. 'Lina is very furious.'

'I . . . I left with Carlo?' she questioned, her stomach sinking.

'We go dance, come back, you're both gone.' Fredo snorted his annoyance. 'Why you wake me at this time? Call Lina.'

'She's not home.'

'Maybe she found Carlo,' he said slyly. 'If you let him free, I'm sure she would've taken him into *her* bed.'

'Y' know, Fredo,' Brigette said irritably. 'It's not *all* about sex.'

'Ah, my sweet little naïve one.' And he hung up.

So, Fredo seemed to think that Carlo had escorted her home. Maybe so, easy enough to find out. She buzzed downstairs to the night porter. 'What time did I get in?' she asked.

'Must've been around eleven, Miss Brigette.'

'Was I . . . uh . . . was I with someone?'

'A gentleman.'

An inward groan. 'How long was he in my apartment?'

'About an hour.'

Oh, God! Here was the deal. She must have been drunk,

had sex with Carlo, and couldn't remember. *Totally* humiliating.

Yet how was it possible? She'd had too much to drink before and never completely blanked out.

It occurred to her, with a feeling of deep dismay, that she might have been drugged. Some of the models had been talking lately about a dangerous new pill doing the rounds. Rohypnols – known on the street as ruffies. Apparently the pills were colourless and odourless, and guys were slipping them in girls' drinks so they could take advantage of them. One of the effects of the drug was total memory loss.

Could Carlo possibly have done this to her?

She buzzed the front desk again to find out if Lina was home. The porter informed her that, no, Lina was still out.

She didn't know what to do next. She had no proof, although maybe if she went to a doctor they could take a blood test and find out for sure if she'd been drugged.

No. The humiliation wasn't worth it.

She ran a bath, collapsed into the soapy bubbles, and lay there thinking. She was rich, pretty and successful – yet every time she ventured out and let her guard down, something happened.

I'm cursed, she thought grimly. *Exactly like my mom.* Her mother, the heiress Olympia Stanislopoulos, with everything to live for, had died in a seedy hotel room with her current addiction – Flash, a drugged-out rock star.

I don't want to be like my mom, she thought, shivering uncontrollably. *I don't want to end up the way Olympia did.*

She wanted to call Lucky in the worst way. Then she remembered that Lucky was out at an event honouring her in LA. And, anyway, every time she got into trouble she couldn't go running to her godmother.

You are not a child any more, she told herself sternly. *You have to learn to deal with things.*

But how could she deal with this when she wasn't even sure what had happened?

She got into bed, huddled beneath the covers, and eventually fell into a fitful sleep.

☆

20

The screaming sound of an ambulance's siren awoke Lennie with a jolt. He was about to get up and shut the bedroom window because the noise was so goddamn loud when he realized he was not in his own bed: he was *in* the ambulance.

Christ! was his first thought. *What the hell am I doing in an ambulance?*

He must've made a noise, more like a groan, because a medic appeared beside him, carefully lifted his head an inch or two and fed him a few sips of water.

'What happened?' he managed.

'You were shot,' said the medic, a cheerful-looking ginger-haired man. 'Took a bullet in the shoulder.'

'Jesus!' he mumbled, trying to get his mind around this startling fact of life. 'How?'

'Attempted car-jacking. You must've given 'em a fight.'

Car-jacked. Car-jacked. Slowly it started to come back. A girl yelling, waving a gun. Mary Lou clinging on to her necklace. A black boy standing silently in the background.

Fuck! The girl had shot him. She'd pointed a gun and shot him! It didn't seem possible.

'Where's Mary Lou?' he asked weakly, noticing a throbbing pain in his shoulder.

The medic turned away for a minute. 'She your wife?'

'No ... my ... sister-in-law.' He groaned, suddenly remembering. 'Oh, God, she was shot, too. How's she doing?'

'The police will need to talk to you.'

'Why?'

'Find out what happened.'

'Lemme see Mary Lou,' he said, thinking how pissed Lucky would be when she heard. She was always warning him to be more careful. 'Havta call my wife,' he said, closing his eyes. 'Gotta tell her ...'

Suddenly everything began to spin, and he didn't feel so great. This could be because he'd never been shot before.

It was not a good feeling.

☆

'Something's wrong,' Lucky said, suddenly sitting up very straight.

'Shh . . .' Gino said gruffly, nudging her to shut up. 'I like this Baby Face, the guy's got a voice.'

'I know something's wrong,' Lucky said sharply. 'I'm calling home.'

'You can't walk out while the man's singing.'

'I can do whatever I want, Gino,' she whispered fiercely, leaving the table and making her way to the back of the crowded ballroom.

Steven came after her. 'What's going on?' he asked.

'I . . . I don't know, Steven. I've got this weird feeling something's wrong.'

He sighed. 'You and your weird feelings.'

'I have to call home, see if the children are okay.'

'You know they are,' he said, producing his cellphone anyway. 'You shouldn't've walked away from the table,' he added. 'It's your night, Lucky, everyone is watching you. And Baby Face is in the middle of a song.'

'What are you? My keeper?' she snapped, in no frame of mind to have either Gino or Steven telling her what to do.

'*You*'re in a good mood,' he said.

'That's because I need to know where Lennie and Mary Lou are. This isn't like him, and it's certainly not like your wife – she's *always* concerned about getting everywhere on time.'

'I'll call my house,' he said, punching out his number. Jennifer answered and assured him all was quiet. He handed the phone to Lucky. 'Your turn.'

She took the small phone and reached CeeCee. 'Everything okay?'

'Of course,' CeeCee said. 'Why?'

'It's late and Lennie hasn't gotten here. I thought he might have called.'

'I'm sure he would've been in touch if anything was wrong.'

'So you haven't heard from him?' Lucky said, turning her back on a hovering photographer.

'Wait a minute,' CeeCee said. 'The other line's ringing. Shall I get it?'

'Yes,' Lucky said abruptly. Sometimes she experienced hunches, feelings that enveloped her, feelings she couldn't explain. She had one now. It was like a black cloud hovering overhead, and she *knew* something bad was about to happen.

A few moments later CeeCee came back on the line. 'It . . . it's about Lennie,' she said, sounding upset.

Lucky felt a cold chill. 'Yes?' she said, fearing the worst.

'He . . . he was shot in a robbery. They've taken him to Cedars.'

'Oh, my God!' Lucky said.

Steven grabbed her arm. 'What?' he demanded.

'Lennie's been shot. He's at Cedars.'

'What about Mary Lou?' Steven asked urgently. 'Was she with him?'

'CeeCee,' Lucky said, desperately trying to stay calm, 'was Mary Lou with him?'

'They . . . they didn't say.'

'What *did* they say? Is it bad? Is he going to be okay?' WILL HE LIVE? screamed silently in her head.

'He's being taken to emergency.'

'Stay with the children,' Lucky said, trying to think straight and not panic. 'Do *not* tell them. I'm on my way to the hospital.' She clicked off the phone. 'I don't believe this,' she said, shaking her head. 'I *knew* something was wrong. I fucking *knew* it.'

'Where's Mary Lou?' Steven said.

'Probably looking after him, you know how she is.'

Steven nodded, praying that this was the case.

'Let's go,' Lucky said.

'What about Gino?'

'Go back to the table, say I'm not feeling well, and tell Gino to take Bobby home after the show. Hurry. I'll get the limo and meet you in front.'

Oh God, that feeling in the pit of her stomach never lied. How many times had she begged Lennie not to drive the Porsche in bad areas of town? He'd laughed at her. 'You're such a panicker,' he'd said. 'Always worrying something's going to happen.'

'I'm smart, Lennie,' she'd answered. 'And if *you*'re smart you can stop stuff from happening.'

'Yeah, yeah, sure.' He'd laughed. 'Miss Know-it-all.'

'You think getting mugged is planned, Lennie? It doesn't happen that way. Crime is a spur-of-the-moment thing, you've *always* got to be on the alert. Gino taught me that.'

'I'm careful,' he'd assured her.

'No, you're not. You're in a world of your own – always thinking about the script you're working on, your movie . . .'

And so they'd argued. And now this had happened.

She hurried out of the hotel and into the limo. Steven joined her a few moments later.

'Let's go, driver,' Lucky said. 'And break records. We need to be there like now!'

21

'You're a right little bitch,' Lina said, her face contorted in anger, not at all her usual friendly self.

Brigette stood at Lina's door, makeup-less, clad in leggings and a baggy sweatshirt. She looked miserable.

Lina, heading for a major hangover and clutching a short scarlet robe around her, resembled the wild woman of Borneo. Her black hair was standing on end and her skin was all blotchy. Without her immaculate makeup she was certainly not the exotic, feline supermodel featured in all the fashion magazines.

'Let me in,' Brigette insisted, shoving past her. 'Something happened.'

'You bet your skinny arse something 'appened,' Lina said crossly. 'You *knew* perfectly well *I* fancied Carlo, yet *you* ran off with 'im. You can't do that to a girlfriend an' expect t' get away with it.'

Brigette marched into the kitchen, shaking her head. 'You don't understand,' she said.

'Sure I do,' Lina said, following her. 'I understand plenty. And now I want to go t' bed an' get some sleep, so piss off.'

'No, no – you *don't* understand,' Brigette assured her, sitting down at the kitchen table and putting her head in her hands. 'I was drugged.'

Lina stopped short. 'You were *what*?'

'I think Carlo slipped a pill into my drink.'

'What kind of pill?' Lina said suspiciously.

'You know, ruffies. Whatever those stupid drugs are that guys give girls so they can rape them.'

'C'*mon*,' Lina said disbelievingly. 'Carlo doesn't 'ave to drug anybody for sex. Look at 'im – 'e's a babe, 'e can 'ave whoever 'e wants. He could've 'ad *me* if *you* hadn't dragged 'im off.'

'You don't get it,' Brigette said excitedly, sitting up straight and banging her fist on the table. 'I *didn't* drag him off. I don't remember anything.'

'Not *anything*?' Lina said cautiously.

'I don't remember coming home, or leaving the club – nothing. I woke up just now, and I'm covered in bruises.' A long pause – then, 'I *know* somebody made love to me.'

'Shit!' Lina said, frowning.

'There's no way I'd take a guy from you,' Brigette continued earnestly. 'I swore off sex ages ago. *You* know that. I don't even *like* sex.'

Lina nodded. 'I'll pour us a brandy an' get Fredo over here.'

'We can't tell him,' Brigette said, panicking. 'We can't tell anybody.'

'If Carlo did what you *think* he did,' Lina raged, 'then 'e's a right bastard, an' I'll personally kick his scummy balls all the way to Italy an' back! But first we gotta find 'im, an' that's where Fredo makes 'imself useful.'

'This is the most embarrassing thing that's ever happened to me,' Brigette wailed.

'No, it's not,' Lina said firmly. 'Remember Michel Guy? *That* was the most embarrassing. *This* is something you can deal with.'

'How?' Brigette asked, feeling powerless. 'I don't even know where he's staying.'

'I told you,' Lina said, attempting to smother a yawn. 'Fredo will know.'

'You must think I'm such an idiot.'

'Revenge, baby,' Lina said, nodding vigorously. 'Think about *that*.'

'I don't know . . .' Brigette said unsurely.

'Oh, yes,' Lina's eyes were gleaming at the thought, 'I'm *really* into revenge.'

'You are?'

'It's the only way, ain't it?'

'Maybe . . .' Brigette said, thinking that Lucky always said the same thing.

'Stop worrying,' Lina said. 'We're gonna get the wop bastard, or I'm not a bleedin' supermodel!'

By the time Fredo put in a reluctant appearance, Lina had slipped into a T-shirt and ripped jeans, hidden her unruly hair beneath a Chicago Bears baseball cap, and added Dolce & Gabbana oblique shades.

'Where's your freakin' cousin?' she demanded, before he was half-way through the door.

'Excuse me?' Fredo said, wondering what his handsome cousin had done now.

'Where's the bastard stayin'?' Lina shouted.

Fredo gave a vague shrug. 'I don't know. He leaves in the morning. And why you get me out of bed?'

'Ha!' Lina said, outraged. 'Where's 'e goin'?'

'Why you so mad?' Fredo asked. 'And what's the matter with *you*?' he said, glancing at Brigette, who was now sitting on the couch in the living room, her knees pulled up to her chin.

'I'll tell you why we're mad,' Lina said furiously. ''E bleedin' raped her, didn't 'e?'

'Don't be ridiculous,' Fredo said, his bushy eyebrows shadowing his eyes with a deep frown.

'It's not ridiculous,' Brigette said flatly. 'I'm sure Carlo must've slipped a pill in my drink.'

'I do not believe this,' Fredo said, blinking rapidly. Actually, he believed it only too well.

'You'd better,' Lina said angrily, ''cause she's gonna bleedin' sue 'im. An'—'

'No, I'm not,' Brigette interrupted.

'Yes, you are,' Lina said, silencing her with a stony stare.

Fredo didn't know what to say, so he remained silent, figuring that was the safest way to play it. All he wanted to do was go home and get into bed. Lina was scary when she was angry.

'So . . . the scumbag is goin' back to England and his fiancée, I suppose,' Lina sneered disparagingly. 'There *is* a fiancée, isn't there?'

'As far as I know,' Fredo said, gesturing vaguely.

'Who *is* this arsehole anyway?' Lina demanded. 'And why'd you drag *us* out with him?'

'Yes,' Brigette said, joining in. 'You said he was a prick, so why did you introduce us?'

'Sorry,' Fredo said, throwing up his hands. 'Carlo and I, we grew up together in Roma.'

'How come?' Lina said.

'When my mother died, I was sent to live with Carlo's family. His father is my mother's brother,' Fredo explained. 'Carlo was always the handsome one. Me, I was looked upon as merely the stupid cousin. So when I came to America and make the big success, I was finally able to impress him. Every time Carlo visits, I introduce him to beautiful models. This way *I* am the important one now.'

'He's a bastard,' Lina said shortly. ''E fuckin' raped 'er, an' you'd better do somethin' about it.'

'I told you,' Fredo said. 'Carlo leaves tomorrow, and I don't know where to reach him.'

'You know what,' Brigette said, suddenly jumping to her feet. 'Let's forget about it. I never want to see him again, or hear his name mentioned. Okay, Fredo? Lina?'

'You're gonna let it drop?' Lina said in disgust. 'Do nothing?'

'Yes,' Brigette said, making up her mind. 'As far as I'm concerned, it's over.'

'If Carlo did what you say he did, then I am very sorry,' Fredo said, thinking that what Brigette claimed was probably true, because Carlo had never been a man to be trusted.

'So you should be,' Lina muttered ominously.

By the time Fredo left, Brigette felt a lot calmer. She went back to her own apartment and took a shower, frantically scrubbing her skin, wondering what kind of advantage Carlo had taken of her while she was passed out.

Then she decided it was better that she didn't know. And she got back into bed and tried to sleep. Early in the morning she and Lina were leaving on a photo shoot to the Bahamas. She'd soak up the sun, enjoy posing for the photographs, and forget all about her ordeal.

If there was one thing Lucky had taught her it was always move on, never get dragged down by the past.

And that's exactly what she planned on doing. She was moving on.

22

Detective Johnson stood beside Lennie's bed. He was a tall, awkward-looking man in his forties, with an austere Marine crew-cut, and heavy steel-rimmed glasses. He stared down at Lennie, slightly uncomfortable because he knew Lennie Golden was famous, and that would make this case all the more difficult. Before long the press would be swarming, especially if Mary Lou Berkeley died – which right at this moment seemed to be a possibility. A team of doctors was working on her in the operating room, but right now it didn't look too good.

'They came at us out of a dark-coloured jeep,' Lennie said. 'Two of them, a girl and a boy.'

'How old?' Detective Johnson asked, making copious notes in a looseleaf notebook.

'Teenagers. Seventeen, eighteen. I dunno,' Lennie said, shifting uncomfortably. 'Has somebody contacted my wife?'

'She's on her way.'

'How's Mary Lou doing?'

'Holding on.'

'Shit!' He groaned. 'How serious is she?'

'We're ... hopeful,' the detective said, clearing his throat. 'Uh ... Mr Golden, I know this isn't the ideal time, but the sooner I get the facts ...'

'Yeah, yeah, of course,' Lennie said, still in semi-shock.

'Two teenagers,' Detective Johnson said, prompting him. 'White? Black? Asian?'

'Uh ... the girl was white. She was the one waving the gun at us. In fact, she was the one doing all the talking.'

'Talking?'

'Y' know, she was demanding Mary Lou's jewellery. Threatening to blow her fucking head off if she didn't give it up. That kind of movie-speech stuff.' He laughed bitterly. 'I couldn't write it if I tried.'

'And the boy was—'

'Black. Didn't say a word. Kind of hung behind her like he wasn't into it.'

'That's unusual.'

'*She* was definitely in charge.'

'And so?'

'So Mary Lou reached up to take off her necklace, and the clasp got stuck or something. That's when the girl leaned in and dragged it off her neck.'

'Yes?' Detective Johnson encouraged.

'It's . . . it's kind of a blur after that. We heard a police siren in the distance. The girl wanted Mary Lou's earrings and she wouldn't give them up. I guess she felt brave 'cause the siren sounded like it was getting nearer.'

'Is that when the girl shot her?'

'No. She hit Mary Lou across the face with her gun, and I kinda lost it—'

'Lost it?'

'I tried to reach *my* gun, which was in the glove compartment. Then she shot Mary Lou, just like that. In cold fucking blood.'

'What did the boy do?'

'Nothing. He was standing behind her. She shoved the necklace at him and he put it in his pocket.'

'And then?'

'She started ripping the earrings out of Mary Lou's ears, so I went for her. That's when she shot me. After she fired the gun, they ran . . .'

'Back to the jeep?'

'Yeah . . .'

'Did you get the licence-plate number?'

'Don't remember it,' Lennie mumbled, feeling dizzy.

'Anything would help.'

'I – I can't be sure.'

'Excuse me, Officer,' said a stern-faced nurse, moving close and taking hold of Lennie's wrist to check his pulse. 'It's time for you to go.'

Detective Johnson nodded. 'Get some rest,' he said to Lennie. 'It'll help. I'll come back in the morning. When I do, I'd like you to take a look through some books and talk to our sketch artist.'

'Sure,' Lennie said.

'Thanks, Mr Golden.'

'When can I see Mary Lou?'

'Someone will let you know.'

'Jesus!' Lennie sighed. 'This is surreal. Like it never really happened.'

'Common reaction,' Detective Johnson said. 'I'll be back tomorrow.'

'Not too early,' the nurse said snippily. 'This patient needs his rest.'

☆

Lucky raced into the hospital, Steven right behind her. Reception directed them to the intensive care unit.

Travelling up in the elevator neither of them said a word. Lucky was praying that Lennie would be okay, and Steven was too busy wondering why Mary Lou hadn't called. She had the number of his cellphone, which she knew he always kept on, so he couldn't understand why he hadn't heard from her.

They got out of the elevator and hurried down the corridor to the nurses' station.

'Lennie Golden,' Lucky said, to a tall, thin, black nurse.

'Mr Golden's been moved out of Intensive Care into a private room,' the nurse said. 'He's doing fine.' She stepped out from behind the desk. 'Please follow me.'

Steven put his hand on her arm. 'Where's Mary Lou Berkeley?' he demanded. 'She was with Mr Golden when he was shot.'

The nurse glanced at him. 'And you are . . . ?'

'Her husband.'

'Uh . . . Mr Berkeley, you should speak to Dr Feldman.'

'Who's Dr Feldman?'

'He's looking after your wife.'

He felt his stomach drop. 'So she *was* hurt?'

'If you wait right here I'll page the doctor,' the nurse said. 'Mrs Golden, you can come with me.'

Lucky quickly kissed Steven on the cheek. 'I'm sure she's fine,' she said encouragingly. 'I'll see Lennie, then I'll come find you.'

'Right,' Steven said, attempting to keep it together, although inside he was petrified. What if something bad had happened to his precious Mary Lou? What if she'd been shot too?

No. It was impossible. He was thinking the worst when everything was going to be okay.

The power of positive thinking. It worked every time.

☆

Lucky hovered over Lennie's bed. He looked pale and shaken, but very much alive. He winked at her.

'Oh, God, Lennie!' She sighed, grabbing his hand and squeezing it tightly. 'You've got to stop pulling these stunts. I can't take it any more.'

He grimaced. 'We got held up by a couple of kids. They came out of nowhere.'

'I don't want to say I told you so, but for Chrissakes get rid of that fucking Porsche.'

'My wife the nag,' he said, summoning a weak grin.

'What happened to Mary Lou?' Lucky asked. 'Where is she?' From the look on Lennie's face, she knew it was not good news. 'Oh, God.' She groaned. 'How bad is it?'

'Dunno,' he said. 'Can't seem to get any information.'

'Damn,' Lucky said. 'Now that I know you're okay, I'd better go find out.'

☆

Dr Feldman looked Steven straight in the eye and said, 'I'm not going to lie to you, Mr Berkeley. Your wife has suffered serious damage from the bullet, which is lodged extremely close to her heart. She's lost a tremendous amount of blood, and I'm sorry to tell you that she's also lost the baby.'

'What?' Steven said blankly.

Dr Feldman cleared his throat and looked uncomfortable. 'You *did* know that your wife was pregnant?'

'I . . . I didn't.'

'She was in the early stages . . . no more than two months.'

'Can I see her?' he asked, his mind in turmoil.

'She's very weak, Mr Berkeley.'

'Can I see her?' he repeated forcefully. 'I want to see her *now*.'

'Certainly,' the doctor said, taking a step back.

Steven followed the man down the corridor to Intensive

Care. The doctor was droning on about the bullet being lodged in a place they hadn't been able to get to. And since she was in such a weakened state they were not going to try again until she'd had a blood transfusion. However, this would have to take place soon, because the bullet was blocking certain functions and it was essential they remove it, otherwise . . .

Mary Lou was in a semi-conscious state. Her beautiful big brown eyes flickered when she saw Steven, and she made a vain attempt at a smile.

'Baby,' he whispered, bending over her. 'My sweet, sweet baby.'

'I'm sorry . . .' she murmured. 'Wasn't my fault . . .'

'Nobody said it was,' Steven said, brushing a lock of hair off her forehead.

'You do know that I love you,' she said very softly.

'Yes. I do know that, baby.'

'If only . . .'

'If only *what*?' he said, leaning closer.

And she opened her eyes very wide and gazed into his. 'Take . . . care . . . of . . . Carioca.'

Then she began to convulse, and as Steven screamed for help, she quietly slid away.

By the time Lucky reached them, Mary Lou was gone.

23

Early in the morning Brigette and Lina shared a limo to the airport, both hiding behind oversized dark glasses – the supermodel staple. Lina attempted to bring up the subject of Carlo, but Brigette shushed her with a finger to her lips. 'I don't care to discuss it,' she reminded her friend. 'Whatever happened is over. Please don't make me sorry I told you.'

'Ha!' sniffed Lina. 'If you can't tell *me*, who can you tell? We're friends – remember?'

'The only reason I told you was because I didn't want you thinking I'd chased after him when I knew *you* were interested.'

'I probably 'ad a narrow escape,' Lina mused. 'Rape ain't my cuppa tea.'

'Me neither,' agreed Brigette, wondering how Lina could be so insensitive, but forgiving her anyway. 'Let's make a pact that we'll never mention it again.'

'Cool with me,' Lina said.

Brigette felt a lot calmer. She'd made up her mind to put the Carlo incident firmly in the past where it belonged.

'I'm looking forward to seein' a bit of sunshine,' Lina remarked, staring out of the limo window at the windy New York gloom. 'Growin' up in England, it bloody rained every day. Bleedin' rain drove me bonkers.'

'Ever thought of living in LA?' Brigette ventured.

'Nah,' Lina said, with a wild chuckle. 'I'd be dead within a year. All those temptations. You *do* know that me willpower's non-existent!'

'Like there aren't temptations in New York?' Brigette said.

'I'd get carried away in LA,' Lina explained. 'Anyway, when I'm a movie star I'll 'ave to spend more time there.'

'You should meet Lucky,' Brigette remarked. 'She's got a kick-ass attitude you'd love.'

'I bet.'

'I wish I could be more like her.' Brigette sighed. 'She's got it together. Career, husband, kids. Lucky has it all.'

'Who's she married to?'

'Lennie Golden – he *used* to be my stepdad.'

'Sounds complicated.'

'I suppose it is – *was*. You see, he was married to my mom for a short while – who happened to be Lucky's best friend.'

The limo entered the private part of the airport. They were flying to the Bahamas on a chartered plane, courtesy of *Sports World International*, who were organizing the photo shoot for their once-a-year sportswear issue. This year they had six girls going to the Bahamas, accompanied by Sheila Margolis, the *Sports World International* den mother. Also along was their star photographer, Chris Marshall.

'I'm totally into Chris.' Lina sighed. 'Wish he wasn't married.'

'Since when did that make any difference to you?' Brigette remarked.

'It does when 'is wife comes on the trip,' Lina said, lighting a cigarette. 'Remember? The old bag was there last year.'

'Maybe this year you'll get lucky.'

'Yeah,' Lina said ruefully. 'Lucky or unlucky – depending 'ow you look at it.'

'What does *that* mean?'

'I could go for him big time,' Lina said, eyes lighting up at the thought. 'We come from the same background an' all. He was born, like, five minutes away from me. We got history.'

The limo drove across the tarmac to the plane, where Sheila Margolis waited to greet them. Sheila organized the shoot, watched every detail, and kept a beady eye on everyone. She was plump, friendly and well liked. The girls never crossed Sheila – they wouldn't dare. She was the one who made sure they weren't out partying all night, got their sleep and had plenty of energy for the gruelling shoot under the hot Bahamian sun. For six days she kept them under control, and on the last night everyone partied – including Sheila, who last year had been discovered at seven a.m. emerging from the room of a black basketball star, much to Lina's chagrin, because Lina had wanted him for herself, and couldn't imagine what he'd seen in the hardly glamorous Sheila.

'Hi, Sheil,' said Brigette, emerging from the limo and kissing Sheila on both cheeks.

'Hello, darlings,' Sheila greeted them, beaming.

Lina kissed her too. 'Where's Chris?' she asked casually.

'Already aboard,' Sheila said, adding a succinct, 'and keep your hands to yourself, Lina, dear. His wife's not with him this trip.'

'*Ooooh*,' Lina said, with a wicked laugh. 'There *is* a God.'

As they stood talking to Sheila, another limo drew up, and out got Annik Velderfon, the famous Dutch model. Annik was tall and wide-shouldered with a magnificent sweep of long blonde hair and a toothy smile. 'Hello, girls,' she said.

'Hello, Annik,' they chorused.

Annik began conferring with her driver, who was busy unloading her matching Vuitton luggage.

'She's got about as much personality as a dead salmon!' Lina muttered.

'Now, now,' chided Brigette, stifling a giggle.

'C'mon,' Lina said. 'Let's grab the best seats.'

Chris stood up when he saw them coming. Chris was

English, a Rod Stewart clone but younger, with a cheeky smile and plenty of attitude. ''Ello, ladies,' he said, his thick Cockney accent matching Lina's. 'Fancy an 'orrible time?'

''Ello, darling,' said Lina, swooping in for a big intimate hug. 'I hear you left wifey-pie at home.'

'The old bird's pregnant,' Chris announced, stopping Lina in her tracks.

'Oh, that's just great!' she said, with a disappointed grimace. 'I s'pose that means you're off limits again.'

'Sorry, darlin',' Chris said, chuckling. 'The butler did it!'

'Who else is coming today?' Brigette asked.

'There's you,' Chris said. 'Lina, Annik, Suzi, and ... oh, yeah ... Kyra.'

'Good, I like Kyra,' Lina said. 'She's got balls – just like me!'

'Where d'you keep 'em?' Chris asked, with a cheeky wink.

'Wouldn't *you* like to know?' Lina answered, with a flirty smile.

And so it starts, thought Brigette.

'I forgot,' Chris said. 'Didi Hamilton's on this trip too.'

'Shit!' Lina said, pulling a disgusted face. 'The poor man's me.'

'Don't be like that, darlin',' Chris said. 'Didi looks nothing like you.'

'She's black, isn't she?'

'You tellin' me all black girls look alike?'

'Only in the dark,' Lina deadpanned. She was quite jealous of Didi who, at nineteen, was seven years younger than her, very skinny, with exceptionally large boobs – which Lina had tried to convince everyone were silicone-enhanced.

'She's the road version of you,' Brigette whispered. 'No style.'

'Thanks a lot. I don't need a freakin' road version of me on this trip,' Lina grumbled, sulking.

They found seats and settled in.

Kyra Kattleman arrived next. Kyra was Australian, over six feet tall, with a mane of reddish brown hair, a surfer's body, big extra-white teeth, and a high, squeaky voice. She'd recently married a fellow model. 'I'm exhausted!' she said, flopping into a seat. 'Anyone got illicit drugs? I need a boost.'

'Who doesn't?' grumbled Lina.

Sheila Margolis bustled aboard. 'Somebody's missing,' she said, looking around and frowning.

'Didi's late,' Chris said.

'As usual,' Lina added.

'No, not Didi, someone else,' Sheila said.

'Suzi,' Kyra said. 'I spoke to her last night.'

'Suzi's always on time,' Sheila said, worrying.

'She probably got held up in traffic,' Lina said. 'It's a bitch getting here at this time.'

Most of the girls were secretly envious of Suzi, who'd recently starred in a Hollywood movie and was currently engaged to a sexy movie star.

'Suzi's a wanker's dream,' Lina had once said about her. 'Totally non-threatening. They can come all over her an' she'll never complain!'

Suzi arrived two minutes later, apologizing for not being on time. She brought flowers for Sheila, a rare photography book for Chris, and home-made cookies for everyone else.

'If I didn't know 'er better, I'd swear she was kissing arse,' Lina whispered.

'No,' Brigette said. 'She's just thoughtful.'

'Bitch!' Lina said.

After Suzi's arrival, they all sat for another twenty minutes before Didi put in an appearance.

Didi sauntered on to the plane as if she had no idea she'd kept them all waiting, infuriating Lina. Naturally she had twice as much luggage as everyone else, so they had to wait even longer while it was loaded aboard.

'You're late,' Lina snapped. 'Don't worry about keeping us all sitting around like a bunch of spare pricks at a wedding.'

'You're always in such a bad mood,' Didi said, blowing finger kisses at Chris. 'Going through the menopause?'

'*What* did you say?' Lina demanded, furious. 'I'm twenty-six, for Chrissakes.'

'Oh . . . sorry,' Didi said, all girlish innocence. 'You seem so much older.'

The two black supermodels glared at each other.

This is going to be fun, Brigette thought.

Lina fastened her seatbelt, seething. 'I'm not goin' on another fucking location with that cow!' she muttered ominously. 'This is *it*.'

'Ignore her,' Brigette said.

'She's always effing with me. Did you *hear* what she said?'

'Everyone knows she's only trying to piss you off,' Brigette said, trying to calm her down.

'I don't 'ave to take her shit,' Lina said broodingly. 'Who needs to be in stupid *Sports World International?* I'm gonna bleedin' *kill* if she gets the cover an' I don't.'

'She won't,' Brigette said reassuringly.

'Easy for *you* to say, you made the cover last year. I've *never* been on the bleedin' cover, 'ave I? Guess I'm too black.'

The plane began taxiing down the runway.

Brigette leaned back in her seat and closed her eyes. Every day she thought the same thing. *This is the start of a whole new life.* But where was her life taking her? The only time she seemed to be living was in front of a camera. And a press-clipping book of magazine covers and fashion layouts would not keep her warm at night.

She was never going to find a man she could trust, one who would treat her nicely. They'd all proved themselves to be untrustworthy time and time again. And yet she'd like nothing better than to meet the right one. Settle down, have a family. Be normal.

Oh, well . . . she had her career, and for now that would just have to do.

☆

One thing Brigette loved was the excitement of being on location, hanging out in a place that completely took over her life. When she got up in the morning she didn't have to make any decisions. There were people to do her makeup, style her hair, choose the outfits she was to wear that day. Everything was taken care of.

Then there was the camaraderie with all the other girls. Brigette got along with everyone. Supermodels – a rare and exotic breed. Leggy girls with slim bodies, manes of shiny hair, luminous skin, gorgeous smiles and plenty of attitude.

Early in the morning, Brigette and Lina took a long power jog along the beach before raiding the hotel room where all the clothes for the upcoming shoot were kept. Today they were starting off with a group shot, so naturally Lina had decided to outshine everyone. She sorted through the hanging racks of outfits, finally picking an outrageous leopard thong bikini with matching sarong skirt. 'This'll do,' she said, stripping off her shorts and tank top and putting on the sexy bikini. 'Think Chris'll like me in this?'

Brigette shrugged. 'Dunno and don't care.'

'Ha! Thanks for your support,' Lina said, prancing like a thoroughbred horse waiting at the gate.

'You know I support you,' Brigette said patiently, 'only it beats me why you have this sick desire to sleep with married guys. What's the kick in *that*?'

'Knowing they want me more than anybody else,' Lina said, licking her full lips. 'And that sometimes they can 'ave me, an' sometimes they can't.'

'Don't you ever think about their wives? And what you're doing to them?'

'What am *I* doing if the wife don't know about it?' Lina said defiantly.

'How would *you* like it if it was your husband sleeping with some beautiful model?' Brigette asked, attempting to reason with her, although she knew it was useless.

'Wise up, Brig,' Lina said, with a casual shrug. 'I couldn't care less. What kind of idiot expects any man to be faithful?'

'You don't think it's possible?'

'Men are dogs, baby,' Lina pronounced, with a knowledgeable nod. 'Offer 'em a blow-job an' they're yours. It don't matter who it is. Politicians, movie stars, the man in the street. Trust me, they're all the bleedin' same.'

'You honestly believe that?'

'Yeah. An' if you don't, then you're naïve,' she said, barely smothering a huge yawn. 'But, then, of course, I'm forgetting – you *are* naïve. For a girl who's gonna inherit all kinds of money, you're *way* not street smart. When *do* you get it all?'

'I have enough now to keep me very happy,' Brigette said, reluctant to discuss her money, because she hated any reference to her role as an heiress.

'Yeah, but don't you score, like, billions of dollars or something?' Lina enquired, pushing it.

'When I'm thirty,' Brigette said, thinking that she wasn't looking forward to that day for a variety of reasons. Big money brought big problems.

'Hmm ... you'd better not let that little piece of

information out the bag,' Lina said, offering advice, ' 'cause if you do, guys'll be storming your life.'

'You think that's the only reason men would be after me?' Brigette asked, slightly irritated.

'Don't get shirty,' Lina said, yawning again. 'Y' know what I mean. You're gorgeous anyway. You can have whoever you want, money or no money.'

'Trouble is,' Brigette said wistfully, 'there's nobody I want.'

'Oh, that's right, I forgot, you're Miss Particular,' Lina said, still posing in front of the mirror. 'The good thing is you an' I get along so well 'cause we appeal to different types. You all blonde an' bubbly, and me – like some exotic prowling black panther.' She giggled at her own description. 'D'you think men find me . . . dangerous?'

'You scare the crap out of them, Lina,' Brigette said crisply.

'Scare the crap out of who?' Kyra asked, entering the room.

'Lina scares men,' Brigette said. 'She's got that predatory look.'

'You mean that carefully cultivated eat-shit-and-die look?' Kyra said, tossing back her luxuriant mane of hair as she approached the clothes rack. 'It sure works wonders on the runway.'

'Secret of me success!' Lina giggled. 'Let's see now . . . It got me four rock stars, one moody film star, a tennis player, two billionaires—'

'Enough!' Kyra shouted, in her high-pitched, squeaky voice. 'You're making me jealous. Before I got married I only had *one* rock star, and he was a dud in bed.'

'Who was that?' Lina enquired.

'Flick Fonda.'

'Bingo!' Lina screamed triumphantly. '*I* just 'ad 'im! You'd think with his studly reputation, an' all that gyrating on stage, he would've been a major performer.'

'Big dick. Has no clue what t' do with it,' Kyra said matter-of-factly.

'Right!' Lina yelled her agreement. 'Calls it 'is joystick. An' the only one to get any joy is *'im*!'

'Since you're always complaining about rock stars,' Brigette said, joining in. 'Why sleep with them?'

'There's too many women around waiting to service 'em,' Lina said. 'Same reason most models are boring fucks.'

'Excuse *me*,' huffed Kyra, quite insulted.

'Beauty's not always a good thing,' Lina continued. 'When I'm with a bloke, I give it me all!'

'So I've heard,' Kyra said, with an insinuating giggle.

'*Especially* if they buy me presents,' Lina added, tapping one of her diamond-stud earrings.

'What *is* this thing you've got with presents?' Brigette said, genuinely puzzled. 'You can afford to buy yourself anything.'

'I know,' Lina said airily. 'Think it's 'cause I was deprived as a child, or some such crap.'

Sheila bustled into the room followed by Didi and Annik. 'Brigette, dear,' she said, 'can I talk to you a moment? It's . . . personal.'

Lina raised an eyebrow. 'Personal?' she said, as if she was entitled to know everything that happened to Brigette.

'Come with me, dear,' Sheila said, leaving the room.

Brigette followed. 'What's up, Sheil?' she asked.

'We uh . . . had a call from your godmother, Lucky Santangelo.'

'You did?' Brigette said, surprised.

'She tried to reach you at your apartment, but of course you'd left,' Sheila went on. 'Then she contacted the agency, and they got in touch with me here.'

'What is it?'

'There's been an unfortunate accident, dear. And Lucky wanted to be sure you heard about it before it's all over the news.'

'Is Lucky all right?' Brigette asked, her stomach doing a crazy somersault.

'She's fine,' Sheila replied, pausing for a moment. 'It's simply that . . . well, Lennie Golden and his sister-in-law, Mary Lou, were the victims of an attempted car-jacking.'

'Oh, God!' Brigette gasped. 'Are *they* all right?'

'Lucky would like you to call her.'

A car-jacking, Brigette thought. *One of the reasons not to live in California.*

She rushed back to her room and immediately placed a call to Lucky.

'Be here Monday,' Lucky said quietly. 'I'm sorry to tell you this.'

'What?' Brigette demanded, filled with foreboding.

'Uh ... Mary Lou is dead. I know she'd want you at her funeral.'

Brigette hung up the phone in shock, too startled to cry, too numb to do anything.

Poor Steven. Poor little Carioca.

And there was absolutely nothing she could do.

BOOK TWO

Six Weeks Later

24

'**Dinner is served,** Mr Washington.'

'Thanks, Irena,' Price Washington replied, strolling into the formal dining room of his Hancock Park mansion and sitting down at the long table set for two. 'Didja call Teddy?'

'He's coming,' Irena said, unfolding a pristine linen napkin and placing it on his lap.

Price Washington was a superstar comedian. Tall, rangy and very black, he was not exactly handsome, but with his gleaming shaved head, full lips and heavily lidded bedroom eyes, he had a look plenty of women found irresistible.

At thirty-eight and currently single, Price was at his peak. His on-the-edge HBO comedy specials were legend, and his in-person performances were always sold out months in advance. Recently he'd starred in a television sitcom that had made him even more famous, and soon he was set to embark on a movie career, which people in the business seemed to think would surpass even Eddie Murphy's raging success.

Irena Kopistani had been his housekeeper for over nineteen years. She was a thin, austere white woman of forty-eight, exactly ten years older than Price. Quite attractive, she was five feet six, with pointed features and straight brown hair, usually worn back in a bun. He'd hired her when he was nineteen years old and out of his mind on drugs. She'd arrived for an interview at his recently purchased Hancock Park mansion, and he'd said, 'Start today,' even though he had no idea what he was doing or who he was doing it to.

At the time, Irena had recently immigrated to America from her native Russia, so she was happy to land any job, especially as she had no references. She moved into the maid's quarters above the garage, and tried to make order out of the chaos that was Price's life.

Over the years she'd succeeded. Now Price could not contemplate being without her. Irena kept him straight. She watched over him with a steely eye. She was always on his side, ready to defend and protect. He'd missed her while he'd been making his sitcom in New York, but somebody had to stay in LA and take care of the house, and there was nobody he trusted more than her.

Sometimes Price couldn't help marvelling at how his life had turned out. Born in the Watts area of LA to a mother who already had three children by three different men, he was raised in abject poverty with no father. His mom had been a real ballsy woman, who by sheer force of will had kept him out of the gangs. And how had she done that? She'd slapped him around so hard that he still had the scars to prove it. She hadn't taken any shit, his mom.

Unfortunately she'd died before he'd achieved any kind of success. When he was fourteen she'd gotten hit by a sniper's bullet crossing the street, and he'd been sent to live with a cousin.

Losing his mother was his one big regret, because she would have derived so much pleasure from his fame and success. Not to mention his grand mansion where she would've had a fine old time.

Not that he didn't enjoy it himself. Once he'd gotten past the drug years it was all a fantasy. Although getting married so young and fathering a son probably had been a mistake. He loved Teddy, but Price was still only thirty-eight, and the responsibility of raising a sixteen-year-old hung heavy.

The trouble with Teddy was that he took everything for granted. He had no clue what it was like growing up on welfare with rats running over your feet while you slept, and having to endure the constant struggle to get enough to eat. Teddy had it too easy. Problem was he was too young to realize his good fortune.

Price knew that God had smiled on him. He had money, fame, happiness – well, not really happiness, because he wasn't exactly ecstatic living by himself in his big old mansion with nobody to keep him warm at night. But he figured that *one* day he'd find the right woman.

He'd been married twice. Both wives had taken up residence in his Hancock Park mansion. Both had tried to force him to fire Irena. He'd stood firm.

Ginee and Olivia. Two witches.

Ginee, black and beautiful, and stoned out of her mind most of the time. He'd lived with her on and off for several years, then made the mistake of marrying her when she'd gotten pregnant with Teddy.

And Olivia. White, blonde and stacked – a ten-month mistake that had cost him dearly.

He knew he had a thing about beautiful women. And he also knew it was about time he got over that particular addiction.

Teddy, dressed in baggy, falling-down pants and an over-sized hooded Tommy Hilfiger sweatshirt, slouched into the room. Price scrutinized his son. Lately he had a feeling that something was going on with the boy, although he couldn't figure out what. A few weeks ago Teddy had arrived home way past his curfew and totally wasted. Price had punished him by not allowing him to leave his room for a week except to attend school. Since that time, Teddy had turned moody and difficult, and he'd developed a real smart mouth.

Irena had agreed with his punishment of Teddy. She understood how difficult it was raising a teenager. She had a daughter, Mila, who'd been born in America. Price didn't see much of the girl, who kept to herself. What he did see, he didn't like. Mila had a bad attitude. She'd been brought up in their household as part of the family, but every time he ran into her she still struck him as an outsider. He discouraged Teddy from hanging with Mila. She was bad news – Price recognized the type.

Teddy flopped into a chair.

'How'd you do at school today?' Price asked, rubbing the bridge of his nose.

'All right,' Teddy said.

Price often wondered if he spent enough time with the boy. Hey, if he wasn't working so hard maybe they could spend more time together, but work came first. It had to. Work paid the bills and kept him straight. Irena, with a little help from his shrink, had taught him that the high he got from working was a better buzz than the one he got from doing drugs.

'Y' know,' Price said, trying to get a dialogue going, 'a good education's everything.'

'You keep on telling me that,' Teddy muttered, his eyes looking everywhere except at his father. 'Only *you* don't get it. I don't *wanna* go to college.'

'No, *you*'re the dumb shit who doesn't get it,' Price said warningly. 'You're goin' whether *you* want to or not. If *I*'d had the opportunity to attend college, I would've considered myself the luckiest dude around. But no, Teddy, *I* hadda bust my ass workin'. *I* was out in the street pimping girls when I was fourteen. How d'you think *I* made it? Sheer guts an' ambition, nothing more. I didn't have no education. You're gonna have that advantage.'

'Don' want it,' Teddy said, scowling.

'You know somethin'? You're an ungrateful little prick,' Price snapped, wishing he could whack his son like his mom used to do to him.

Somehow he controlled himself: his shrink had warned him never to get physical with Teddy, she'd assured him that repeating patterns never worked.

Jesus! Raising a kid today was a bitch. It didn't matter that he was famous, that he knew what went on out there in the real world. Okay, so he was Price Washington, big fucking star. But he was well aware of how it was for other black men. They still had to struggle with the racism that was rampant in every large city across America, and anyone who denied it was living in an unreal world.

'Listen to me, son,' he said, attempting to be patient. 'Education's *it*. If you have knowledge, you got the shit.'

'How much education did *you* need to get up on stage and say motherfucker fifty times a night?' Teddy said, glaring resentfully at his famous dad.

Price slammed his fist on the table. 'Don't you have no goddamn respect, fool?' he shouted. 'I'm your father, for God's sake. Gettin' up on stage is what I do. That's how I make money to put food on this table.'

'I don't give a crap,' Teddy muttered.

'You don't give a crap,' Price repeated, his voice rising menacingly. Goddamn it, he wanted to whack this kid so bad. 'I thought takin' you with me to New York might've done you some good. Forget about it. Since we're back, you're worse than ever.'

'That's 'cause you won't let me do what I wanna do,' Teddy said, staring at the tablecloth.

'Uh-huh, and what exactly *is* it that you wanna do? Sit around the house all day watchin' videos? Or maybe join a gang? You can do that. Go downtown, hang with the dudes in Compton, get yourself shot. That's what black guys are *supposed* to do, right?' He sighed, thoroughly disgusted. 'The young black men of America are killing each other, an' I've given *you* a life like you can't believe, an' all *you* do is hand *me* shit.'

'Why don't you ever let me see my mother?' Teddy demanded.

' 'Cause she's a whore,' Price said, not prepared to discuss it.

'She used to say that 'bout you.'

'That's not smart, boy,' Price said furiously. 'She's a whore who fucked other men in *my* bed. An' when I divorced her she didn't want you. Are you listenin' to me? She signed a paper *sayin'* she didn't want you.'

'You paid her.'

'Sure I did. An' the whore took the money an' walked.' Price didn't know what to say next. What could he say to a sixteen-year-old kid who thought he knew it all? Since he'd decided never to beat him, all he could do was encourage him. And that's what he was trying to do, encourage the dumb little shit to get himself an education. As for wanting to see his mom, what kind of garbage was *that*? Ginee hadn't seen Teddy in twelve years. And, knowing Ginee, she didn't give a damn.

Irena entered the room, her thin face impassive. Irena never interfered between him and his son. She'd tried once, and he'd told her to stay out of family business. Irena knew her place. She was his housekeeper. She organized the workforce that cleaned his house, ironed his shirts, washed his shorts, folded his socks. Irena bought the groceries, drove the car, ran errands, that's what Irena did. And she was good at it.

Both of his wives had hated her. They'd resented that he'd allowed her kid to be raised on the premises, even though

Irena and Mila lived above the garage in the back. It was *his* prerogative if he wanted someone living there, someone who took care of everything when he wasn't around. And Irena was a good cook, too, although some of the Russian shit she dished up didn't exactly appeal to his palate. Over the years he'd trained her not to cook that way. Simple foods were what he liked: steaks, fried chicken, salads. Now she had it down.

'Don't forget,' he said to Irena, 'tomorrow night the guys are comin' by for poker. Pick up some of that Jewish shit – y'know, smoked salmon, bagels, all of that crap. They like it.'

'Yes, Mr Washington,' she said, serving him from a heaping platter of grilled lamb chops, mashed potatoes and green beans.

When she reached Teddy, he pushed his plate away. 'Not hungry,' he mumbled. 'Don't wanna eat.'

'If I didn't know any better, I'd swear you was doin' drugs,' Price said, staring at him accusingly.

'*You* should know,' Teddy countered, remembering the many years his dad had been a total addict.

'I'm gettin' damn sick of your mouth,' Price said, narrowing his eyes.

'And I'm sick of *you* telling me what to do,' Teddy said sullenly.

That was it. Price had had enough. 'You're not hungry?' he roared, getting up from the table and throwing down his napkin. 'Then go to your room, an' don't let me catch a glimpse of your smart ass again tonight.'

Teddy shoved his chair away from the table and slouched out of the dining room.

Price looked at Irena. She returned his look.

'Kids,' he said, with a helpless shrug, sitting down again.

'I know what you mean, Mr Washington,' she agreed.

He reached out his hand. 'C'mere a minute.' She took his hand and moved closer. 'You miss me while I was gone?' he asked, his voice softening.

'Yes, Mr Washington,' she said. 'The house was very quiet.'

'Yeah?' he said, reaching up and touching her left breast, fingering the nipple in a familiar fashion. 'You must've missed me plenty, huh?'

She took a step back, her face expressionless. 'Yes, Mr Washington.'

He chuckled. 'Okay, sweetcakes, maybe later tonight you'll tell me exactly how *much* you missed me.'

Irena kept the same stoic expression. 'Yes, Mr Washington.'

☆

Upstairs, Teddy paced around his room like a rat on a treadmill. Ever since that fateful night six weeks ago, he couldn't get the horrible scenario out of his head.

Two people sitting in a car. Two people not doing any harm to anyone.

And Mila. Blowing the woman away. Grabbing her jewellery and running.

Blood. Teddy kept on seeing the blood soaking the pretty black woman's white gown.

Jesus! And she was a sister too, which made it even worse.

Mila had told him to forget about it. Once they were back in the jeep she'd started yelling about how it was an accident and nobody's fault. But he *knew* the horrible truth. It had been no accident. Mila had brutally shot two people, and the woman had died.

The next day it was all over the news on account of the two people she'd shot being famous. Maybe his father even knew them! That thought really freaked him.

'We're gonna get caught,' he'd told Mila. 'They're gonna find us.'

'They can't,' she'd answered, staring him down. 'There were no witnesses.'

'They'll find us,' he'd repeated. 'The gun – where'd you get it?'

'It doesn't matter.'

'They could put a trace on it.'

'How? They don't *have* the goddamn gun.'

'Where'd you hide it?'

'You think I'm stupid?' she'd sneered. 'I got rid of it.'

'What about her jewellery?'

'Don't worry, when the time comes you'll get your share of the money.' And she'd glared at him with a savage look in her eyes. 'Don't *ever* open your mouth, Teddy Washington. 'Cause if you do, I swear I'll kill you.'

He lived in fear. Fear of his father finding out, and fear of Mila and her threats.

If she was capable of shooting two people, then she was certainly capable of killing him.

Teddy had nowhere to turn.

25

The unreal tragedy had affected all of them. The days drifted into weeks and Lucky was glad she'd made the decision to leave Panther because it gave her time to spend with Lennie and Steven, both of whom desperately needed her – especially Steven, who was totally devastated by the death of his wife.

She'd placed people she trusted in positions of power at Panther. Since her departure there was not one person running the studio, there were three. Which meant that no decisions could be made without all three of them consulting each other, and since she was on the board, it meant that she was still very much involved. She certainly didn't want the studio being less of a power simply because she'd left. After all, she hadn't sold Panther, she'd merely stepped down as studio head, and this way gave her an option if she ever chose to resume control. She'd decided that if in a year she was no longer interested, then she'd sell. She'd make that decision when the time came.

Carioca Jade was staying at their house, comforted by her cousin Maria. The two little girls were inseparable, sleeping in the same room and spending all their time together. *Thank God they have each other*, Lucky thought, remembering how she and her brother, Dario, had clung together when their mother was murdered.

Physically Lennie had recovered quickly. His gunshot had been a surface wound and not that bad. It was the shock of losing Mary Lou that he couldn't seem to get over. 'There's nothing you could've done,' Lucky kept assuring him.

'I shouldn't've gone for my gun,' he said, going over it time and again. 'It was a mistake that cost Mary Lou her life. It's like the worst fucking nightmare in the world.'

Lucky didn't know what to say. He was right, it *was* a nightmare, one they were both trapped in.

Orpheus Studios had shut down production on Lennie's movie until they could recast Mary Lou's role. It might not even get recast because it would put the film way over budget. Lennie had vowed not to return as director. 'I refuse to direct it with another actress,' he'd said. 'Let them get somebody else.'

She'd noticed that he didn't want to leave the house, which is exactly what had happened after his kidnapping. The only time he went out was to take long solitary walks along the beach. He never asked her to go with him, and she didn't volunteer, because she knew he preferred being alone.

He'd hardly mentioned her decision to leave the studio. 'I *wanted* to tell you,' she'd explained, 'but then I thought it would be better to surprise you.'

'It's a surprise all right,' he'd said. And that had been his only comment on the subject. She knew he was pissed.

Now she was at home with him every day, and for the first time in their marriage things between them were strained. They weren't even making love, and she didn't know what she could do to make the situation better.

She understood that he was suffused with guilt, but he had to get over it sometime.

Steven was in a complete depression. Like Lennie, he blamed himself. '*I* should have gone to the location and picked her up,' he kept on saying. 'It was my mistake. I thought she'd be safe with Lennie.'

They both called Detective Johnson on a daily basis. 'We're not the kind of people who can sit back and do nothing,' Lucky informed the detective. 'We expect action.'

Detective Johnson assured them he was doing his best. He'd interviewed Lennie several times to go over things. Unfortunately, Lennie could only remember so much. And, try as he might, he could not recall the licence-plate number of the jeep.

'We've got it down to about six thousand black jeeps registered in California,' the detective told them. 'That's if the jeep *was* black. It could've been dark green or blue, even brown.'

'That's encouraging,' Lucky said, unimpressed with his so-called detective work. 'How do you plan on finding the right one?'

'We're working on it, Miss.'

'Don't call me Miss.'

'Sorry, *Miz* Santangelo.'

Lennie spent many hours with a police sketch artist and who'd come up with a computer likeness of the two suspects. 'She doesn't look any older than Bobby,' Lucky said, staring at the girl's picture. 'To think that teenagers with guns can snuff out a life just like that. There should be a law against it.'

'There *is* a law against it,' Lennie said grimly. 'If you carry a gun, you're supposed to have a licence.'

Lucky decided it might be good for Lennie to get out of Los Angeles for a while. 'How about a trip to New York?' she suggested. 'Remember? The early days – you and me in my apartment?'

'And my big old loft,' he said, with the glimmer of a smile. 'The one you made me sell.'

'I could try to buy it back.'

'Don't be silly.'

'Y'know, Lennie,' she said. 'I keep on flashing back on the night you were shot. Going to the event and you not being there, then hearing about the shooting. Losing Mary Lou is bad enough, but if I'd lost you ... I wouldn't have been able to go on.'

'Yes, you would,' he said. 'You're a survivor. You've survived a lot of shit in your life.'

'So have you, Lennie, and believe me, we'll survive this together. It's like being robbed – somebody breaks in your house, takes your things and runs off into the night. If you caught 'em, you'd feel a hell of a lot better.'

A few days later she contacted Detective Johnson. 'I've been thinking,' she said. 'How about if we hire our own detective agency to help you with this investigation? I'm sure you're short on man-power.'

'I'd have no objections.'

'Would you co-operate?'

'Of course.'

'Then I'll do it. Oh, yes, and I want to post a reward for information.'

'Sometimes that can be helpful. Sometimes not.'

'Let's try it,' Lucky said.

Fuck the system, she thought. One way or another, they were going to catch the killers.

And a reward of one hundred thousand dollars might be the answer.

26

Brigette had been back from LA for a month when she announced, 'I'm taking off for a few weeks.'

'And where are you goin'?' Lina asked, sitting cross-legged on the floor of her apartment, painting her toenails in complicated zebra stripes.

They were having a girl's night in, with Alanis Morissette on the stereo, and a large, half-eaten pepperoni pizza on the table.

'I promised Lucky I'd go to Europe with her,' Brigette said vaguely, not wanting to get too specific.

'Sounds good t' me,' Lina said. ''Ow's Lucky doing?'

'*She*'s okay. Steven's a wreck.'

'It must be awful,' Lina said, taking a swig from a can of Diet Coke.

'It is. You should see him, it's like he's in a permanent daze. And Lennie isn't doing much better 'cause he blames himself. Thinks he could've done something to stop it.'

'Could he?' Lina asked, still painting.

'Not according to Lucky. They had this crazy girl waving a gun in their faces. Can you imagine what it must've been like? They were totally trapped.'

'I'd *freak* if I 'ad a gun in *my* face,' Lina said. 'I'd, like, lose it big time.'

'So would I,' Brigette agreed.

'An' especially it bein' a girl an' all,' Lina added. 'That's like a double whammy – y' know, it's *really* messin' with his machismo.'

'I know,' Brigette agreed.

'They got any leads on who did it?'

'Lennie doesn't remember much.'

'Talk about fate,' Lina said, picking up the remote and clicking on the TV *sans* sound. 'One moment you're sitting in your car, the next you're lying there – dead.'

'Mary Lou was such a sweetheart,' Brigette said. 'Kind and thoughtful. Always nice to everyone. You should've *seen* the turn-out at her funeral.'

'I used to watch her on that sitcom she did years ago,' Lina said, flipping channels.

'The saddest thing of all is that Steven and Mary Lou were *so* happy together.' Brigette sighed. 'And then there's little Carioca, she's only eight, and now she's got no mother. It's a tragedy.'

'Terrible,' Lina said. ''Ow old were you when *your* mum died?'

'Fifteen,' Brigette answered flatly. 'I was better off than Lucky – she was five when she found *her* mother floating in the family swimming-pool, murdered.'

'*My* mum drives me insane,' Lina said, holding out her foot and admiring her freshly painted toenails. 'Although I s'pose I shouldn't complain.'

'I'd have liked nothing better than to have known my mother properly,' Brigette said wistfully, remembering the few good times. 'You should make the most of yours.'

'Fifteen's not that young,' Lina remarked. 'At least you got to spend time with her.'

'Not really,' Brigette said pensively. 'Olympia was never around when I needed her.'

'Where was she?'

'Where was she?' Brigette repeated, recalling the blonde bombshell who'd never wanted to miss a thing. 'Good question. London, Paris, Rome, Buenos Aires. Olympia was the original jet-setter – always flying somewhere for a happening party or a new lover. She had boyfriends, husbands and too much money. I was shunted away to a boarding school in Connecticut which I hated.'

'*Quelle* drag.'

'It certainly was.'

'You can 'ave *my* mum if you like,' Lina joked. 'The old bag keeps on threatenin' to visit.'

'What's wrong with that?'

'She's a colossal pain in the butt.'

'I don't understand. How can you have a problem with her when she doesn't even live here?'

'She 'ad me when she was fifteen,' Lina explained. 'She's forty now, an' still a looker.'

'You should be proud of her then.'

'No, no, you don't get it,' Lina said excitedly. 'The thing that pisses me off most is that sometimes she bloody imagines she's *me*!'

'What does *that* mean?'

'Well, she does all these modelling jobs for magazines an' the English papers. An' the copy always reads Lina's mum this an' Lina's mum that, an' isn't she lovely – just like her famous daughter. That kind of crap drives me bonkers.'

'You shouldn't begrudge her,' Brigette said, wishing that she still had a mother, someone she could trust and confide in. 'She's only trying to emulate you. It's flattering.'

'It is?' Lina said.

'Anyway,' Brigette said, reaching for a second slice of pizza, 'I called the agency and got out of the Milan shows.'

'You did *what*?' Lina wailed. 'Milan's such an adventure. All those horny Italians with their dicks 'anging out!'

'It's more important that I spend time with Lucky.'

'You mean she's taking off and leaving Lennie behind?' Lina said, standing up and stretching.

'He's not exactly in a travelling mood.'

'Poor bastard.'

'So,' Brigette said, 'I'll fly to Europe with Lucky, then probably head back to LA for a while.'

'I'm learning to shoot when *I* get to LA,' Lina announced. 'Which might be sooner than you think, 'cause *I* got an audition for a role in the new Charlie Dollar flick.'

'You have?'

'*Not* that I usually audition,' Lina said quickly. ''Owever, according to my agent, the studio is after a name actress, an' Charlie wants *me*! So, if it comes off, I'll fly out to LA for a couple of days an' meet the man 'imself.'

'I saw him at Lucky's while I was there,' Brigette said. 'He's kind of a weird and wonderful character.'

'Oooh!' Lina said, licking her lips. 'I get off on weird!'

'You can't possibly sleep with him,' Brigette admonished. 'He's almost sixty.'

'So?' Lina said with a mischievous grin. 'I've 'ad older.'

Brigette couldn't help laughing. 'You're incorrigible,' she said.

'I'll take that as a compliment,' Lina replied.

'Well,' Brigette said, jumping up, 'I guess this is a wrap.'

'*When* are you leaving?' Lina asked, following her to the door.

'Tomorrow.'

'I can't believe it!' Lina exclaimed. 'You almost sneaked off without telling me.'

'I just told you.'

'Hmm . . .' Lina said, considering it. 'Maybe I should come with you.'

'Maybe you shouldn't,' Brigette said, grabbing her purse from the hall table. 'You're expected in Milan.'

'I don't *havta* go,' Lina said. 'I can tell 'em to go fuck 'emselves if I want. Then I'll go see Charlie early.'

'The thing is,' Brigette said, 'much as I love your company, I *should* spend time with Lucky by myself.'

'Okay, okay,' Lina said huffily. 'You don't havta draw me a picture.'

They hugged each other, making fervent promises to keep in touch. Both of them knew they wouldn't. Life in the modelling world was always frenetic, they'd meet again soon enough.

Brigette returned to her apartment, put on the Smashing Pumpkins' *Siamese Dream* CD, then began packing, throwing clothes into a suitcase without much thought because her mind was elsewhere.

She was not telling Lina the truth. The truth was painful and very private.

Lucky had no plans to travel to Europe, but *she* did.

She was going to London.

She was confronting Carlo.

And maybe – just maybe – she'd tell him she was pregnant.

27

Lucky's friends rallied. Venus was particularly concerned. 'Are you *sure* you know what you're doing?' she said, while they were having lunch at Le Dôme one day.

'Absolutely sure,' Lucky replied, munching a Chinese chicken salad.

'But you've given away your power base in this town,' Venus said, dazzling in a skin-tight snakeskin dress.

Lucky stared at her platinum blonde friend with a quizzical expression. 'Who needs a power base? *I* certainly don't.'

'Yes, you do,' Venus said excitedly. 'You have to realize,

you were like Superwoman in this town. You could get anybody you wanted to come to a party, meet anyone in the world. Owning a Hollywood studio is like being the fucking President, for Chrissakes.'

'Not quite the same,' Lucky said, with a wan smile. 'However, I get the analogy. Besides, you're forgetting, I still *own* the place.'

Venus downed a quick shot of vodka. She never drank when she was with Cooper, because since the birth of their child he had liked to view her as virginal. 'Have you spoken to Alex?' she asked, picking up her sunglasses.

'No,' Lucky said slowly. '*Should* I have?'

'I thought you two were best friends.'

'You and *I* are best friends,' Lucky said patiently, knowing exactly where Venus was going. 'Alex is just, you know ... someone Lennie and I pal around with.'

'Ha!' Venus exclaimed. 'Don't give *me* that crap. You like him, I *know* you do.'

'I'm married to Lennie,' Lucky said evenly. 'There's no other man that even remotely interests me.'

'God, you're good,' Venus said admiringly. 'You've even got yourself convinced.'

'What *are* you talking about?'

Venus nodded knowingly. 'Everyone sees the chemistry between you and Alex.'

'The only people Alex has chemistry with are his never-ending supply of Asian beauties,' Lucky said, wishing Venus would get off the subject. 'He doesn't like American women. Haven't you noticed?'

'That's true,' Venus agreed. 'Only *you*'re the exception.'

'Can we drop it?' Lucky said, starting to get irritated. 'I haven't heard from him. He's probably feeling left out that I didn't discuss this whole studio thing with him. But, hey, since when do I have to do things by committee?'

'You don't. Although usually with friends you tell them stuff. *Especially* before they read it in the newspapers, or hear about it at an intimate dinner for five hundred people.'

'So you think he's pissed with me?'

'As a matter of fact, I do.'

'You're wrong, Venus. He's been to see Lennie a couple of times.'

'And?'

'And what?' she said, exasperated. 'Will you stop making a meal out of this.'

'Speaking of food,' Venus said, knowing when to move on, 'Cooper and I are planning an anniversary party. We'd like you and Lennie to come.'

'When is it?'

'Next week.'

'We might be in New York.'

'What are you doing there?'

'I thought a change of scenery would be good for Lennie. He's still depressed. It's difficult – how would you feel?'

'Like shit.'

'Right. And there's nothing I can do,' Lucky said, shrugging helplessly. 'He's in the same mood he was in after the kidnapping – moody and withdrawn. It took me months to get him to communicate last time. Now this.'

'How is he with the kids?'

'Quiet. They don't get it. I have to keep telling them Daddy's got a headache. Christ! You'd think it was *him* who'd lost his wife.'

'What are you going to do?'

'I'd like to get him to a shrink. Not that I believe in them, but somebody's got to help him.'

'I have a great shrink,' Venus said, her face brightening.

'Of course you do.'

'She got me through that whole stalker drama a few years ago. I'll give you her number.'

Lucky nodded. 'Sounds like a plan.'

Venus waved at John Paul DeJoria and his exquisite wife, Eloise, as they entered the restaurant. 'He owns all those Paul Mitchell hair products,' Venus said. '*Love* their stuff.'

'I've got to go,' Lucky said. 'I'm meeting the kids.'

Venus nodded. 'Think I'll join Eloise and John Paul.'

☆

Later that day Lucky collected Maria, Carioca and little Gino from school, then took them to the Hard Rock, where she ordered them double chocolate milkshakes and burgers with everything on. The kids were totally excited, chattering to each other as they stuffed their mouths.

Lucky watched them. Playing mom full-time was a whole new experience, and although she adored her children, she wasn't sure family outings were a permanent staple for her. She needed action and excitement. She needed to be doing something creative. And for the first time she had doubts about leaving Panther.

She sat in the restaurant observing the passing crowd. *Somewhere out there is the person who shot Mary Lou and Lennie*, she thought. *And one day soon they'll be found and punished. That's for sure.*

She was determined they'd be caught. And when they were, she expected to see justice.

And if she didn't . . .

Well, there was always Santangelo justice.

And Santangelo justice was something Lucky would not hesitate to use.

28

Brigette sat in a first-class seat on a British Airways flight to London. She could have watched a movie, or read a magazine, but she chose to do neither, because all she could think about was confronting Carlo.

The fact that she was pregnant had confirmed her worst fears. If she and Carlo had made love and she'd been a willing participant, she would have remembered it. But she didn't. And that was proof enough that he'd drugged her.

Brigette did not believe in abortion. Once, when she and her mother were having a fight, Olympia had told her that she'd tried to get rid of her before she was born. Brigette knew she could never do that to her unborn baby. It wasn't right, and she wished her mother had never shared that story with her.

It wasn't as if she was running to Carlo, saying, 'Oh, I'm pregnant, please give me the money to get an abortion.' She had a fortune of her own, she needed nothing from him. All she wanted to do was look into his eyes and find out what the lying scum had to say for himself.

A few days earlier she'd gone over to Fredo's studio, and while he was busy on the phone she'd checked out his

Rolodex, found Carlo's address and phone number in London and copied them down. Once she'd done that she'd felt more in control of the situation.

She hadn't told Lina, because Lina would have relished every moment and probably begged to join in.

What am I going to say to Carlo when I catch up with him? she thought. *Who knows? When I see him I'll come up with something.*

Suddenly she flashed back on the night Santino Bonnatti had kidnapped her and Bobby, sexually abusing them both. How had she dealt with *that* drama?

She'd reached for a gun and blown him away.

She shuddered at the memory.

Revenge is sweet. Lucky had taught her that. It was a lesson she'd learned well.

She leaned back in her seat and closed her eyes. Soon she'd be there, ready to deal with anything.

☆

Heathrow airport was crowded as usual. Special Services met her as she alighted from the plane and whisked her through Customs. Outside the airport a car and driver were waiting to take her to the Dorchester, her favourite hotel. In fact, under different circumstances, London was her favourite city.

After a short drive into town, she checked into the Dorchester, ordered room service, ate in front of the television, then climbed into bed and slept for fourteen hours. Brigette knew how to beat jet lag better than anyone.

She awoke at eight a.m. refreshed and ready to face anything.

The first thing she did was call Lucky in LA. Lucky wanted to know what she was doing in London. 'Work,' she said vaguely. 'I might go on to Milan.'

'Take care,' Lucky said. 'And don't forget to have fun.'

'I always do.'

'Keep in touch.'

'Oh, I will.'

Thoughtfully she put down the phone.

Carlo Vittorio Vitti, here I come. I hope you're ready, because two can play games, and believe me – I am in the mood to play.

☆

Most days Carlo Vittorio Vitti lunched at either Langan's or Le Caprice. He had his own table in both establishments, and was popular with the waiters and maître d's because he was an excellent tipper. Carlo understood the importance of taking care of the service people. It stood him in good stead.

He usually lunched alone, preferring his own company to other people's. It was enough that he was stuck in London in a boring job simply because his family had banished him on account of the scandal. He didn't need to mix with boring people as well.

Ah, the scandal. What was so bad about conducting an affair with a politician's young wife – who would inherit everything when her eighty-year-old husband died? Well, her husband *had* died – under mysterious circumstances, and suddenly every finger was pointed toward *him*.

It didn't matter that nobody could prove he'd had anything to do with it. What *did* matter was that he'd brought his family's name into prominence in a disgraceful way. He was Count Carlo Vittorio Vitti and, as such, he was quite a catch in Rome. But after the scandal he became a pariah, and his family couldn't wait to get rid of him. His father had promptly shipped him off to London and the mind-numbing job at the bank.

In the meantime, his young lady love, the widow Isabella, had eloped with an overweight opera star and, to his chagrin, he, Carlo, had ended up with nothing.

He'd arrived in London in a brooding fury. How had this happened? All his life he'd never had to work. He was a count. Counts did not do menial jobs. And although his family was piss poor, they at least had distinguished lineage dating back hundreds of years.

Carlo hated working. Especially in a bank surrounded by real workers. It was humiliating, not something he enjoyed at all.

He knew what he had to do, and that was to find himself a very rich woman. If he could manage that, he'd be free of his family for ever.

Of course, it had to be the right woman. Not just anyone would do for Count Carlo Vittorio Vitti.

Currently he was engaged to the homely daughter of a captain of industry. He didn't love the girl; in fact, he didn't even particularly like her. However, she *was* due to inherit a fortune, and she loved him dearly, so if nothing better came along, he would be forced to marry her, because the monthly pittance he received from his father and his meagre salary from the bank simply did not cut it.

On his last trip to New York, his boringly plebeian cousin, Fredo, had attempted to fix him up with two models. Fredo was always trying to impress him because Fredo had always wanted to *be* him. Unfortunately for Fredo, nothing he did impressed Carlo.

One of the girls was named Brigette, and there was something about her that immediately rang cash-register bells in Carlo's head. When the girls went to the ladies' room, Fredo had kissed his fingers, made a suggestive sucking noise and said, '*Bellissima*, huh? *Bella! Bella!*'

'Who is the blonde one?' Carlo asked. 'She's not just a model, is she?'

Fredo leaned towards him, speaking in a conspiratorial whisper. 'Brigette doesn't like people knowing,' he said. 'But the truth is, she's a Stanislopoulos.'

'Of the Stanislopoulos fortune?' Carlo enquired, perking up considerably.

'Yes,' Fredo replied. 'Eventually she will inherit everything. But don't mention that you know.'

'Of course not,' Carlo said smoothly. And as Brigette made her way back to the table, he saw his future.

Carlo was not a foolish man. At thirty-one, he'd been around and knew women very well. Because of his title and elegant looks, women were constantly throwing themselves at him – just like the black girl with Brigette, he could have her any time he wanted. He considered most women to be worthless whores, cheap *puttane* not worth a second glance.

However, as soon as he learned who Brigette was, he made a plan. And because he was in New York for only two days, his plan had to be executed quickly. In his pocket he kept a packet of little white pills, using them when he couldn't be bothered courting a girl all night. One dropped in her drink, and she was his. Not that he needed to drug his conquests, but it was so much easier this way, and did not involve conversation and false declarations of love.

Instinctively he knew that Brigette was not the kind of girl to jump into bed on a first meeting, so shortly before they left the club, he slipped half a pill into her drink. When they reached her apartment she was in an extremely relaxed state, and it was easy to make love to her.

He left before she awoke. He knew exactly what he was doing, using just half a pill. He wanted her to remember this one night of passion. He wanted her to fret and wonder why he hadn't called.

If she was like every other girl he'd slept with, she'd be waiting by the phone, holding her breath until she heard from him.

Mission accomplished, he flew back to London and his fiancée. But his mind was full of Brigette and what a match they would make.

Calculatingly he decided to give it three months, then he'd return to New York and sweep Brigette up into his arms like a conquering hero. By that time she'd be easy pickings.

In the meantime he needed capital, so he worked on his fiancée, persuading her to buy an antique diamond pin she didn't need, and pocketing the hefty commission he got from the dealer. He then asked her for a short-term loan, explaining that money he was expecting from Italy had inexplicably been held up.

She would do anything for him, this unattractive thirty-three-year-old heiress who still lived at home with her equally unattractive parents.

Unfortunately for her, she wasn't rich enough. Why have her when he could have a beauty who was due to inherit the world?

29

Basically Teddy was living his life in fear. Nothing new about that, because the truth was he'd always been a fearful kid – ever since his mother had taken off when he was only four years old.

'Goodbye, Teddy,' she'd said, drunk and full of venom, her luggage stacked in the front hall. 'See if *you* can get along with this whoremongering bastard who calls himself your father!'

Nice words for a four-year-old to remember his mother by.

After that there had been a series of nannies, who never stayed long because they couldn't stand being around Irena, who made their lives miserable.

And then, when he was just eight, along came Price's wife number two – a blonde with a huge bosom and a habit of hugging Teddy too close. She was forever whispering in his ear that he should live his life like a white boy and forget about being black. She told him about racism and hate and that he didn't want to get called a nigger, so maybe he should try bleaching his skin like Michael Jackson.

When Price heard what she'd been filling his son's head with, he'd gone berserk and informed her she was the world's biggest idiot. A few months later she was history.

At an early age, Teddy became used to treading carefully. And since his dad was always on the road doing stand-up, Teddy's only real companion was Mila. He looked up to her because she was two years older than him and tough. But she never let him get close, always treating him with a mixture of disdain and disinterest.

Now this terrible thing had happened, bonding them together for ever. And he was scared.

He drove his jeep reluctantly, taking it out of the garage only when absolutely necessary. He started leaving the house later and later, riding the bus to school. Every day he expected the cops to turn up at their front door and arrest both of them.

'What's wrong with your car?' Irena asked, because Irena was a witch – she never missed a thing.

''S making a weird noise,' he lied, wishing she'd butt out for once.

She immediately told their night-time guard, who informed him in front of his father that he'd checked out the jeep, and there was absolutely nothing wrong with it.

'I bought you the goddamn car two months ago,' Price complained. 'If there's somethin' wrong with it, why didn'cha tell me? We could've sent it back.'

'Thought I heard a rattle,' Teddy muttered. 'Nothin' serious.'

'Serious enough for you to start ridin' the bus,' Price said.

'I *like* taking the bus,' Teddy said truculently. 'That's the only way I get t' meet real people.'

'Y' know, Teddy,' Price said, staring at him accusingly, 'if I *ever* catch you doin' drugs, I'll whack your ass so bad you won't be able to sit down for a week. You listenin' to me, fool?'

'Yeah, Dad, I hear you.'

'You'd better,' Price said ominously.

Teddy's main priority was staying out of Mila's way, which was easier since she'd gotten a job at a local burger joint and was no longer in school. Whenever their paths crossed, she glared at him with a scary malevolent look in her eyes. He was a witness to her crime, and she *knew* that he *knew* she was guilty, and that it wasn't his fault.

Occasionally she sidled close enough to make a few threats. 'Remember what I told you, fuck-face. Don't open that puny dumb mouth of yours, 'cause if you *ever* say anything, I'll kill you. You can depend on that.'

He didn't know what to do. He would've liked to have gotten it all out in the open, gone to the cops and confessed everything. The only problem was that if Mila didn't do it first, his father would most certainly kill him. Price's rage would be unbearable.

He spent hours trying to figure out how it had happened. Where had Mila gotten the gun? And the biggest question of all, why had she used it? The two people in the car weren't doing anything to them, they hadn't even put up a real fight.

Every day he pored over the newspapers, trying to find out anything he could about the two victims. One thing he knew for sure: Lennie Golden had recovered, Mary Lou Berkeley was dead.

He studied Mary Lou's pictures in the newspapers and magazines, clipping everything he could about her and hiding it under his mattress for further review. She was so pretty. What had she done to deserve Mila blowing her away?

His school grades suffered. He couldn't sleep at night and couldn't concentrate during the day. He knew that any moment his dad was likely to get on his case, so to ease the tension he started smoking a little weed he scored from a boy at school. At least it took his mind off the horror of what had taken place.

It didn't take long for Price to catch on. One day Teddy arrived home to find him standing in his room. 'What the *fuck* is this?' Price demanded, holding up a couple of half-smoked joints that Teddy had hidden in his closet.

'C'mon, Dad,' Teddy whined. ''S better than mainlining heroin or gettin' into crack – like *you* used to.'

'What *I* used to do has nothin' the fuck t' do with *you*,' Price yelled, eyes bulging. 'Don't look at me to be your example in life, 'cause I ain't no shinin' angel.'

'Never said you were,' Teddy muttered.

And outside his room he saw Mila flit by, ever watchful.

He knew she was listening, spying on him to see if he'd weaken.

He had a plan.

He was going to take off.

It was the only answer.

☆

Mila Kopistani did not know who her father was, but she had her suspicions. Irena, her mother, refused to discuss it. All she'd managed to get out of her was that her father was a Russian ex-boyfriend who'd visited America, knocked Irena up, and then returned to his homeland. Mila didn't believe her for a moment: there had to be more to it than that.

Growing up, she hadn't thought about it that much. However, once she reached school age and the other girls started questioning her, she'd grown curious. At first, she'd thought her father might be Irena's boss, Price Washington. But no. He was black and she was white, so she'd abandoned that idea. Then she'd considered Father McBain, the priest at the local church. He and her mom seemed pretty damn friendly. 'Impossible,' one of her girlfriends informed her. 'Priests aren't allowed to do it. He can't be your dad.'

Another dead end.

Desperately, Mila tried to discover the truth. Whenever Irena left the house, Mila searched through her things but couldn't find anything worth shit.

Mother and daughter did not have a warm and wonderful relationship. Irena was a cold woman, who ran the house with a rigid hand. Two maids came in daily, and she bossed them about as if she were a queen. She treated the gardener, the pool man and any other workers who came to the house the same way. Nobody liked her except Price, and Mila was sure he only put up with her 'cause she was his faithful work slave. She often wondered if they were sleeping together. Sometimes she thought yes, sometimes no. If they *were* sleeping together, they certainly kept it a secret.

Mila had hated Price's two wives. Ginee, the first one, was as bad a druggie as he was at one time. And his second wife, a bimbo blonde, was a joke. A *Playboy* centrefold with fake tits, cascades of dyed blonde ringlets, and a big stupid smile. Mila had spent many an amusing day pinning the bimbo's naked photographs up all over the school, much to Teddy's embarrassment and humiliation.

Mila had always toyed with Teddy, teased and taunted him. Why not? He was a male, wasn't he? He had a father. She didn't. It wasn't fair.

Everyone at school knew she was only the housekeeper's daughter. It irked her that she had no standing while Teddy had a famous dad. Sometimes she made him pay for it. Unfortunately, he was too dumb to understand that she wasn't his friend, that she actually loathed him. And she loathed her mother too, because Irena had never had any time for her. Her mother always put Price Washington first, like he was a fucking king and they should all bow down to him.

When Mila had taken Teddy out with her that other night, her intention had been to get him drunk and mess with his head. She certainly hadn't *meant* to kill anyone, although she had to admit it was a wild feeling. Snuffing out a life had given her a jolt of tremendous power. Price had lorded it over her and Irena all those years, yet she'd produced a gun and managed to end somebody's life, just like that.

She could do it to *him* if she wanted. She had her own kind of power now.

She wouldn't mind shooting Price.

Shooting him or fucking him.

She couldn't decide which would be the worse punishment.

She'd never attempted to turn her mother's boss on, although she knew she could if she tried. Men chased after her all the time, especially at work where she got several propositions a day. She was young, and well aware how to flaunt it. Tight little tank tops, short clingy skirts – all the better to show off her long legs and big bosom. Her cropped dark hair brought out her hazel eyes, and she piled on the makeup when she wanted to look her most alluring.

Men were always checking her out. A few of them had even gotten lucky. Nobody she gave ten cents about, though: she was saving herself for the one who would take her away from being the housekeeper's daughter.

She never wanted to end up like her mom – some rich, famous asshole's work slave. Mila was after money and power. *She* wanted to be the mistress of the house. *She* wanted to have it all. Sometimes she looked at Teddy and saw him as her future. That's if nothing better came along. If she and Teddy got married when they were older, eventually Teddy would inherit all his father's money which meant he'd be rich because Price Washington must have stashed away a bundle. But marrying Teddy would be her last resort. He was never going to change. Even when he was twenty he'd still be a weak loser.

Right now she was worried about him opening his mouth and spilling everything. It was just the kind of dumb thing he was likely to do.

It occurred to her that being mean to him was not helping her case. So she decided to go in the opposite direction and lure him in. A little sex would go a long way towards keeping him on her side. Sex would make him realize where his *real* loyalties lay.

Yeah. Maybe she'd give him a taste of what he was always lusting after. That way she'd have him totally hooked.

Either that or she'd shut his mouth permanently.

Mila could not make up her mind which would be better.

30

Lucky took out a full page ad in the *LA Times*, offering a hundred-thousand-dollar reward for information concerning the hold-up and Mary Lou's murder. She also had posters printed and pasted all over the city, concentrating on the mid-Wilshire area, where the crime had taken place. And on either side of the reward sign were the computer-generated images of the two suspects the police sketch artist had come up with.

Detective Johnson warned her they'd be dealing with a lot

of cranks and crazies. 'People crawl out of the sewers when they smell money,' he said.

'So be it,' Lucky said. 'Let 'em come. I've got a hunch that, for a hundred grand, we're about to get some answers.'

'I don't usually condone doing this,' Detective Johnson said. 'Makes people greedy. Gives us a lot of extra work, too.'

'Hey,' Lucky said restlessly, 'if it gets results, what do you care?'

She went home to Lennie, who was in his usual blue funk, sitting upstairs in the master bedroom flipping channels with the remote. 'It's a good job I love you,' she said, flopping down on the couch next to him, wondering when he was going to snap out of it.

'Huh?' he said, still changing channels.

'I said,' she repeated, 'that it's a good job I love you.'

'What's *that* supposed to mean?' he said, staring at the TV. 'You had enough?'

'Enough of what?'

'Me.'

'I want the *real* you back, Lennie,' she said softly. 'Is that a major felony?'

'I can't help the way I feel.'

'You should see somebody.'

'Who?'

'There's this woman – she's a shrink and, uh ... it'd be a good idea for you to talk to someone, and get it all out.'

'Fuck!' he said, standing up. 'You *know* I don't believe in that crap.'

'Nor do I, but I think you need it.'

'How come *you* don't?' he said belligerently.

''Cause I'm not the one sitting around the house sulking,' she answered, not happy with the way this was going.

'Sulking?' he repeated, furious. 'I was with a woman who got blown away, and you think I'm *sulking*. What the fuck is wrong with you, Lucky?' And with that he marched out of the room.

She shook her head. This was getting ridiculous. Lennie's anger was out of control, and there seemed to be nothing she could do.

She went downstairs to the family room, where the kids were excitedly getting ready to visit Gino and Paige in Palm

Springs for the weekend. Carioca was going with them. Bobby was not. He finally had a date with the sitcom star he'd been lusting after. And then in the morning he was flying to Greece to spend time with some of Dimitri's relatives.

'Where are you taking her?' Lucky enquired, playing good mom, although Lennie had deeply disturbed her with his non-stop bad mood.

'Dunno,' Bobby said. 'Can I borrow your Ferrari?'

'Are you insane?' Lucky said, trying to decide if now was the time to give him a lecture on safe sex and the use of condoms. 'You're not borrowing my Ferrari. You've got your jeep.'

'Everyone has a jeep.' Bobby groaned. 'Why couldn't I have gotten a Porsche?'

'So you could've been held up like Lennie?'

He shrugged. 'I feel stupid taking a girl like her out in a jeep. She's, like, a big TV star, Mom.'

'Bobby!' Lucky said forcefully. 'I hope you're not turning into a Hollywood kid. A jeep is cool, so don't give me any more of your crap.' Now it was her turn to march out of the room. In the background she heard Maria imitating her. 'Don't give me any more of your crap, Bobby,' squeaked Maria, before dissolving into fits of giggles with Carioca.

Lucky couldn't help smiling. Maria reminded her of herself when she was a kid, feisty and bold, never afraid of anything.

After seeing them off, she looked for Lennie and found him standing on the deck overlooking the ocean. Sliding open the heavy glass doors she went and stood beside him. 'Don't let's fight,' she said, putting her hand on his arm. 'Fighting doesn't help anybody – especially Steven. He's coming for dinner tonight.'

'No, no, I can't see him,' Lennie said, panicking. 'Every time I see him it makes me feel worse.'

'That's pretty damn selfish. Steven's all by himself. Remember – he lost his *wife*?'

'Fuck!' Lennie shouted. 'I can't do this any more.'

'Do what?'

'Any of this shit. I'm taking a drive.'

She almost stopped him, but didn't. She'd never been the clinging type.

On the other hand, she wasn't about to sit around waiting

for him to come home so he could scream at her some more. If she wasn't so goddamn understanding, she'd be screaming back.

She called Steven at his office. 'Would you mind if we switched to a restaurant tonight?' she said. 'Just the two of us?'

'I'd like that,' Steven said. 'How come?'

'The kids have gone to Palm Springs, and Lennie's not feeling great. So how about you and I go to La Scala and tell each other our problems?'

'You got problems, Lucky?'

'Not as big as yours, Steven. I'll pick you up at the office.'

An hour later they sat in a cosy booth in La Scala, eating spaghetti and chopped salads.

Lucky stared at her half-brother intently. 'Steven,' she said, placing her hand over his, 'I want you to know how much I love you and that I truly feel your pain. I wish there was something I could do, but obviously there isn't.'

'I love you too,' Steven said. 'But loving you doesn't bring back Mary Lou.'

'The reason Lennie isn't here,' Lucky continued, 'is because he's consumed with guilt. I'm trying to help him get over it, but it's not easy.'

'Lennie has nothing to feel guilty about.'

'I keep on telling him that.'

'Should I talk to him?'

'No. He's a big boy, he'll have to figure it out on his own.'

'If you change your mind, just say the word. I can talk to him.'

'Let's see how it goes. The important thing is how are *you* doing?'

'I have good days, mostly bad nights.' He gave a hollow laugh. 'I'm getting through it.'

'It's not easy.'

'Tell me.' He picked up a piece of bread and tore it into pieces. 'How's Carioca?'

'Sensational. When do you want her back?'

'She's better off with you, Lucky. She has such a good time being with your kids. What can she do with me? Sit in the house by herself?'

'You're her father,' Lucky said quietly. 'She loves you.'

'I *know* that. But if you could keep her a little longer . . .'

'I will, only you've got to remember that it's tough for her, too. The last thing you want is for her to feel abandoned. Believe me, I know what that's like.' She paused while the waiter refilled their wine-glasses. 'I'll never forget the day I discovered my mother floating on that raft in the swimming-pool . . .' For a moment her black eyes clouded over. 'Everything stopped. You can't imagine . . .' Another pause. 'Maybe you can.'

'When I think about what you went through, Lucky, it gives me the strength to keep going.'

'I still miss her,' Lucky whispered softly. 'The pain never goes away, it's always there, it simply gets pushed into the background.'

Steven squeezed her hand. 'Love you, sis.'

She managed a wan smile. 'You too, bro.'

By the time she returned to the house, Lennie was in bed asleep. She hovered beside their bed for a moment, wondering if he was faking it. Since he didn't stir, she decided he wasn't.

This is what marriage is all about, she thought. *For better or worse.* Right now it was for worse, and she had to get him better. If they could only find the attackers, she was sure that would help Lennie feel good again.

Tomorrow she'd badger Detective Johnson, something he was getting used to because she did it every day. And she couldn't care less if he was getting sick of her, since she was convinced that unless she kept bothering him, this case would never get solved.

She went into her bathroom and slipped into black silk pyjamas. Tonight sex with her husband, the love of her life, might be nice. And there was no reason why they shouldn't make love. By withholding himself sexually, Lennie was punishing *her*, and she didn't appreciate it one bit.

She climbed into bed and snuggled up behind him.

He groaned in his sleep and moved away.

This was a first.

Lucky had always been under the impression that she had the perfect marriage. Maybe she was wrong.

She closed her eyes, attempting to sleep. But sleep was a

long time coming, and by the time she did drop off she was hurt and angry.

Lennie better get his act together or, as far as she was concerned, they were heading for serious problems.

31

Brigette had breakfast in the living room of her hotel suite with Horace Otley, a short, sweaty-palmed man in his mid-forties, who looked like an out-of-work hack for one of the tabloids. However, Horace was not an out-of-work hack. Horace was probably the best private detective in England.

Brigette had hired him two weeks ago from America.

'It'll cost you,' Horace had told her over the phone.

'I don't care,' she'd answered. 'Privacy is my main issue. I'll want you to sign an agreement that you'll never reveal anything about this investigation.'

Horace had agreed, so she'd had one of her lawyers draw up a paper and fax it to him. Horace signed and faxed it back. After that she'd faxed him Carlo's full name and where he worked, and requested every bit of information Horace could come up with. Now here they were, finally getting together.

'It's nice to meet you, Mr Otley,' Brigette said politely.

He bobbed his head, quite startled to be faced with such a gorgeous female, and a famous one too. Naturally he recognized her, and so he should, considering she'd appeared on magazine covers the world over.

'I didn't realize who you were when you hired me,' he said, thinking that he couldn't wait to tell his life partner, Will, about *this*. Will would *cream* when he heard who Horace was dealing with.

'That's all right,' she said. 'Now perhaps you understand my need for privacy.'

'I protect *every* client's privacy,' Horace said pompously. 'Every one of them is just as important to me, whoever they might be.'

'That's nice to know, Mr Otley. Would you care to order breakfast?'

He put on a pair of wire-rimmed spectacles and perused

the menu, deciding on toast, eggs, bacon, sausages and grilled tomatoes.

'Sounds good to me,' she said, calling room service and ordering the same.

Soon she was picking at her food while Horace stuffed his into his mouth as if he hadn't eaten in weeks. 'I've got every bit of information you could possibly need,' he said, between mouthfuls.

'Excellent,' she said, sipping orange juice.

'Carlo Vittorio Vitti. *Count* Carlo Vittorio Vitti – you did know he has a title?'

She nodded.

'Yes, he's a count,' Horace said, 'although the family has no money.'

'Are you sure?'

'His parents reside in Italy, in a run-down palace outside Rome. They're down to two servants and a chauffeur. Both parents are alcoholics.'

'Sounds like a pleasant family.'

'Carlo was sent to London eighteen months ago.'

'How come?'

'There was a big disgrace in Italy.'

'What was it?'

'Carlo was seeing a twenty-year-old married woman, whose eighty-year-old husband was found asphyxiated in his own garage. The suspicion fell on Carlo.'

'Why? *Did* he do it?'

'There was talk . . . scandal. Before the police acted, his father sent him here to London, which, from what I can ascertain, he hates. He's looking for a rich woman. He's found *one*, but she's not his ideal. However, they *are* engaged.'

'So he *is* engaged?'

'She's a dog,' Horace said, chewing on a piece of bacon. 'Need I say more?'

'That's not a very nice thing to say, Mr Otley,' Brigette scolded. 'A woman might not be the best-looking in the world, but she can have a lovely personality.'

'This one doesn't.'

'How do you know?'

'I have my sources,' he said smugly.

'What about photos?'

'Yes. I have some with me.' He bent down, fishing in a battered leather briefcase, producing an eight-by-ten manila envelope from which he slid several pictures.

Brigette inspected the photos. There was Carlo, undeniably handsome in a blue blazer and grey pants, standing with his arm around a short, plumpish woman who was not at all attractive.

'Is *this* his fiancée?' she asked, hardly able to hide her surprise.

'That's her,' Horace said.

'Hmmm . . . well, I suppose he could've done better.'

'Not money-wise,' Horace said, with an odd little chuckle. 'There aren't that many good-looking heiresses around.'

Brigette pushed away her plate and got up from the table. 'What else can you tell me about him?'

'He's a loner, his father pays his bills, keeps him on a short leash because, as I said before, they're low on cash. From what I understand, Carlo is waiting to return to Rome when the scandal dies down. Either that or he'll marry this English-woman, especially if her father makes him an offer he can't refuse regarding the family business.'

'What's her name?'

'Fiona Lewyllen Wharton. She's heiress to a paper empire.'

'Is there a lot of money?'

'Enough to keep Carlo happy although, from what I hear, *she* doesn't.'

'Why do you say that?'

'Fiona never stays over at his apartment, nor he at her family home – she still lives with her parents in a house in Eaton Square. But he has been known to send for high-class call-girls at midnight. They visit his apartment, stay an hour, and leave.'

'Really?' Brigette said.

And in her mind she was already forming a plan.

32

'**We're getting** inundated,' Detective Johnson said.

'Anything worthwhile?' Lucky asked, not at all satisfied with the way the investigation was progressing, but trying not to blow her cool.

'We're sifting.'

While he was sifting, Lucky had her own team of detectives going from house to house, questioning all jeep owners within a five-mile radius of the hold-up, showing the sketch artist's rendition of the two suspects. If only Lennie could remember at least one of the numbers on the licence plate. But he couldn't, his mind was a blank.

With the children safely in Palm Springs at their grand-father's house, and Bobby away in Greece, Lucky made a concentrated effort to spend more time with Lennie, hoping she could persuade him to visit Venus' shrink.

Getting him to agree was impossible: he refused to even consider it.

She held her temper and attempted to go along with whatever he wanted to do. Eventually, she knew, he would return to being the man she loved.

'That's okay, Lucky,' he said, when one day she offered to accompany him on one of his marathon walks along the beach. 'Truth is, I'd sooner be alone.'

'You would?' she said, somewhat uptight.

He didn't seem to notice her reaction. 'Uh-huh,' he said evenly.

'If that's the way you feel . . .'

'I'm allowed to feel, aren't I?' he snapped.

'Keep it up, Lennie,' she said, her patience faltering. 'You can be alone permanently if that's what turns you on.'

'Is that what you *want*?' he countered. ''Cause if so, it's easy enough to arrange.'

She'd been trying to avoid a fight, but obviously Lennie was heading in that direction – in fact, he seemed determined to get into an argument.

'You're acting like a jerk,' she said. 'Nothing ever pleases you.'

'Can I help it if I prefer to be by myself?'

No, she told herself, staring at him. *I will not get into a fight with this man who I love. I refuse to. And he will not goad me into it.*

'Have you given any thought to New York?' she asked casually. 'We could go for a long weekend and *try* to have fun?'

'Fun?' he said, shaking his head in disbelief. 'Mary Lou's ten feet under and *you* want to have fun?'

'Jesus, Lennie,' she snapped, 'you're really pushing.'

'*I'm* pushing?'

'This feeling sorry for yourself shit has to stop. How long do you think we can take it?'

'Who's we?'

'Me, the kids, anybody who tries to get close to you. You've shut off, Lennie. Just like you did after the kidnapping.'

'I'm sorry if Mary Lou getting killed is inconveniencing everyone,' he said stiffly. 'The timing was wrong, huh? You decided to dump the studio and sit around having *fun*, but unfortunately things haven't worked out the way you planned. And while we're on that subject, it would've been nice if you'd discussed leaving the studio with me *before* you announced it to the world. Do *I* make major decisions without including you?'

'So *that*'s what you're burning up about?'

'No, I'm merely saying I remember once before you made a major decision without asking me – and that was to *buy* the goddamn studio in the first place.'

'Let's not fight, Lennie.'

'Why? You've been following me around for the last six weeks looking for a fight.'

'You are so full of shit!' she responded, outraged that he should be this unfair. '*You*'re the one who's looking for a fight.'

'No. I'm the one who merely wants to be left alone. Is that too much to ask?'

'Yes, Lennie, it is,' she said angrily. 'You have a life, a family, and a wife. Do you know that we haven't made love in nearly two months?'

'Ah, so that's what this is all about – sex.'

'It's not sex, Lennie. It's about being together and loving someone.'

'I should've known you would have focused on the sex.'

She stared at him as if he were a stranger, because that's the way he was acting. 'If you could remember the goddamn licence-plate number, perhaps we could catch the killers and get on with our lives,' she said, needling him.

'You think I'm forgetting on purpose?' he said, furious.

'No. But you say you thought you saw it, and yet you can't even remember the first letter.'

'That's not my fault.'

'Y' know, Lennie – I don't care to be around you when you're like this.'

'I think I should move out for a couple of days,' he said. 'Get my head straight without you, since I'm making you so miserable.'

'Move out and what?' she challenged.

'Get laid, get drunk,' he said, waving a verbal red flag. 'Who the fuck knows? I'm fed up with you watching every move I make. You're a very controlling woman. Maybe what I need is some freedom.'

'Screw freedom,' she said vehemently. 'We're married. Being married is togetherness. If it's freedom you want, then let's get a divorce.'

She could hardly believe the words had come out of her mouth. She loved Lennie, they'd been through so much together, yet if he was going to behave like an asshole, she wasn't about to take it.

'Fine with me,' he said, just like that.

Did nine years of marriage mean nothing to him? Was he simply prepared to walk? This situation was getting out of control. But, hey, she'd never been the little woman sitting at home waiting to take crap from some man. She was Lucky Santangelo, and she lived life by *her* rules. If he was so anxious to go, let him.

'I'm outta here,' Lennie said. 'I'll call in a few days when you've calmed down.'

'When *I*'ve calmed down?' she said. 'You've got it wrong, Lennie.'

'No. I can see what's happening here. I'm caught in a trap with you. I'm in prison.'

'*You*'re the one who never wants to leave the beach,' she said heatedly. '*You*'re the one who sits in the house every day. If it's a prison, it's yours – not mine.'

'So what is it you *want* me to do, Lucky? Go out with your Hollywood friends – Venus, Charlie Dollar and that group? They're not my kind of people.'

'Since *when*? You love Venus, and you've always got along great with Charlie.'

'How come you're not mentioning your close friend, Alex,

who's only nice to me 'cause he's got a hot nut for you? *And* everyone knows it.'

'Now you're really talking crap.'

'You know it's true. Anyway,' he said abruptly, 'I don't want to discuss it any more. I'm leaving.'

'Go ahead,' she said coldly.

And he did. He went upstairs, threw some clothes in a bag, walked downstairs and out of the house.

Lucky shook her head in disbelief. She loved this man. She'd loved him from the moment they'd met in Las Vegas and had an erotic first encounter. And when they'd re-met a year later, she was married to Dimitri and he to Dimitri's daughter, Olympia. What a tangled web. But they'd loved each other – fiercely, passionately. They'd had two children together, and now he'd walked out. Impossible.

What was she going to do now? Cry?

No fucking way. She was a Santangelo. Santangelos didn't cry.

Besides, as soon as Lennie got his head straight, he'd realize what a mistake he'd made and come running back.

And if he didn't?

Well ... much as she loved him, Lucky Santangelo was a survivor. And she would go on – with or without Lennie by her side.

33

By chance Brigette ran into Kyra Kattleman in the health spa at the Dorchester. It was a fortuitous meeting as she'd been thinking about who she could have lunch with, and there was Kyra wearing a bright orange leotard, lifting weights with effortless ease, looking every inch the superjock supermodel she was.

'What are *you* doing here?' they both said at once.

'I'm on my way to Milan,' Kyra said, in her incongruous squeaky voice. 'Is that where you're headed?'

'No, actually I have business here,' Brigette explained. 'I ducked out of Milan this year.'

'I'm doing the Valentino show,' Kyra said casually. 'Dear Val says he can't live without me. I'm his favourite.'

'You sound like Lina,' Brigette said, laughing. 'By the way, what are you doing for lunch today?'

'Nothing,' Kyra said, with a casual shrug. 'I was planning a bit of shopping 'cause I'm leaving in the morning.'

'Then let's go to Le Caprice,' Brigette suggested. 'I hear it's fun.'

'I *love* Le Caprice,' Kyra said enthusiastically. 'And we can do the shopping thing after.'

The last thing Brigette felt like doing was going shopping, but she needed Kyra so she rallied. 'Where did you have in mind?' she asked.

'Harvey Nichols – it's *such* a great store, makes Bloomingdale's look sick.'

'Sure,' Brigette said. 'I'll get us a reservation for lunch. Let's meet in the lobby at noon.'

'Aren't you working out?'

'Of course,' Brigette said, heading for the nearest Stairmaster. Working out was boring, but if she wanted to keep a great body it was absolutely necessary. Olympia had verged on the plump side; she would never allow that to happen to her.

Things were falling into position nicely. Lunch at Le Caprice with Kyra and, according to Horace, Carlo would definitely be there.

Good. She didn't plan on wasting a moment.

☆

It was raining in New York as Lina made a wild dash for the airport. Early that morning her agent had called to inform her that Charlie Dollar was leaving for Africa on location, and that the only time he could meet with her was within the next twenty-four hours.

'Don't worry,' Lina had said. 'I'll make it.'

Since her assistant was out sick, she'd called American Airlines, booked herself on a flight, and now she was in a cab on her way to the airport. She glanced at the script her agent had sent over, scanning the role she was supposed to audition for.

The cab driver hit a pot-hole, and she abandoned the idea of reading until she was on the flight.

An hour later she was settled in her seat on the plane, and once more began leafing through the script. The part she was up for was Zoe, the girl next door to Teal – Charlie's character. Zoe's description in the script was of a beautiful, exotic model.

Hmm, that shouldn't be too hard, she thought, reading through Zoe's scenes. In the first scene Zoe heads out of her apartment on the way to the laundry room, bumps into Teal, and a mild flirtation ensues. In a later scene they end up in bed together. *Nudity required*, Lina thought. So what? She'd paraded up and down enough runways in see-through crap – everyone knew what she looked like without clothes, and it was pretty damn spectacular. Besides, all the big actresses were stripping off in the movies, she wouldn't be an exception. No body doubles for Lina: she was prepared to go all the way, *especially* if she was in bed with Charlie Dollar. He had that Sean Connery/Jack Nicholson thing going for him. He was an oldie but a goodie!

The role of Zoe was small, which was a drag. After all, in the modelling world Lina was a major star. But her agent had pointed out that unless she had film on herself, she'd never get a chance. And a flashy role in a Charlie Dollar movie could be it.

She wondered if she should call Brigette's godmother, Lucky, when she got to LA. Then she remembered, Lucky was in London with Brigette. Shame. She'd like to have met her.

The businessman sitting next to her was desperate to make conversation, he kept shooting her knowing looks. She foiled him by hiding behind a Stephen King paperback, which she had no intention of reading, but knew it offered good protection.

She hadn't remembered to order a limo at LAX, so it was into another cab and on to the Bel Air Hotel, where she was greeted by fellow Brit Frank Bowling, the manager, who always looked after her. He gave her a room near the pool, and she unpacked the few things she'd brought with her.

As soon as she was settled she called the LA branch of her agency. 'I'm here,' she announced to Max Steele, her LA agent, whom she'd never met.

'Great, Lina,' Max said, sounding overly friendly. 'Wanna have dinner?'

'No thanks,' she said crisply. 'What I *would* like to know is when I'm supposed to meet Charlie Dollar.'

'I'll set it up,' Max said. 'I might even get good old Charlie to come to dinner.'

'What *is* this?' she asked, slightly irritated. 'A social event or a bleedin' audition?'

Max laughed. 'Don't get upset. It's an audition. This is the way we do things in LA. I'll get right back to you.'

She hung up the phone. One of the disadvantages of being a world-famous supermodel was that everyone wanted to be seen with her. *Especially* agents. They thought it raised their profile. *And that's not the only thing it raises,* she thought, with a ribald chuckle.

Of course, Max Steele might be incredibly attractive, and if he was, she'd be missing out. *Better check him out over drinks,* she thought. Because if she liked him, they might end up in bed. Lina excelled at sex, it was her favourite pastime, and lately she'd been going through a dry spell. Nobody since Flick Fonda, and *he* had been a total waste of time and energy.

Sometimes, when she was feeling very bad, she imagined what it would be like to be a porno star. Oh, God, what a kick – showing off her goods in front of the world! Naughty, naughty!

Not that she'd ever consider it. It was merely one of her erotic fantasies – of which she had many.

☆

Kyra talked too much in her loud, squeaky voice. Brigette wished she'd shut up as they entered the exclusive London restaurant. Jeremy, the man who ran the place, gave them a big greeting, ushering them to a prime table against the wall. Brigette made sure *not* to look around. She didn't want to catch Carlo's eye if he was already there: she wanted *him* to come to *her*.

Kyra ordered a martini and immediately began talking about her husband, a fellow model she'd married a few months ago. 'He's meeting me in Milan,' she squeaked. '*I* got him the job. Calvin wanted him in New York, but I insisted he come to Milan. He's *sooo* hunky. A real man.'

'I know,' Brigette said. 'I've worked with him.' Actually, she'd always thought he was gay.

'Can you imagine what kind of children we'll have?' Kyra said dreamily. 'Do you *know* how cute they'll look?'

Hmm, Brigette thought. *Kyra's about as modest as Lina.* 'I'm sure they'll be very beautiful,' she said.

'I'll get pregnant in two years,' Kyra announced. 'Then I'll give birth in Australia, because my mum would like that.'

'She must be very proud of you.'

'Oh, yes, all my family are. I'm a national treasure in Australia. Me and Elle MacPherson and Rachel Hunter – we're *totally* famous. Not like here where there's supermodels all over the place. Cindy, Suzi, Naomi, *you*. Lina, Didi—'

'You'd better not let Lina hear you call Didi a supermodel,' Brigette interrupted.

'Why? Is she jealous of her?'

'I'd say there's a touch of rivalry. And, besides, Didi hasn't been working that long, she doesn't deserve the title.'

'She's still pretty famous,' Kyra remarked. 'It's those great big tits on that skinny little bod. Guys cream over her.'

'She's famous because she hired a PR,' Brigette pointed out.

'*I* have a PR,' Kyra said, as if it was a given. 'Don't you?'

'No,' Brigette said. 'Publicity is the *last* thing I need.' And out of the corner of her eye she observed Carlo enter the restaurant.

Good, she thought. *Let the games begin.*

34

Teddy spotted the posters first. How could he miss them? How could anyone miss them? They were everywhere. Big freaking posters with a hundred-thousand-dollar reward printed in huge letters right in the middle. Naturally everyone stopped when they saw that. And then they read the smaller print, and when Teddy read it, his stomach did a double somersault.

> ANYONE WITH INFORMATION
> CONCERNING A CAR-JACKING ROBBERY
> ON 1 SEPTEMBER AT THE CORNER OF
> WILSHIRE AND LANGTON WILL BE
> ELIGIBLE TO COLLECT A REWARD OF
> ONE HUNDRED THOUSAND DOLLARS

The reward announcement was bad enough. But there were also pictures – supposedly of him and Mila. Not that the sketches looked like either of them, but there were certain similarities. Mila's narrow eyes and sharp nose. His wide forehead and cropped hair.

He immediately ran to the burger joint where Mila worked and told her what was going on.

She freaked out. 'You'd better keep your mouth shut,' she warned. 'Nobody knows we did it. There are no witnesses. They don't have the number of the jeep, so we're safe. Remember – keep your fucking mouth *shut*, Teddy.'

But even as she uttered those words, her mind was zooming in a million different directions. A hundred thousand dollars. Boy, what she couldn't do with a hundred thousand dollars!

Teddy, meanwhile, was making his own plans. It was definitely time to run: things were getting too hot. Any moment the cops could come knocking at the door, and when his father discovered he'd been involved in a murder . . . Well, it didn't bear thinking about. He shuddered at the memory of that horrible night. If his dad ever found out he would definitely kill him. Price was a maniac when he lost his temper. He expected his son to be perfect.

Teddy decided he'd better get to his mother's fast. He knew she lived in an apartment on Wilshire, and even though he'd had no contact with her in years, he was sure that when he arrived at her door she wouldn't turn him away. He'd make up a story that Price was back on drugs and beating the crap out of him: that way she'd *have* to take him in.

Saturday afternoon he put on his best rapper outfit – baggy pants swaddling his hips, a hooded oversized sweatshirt and high-top Nikes – then attempted to sneak out.

Price was lounging on the couch in the den watching football on TV. 'Wanna catch some plays with me?' he called, as Teddy tried to sidle past.

'Gotta see some friends, Dad,' Teddy said, in a low voice.

'What time you comin' back?'

'Later.'

'Later,' Price repeated, tossing pretzels into his mouth. 'Now, don't you go smokin' no weed with any of your friends. 'Cause I'll know, an' I'll whack the shit outta you. Got it, boy?'

'Yes, Dad,' he said, moving towards the back door.

As he walked out to the garage, Mila appeared from the kitchen, wearing a tight T-shirt with no bra, and a short fake red-leather skirt. She'd dyed her dark hair a startling shade of white blonde and cut it even shorter so that it looked like a crew-cut. He knew why.

'Where you goin', Teddy?' she asked.

He couldn't take his eyes off her nipples, they were sticking out under her T-shirt, demanding attention.

She saw him looking and stuck them out even further.

'Gonna hang with some friends,' he mumbled, not about to confide in *her* – she'd be the last one he'd tell.

'Shame,' she said, chewing on a hang-nail. 'Thought we'd do something today.'

She'd hardly spoken to him since the night of the murder, except to warn him of the dire consequences if he opened his mouth. 'Like what?' he ventured, frightened of her, yet at the same time drawn to her.

'Dunno,' she said, with a casual shrug. 'Take a drive, catch a movie.'

'Not me,' he said, shaking his head. 'Not after the last time.'

'Shit, man,' she said scornfully. 'That's never gonna happen again. I don't even have a gun.'

He didn't believe her, but her nipples were beckoning and he was beginning to weaken. 'You sure?'

'Course I am,' she said, thrusting her tits in his face. 'Besides, you an' I never get t' spend any time together since I'm workin'. Don't you think we should talk?' He nodded. 'You like my hair?' she added.

' 'S okay,' he said.

'How about it?' she said, moving even closer. 'Can we do something together?'

'S'pose I could meet the guys later,' he said.

'That's my Teddy,' she said, giving him a playful punch on the chin. 'Let's go see *The Bodyguard*.'

'Who's in that?' he asked suspiciously.

'Kevin.'

'Kevin who?'

'Kevin Costner, dunce!'

'Who wants to see *him*?'

'*I* do. Anyway, you can jerk off over Whitney Houston. She's in it, too.'

'Okay,' he said, unable to resist.

'Okay,' she mimicked, teasing him. 'I'll go get a sweater.'

He waited patiently, hoping she'd come back soon. He could always go to his mother's in the morning. If he had a chance to be with Mila, he didn't want to blow it, even though she still scared the crap out of him.

She emerged a few minutes later, a blue sweater tied casually around her narrow waist. 'Let's go,' she said bossily.

He looked at her long legs, then at her tits. 'I'll drive,' he mumbled.

For once she didn't argue.

☆

Irena took her boss lunch on a tray. Price was lounging in front of the TV in a tracksuit with no underwear. Irena was well aware that on weekends he never wore underwear, it was one of his little idiosyncrasies.

'Okay, hon,' he said, indicating the coffee table in front of him. 'Put it there.'

'Yes, Mr Washington,' she said.

He glanced up at her briefly, his heavily lidded eyes immediately swivelling back to the TV. 'Teddy's out. Where's Mila?'

'She went with him,' Irena said. 'They're seeing a movie.'

'Nice t' see the kids gettin' along,' he remarked, although he would have preferred Teddy not to hang out with Mila – he still considered the girl a bad influence.

'They should,' Irena said. 'They were raised together.'

'Right,' he said, splaying his legs in front of him.

She couldn't help noticing that he had a semi hard-on, quite obvious in his tracksuit pants.

'Sit down here for a minute,' he said, patting the space next to him. 'Watch the game with me.'

'I have things to do, Mr Washington.'

'I got things for you to do, too,' he said, pulling her down beside him.

Irena was tense. Price Washington was her boss, but he was also, when he felt like it, her lover. Well, not exactly her lover. A more apt description would be that she was his sex slave.

She hated herself for doing everything he asked. She hated herself for being there whenever he felt like getting serviced and none of his girlfriends was around. She knew she was a fool to oblige him. But the sad fact was . . . she loved him.

Price Washington had taken her in when she'd had nothing, just the one small suitcase of possessions that was all she'd brought with her when she'd fled Moscow, where her life had been unbearable. Thank God for the man in the American Embassy who'd befriended her and helped her get an exit visa in her dead cousin's name. They would never have let her out of the country, a convicted prostitute and felon who'd done jail time for killing her pimp, an unspeakable monster who'd grabbed every rouble she'd ever made, and amused himself by carving his name on her buttocks. She'd been lucky and escaped. And when she'd arrived in America, Price Washington was there for her. She would always be grateful.

'Eat your lunch, Mr Washington,' she said stiffly.

'Quit with the Mr Washington shit,' he said, taking her hand and placing it on his crotch. 'There's nobody around.'

She knew exactly what he expected her to do. She was supposed to rub it a little, make it hard, take it out, suck it, put it back and go away. The routine never varied.

'I have work to do,' she said.

'Work this,' he said, moving her hand up and down.

In a way she supposed she should be flattered. Price Washington had many girlfriends, and any one of them would have been only too happy to sit in front of the TV with him all day doing whatever he wanted. But Price enjoyed watching football alone. He liked making his phone bets, hollering at the players on the TV screen, and snacking on a variety of junk foods. Maybe he even liked having *her* around. She didn't know. He never told her.

Once in a while he summoned her to his room late at night when Mila and Teddy were asleep. There were times he even touched her, but not very often. Once, when Teddy was away at summer camp, and Mila was staying with a girlfriend, she'd spent the night in his bed, naked and in total abandon. It had been the most memorable night of her life. After it was over he'd never mentioned it again.

When he'd first started coming on to her it had been in his drug days, those lazy, hazy days when he had no idea what he was doing. She'd dismissed his attentions at first. But even after he was stone cold sober and absolutely straight, he continued from time to time to call on her services.

There weren't any other men in Irena's life. She lived for Price, he was all she cared about.

Of course, there was her daughter, Mila. But Irena was well aware what a devious little bitch Mila could be. There was nothing she could do about it. She'd given up trying.

Although if she was truthful with herself, she'd admit that she'd never really tried in the first place.

Her most fervent hope was that Mila would find a man, get married and go away. And then when Teddy left, she'd finally be alone with Price, and maybe, just maybe, he'd realize she was the only woman who genuinely cared about him.

☆

To Teddy's amazement, Mila snuggled close in the cinema. He couldn't believe it. This was something he'd dreamed about ever since he'd hit puberty, yet he was still scared of her. He couldn't help thinking of her firing the gun . . . killing Mary Lou. At the same time he wanted to grab a feel of those perky little tits and touch those hot sexy thighs. He wanted to shove his johnson at her and have her caress it.

He'd never touched a girl – he was way behind the other dudes in his class, who'd all been making out while he'd been shut in a boys-only school in New York, thanks to Price, who thought that would force him to concentrate on his work.

Price did not want him getting into any of the things that he'd done. Endless women, wild sex, drugs, and booze. Price wanted him to be perfect. And that was impossible.

'Wanna touch my tits?' Mila whispered seductively in his ear.

'Wh-what?' he stammered, sure he hadn't heard correctly.

'Do you?' she encouraged, moving even closer.

'C-can I?'

'Christ, Teddy,' she said forcefully. 'You're such a loser. For God's sake, go for it.' And with that, she grabbed his hand and shoved it up her T-shirt.

Feeling her hard, pointed nipples, he nearly came in his pants. Her tits were the best thing he'd ever felt.

Was this sex? He had a giant hard-on – which was nothing new because he got hard every time he looked at a girlie magazine. Only this was the real thing, this was Mila, and his heart was pounding.

Her hand crept down to stroke his erection. 'Oooh, aren't *you* a big boy?' she said, licking her lips with a snake-like pink tongue. 'My little Teddy – what a surprise!'

They were sitting in the back row, her choice. Whitney Houston and Kevin Costner were emoting on the screen, but who cared? Teddy certainly didn't. Right now he didn't care about anything except his interaction with Mila – the object of his lust.

She snaked her hand down the front of his pants. Flesh upon flesh. He thought he'd died and gone to heaven. Then, without warning, he felt himself squirting all over her hand.

'Ha!' she exclaimed. 'That was quick. Now you belong to me. Did you know that, Teddy? You always belong to the first woman you have.'

'But – but I haven't had you,' he stammered.

'That's okay,' she said matter-of-factly. 'We're just starting. We got plenty of time.'

35

'**I haven't** heard from you in a while.'

'Who's this?'

'You're kidding, right?'

Lucky sighed and held the phone tight. 'Hi, Alex,' she said. 'Your timing is impeccable.'

'What does *that* mean?'

'It means that twenty minutes ago Lennie and I had a big fight and he walked.'

'Walked?'

'You heard it here first.'

'Jesus! This isn't right.'

'Tell me about it. I'm sitting in an empty house with nobody to punch in the face.'

'If it's a face you want, you can have mine.'

'I'm angry and frustrated.'

'Sounds healthy.'

'Are you alone?'

'I could be in ten minutes. Why?'

'Thought I might come over and vent.'

'Want me to drive to your house and collect you?'

'I'm still capable of driving, thankyouverymuch.'

'I'll get out the vodka.'

'I'll see you in ten.'

What am I doing? she thought. *Running to Alex at the first sign of trouble. This is insane.*

And, yet, why shouldn't she go to Alex? Whether Lennie liked it or not, he *was* her best friend. And she couldn't burden Steven: he had enough to cope with.

Besides, her relationship with Alex was absolutely platonic.

Of course, there was that one wild night five years ago . . . but that had been a one-off they'd both agreed to forget about. And, anyway, Alex only went for Asian women, and she was in love with Lennie. There was absolutely no chemistry between her and Alex. Absolutely none.

Before leaving, she called Palm Springs to talk to her children. Instead she got Gino, who informed her they were all eating dinner. 'Everything okay with you, kid?' Gino asked.

'Of course. Why?'

'Somethin' in your voice.'

Oh, he knew her very well indeed, her father. He was a canny old man. 'Don't be silly,' she said lightly. 'I'm enjoying the break.'

'We'll keep the kids as long as you want,' he said. 'They're havin' a good time.'

'Thanks, Gino. And please thank Paige for me.'

Five minutes later she was in her Ferrari on her way to Alex's house. He lived further along the Pacific Coast Highway, in a Richard Meier-designed modern masterpiece. They were neighbours in a way, although neither of them ever dropped by.

He was standing at his front door, waiting for her. 'This is a nice surprise,' he said. 'Sorry to hear that you're so pissed off.'

'Right,' she said, getting out of her Ferrari. 'And so would you be.'

'I'll tell you what the plan is,' he said, holding her arm. 'We'll take my car, 'cause I hate your driving.'

'Take your car where?'

'We're going up the canyon to the Saddlebag Inn, where we will have a leisurely dinner, during which you can tell me everything.'

'I wasn't planning on dinner,' she said, gesturing at her outfit. 'I mean, look at me – I'm in jeans and a sweater.'

'Lucky, I don't know how to tell you this – but you're the most beautiful woman I've ever seen.'

'You're prejudiced, Alex, 'cause I'm your best friend.'

'Could be. But since you're also the smartest woman I know, we won't argue. Here's the deal. My fridge is empty and we both need to eat.'

'I'm not hungry.'

'You'd better be. I was planning a wild night of tantric sex with Pia, but since you've ruined *that* little scenario, let's go satisfy me in some other way.'

She couldn't help smiling. 'Hmm . . . just because I'm not into tantric sex . . .'

'Ha ha!' Alex said. 'I'm amused.'

'I aim to please.'

'Stop carrying on,' he said, 'and get in my car.'

'God, you're bossy,' she grumbled. 'I'd forgotten what it was like being around you.'

'I'm a director,' he said briskly. 'That's the way we are.'

She climbed into his Mercedes and they set off.

As they drove up the canyon, she started laughing.

'Glad to see I've brought a smile back to your face,' he said, glancing over at her. 'Care to share the joke?'

'I'm remembering,' she said.

'What?'

'The last drive we took under adverse circumstances.'

'You mean that drive when we were *supposed* to go see Gino in Palm Springs?'

'That's the one,' she said. 'I was in a freaked-out state

'cause that's when I thought Lennie was dead. But instead it turned out he'd been kidnapped. Only we didn't know that, right?'

'Sounds like a plot from one of my movies.'

'I hope not.'

'If I remember correctly you were *so* wasted. And we ended up in a sleazy bar with some crazy stripper – what was her name?'

'Driving Miss Daisy,' Lucky said, chuckling as she remembered the outrageous black stripper they'd somehow gotten attached to.

'Right,' Alex said, laughing too. 'You insisted I give her a job.'

'And you wouldn't,' Lucky said.

'God!' Alex said, smiling at the memory. 'That was some night. You were totally out of it.'

'And I suppose *you* were stone cold sober.'

'As a matter of fact I was,' he said. 'Had to be. One of us needed to be in control.'

'Sure,' she said.

'Then we had wild sex in that Norman Bates motel in the middle of nowhere,' he reminded her. 'And in the morning you were gone.'

Lucky stopped laughing. 'Alex,' she said, her face serious, 'you were never supposed to mention that. I *was* drunk. I didn't know what I was doing.'

'Never thought I'd hear *you* come up with an excuse like that,' he said, shaking his head.

'It's not an excuse, it's a fact. For all I know we didn't even *have* sex. You probably passed out.'

'Thanks a lot.'

'Did you?'

'What?'

'Pass out?'

'If it makes you feel better.'

They drove in silence for a few minutes, then Alex said, 'You ever tell Lennie?'

'Of course not.'

'Then why does he hate me?'

'He doesn't hate you.'

'Sure he does.'

'That's not true. We're all friends.'

'We *were* all friends for about two months after he reappeared, then suddenly his attitude changed. You must've noticed.'

'He likes you, Alex.'

'Bullshit! I think he knows.'

'There's no way he could possibly know,' she said. 'I never told him.'

'Anyway, what was he doing all that time he was held captive in a cave – jerking off?'

'That's not a very nice thing to say.'

'What about the girl who rescued him?'

'Nothing happened between them.'

'How do *you* know?'

'Because he told me and I trust him.'

'Okay, if *you* believe it, *I*'ll believe it.'

'Can we quit this conversation, Alex.'

'Yes, Lucky, whatever you say.'

☆

Once Lennie was out of the house and in his car, he realized he had nowhere to go. He also realized that Lucky was right, he *was* taking his lousy mood out on her, and any sane person knew that it wasn't her fault.

She'd mentioned divorce. How could she mention divorce at a time like this? The very fact that she'd done so angered him. Christ – didn't she understand what he was going through?

Yes, a little voice whispered in his head. *She understands all right. You're behaving like an asshole, and it's gone on too long.*

Cool down, that's what he had to do. Cool down and get his head together. Go home, apologize, and resume normal life. Because whatever he did could not bring Mary Lou back.

In the meantime, he drove around aimlessly, finally deciding to check into the Sunset Marquis for the night. Being by himself for one night wasn't such a bad idea. After all, he'd endured months of solitary confinement when he'd been kidnapped.

It had taken him a while when he'd got back from that ordeal to face life again. Now this: the setback he'd been praying wouldn't happen.

Mary Lou's image kept dancing before his eyes. So pretty and sweet and talented. What if he'd gone for his gun immediately? What if he'd thrown open his car door and fought with the attackers?

What if, what if, what if . . . The words kept going through his head, driving him insane.

Perhaps tomorrow he'd feel better. He wasn't going home until he did. Lucky deserved better.

☆

Alex allowed her to talk. They sat outside at a table for two, and Lucky let fly with all her problems.

'Maybe I made a mistake giving up my job at the studio,' she said, reflecting on the situation. 'It wasn't that I didn't enjoy what I was doing, I simply felt my responsibility was to spend more time with Lennie and my kids.'

'Do you miss being at Panther?' Alex asked.

'I *think* I do,' she said uncertainly. 'It was hard work, but that's what I enjoy. I've always worked hard. When I was in my twenties I was building hotels in Vegas and Atlantic City. Gino taught me the work ethic, y' know. Get out there and do it – and do it good.'

'If you miss it, you can always go back. After all, you still own the studio.'

'I'd feel kind of stupid going back so soon. I have to give the people I've put in charge a chance.'

'Then what's your plan? You'll go nuts sitting around doing nothing.'

She nodded, picking up her wine-glass. 'You're right.'

'I have an idea,' he said.

'What?'

'Why don't you produce a movie? It's a whole different deal from sitting in an office, fighting off agents and producers. Produce your own movie, Lucky,' he urged. 'Something you feel passionate about.'

'I never thought of that.'

'You'd enjoy the challenge. Besides, you're in the perfect position. You don't have to go through the shit of getting a studio to put up the money. You can greenlight your own project, then produce it.'

'I'm not experienced enough.'

'How about taking on a project with me?'

She laughed drily. 'That would go down well with Lennie.'

'So now you're going to live your life worrying about what Lennie thinks, huh? Where's that independent spirit of yours?'

'Lennie *is* my husband, Alex.'

'I know that, but surely you don't have to ask his permission?'

'To tell you the truth, I think you're right – he *is* a little bit jealous of you. So if we undertook a project together, that might put him over the top.'

Alex shrugged. 'Just an idea.'

'Thanks for the thought anyway,' she said. 'We'd probably drive each other crazy, because I'm *very* opinionated. And so are you.'

'*You*'re opinionated?' Alex said, his lethal crocodile grin coming at her full force. 'Wow! I'd never have guessed.'

Lucky couldn't help smiling back. 'Let's talk about *you* for a while. How's your mother?'

'Dominique's fine. Since she married the opera singer, she leaves me alone.'

'That's nice to know. You must feel good about that.'

'Stop sounding like a shrink.'

'I'd have made an excellent shrink.'

'You'd have made an excellent anything.'

'You always make me feel good, Alex.' She took another sip of wine. 'By the way, how's your love life?'

'You *know* about my love life, Lucky,' he said ruefully. 'They come, they go. *I* come, they go.'

'Alex, Alex, why don't you find a nice girl and settle down?'

'Now you sound like my mother.'

She laughed softly. 'First your shrink, then your mother. Which do you choose?'

'If I had a choice,' he said slowly, 'you'd be a free woman.' A long meaningful pause. 'And you'd be with me.'

☆

36

'**Don't look now,**' Kyra said, speaking out of the corner of her mouth. 'There's a guy sitting at the table to our left who hasn't taken his eyes off me.'

'Really?' Brigette said.

'Yeah,' Kyra said. 'He keeps on staring at me. Of course, I'm used to it.'

Here we go again, Brigette thought. *Kyra and Lina are exactly alike. Apart from the colour of their skin and their accents. Mega egos!*

'I should tell him I'm married, put the poor bloke out of his misery,' Kyra said, fluffing out her hair.

'Why don't you do that?' Brigette said.

'I will when he comes over.'

'What makes you think he's coming over?'

' 'Cause he's getting up now. He's on his way. And, baby, he's *major* cute!'

Brigette picked up her glass of Evian water and took a sip. Kyra was in for a surprise when she saw whom he was really coming over to see.

A moment later, tall and handsome Carlo stood in front of their table. 'Brigette!' he exclaimed. 'How nice to see you. *What* are you doing in London?'

She glanced up as if she was utterly surprised. 'Excuse me?' she said politely. 'Do I know you?'

'Do you know me?' he said with a laugh. 'I am Carlo.'

'Carlo?' she said vaguely. 'Oh . . . *Fredo*'s Carlo. How *are* you?'

His expression told her he couldn't believe she didn't recognize him.

Kyra, meanwhile, was trying to get introduced. 'Friend of yours?' she asked, giving Brigette a sharp nudge.

'Oh, yes, uh . . . Carlo . . . sorry . . .'

'Count Carlo Vittorio Vitti,' he said, kissing Kyra's hand. 'And you are?'

'Oh, come on,' Kyra said, bursting with laughter. 'You don't know who I am?'

'No, I'm sorry – should I?'

'The rest of the world certainly does,' Kyra said, slightly put out. 'I'm Kyra Kattleman.'

'Kyra Kattleman.' He repeated her name, rolling it over his tongue. 'Are you an actress?'

'Oh, Lordy, where do *you* live?' Kyra said, unamused by his total lack of recognition.

Brigette was quite enjoying the exchange.

'So, Brigette,' Carlo said, 'what are *you* doing here in London?'

'Visiting friends,' she answered casually.

'And Fredo didn't ask you to call me?'

'No. Actually, I haven't worked with Fredo lately. It's nice to bump into you though.'

He stared at her, noting that she was even more lovely during the day. Skin like peaches and cream, soft honey-blonde curls, and an exquisite mouth, pouty and inviting. He remembered making love to her, *he* remembered it well. Only she probably didn't recall the details. One of the disadvantages of the little white pills.

'Where are you staying?' he asked.

'The Dorchester.'

'So am I,' Kyra said, joining in. 'Leaving tomorrow for Milan. It's fashion week. Valentino can't do his show without me.'

'Ah,' Carlo said. 'So you are a model?'

'Not *a* model,' Kyra said, fluttering her long lashes. 'A *super*model. You've heard that word, I'm sure.'

'Ah, yes . . . Naomi Campbell.'

Kyra frowned. 'Why does everyone say Naomi Campbell. There *are* other supermodels, you know. Cindy, me, Kate Moss . . .'

'Brigette,' he said, turning his attention back to the woman who was one day to be his wife, 'are you free for dinner tonight?'

She smiled sweetly. 'As a matter of fact,' a pause, 'I'm not.'

'That *is* a shame.'

'Yes, isn't it?'

'How long will you be staying in London?'

'A few days. Depending on what my friends want to do.'

He wondered if they were male or female friends. It would

not do to have a rival enter the picture; he hadn't counted on that. According to Fredo, Brigette was a loner who did not go out a lot. Now all of a sudden she was here in London with a group of friends. This wasn't the way he'd planned it.

'How about dinner tomorrow night?' he suggested.

'Mmm . . .' she said. 'I think I'm busy.'

This was ridiculous. Women never turned him down. 'Perhaps you can change your plans?'

'I could try. Why don't you give me a call.'

'I will,' he said, lifting her hand to his lips. 'You look as beautiful as ever.' He lowered his voice. 'You *do* remember our night in New York?'

'Of course,' she said cheerfully. 'You, me, Lina and Fredo. We went dancing, didn't we? Had a great time.'

Now he was in a quandary. Was it possible that she did *not* remember anything at all about him making love to her? Damn! He'd only given her half a pill, she was supposed to be wondering why he hadn't called her. And here she was sitting in London without a care in the world.

'I will call you later, Brigette,' he said. 'We will talk.' He nodded briefly in Kyra's direction. 'A pleasure.'

'The pleasure was all mine,' Kyra said, adding a succinct, 'By the way, I'm married, so *I* can't have dinner with you either.'

'I'm glad you told me that.'

'Well!' Kyra said, as he walked away from the table. '*Told* you he was staring at me. Good job he knew you, so he had a legitimate excuse to come over.'

Brigette nodded. Things were working out just fine. Soon she would get her revenge on Carlo for taking advantage of her. It was a good feeling.

☆

Lina considered Max Steele a babe, which meant that more than likely she'd fuck him later. That's if Charlie Dollar didn't materialize. If she had a choice between an agent and a star, she'd take the star every time. Law of the jungle.

Max was a partner in IAA, International Artists Agency, a very hot place to be. He was partners with Freddie Leon, the super-agent. She was a bit miffed that Freddie himself hadn't chosen to handle her but, from what she'd heard, Max was almost as good.

He met her at the bar in the Peninsula, and they got along straight away.

'Is Charlie coming?' she asked, crossing her long legs and lighting a cigarette.

Max's eyes were popping. 'Baby, one look at you and he'll be coming all the way to Africa!'

'You're a cute one, huh?' she said, blowing smoke in his direction.

'There's only one cute one here,' Max said with a sly smile. 'And it certainly ain't me.'

She continued checking him out. Max Steele was not movie-star handsome, but he had an abundance of boyish charm, a full head of curly brown hair, an in-shape body, and plenty of charisma.

'So who's the director?' she asked, sipping a rum and Coke through a straw.

'A friend of mine,' Max said, with a wink. 'But you don't have to worry about the director. If Charlie likes you, we're in.'

'Who does the studio want for the part?' she asked, anxious to find out who she was up against.

'They're after a name,' Max said. 'They're pushing for Angela or Lela, even Whitney.'

'Don't be daft,' Lina said, snorting with laughter. 'It's not a big enough part for Whitney. And she *certainly* wouldn't take her clothes off. Bobby would *never* put up with it.'

'You'd be surprised,' Max said. 'Roles for black actresses are not that easy to find.'

'Oh, it's a *racist* thing in Hollywood, is it?' she said, cocking her head to one side.

'It's always been a racist thing in Hollywood,' Max replied, thinking that this girl was a total knock-out.

'Really?'

'You're far more stunning than your photographs.'

She giggled. 'Yeah, like I haven't heard *that* line before.'

'It's not a line,' he said indignantly. 'I'm an agent, I have to be truthful with my clients. If you looked like shit I'd tell you.'

'Sure you would,' she said sanguinely. 'An' the Pope goes rollerskatin' up my arse.'

'Oh,' Max said. 'Charlie's going to *love* you.'

☆

Brigette accompanied Kyra on her shopping trip to Harvey Nichols. She even bought a few things herself – some cool Police shades, a soft pink cashmere sweater and a long silk scarf.

'*Told* you this was a great store,' Kyra boasted, as if she was personally responsible for the array of tempting goods.

Brigette nodded.

'Y' know,' Kyra announced, completely oblivious to the fact that Carlo had only had eyes for Brigette, 'if I wasn't married, I would've gone out with that bloke at lunch.'

'Why?' Brigette questioned.

'*Why?*' Kyra answered, surprised that Brigette would even ask. ''Cause he's a babe. And he's got that count thingy going for him.'

He's a bastard, Brigette wanted to say. *He drugged and raped me, and he's going to pay for it.*

But she didn't say a word.

This was her game now, and she would play it her way.

37

Two things struck Lennie when he awoke. One, he wasn't in his own bed; and two, several numbers were jumping around in his head.

Was it possible that he was finally remembering the licence plate?

He groped for a notepad and quickly jotted down the numbers – three of them. Not enough, but better than nothing. Then he called his wife.

Lucky answered, sounding sleepy.

'It's me,' he said, very upbeat as if nothing was going on. 'We should talk.'

'That's what I've been trying to do for the last six weeks,' she said, waking up with a start.

'Okay, okay,' he said. 'I admit it's my fault. No need to get belligerent, I'm trying to be nice here.'

'*You*'re trying to be nice?' she responded hotly, struggling to sit up. 'Wasn't it *you* who walked out last night?'

'I know, honey,' he said soothingly, 'and I got a feeling it was a good thing 'cause it gave us space. And guess what?'

'What?' She sighed, thrown by his sudden change of mood.

'I came up with a couple of numbers that I'm sure were part of the licence plate.'

'Have you called Detective Johnson?'

'Not yet.'

'What're you waiting for?'

'To speak to you first. Can we meet for breakfast, or shall I come home right now?'

'No, Lennie,' she said sternly, not about to forgive him so fast. 'You walked out last night. You're right, we both need space.'

'But I miss you, baby.'

She felt herself beginning to weaken, Lennie had that effect on her. 'I miss you, too,' she said quietly.

'I'll be there in twenty minutes.'

'No,' she said quickly. 'I'll meet you for breakfast.'

'If that's what you want.'

'Yes. Where are you?'

'At the Sunset Marquis. Hurry.'

'As soon as I'm dressed. In the meantime call Detective Johnson.'

Thoughtfully she put down the phone. Maybe Lennie was right, one night apart and he realized how wrong he was. Thank God! Because she couldn't stand fighting with him, it drove her crazy.

Before she could get out of bed the phone rang again. She grabbed it. 'Okay, okay – I'm on my way,' she said.

'You are?' Alex said.

'Oh – it's you.'

'Oh, it's me. Does that indicate that you've heard from your husband.'

'What're you? A psychic?'

'Kind of.'

'Okay, you're right. He called, wants to meet. And I must say he sounds a whole lot better.'

'I couldn't be happier,' Alex drawled sarcastically.

'Don't be a prick. Be happy for me.'

'I prefer it when you're separated.'

'It didn't even last twenty-four hours.'

'Shame.'

'Quit being such a smartass.'

'And she continues to entice me with her masterful use of the English language.'

'Anyway, Alex, thanks for last night, you helped as usual. Talking to you is the best.'

'You know I'm *always* here for you, Lucky.'

'And it's much appreciated. Oh, yes, and the good news is that I won't be bothering you again. You're free. You can call up Mia or Pia, or whatever her name is, and get into that tantric-sex thing you mentioned.' A meaningful pause. 'By the way, is it worth it?'

He gave a dry laugh. 'When you're ready to find out, let me know.'

'Oh, and, Alex,' she added casually, 'not that it's a big secret or anything, but I'd sooner not piss Lennie off, so let's keep last night's dinner between us.'

'Damn! And I was gonna call the *Enquirer*.'

She hung up smiling, and dressed quickly. She was excited at the thought of seeing Lennie, it was almost as if she was embarking on a date with him.

Before leaving the house she called Steven. 'How's my favourite brother today?' she asked cheerfully.

'Still here,' Steven said. 'I was thinking of driving down to Palm Springs to visit the kids.'

'Sounds like a great idea to me.'

'Want to come?'

'I would, but it seems like I only just got rid of them. And actually . . . I was planning a romantic weekend alone with Lennie.'

'Think I'll call Gino, tell him I'm on my way.'

'By the way, before I forget, Venus and Cooper are having an anniversary party on Monday. They wanted me to ask if you'd drop by.'

'Thanks anyway, but I'll pass.'

She had hoped he'd say yes. As far as she knew he'd gone nowhere since Mary Lou's death. 'Isn't it time you got out?'

'Lucky,' he answered slowly, 'it hasn't been long enough.'

'I know you need time, Steven, but eventually you'll have to meet other women.'

'No,' he said fiercely, 'I had enough women before Mary Lou. She *was* my life, my prize. I'll never be able to replace her. And I have no desire to do so.'

'That's how you feel now, but don't forget that old cliché, time heals everything.'

'It doesn't heal, it covers up.'

'Whatever you say,' she said, backing off, because the worst thing she could do was push him. 'Have a good drive to Palm Springs. Kiss my babies for me, and hug Carioca.'

'I will.'

'Uh . . . Steven, maybe when you leave Palm Springs you should take her home with you, spend time together. Y' know, daddy and daughter, that kind of deal.'

'She likes staying with you, Lucky.'

'And we love having her, but she can't stay here for ever, because that's not good for either of you.'

'Okay,' he said impatiently. 'I get it.'

He knew she was right, his daughter should be with him. But he didn't need it shoved in his face. It was difficult enough getting through each day. And the sad thing was that every time he looked at Carioca she reminded him of Mary Lou.

'By the way, I have excellent news,' Lucky added.

'What?'

'Lennie came up with a couple of numbers from the licence plate.'

'That *is* good news.'

'I kind of threw him out last night, and I guess sitting alone in a hotel room gave him time to think.'

'You threw Lennie out?'

'It was a mutual deal. I told you before, he's having a lot of trouble with this.'

'We both are, Lucky,' Steven said grimly. 'We both are.'

☆

When Lucky walked in Lennie was sitting at a table near the hotel pool. He jumped up and waved. She waved back, dodging her way around palm trees to reach him.

'Hello, you,' he said, holding out his arms, half an embrace, half a gesture of apology.

'Hello you, too,' she said, falling into them. He gave her a long, lingering soul kiss. 'Wow!' she said, backing off and gasping for breath. 'Where did you come up with *that*?'

'You're my wife, aren't you? I'm entitled.'

'Hmm . . .' she said, thinking that he looked more relaxed than he had in weeks. 'Did you call the detective?'

'I did.'

'And?'

'He told me it's a big help.'

'This ain't bad,' she said, looking around, checking out the small hotel.

'I figured if I was taking off I may as well do it in style,' he said. 'This hotel is full of horny models and English rock stars. Better vibe than the fancier places.'

Lucky regarded him with a quizzical expression. 'Okay,' she joked. 'I'll take the rock stars – you can stick with the horny models.'

He scratched his chin. 'Wanna see my room?'

'Is it worth seeing?'

'You tell me,' he said, taking her by the hand and leading her along the side of the pool to one of the bungalows.

Inside the room the shades were drawn, the bed rumpled. 'So . . .' she said casually. 'Did you get laid and drunk?'

'Oh, yeah, sure,' he said, gesturing across the room. 'Can't you see all the signs? Empty bottles, women's panties, drug paraphernalia.'

'Lennie, Lennie,' she said, shaking her head and smiling. 'What am I going to do with you?'

'What're *you* gonna do with *me*?' he said, perplexed. 'The question is, what am *I* gonna do with *you*?'

She sighed. 'Don't let's get into that game again.'

'What game?'

'Repeating everything.'

'Okay,' he said. 'Let me tell you what happened. I woke up this morning, and it was like I was struck by a ray of light. I *saw* the jeep driving away. I *saw* the licence plate, and those numbers came to me. If I keep thinking about it, I'll come up with the rest of them. You're right. When those murderers are caught, I'm gonna feel totally different.'

'Revenge has always worked for me,' Lucky said. 'Lock 'em up and throw away the key.'

'I want to help make it happen,' Lennie said. 'I want my day in court.'

Lucky sat down on the edge of the bed, testing the mattress. 'Nice room,' she said, 'but now I'd like you to come home.'

'I'm ready.'

'This is good, 'cause I sent the kids away so we could have a romantic weekend.'

He came over and stood in front of her. 'I'm sorry for walking out and acting like a jerk. I kind of got stir crazy, and took it out on you.'

She reached up and touched his cheek. 'And I'm sorry I didn't tell you about the studio. You're right, Lennie, I was wrong. I did it to you once before and you went crazy – I remember that now.' A long beat. 'Y' see, I thought I'd surprise you. Then after, I realized we should've discussed it.'

'Right.'

'But you know me, I have a thing about making my own decisions. Thing is, I've never *had* to answer to anyone.'

'Do you know?' he said. 'We've been married nine years.'

'I know that.'

'And right now I feel as if we've been married nine minutes.'

'Me, too.'

'I know I haven't been much fun to be around lately, but believe me, I'll make it up to you.'

'Promise?'

'You got it. Anything you want.'

'Anything?' she teased.

'You,' he said, smiling, 'are such a turn-on.'

'I am?' she said, toying with his zipper. 'Tell me more, Lennie.'

'Well, all I have to do is look at you . . .'

'And?'

'. . . and Elvis is back in town.'

She burst out laughing. 'Such a way with words!'

'Remember our first hotel room?' he said.

'How could I ever forget?' she said, laughing. 'Vegas.'

'And you walked out on me.'

'That's 'cause you thought I was a hooker.'

'You acted like one.'

'Thanks a lot,' she said indignantly. 'I was single. I saw something I liked and went for it. What's wrong with *that*?'

'You always lived your life like a man, didn't you?'

'Seems to me men have always known how to have a good time.'

'And you, my little darling, have always had a good time, too.'

'And you, my little sweetheart,' she countered, 'were never exactly a virgin. In fact . . . the word *stud* comes to mind. You and your never-ending parade of blondes.'

Now they were both laughing as she pulled him down on the bed beside her.

'Lucky, Lucky,' he sighed, 'I love you more than anything in the world.'

'You too,' she whispered.

'And I *never* want to hear the word divorce come out of your mouth again.'

'I promise.'

'You do?'

'I do.'

And then they were kissing, and soon they were caught up in passion and love and everything nice.

Lennie was back, and it felt indescribably good.

38

At Brigette's request, Horace Otley came up with a detailed report of Fiona Lewyllen Wharton's movements. According to Horace's report, Fiona worked at an art gallery off Bond Street, and every Saturday morning she had a standing appointment at a nearby hairdresser's with a stylist named Edward.

Brigette made an appointment for herself. It wasn't difficult because once she announced who she was the salon were so thrilled to accommodate her that they would have cancelled anybody. As it happened, she made her appointment fifteen minutes before Fiona was due to appear.

Carlo had called her several times since bumping into her

at lunch. She'd instructed the hotel switchboard to inform him that she was not available, which she knew must be driving him crazy. Carlo was not a man used to being turned down.

The one thing Brigette didn't think about was being pregnant. She pushed the thought out of her mind – it was too disturbing. Right now she had to concentrate on dealing with Carlo.

She arrived at the hairdressing salon on time. There were several stylists working hard, and a few assistants who couldn't help staring at her.

Edward was a sweet-faced, fair-haired boy who could hardly believe his luck. 'My goodness, who recommended me?' he gasped. 'I'm so *flattered*.'

'Someone at the hotel,' Brigette answered vaguely. 'I was told you're good with long hair.'

'Oh, you've got beautiful hair,' he exclaimed, picking up a strand. 'Absolutely fab. And what would her loveliness like me to do to it today?'

'A wash and blow-dry would be great.'

'Certainly. And may I take this opportunity to tell you that we're all big fans of yours here?'

Fiona Lewyllen Wharton entered the salon a few minutes later. She was a plump brunette, not quite as homely as she looked in her photographs, but hardly a beauty. She wore an unflattering tweed suit, patterned tights and comfortable pumps. Her legs were sturdy.

Brigette was sitting in Edward's chair getting her hair blow-dried.

'Are you running late, Edward?' Fiona enquired, in a louder-than-usual voice.

'No,' Edward answered, flitting around Brigette with his blow-dryer. 'By the time you're washed I'll be ready for you.'

Brigette met Fiona's eyes in the mirror. 'I'm *sorry*,' she said. 'I do hope I haven't taken your appointment.'

Fiona frowned and glanced at Edward, who looked embarrassed. 'I crammed Brigette in,' he explained quickly. 'She's a big New York model, and uh . . . we wanted to accommodate her. You don't mind, do you?'

'You mean she's taken my appointment?' Fiona said, obviously not pleased.

'No, no, she was here earlier. You'll only have to wait five minutes.'

'It doesn't matter,' Fiona said. 'However, I do have somewhere special to go tonight.'

'Wish I did.' Brigette sighed wistfully. 'I'm in London for such a short time, and I hardly know anybody.'

'Can't imagine you sitting home knitting socks, dear,' Edward said boldly.

Fiona emitted a horsy laugh. 'Weren't you on the cover of *Vogue* last month?' she asked, peering at Brigette in the mirror. 'Mummy takes it.'

'That was me,' Brigette said.

'You must be terribly famous in America.'

'She's terribly famous everywhere,' Edward pointed out.

'And what do *you* do?' Brigette asked politely.

'Oh, me – I work in an art gallery.'

'What kind of art do you sell?'

'Old masters,' Fiona said airily, as if it was the only thing any art gallery could possibly sell.

'How fascinating,' Brigette said. 'Do tell me all about it.'

Fiona's eyes lit up, it wasn't every day a famous New York model wanted to know about *her*.

By the time Edward had finished blow-drying Brigette's long hair, she and Fiona were fast friends. Brigette had a way of bringing people out, getting them to speak about themselves. It was probably why she was so popular with Lina and the other girls. She never talked about herself, always listened.

Fiona was quite flattered. 'I have a super idea,' she said, full of enthusiasm. 'Why don't you come over to Daddy's tonight? Every Saturday we have a little soirée. Daddy calls it our salon. Mummy calls it Daddy's liquorice all-sorts.'

'That's an English candy,' Edward said, *sotto voce*.

'We invite fifteen or twenty interesting people,' Fiona continued. 'Sometimes they're politicians, and once we had Fergie – she's charming, quite amusing, too. Will you come?'

Brigette glanced at Edward, who nodded encouragingly. 'Well, I . . . I don't know,' she said. 'I mean . . . I hardly like to intrude.'

'Daddy will be delighted to have you,' Fiona said, with another horsy laugh.

'Then I'd love to come,' Brigette said. 'That's very kind of you.'

'I'll write down the address,' Fiona said. 'About seven thirty. Cocktail attire.'

Brigette nodded. 'Seven thirty it is.'

☆

Dinner at Morton's. A good table near the front of the room against the wall. Max Steele was showing off.

'Where's Charlie?' Lina asked, as they were finishing their main course of delicious swordfish.

'He'll be here,' Max said confidently. 'Charlie's got a reputation for running late. In fact, if I didn't want to avoid insulting you, I'd say he runs on black time.'

'Black time?' Lina said, pushing a piece of fish across her plate.

'Well, y' know,' Max said easily, picking up a French fry with his fingers, 'black people do things by their own clock.'

'Are you a racist?' she asked sharply, like he'd admit it if he was.

'That's the second time you've mentioned the word racist,' Max said, throwing his hands in the air. 'I'm sitting here with *you*, aren't I?'

'Bloody 'ell,' Lina said indignantly. 'You should be so *lucky* to be sitting 'ere with me. Men give their right balls to sit with me.'

'Modest,' Max said. 'I like that in a woman. If you can act, we'll own the world.'

''Course I can act,' Lina said, like it was a given. 'What do you *think* I'm doing when I'm poncing up and down those stupid runways. *That*'s acting. I put on my drop-dead-you-morons face, an' give 'em what they want.'

'And what is it they want?'

'They wanna see girls who look better than everyone else. You've gotta admit it, Max, right now models are a lot more glam than all those scrungy actresses up on the screen. Who've *you* got to write 'ome about? Holly Hunter and Meryl Streep. Ha! Great actresses, but not exactly drop dead gorgeous. It's the models who 'ave all the glamour today.'

'I disagree,' Max said. 'How about Julia Roberts and Michelle Pfeiffer?'

'Okay, I'll give you them, only that's about it.'

'Can't wait to see you and Charlie together,' he said. 'This'll be some combination!'

'If he ever bleedin' turns up,' Lina said huffily.

'He will,' Max said confidently.

Half an hour later Charlie ambled in, wearing one of his favourite Hawaiian shirts, baggy white pants, dark shades and his usual shit-eating grin. 'Hey,' he said, slapping Max on the back, 'what's goin' on in Agent Land?'

'Hey,' Max said, standing up, 'meet Lina.'

Lina gave Charlie a long, penetrating look.

'Quite an eyeful!' Charlie said. 'Five feet ten and—'

'Eleven,' she interrupted.

'Dark hair and big . . . eyes. Just my type.'

Lina narrowed her cat like eyes. 'Hmm . . . let me see. Fifty-something, chubby, an' ever so talented.' She grinned. 'Just my type, too.'

'Okay, doll,' Charlie said, nodding. 'I can see you and I are gonna get along like a gang of hookers at a sailors' convention in Puerto Rico.'

'I've been wanting to meet you,' she said, hoping she didn't sound too much like a fan. 'I think you're smashing.'

'Smashing, huh?' Charlie said, raising an extravagant eyebrow. 'In that case, I'm gonna join you good people.'

And with that he pulled out a chair and sat down.

☆

The Lewyllen Whartons lived in a luxurious, well-appointed five-storey townhouse in Eaton Square. A butler answered the door and ushered Brigette in.

She looked around for Fiona, who came running over to greet her. 'Welcome,' Fiona said, as if they were old friends. 'I'm so glad you're here.'

'It was nice of you to invite me,' Brigette said.

'Come,' Fiona said, leading Brigette into the formal living room to meet her parents.

Editha, her mother, was a small, wispy blonde woman, and Leopold, her father, was large, bald and blustery.

'This is my new friend, Brigette,' Fiona announced proudly. 'She's a top model, you know. She was on the cover of American *Vogue* last month.'

'How nice,' Editha said, completely unimpressed as she turned away to talk to someone else.

Brigette couldn't help noticing that Leopold was giving her a different kind of look – the kind of look that made her feel as if she was standing naked in front of him. 'Delighted to welcome you, dear,' he said. 'Fiona, introduce your friend to some of the other guests.'

'I'm delighted to be here,' Brigette said. 'It's so nice of you to invite me.'

'Any friend of Fiona's is a friend of ours,' Leopold said, not even attempting to shift his gaze from her breasts.

She had chosen to wear a simple black Isaac Mizrahi dress, not too low-cut, just enough to attract the attention of every man in the room. Fiona was in fussy brown velvet with a long skirt and wide sleeves, a most unfortunate choice, Brigette thought.

'You *have* to meet my fiancé first,' Fiona said, taking her arm and pulling her across the room. 'He's over here. He's an Italian count, you know. We're getting married next year.'

'How wonderful,' Brigette murmured, feeling her heart start to beat rapidly.

Carlo had his back to them as they approached. He was busy talking to a distinguished-looking man and a somewhat bored redhead.

Fiona tapped him on the shoulder. 'Darling, I'd like you to meet my new friend, Brigette.'

Carlo turned around. Their eyes met. He stared at her for a second or two before saying, 'A pleasure to meet you, Brigette.'

'Oh,' she responded, not letting him get away with a thing, 'Carlo – it's you!'

'Me?' he said, trying to warn her with his eyes that he would prefer it if they did not acknowledge knowing each other.

'Brigette,' she insisted. '*You* remember – I bumped into you at lunch the other day, and you reminded me of that fantastic night we spent together in New York.'

Fiona looked from one to the other, confused. 'Do you two *know* each other?' she asked, her expression sagging.

Carlo shrugged. 'Brigette must be mistaking me for some-one else,' he said coolly. 'We have never met.'

'No mistake,' Brigette said, nailing him – although this was only the beginning. 'You're Count Carlo Vittorio Vitti, Fredo's cousin. You came up to me in Le Caprice the other day. Surely you can't have forgotten?'

Carlo gritted his teeth. What a bad coincidence *this* was. 'Ah, yes,' he said stiffly. 'Of course. Brigette. *Now* I remember. You were with my cousin, Fredo.' He turned quickly to Fiona. 'I told you about that dinner for twenty people I went to with Fredo in New York. Brigette was one of the guests.'

'Oh,' Fiona said unsurely. 'I don't remember.'

'Small world,' Brigette said, feeling bad because she hadn't expected to like Fiona. And not only did she like her, she felt sorry for her, too.

Still ... it was better that Fiona discovered what a two-timing rapist-scumbag-rat her fiancé actually was before she went ahead and married him.

'This is a beautiful house, Fiona,' Brigette said. 'Would you mind if I took a look around?'

'Not at all,' Fiona said.

And Brigette turned and walked away, leaving Carlo to explain the situation to his fiancée.

39

'**Hold this,**' Mila said, throwing the gun at Teddy.

He caught it, a look of abject amazement on his face. 'You told me you'd gotten rid of it,' he said, thoroughly alarmed.

'I was going to, then I figured it was safer to wait,' Mila explained, giving him a sly sideways glance.

He tossed the gun on to the middle of her bed. 'You gotta get it outta here,' he said, panicking. 'What if the cops come and search?'

'You're so right,' she agreed. 'I will.'

They had just returned from the movies, and Mila had smuggled him out to her room in the back. 'Irena's watching TV,' she'd said. 'The old crow never comes in here anyway. This is *my* place, an' she knows it.'

He looked around her room, sparsely furnished with just

the essentials and bare walls. A tattered red scarf was draped over one lamp, while another faded one hung half-way across the window. Her clothes were piled on a chair, with her shoes in an untidy jumble underneath.

Teddy thought of his own cosy room – walls covered in posters, piles of books everywhere, a large-screen TV; and an Apple computer. Not to mention a stack of CDs and videos, and a radical new stereo. He had everything, while she had nothing. Suddenly he felt incredibly guilty.

'I'm thirsty,' she said. 'Wanna sneak down to the pool bar an' get us a couple of beers?'

'Okay,' he said. 'But you gotta promise you'll dump the gun.'

'I will,' she said guilelessly.

He left her room and hurried to the pool bar, hoping he wouldn't bump into the dreaded Irena.

When he came back the gun was gone. 'What didja do with it?' he asked, handing her a bottle of beer.

'Put it somewhere safe,' she said mysteriously. 'I'll get it out of here tomorrow.'

'Promise?'

'You got it, Teddy.'

Teddy drank from his bottle of beer, surreptitiously edging closer to her. They were a couple now: nothing and no one could come between them.

'I'm tired,' she said, yawning in his face. 'I need sleep.'

'Don't you want me to stay?' he asked, disappointed.

'You've had enough excitement for one day,' she said, yawning again.

'Stop talkin' to me as if I'm a kid,' he said, annoyed that she still treated him with no respect. 'I've proved to you I'm not.'

'Okay, okay,' she said, stifling yet another yawn. 'Don't get your stones in a twist, there's always tomorrow.' As she spoke, she hustled him towards the door, finally shoving him out.

As soon as he was gone, she opened the drawer where she'd hidden the gun, carefully wrapped in a small towel. Teddy was the dumbest shit alive. He had no clue that he'd gotten his prints all over it.

'Oh, Teddy, Teddy,' she murmured. 'When are you gonna wise up?'

☆

Price had a choice: he could stay home and relax, or he could call one of three women he was currently dating.

He thought about them for a moment. There was the actress, black and extremely beautiful in a kind of uptight way. She'd recently gone through a very public divorce, and all the tabloids were telling tales and calling her a maniac. She was sweet as pie to him, but he didn't want to get involved with *another* maniac – his first wife was quite enough.

Then there was the very famous white actress, older and hungry. He had a strong suspicion she was only dating him because he was black.

The third prospect was Krissie, an ex-*Penthouse* Pet with a body to die for. Unfortunately she was irredeemably stupid. Recently interviewed on TV as to what her favourite beauty aid was, she'd fluttered her long eyelashes and said, 'I simply can't *live* without my eyelash curlers.' A brain she wasn't, although he had to admit that she used those eyelashes to good effect when giving him a masterful blow-job.

Still, staying home seemed like the best idea of all. He'd have Irena cook him up some fried chicken and her special potatoes, then he'd get into bed and watch a movie. In a few days he was due to play Vegas, and that was hectic time. He got so hyped up after a performance that the only way he could calm down was to be with a woman. Sex was his last drug of choice – that and an occasional joint. Especially after a live performance.

He wondered if Teddy was home. If he was, they could eat together. Price prided himself on being a good father. He kept a watchful eye on Teddy and didn't let him get up to much. Thank God the only thing Teddy seemed to have gotten into was smoking a little grass. No big deal.

Price wandered into the kitchen, where Irena was busy cleaning out a cupboard. 'What're you doing?' he asked.

'The maids are never thorough enough for me,' she said, scrubbing out the cupboard with a stiff wire brush, exerting herself well beyond the call of duty.

'Isn't that what *they* get paid for?' he remarked.

'Yes, Mr Washington. However, I prefer to see that everything is perfect.'

One thing about Irena, she kept a spotless house. She also had a very nice ass, which he sometimes took advantage of. She didn't object. In fact, she seemed disappointed if he *didn't* pay her attention.

As far as Price was concerned, Irena Kopistani was one lucky White Russian. She lived under his roof, serviced him whenever he felt like it, *and* got paid. Other women would pay *him* for the privilege.

Plus he knew he was a great boss. He'd never complained when she'd gotten pregnant and had a kid, never badgered her with questions about who the father was. He'd noticed that no man ever came around to visit, which didn't bother him at all. Who needed some strange dude sniffing around? He liked the fact that she was all his, available whenever he wanted.

Once a year he raised her salary, which kept her happy, because one thing he knew for sure, he couldn't manage without her.

'Think I'm gonna be eating at home tonight,' he said. 'Where's Teddy?'

'I have no idea,' she said.

'Is he back from the movies?'

'I don't know,' she said, still scrubbing.

'Y' know, sometimes you could talk a little more,' he said. 'You're not exactly the most communicative person in the world.'

She stopped her work and looked up at him. *I'm your sex slave*, she wanted to say. *You use me in every way. Now you want me to talk too?* But she didn't say a word. 'I will buzz Teddy in his room,' she said, moving over to the intercom.

At that moment, Teddy entered the kitchen.

'Hey, boy,' Price said, pleased to see him, 'how was the movie?'

'Pretty cool,' Teddy said, wishing his father would stop calling him 'boy'. He wasn't a kid any more, he'd proved that today.

'Whaddya see?'

'The Bodyguard.'

'Whitney Houston, huh? Now *there*'s a body I wouldn't mind guarding!'

'Didja ever meet her, Dad?' Teddy asked, just to be polite because, after his mind-blowing experiences with Mila, the last thing on his mind was Whitney Houston.

'Run into her and Bobby at a couple of events,' Price said casually. 'What're you up to for dinner?'

'Nothing,' Teddy said, unable to think of a quick enough excuse.

'So we'll do the father-son thing. You'll eat with me.'

'Yes, Dad,' Teddy said glumly, trapped.

'I'll send Irena out to rent a video. Anything you wanna see?'

'I got homework,' Teddy said. After dinner he planned to go to his room and think about what had taken place that afternoon. Mila allowing him to touch her tits. Coming in his pants. Jeez! Just thinking about it got him horny. For the time being, running away was put on a back-burner.

'Dining room, seven o'clock,' Price announced. 'Try to be on time for once.'

'Sure, Dad,' Teddy said, making a fast exit.

As soon as Teddy was gone Price began rubbing his crotch. Irena might not be as foxy as his trio of girlfriends, but she sure gave a hell of a blow-job. So maybe later, when everyone was asleep, he'd buzz her to come up to his room. He might even fuck her, give her the thrill of her life.

The truth of the matter was that he enjoyed sex with Irena more than with any of his transient dates. And wasn't *that* something to admit?

Only to himself, of course.

Irena was his guilty secret, and that's the way it had to stay.

40

They spent the morning making love in Lennie's hotel room.

'This is totally wild and wonderful,' Lucky said, rolling across the bed and stretching luxuriously. 'We should do it more often. I gotta tell you – hotels are dead sexy.'

'They certainly are,' Lennie agreed, stroking her thigh.

She laughed softly.

'What's up?' he asked. 'Did I say something funny?'

'I feel like I'm cheating on my husband.'

'If I ever find you cheating on your husband, you're a dead woman,' he said, mock-threateningly.

Running her fingers lightly across his chest, she leaned close to his ear and whispered, 'Would you kill me, Lennie? Would you really do that?'

'Believe me,' he said sternly, 'you don't wanna try it.'

'Then you'd better remember it's mutual.'

'Right,' he said, laughing. 'Knowing you, you'd cut off my dick and keep it in a jar by the bed.'

'No, I wouldn't,' she said, laughing back. 'I'd drop it down the waste-disposal.'

'You're a dangerous woman,' he said, shuddering.

'Never said I wasn't.'

'I'm starving,' he said, sitting up. 'Shall we order room service?'

'I was thinking that maybe we should go home.'

'Why? I'm perfectly happy here.'

'You are?'

'I get off on hotel living. It's impersonal, kind of like a time-suspension deal.'

'Yes, well, don't forget, we've got three kids to think about. You're a family man, Lennie. Mr Married.'

'Ouch!'

'Is it that painful?'

'Not when I'm with you.'

'What do you want to eat?' she asked, climbing out of bed, searching for a menu.

He lay back, watching her slender body as she crossed the room, naked and still as beautiful as the first time he'd seen her. 'I'll have an omelette.'

'An *omelette*?' she exclaimed, running a hand through her unruly black hair. 'What kind of girly food is *that*? *I* need a hamburger.'

'That's 'cause *you*'ve got a voracious appetite,' he pointed out. 'In every way.'

'Then aren't *you* the fortunate one?' she said, finding a menu on the desk and hurrying back to bed.

'That's me,' he said, grinning.

'That's you,' she agreed, straddling him and pinning his shoulders to the bed, thinking that it was so damn good to have him back. He'd been missing since the hold-up. Now here he was, the Lennie she knew and loved.

For a moment her thoughts turned to Alex. She'd enjoyed being with him last night, but they were just friends. Nobody could ever come between her and Lennie. They were truly bound together.

'When you were kidnapped,' she said casually, 'what did you think about every day?'

He regarded her quizzically. 'You're asking me five years later?'

'You must have thought of *something* – you can't have just sat there, staring at walls.'

'I thought about *you*, Lucky,' he said, his face serious. 'You and the kids and coming home. That's *all* I thought about.'

'And the girl who helped you escape – what was her name?'

'Uh ... I don't remember.'

'Yes, you do.'

'I think it was Claudia.'

'Ah, yes ... Claudia.' A long beat. 'Did you have any ... feelings for her? I mean, there you were, trapped in a cave, and she was your only human contact.'

'Why are you asking me this now?'

'Sometimes I get to thinking about it,' she said slowly. 'I was alone here, I thought you were dead ...'

'What are you getting at?'

'I simply wondered if anything happened between the two of you.'

He shook his head. 'Now I know you're crazy.'

'Was she pretty?'

'*What?*'

'Well, was she?'

'If it'll make you happy, she was a dog,' he lied.

'Shame,' she murmured.

'C'mon, Lucky,' he said sharply. 'It's bad memories, and I do not care to talk about it any more.'

'Okay, okay, I understand,' she said, kissing him fervently. 'Pass me the phone. I'll do the ordering.'

☆

Alex Woods did not call Pia. The truth was that any woman paled in comparison to Lucky Santangelo, so even though he was prepping a new movie, and that was *all* he should have been thinking about, his thoughts lingered on Lucky. Ever since that one wild night in the desert he'd known she was the woman for him. And yet he'd had to stand by, an observer, as she welcomed Lennie home; he'd had to watch their relationship flourish. He'd also been a guest at their house many times, had seen Lucky in every situation – as boss of Panther Studios, mother of her three children, god-mother to Brigette. She was a remarkable woman, and as far as he was concerned she could do anything.

He'd really meant it when he'd suggested she should produce a movie. In fact, he'd welcome her savvy and know-how on any one of his projects.

In his heart he knew that Lennie would never allow it, because Lennie was well aware of how he, Alex, felt about Lucky. It was a man thing: instinctively you knew when another man was checking out your woman.

Not that Alex didn't like Lennie, he considered him an okay guy. But not okay enough for Lucky. He, Alex Woods, was the man she should really be with.

Alex had never married nor had children. His mother, the formidable Dominique, continually berated him for that. 'You *should* be married,' she often scolded. 'It's not normal for a man of your age to be alone.'

Hey, he wanted to say, you're *not fucking normal. You're the one who sent me to military school and treated me like a piece of shit all my life. That is, until I finally made it. Then, all of a sudden, I was your son again and you wanted everyone to know it.*

But he never said anything. She was getting old. She was married now and not such a domineering presence, thank God!

One thing he knew for sure: he certainly wasn't looking for a woman who reminded him of dear old Mama.

He often thought with wry amusement about his first

encounter with Lucky. The movie he was involved with at the time – *Gangsters* – was in turn-around, and Freddie Leon, his agent, had suggested they run it over to Panther Studios, where Lucky had recently taken over. He'd walked into her office and been faced with this indescribably powerful and beautiful woman. Tall and slender, with a tangle of jet curls framing an incredible face, dangerous black eyes and a seductive smile.

The meeting had gone well, except that just as he was about to leave she'd stopped him at the door and said, 'I'm aware that Paramount passed on your movie because of the graphic violence, and I'm not asking you to tone it down. However, about the sex – the script makes it clear several of the actresses are naked in certain scenes, yet it seems our hero and his friends remain modestly covered.'

'What's the problem?' he'd asked, genuinely not getting it.

'This is an equal opportunity studio,' she'd said. 'If the females take it off, so do the guys.' He'd stared at her like she was a crazy woman. 'Let me put it this way, Mr Woods,' she'd added. 'If we get to see tits and ass, we get to see dick. And I'm *not* talking Dick Clark.'

He'd left her office outraged, complaining to Freddie all the way to his car. Freddie had laughed at him, so had his two Asian assistants – Lili, a softly pretty Chinese woman who'd been with him for ever, and France, who'd since departed.

Yes, Lucky Santangelo had managed to shock him, something that few women had been able to do. And yet, he'd fallen in love with her then and there.

He'd never forget the one magical night they'd spent together. Never. No woman could ever live up to Lucky. She was the woman he'd been searching for all his life, and when things seemed to be on track and moving along at a good pace, Lennie had come back into the picture, returning from the dead so to speak.

So now Lucky was his friend. But he wanted more than that.

He wanted her to be his everything.

☆

They returned home around six. Lucky hurried straight to the answering-machine, where there was a message from Detective Johnson acknowledging the licence-plate information. She listened to his message, then clicked off the machine. 'Let's hope they can finally get some action going,' she said. 'Those guys are useless.'

'You think?'

'I *know*. They should've made an arrest long ago.'

'Can you believe how quiet it is here without the kids running around?' Lennie remarked.

'It sure is,' she agreed.

'Kind of like old times, huh?' he said, throwing himself down on the couch and smiling lazily. 'And, my darling wife, I have a great idea.'

'Wanna share it?'

'Well ... how about you take off your clothes, and walk around naked?'

'I don't believe you!'

'C'mon, Lucky, humour me.'

'You're such a little voyeur,' she said. 'No way am I parading around like a hooker.'

He grinned. 'I love it when you turn prudish.'

'Okay, okay, here's the action,' she said, happy to see a smile on his face. 'I'll take *my* clothes off if you do the same.'

'It's a deal!' he said, leaping up and immediately starting to unbutton his shirt.

Lucky smiled and began humming stripper music. After a few moments, when he was down to his underwear, she collapsed in fits of laughter. 'You'll never make it as a male stripper,' she gasped. 'Sorry!'

'Why not?' he said indignantly, flexing his muscles while macho posing in his jockey shorts. 'I've got moves you haven't even seen.'

'And I don't want to.'

'I'm insulted.'

'Go back to acting, Lennie,' she said, choking with laughter. 'You're such an actor in real life.'

'Come here, woman,' he said, holding out his arms. 'There's something wrong with this picture. I'm down to my

Calvins, and you're still fully dressed.' She ran into his arms and he hugged her to him, crushing his mouth down on hers. 'I've missed you so much,' he said. 'You gotta forgive me for behaving like an asshole. I think I'm out of it now. Normal life will resume.'

'It doesn't matter,' she whispered. 'I love you anyway. I always have and I always will.'

'You do realize how precious time is?' he said, holding her close. 'One moment we're here, the next gone. I've decided I don't want you out of my sight ever again.'

'It's you and me, babe,' she murmured. 'We're destined to be together for ever. Soulmates.'

'Soulmates,' he repeated. 'You don't have to tell me twice.'

41

Brigette explored the house, talked to some of the guests, endured Leopold Lewyllen Wharton peering down her neckline, and found herself seated next to him at dinner, an elderly Member of Parliament on her other side. She'd never been so bored and restless. But, as she reminded herself, she wasn't in London to enjoy herself, she was here to make sure Carlo paid for what he'd done.

There were three tables, each seating ten people, so it wasn't until after dessert, when she got up to go to the ladies' room, that she bumped into Carlo again.

He caught up with her outside the dining room. 'What are you doing here?' he demanded.

'Excuse me?' she said innocently, noticing that he seemed disturbed. *Good.*

'Why did you tell Fiona we knew each other?' he continued, the expression on his handsome face quite agitated.

'I wasn't aware it was a secret, Carlo,' she said coolly. '*Is* it a secret?'

'Well . . .' He obviously didn't know what to say. 'Because of what happened between us . . .'

She fixed him with her big blue eyes. 'What *did* happen between us?'

'Surely you remember?'

'No. Why don't you tell me?'

'We made love, Brigette,' he said, lowering his voice. 'And, if I may say so, you enjoyed it a great deal.'

'Oh, God!' she said, pretending to be upset. 'I had no idea you really were engaged. What'll Fiona *say* when you tell her?'

He took a step back. 'I am not planning on telling her.'

'You *have* to,' she said, widening her eyes.

'I do not *have* to do anything,' Carlo answered churlishly. Maybe it was her imagination, or did she see a bead of sweat on his perfect brow?

'Oh dear, I must have had too much to drink,' she apologized, fanning herself with her hand. 'Champagne's my downfall. Although I seem to recall that at the dinner in New York, you told us all that you *weren't* engaged.'

'True,' he said quickly. 'Fiona and I had broken our engagement for a few days.'

'How convenient.'

'Believe me, Brigette,' he said, ignoring her stab at sarcasm, 'it is best to say nothing.'

'Why?' she said, staring at him.

'Meet me for lunch tomorrow and we will discuss it.'

'You mean the three of us will have lunch?' she asked, still playing the innocent – albeit a sexy one in her low-cut dress.

'No,' he said sharply. 'Just you and me.'

'Well . . .' she said, pretending to consider it. 'If you think it will help . . .'

'In the meantime,' he said, in a stern voice, 'do *not* mention the night we spent together in New York.'

'How can I mention it,' she asked ingenuously, 'when I don't even remember it?'

He leaned closer, sure that soon they would be a couple, and with her kind of money behind him he would rule the world. 'You're still as lovely as you were that one magical night, Brigette,' he whispered. 'I will remind you of things we did together. You will want to do them again.'

'I can't sleep with a man who is already taken,' she said primly. 'If you wish to see me again, then you must break your engagement immediately.'

'I know,' he said. 'The moment I met you, I realized it was over between Fiona and me. I am an Italian count. *You*, my sweet Brigette, will be my contessa.'

'There's something I don't understand,' she said, frowning.

'What, my darling?'

'If we had such a wonderful time in New York – and I'm sure we did, although I'll have to take your word for it – how come you didn't call me?'

'It's complicated,' he said. 'Fiona's father has been discussing my joining his company.'

'Really?'

'Tomorrow I will explain everything.' A pause, while he gave her the benefit of a long, lingering look. 'You *will* meet me, won't you?'

She nodded her agreement, knowing that soon she would have Count Carlo Vittorio Vitti *exactly* where she wanted him.

☆

'I love you,' Lina said.

'*What?*' Charlie managed, his eyebrows shooting up in alarm.

'I always say that,' Lina said, shrieking with hysterical laughter. 'I get off on seeing the panic rise.' She rolled off Charlie, stretching out one of her long arms to grab a cigarette from the bedside table. 'Course, I never mean it.'

'Shitcakes!' Charlie exclaimed, shaking his head in bewilderment. 'You really do dance your own tango.'

'Takes two, don't it?' she said, lighting up.

He regarded her with a certain amount of puzzlement. 'You're very . . . energetic.'

'Oooh,' she said mockingly, flinging back a curtain of long, straight black hair. 'Tired you out, 'ave I?'

'I'm a movie star, baby,' he deadpanned. 'Movie stars never get tired or go to the bathroom. Surely you knew that?'

'I'm a supermodel, darlin',' she said, handing him her cigarette for a drag. 'We never get tired either. We always gotta look gorgeous an' be nice to people.'

'How convenient for you,' he said drily.

'Screw being nice,' Lina said vehemently. 'Sometimes I wanna kick 'em in the 'ead. Specially some of those bitches who call themselves fashion editors. They're the worst.'

'You're forthright,' Charlie said. 'I like that in a super-model.'

'No point in beating around the bush, is there?' she said.

'I'm a little Cockney girl from London who made good. Now I wanna make even better.'

'Ambition. Another admirable quality.'

'So,' she said, giving him a penetrating stare, 'am I gonna be in your movie or not?'

He blew lazy smoke rings in her direction. 'Is that why you fucked me?'

'No,' she said, taking back her cigarette. 'I fucked you 'cause you was there.'

Even Charlie was puzzled by that one. 'Explain?'

She giggled. 'Me mum would have a freaking fit if she knew I was in bed with Charlie Dollar. She *loves* you, thinks you're the best thing since a bit of toast and marmalade.'

'How about Grandma?' Charlie drawled sardonically. 'She love me, too?'

Once again Lina shrieked with laughter. 'You're funny,' she said. 'I thought all you American movie stars 'ad no sense of humour.'

'Depends on which American movie stars you've been sleeping with.'

Lina stretched languorously. 'I love sex, don't you? 'S better than a sleeping pill any day.'

'You're not planning on spending the night in big bad Charlie's bed, are you?' he asked, worried at the thought. 'I have a sometime girlfriend who's likely to walk in on us and shoot you dead. She's a devil with a gun.'

'It's usually the wife I'm watching out for,' Lina remarked, completely unconcerned.

'Sorry,' Charlie said. 'I'm all out of those at the moment.'

Lina kneeled up on the bed, hugging a pillow to her chest. 'Do you think Max is pissed?'

'About what?'

'About me coming home with you.'

'Not Max – he's used to it,' Charlie said, opening his bedside drawer. 'Here's the deal. You've got an agent on one side and a movie star on the other. Who do *you* think's gonna get the girl?'

'He's kind of cute,' Lina mused.

'You wanna fuck him, too?' Charlie enquired, taking out a plastic bag and a neat stack of cigarette papers.

'Why?' she said boldly. 'You into threesomes? 'Cause if

167

you are, we can call him up, see if he'll give us ten per cent of his dick!'

Charlie roared with laughter. 'I have here some very fine grass,' he said, starting to roll a joint. 'That's, of course, if you're interested.'

Lina grinned. '*Now* you tell me.'

42

'**Is Steven coming?**' Venus Maria asked.

'He's not,' Lucky said. 'I invited him, but he feels it's too soon.'

They were talking in the gym of Venus's ultra-modern house in the Hollywood Hills. Lately Venus had been on Lucky's case about working out with her. 'I hate exercise,' Lucky had said. 'It's boring.'

'You're not twenty any more,' Venus had pointed out. 'You *have* to work out – unless you want to turn into a fat slob.'

'Ha!' Lucky had replied. 'All you want is company in your quest for perfection!'

Now they were sitting on a bench in their workout clothes, waiting for Sven, Venus's personal trainer.

'You've gotta tell Steven that it's never too soon to get back into life,' Venus said briskly. 'Look at me after that horrible experience with the stalker at my house. I was back doing things immediately.'

'Yes,' Lucky said, 'but that was only a stalker. This is the murder of Steven's wife we're talking about. And, of course, he's broken up about the baby – who wouldn't be? He didn't even know Mary Lou was pregnant. I can understand why he doesn't want to go out.'

'Maybe *I* should go talk to him myself,' Venus decided. 'He's always liked me.'

'No,' Lucky corrected. '*You*'ve always liked *him*. If you didn't have Cooper, I'm sure Steven would've been a contender.'

'He *is* gorgeous,' Venus admitted. 'Didn't you tell me that when you first met, and you had no clue he was your half-brother, you had kind of a big flirtation?'

Lucky chuckled at the memory. Nineteen seventy-seven.

The big New York power outage, and her and Steven trapped in an elevator together. Pure fate. Neither of them had had any idea they were related. 'It could have been a lot more than a flirtation,' she said, 'but Steven's always been so straight. Apart from when he was married to that Puerto Rican maniac.'

'Can you imagine,' Venus said, 'if anything had happened between you and him?'

'No, I can't,' Lucky said briskly, reaching for a cigarette. 'Mind if I smoke?'

'You know I do,' Venus retorted. 'Anyway, I thought you gave it up.'

'I give it up, then I do it again,' Lucky said, gesturing helplessly. 'It's kind of a see-saw deal.'

'Smoking is bad for you,' Venus said sternly.

'You're becoming *such* a boring health nut,' Lucky replied, lighting up and taking a long, deep drag. 'You've even got Cooper working out, and *he* was the run-around stud of all time.'

'Ha!' Venus exclaimed. 'How about Lennie? In his movie-star days he didn't exactly keep it zipped up.'

'Ah ... but he wasn't Cooper Turner,' Lucky responded, with a mischievous grin. 'Cooper's legendary in this town. Him and Warren Beatty.'

'I suppose he is,' Venus said, smiling proudly. 'Of course,' she added, after a thoughtful pause, '*I* wasn't exactly hiding in a convent.'

'True,' Lucky agreed. 'Miss If-it-moves-I'll-fuck-it!'

'I like being married though,' Venus said, stretching her arms in the air. 'It's ... comfortable.'

'That's 'cause you're never peering out of your marriage to see what you're missing,' Lucky said wisely. 'You and I both experienced everything, so did our husbands. Which means we never missed a thing.'

'Been there, done that,' Venus said, with a crazed giggle.

'There should be a law against getting married too young,' Lucky said. 'Thirty for women. Thirty-five for men. Seems reasonable to me.'

'According to Gino,' Venus said. 'You were so wild he *had* to marry you off at sixteen. The other night he was telling *insane* stories about you.'

'Here's the thing about Gino,' Lucky said, stubbing out her

cigarette after two drags. 'Never believe a word he says. Gino likes to embellish.'

'Seems you had almost as much fun as me.'

'*Nobody* had as much fun as you,' Lucky remarked drily. 'You *invented* the word party!'

'Hmm . . .' Venus said, savouring the fond memories. 'Sometimes I miss being single . . .'

'Do you really?'

'Nope. But it sounds good.'

Sven arrived, cutting short their conversation. He was a tall well-built Swede with muscles to spare. 'Ladies,' he said, with what Lucky considered to be an evil sneer. 'Are we ready to be tortured?'

'No,' Lucky said irritably, 'I'm ready for another cigarette. I had a hard weekend.'

'How hard?' Venus asked provocatively.

'Hard enough,' Lucky replied, smiling. 'Lennie has returned to the land of the living. And how!'

'I'm glad to hear it.'

'So am I.'

'After we've worked out,' Venus said, 'I think I'll call Steven. In fact, I might even visit him at his office.'

'*That*'ll cause a riot,' Lucky said. 'You – walking into the law offices.'

'Steven represented me on a couple of things,' Venus said. 'They're used to me.'

Lucky shook her head. 'Nobody's used to you, Venus. You're an original.'

'That is true,' Sven said, flexing his considerable muscles. 'Now, ladies, enough time wasted. Let us get to work!'

☆

Steven was gazing out of his Century City office window, when his secretary announced that Venus Maria was there to see him.

'Does she have an appointment?' he asked.

'No, Mr Berkeley. She said she'll only take five minutes of your time.'

'Okay.' He nodded, knowing that if Venus was on the premises there was no getting rid of her. 'Show her in.'

Venus entered his office in a body-hugging Claude Mon-tana purple dress, platinum hair in a straight bob, huge black shades obscuring her eyes. 'I'm here,' she announced.

'I can see that,' he said, getting a whiff of her exotic perfume.

'I'm a walking, talking personal invitation,' she said, with a seductive smile.

'For?'

'Our party tonight,' she said, removing her sunglasses. 'You're coming,' she added, perching on the edge of his desk.

'Venus,' he said patiently, 'I explained it to Lucky. It's too soon.'

'You'll bring Carioca,' she said, matter-of-factly, as if it was a done deal. 'There'll be a special kiddies' table. Chyna has personally requested Carioca's presence. You're not going to deprive your daughter, are you?'

'Stop making it difficult for me,' he said.

'I'm not making it *that* difficult, Steven. I want you there. Anyway . . . I'll be hurt if you don't come.'

'Well . . .'

'Good,' she said, getting off his desk and undulating her way to the door. 'We'll expect you both at seven.'

☆

On her way back to the beach Lucky stopped by the police station. She paced impatiently around Detective Johnson's office, waiting for him to put in an appearance.

He arrived a few minutes later, styrofoam cup of coffee in one hand, the traditional jelly doughnut in the other.

'I do hope I'm not disturbing your breakfast,' she said sarcastically, annoyed because in spite of everyone's efforts there were still no results.

'Glad you're here,' he said, not meaning it. Lucky Santangelo was on his case day and night. The woman was slowly driving him nuts. 'The plate numbers are a help,' he said, taking a swig of coffee. 'We're narrowing down the list.'

'How about the reward?' she asked. 'What's going on with that?'

'We're snowed under with false information,' he said, settling behind his desk and clearing off a stack of papers so he could put his coffee down. 'There was one interesting phone call, though.'

'From?'

He paused, took a bite of his doughnut. 'A girl claiming she knows who did it.'

'What makes this phone call different?'

'She had details other people wouldn't know.'

'Like what?' Lucky said, staring at him.

'Well,' he said, a dribble of jam making its way down his chin, 'she knew exactly how the car was positioned, the dress Mary Lou had on . . .'

'Are you bringing her in?'

'She told me she could give us the shooter, but first she wants to make sure she gets the reward. I informed her that's not the way things work.'

'How did you leave it?'

'She'll call again.'

Lucky attempted to curb her anger. 'You mean you had her on the phone and you let her go?'

'We tried putting a trace on her call, but by that time she'd hung up.'

'Did you get her name . . . anything?'

'No. But we'll hear from her again,' Detective Johnson said confidently. 'She wants the money.'

Lucky was furious. What kind of detective work was *that*? People were just plain incompetent, including the police – *especially* the police.

She drove to the beach breaking speed records, checking in on her car phone with the private detective firm she'd hired. They were also useless. In spite of plenty of time and unlimited money they'd come up with nothing.

The house was quiet when she arrived home; the children weren't due back from Gino's until later.

'Lennie,' she called out, throwing down her purse.

'In here,' he yelled.

She went into his office and was delighted to find him positioned in front of his computer – an excellent sign, considering he hadn't gone near it since the shooting.

Walking up behind him, she began massaging his shoulders. 'Working on something good?' she asked.

'I'm planning a film about violence,' he announced. 'Random violence on the streets today. What do you think?'

'Terrific idea.'

'Yeah,' he said, nodding vigorously. 'Y' know, one of the things that struck me most about what went down was the unbelievable hate in the girl's voice. How did she get like that? What made her learn to take off on total strangers? It's something worth exploring.'

'I'm so happy to see you working again,' Lucky said, kissing the back of his neck.

'How about *you*?' he said, turning around. 'What are *your* plans now that you've given up the studio?'

'It's not that I've given it up,' she explained. 'It's simply that I'm not interested in doing that any more. Eight years running a studio, dealing with everyone's egos on a daily basis. It's a goddamn lifetime, and frankly I've had it.'

'I know you, Lucky,' he said. 'You'll never be happy sitting around doing nothing.'

'I do have kind of an idea . . .' she said, wandering over to the window and gazing out at the ocean.

'Tell me,' he said.

She turned around and faced him. 'I was thinking I might produce a movie.'

He laughed derisively. '*You* don't know anything about producing.'

'I ran Panther for *eight* years,' she said, frowning. 'I know plenty.'

'Physically producing a movie is completely different from sitting in an office greenlighting other people's projects,' he pointed out.

'Are you saying I *can't* do it?' she said, narrowing her eyes.

'You can do anything you set your mind to, as long as you realize it's not as easy as it seems.'

She hated it when Lennie tried to tell her what to do, but since she was on a mission to make him feel better about himself she held back a snappy retort. 'Hey,' she said, being nice, 'how about *you* write me a movie and *I*'ll produce it?'

'Oh, no,' he said, shaking his head like it was the worst idea he'd ever heard. 'Working together, the two of us – bad, bad idea.'

'Why?' she said, trying to stay reasonable even though he was beginning to irritate the hell out of her.

'Because I hate every producer I've ever worked with,' he said shortly. 'They try to cast people I don't want. They're always trying to cut my budget – not to mention screwing with my actors. They get in my way. No, no, no, let's not get into *that*.'

'Then how would you feel if I produced a movie with someone else?' she asked, thinking of Alex.

'Hey, that's your decision.'

It was always her decision until he didn't like it. Lennie was difficult that way. 'I'm trying to discuss things with you, see how *you* feel about it,' she said calmly.

'Whatever you want, sweetheart.'

'You're *sure*?'

'Absolutely. Oh, and, Lucky,' he said, giving her a little more attention, 'thanks for this weekend. It was beyond great.'

'Yes, it was,' she said, smiling at the memories of wild hotel sex. 'When we're good, we're *very, very* good.'

He began to laugh. 'And when we're bad, we're a freaking *mess*.'

She laughed too. 'No, *you*'re a mess.'

'No, *you* are.'

'No, *you*,' she countered, playfully punching him on the chin.

'I'm hungry,' he said. 'Think you can fix me one of your great tuna sandwiches?'

'What am I? The cook?' she said, exasperated.

'You *do* know that in most civilized countries wives fix husbands lunch?'

'Screw you!' she said affectionately. 'Make your own sandwich.'

'Love you, too,' he said, grinning. 'Easy on the mayonnaise.'

'Lennie!'

'Please?'

'Okay,' she said grudgingly. 'Just this once.'

'Thanks, babe,' he said, turning back to his computer.

And, as much as she loved her husband, Lucky knew that being a homebody was not for her.

☆

43

Lunch with Carlo, and Brigette thought that she played him pretty smoothly as they sat side by side in San Lorenzo, a fashionable Italian restaurant in Knightsbridge.

What are you doing?

Getting my revenge. Just as Lucky taught me. Because revenge is sweet. And then I'll worry about being pregnant.

Carlo was continuing with his well-worn line about how the moment he'd set eyes on her he'd known his engagement was a sham and that he would have to end it immediately. He wasn't exactly smooth, corny was more like it.

But she pretended to fall for it, all the while watching him carefully, wondering how such an attractive man could be such a rat.

'Fiona seems nice,' she said carefully. 'However, if you're sure this is the way you feel . . .'

'When I returned to London after meeting you,' he said, 'I knew I must finish with Fiona and move to New York.'

'But first you had to break your engagement,' she said, twirling spaghetti around her fork.

'I'll do it now.'

'What about her father and the business you were discussing?'

'It is not important.'

She picked up her wine-glass and took a sip. 'Will you tell her what happened between us in New York?'

'That is not a good idea,' he said, thinking that it was an extremely bad idea. What if, by some fluke, things didn't work out with Brigette? He had to have Fiona to fall back on. And her father. *And* her father's money. 'When do you leave?' he asked.

'Tomorrow.'

'Then tonight I shall come to your hotel, and we will make it a night to remember.'

Oh, yes, Brigette thought. *We certainly will.*

☆

Breakfast at the Bel Air Hotel in the dining room.

'You got the part,' Max Steele said, as Lina sashayed in

and sat down, causing most people to stare. In a town filled with stars, Lina still stood out.

'I know,' she answered, with a wicked grin. 'All eight inches!'

Max spluttered out a mouthful of coffee. 'So it's true about Charlie?'

'For an old man, 'e rocks,' she said, winking roguishly.

Max took another gulp of coffee. 'Don't *ever* let Charlie hear you call him old.'

'Why?'

'Ego. It's big.'

'Just like his—'

'Okay, okay,' Max interrupted. 'I don't need details. The good thing is he thinks you're perfect for his movie. Doesn't even want to see you on video.'

'I can finally say it, Max,' she said, with a Cheshire-cat grin. 'I slept with a star an' got a role in 'is film.'

'It doesn't make any difference whether you slept with him or not,' Max assured her. 'It's a done deal. He likes you.'

'What about money?' Lina asked, making eye-contact with a hovering waiter who was undeniably cute.

'Leave that to me. It won't be a lot but, at this stage in your career, exposure is more important than money.'

'I'll 'ave to trust *you* on that,' Lina said, abandoning her mild flirtation with the waiter and concentrating once more on Max.

'Tomorrow you'll meet with the wardrobe people,' he said. 'My assistant will set a time.'

'It'll 'ave t' be early,' she said, gulping back a yawn, ''cause I'm flying to Milan in the evening.'

'What a life!' Max said admiringly.

'It beats packin' plastic raincoats, which was my first job. We called 'em the wankers' special!'

'*I* started in the mail room at William Morris,' Max said.

'Didn't we do well!' she said, with another Cheshire-cat grin.

Max signalled for a refill of coffee. 'Charlie's leaving this afternoon,' he said. 'You got to him just in time.'

Lina picked up a muffin and took a healthy bite. 'I always 'ad great timing,' she said, favouring the waiter with another quick glance. He *was* quite delicious in an early Brad Pitt sort of way. If only she had a few moments to spare . . .

'I believe it,' Max said.

'So tell me, Max,' Lina said, a predatory look in her saffron eyes, 'what are you an' I doin' tonight?'

'You don't believe in sitting around, do you?' he said. He'd been around Hollywood for years, but this girl was something else.

'Why waste a great opportunity?' she said, with another wicked grin. 'Unless, of course, you're busy . . . or scared of comparisons . . .'

'*Me?*'

'*You.*'

'Got a hunch I can handle any comparison you have to offer,' he boasted.

'Oooh, good. I'm gonna get lucky twice, huh?'

'If you feel like it,' he said, 'there's a party tonight you might enjoy.'

'I *love* parties. Who's giving it?'

'Venus Maria and Cooper Turner. They're celebrating their anniversary.'

'I met Cooper when 'e was single,' Lina said. 'Chased me all over Paris 'e did.'

'Did he catch you?'

She rolled her eyes mysteriously, remembering a long drunken night of great sex. 'Wouldn't *you* like t' know.'

'You'd better not remind him of it.'

'I'm a big fan of Venus Maria,' she said. 'Used to dress up like 'er when I was a kid.'

'How old *are* you?' Max asked, waving at a fellow agent who was breakfasting with Demi Moore.

'Twenty-six.' She pulled a miserable face. 'That's old, ain't it?'

'Twenty-six is not particularly old,' he said. 'Only don't go telling people in Hollywood you admired them when you were a kid – it's the worst thing you can do. This is Ego City, everyone wants to be perceived as young.'

'I wrote Venus a fan letter once,' she admitted.

'I repeat,' Max said sternly, '*don't* tell her.'

''Ow old is she, anyway?'

'Only a few years older than you and, trust me, she would *not* appreciate you informing her that you used to admire her when you were a kid.'

'Girls say that to me all the time,' Lina said, fidgeting restlessly.

'How do *you* like it?'

' 'S okay if they're twelve!' she said, blowing a kiss at Frank Bowling, who was hovering at the door with a group of Arab dignitaries. 'Gotta go shopping,' she said, pushing her chair away from the table. 'Must buy something knock-out for tonight. Will the party be jammed with movie stars?'

'Who do you want to meet?' he asked, amused.

'Let me see now ... Hmm ... I've always fancied Robert De Niro. 'Course, I *love* Denzel too. An' I wouldn't kick Jack Nicholson out of bed.'

'Into older men, huh?'

'Experience an' stamina. Turns *me* on every time.'

'Didn't you say tonight was *my* night? You're not dumping me for a movie star, are you?'

'Well ...'

He clicked his fingers for the check. 'You're quite an operator, Lina.'

A final grin as she headed towards the door. 'So I've been told.'

☆

The scene was set. Soft music, candlelight, and Brigette in a silver slip dress that left nothing to the imagination.

Carlo was exactly on time, which was good, because she'd counted on him being prompt. He called from the lobby, and she asked him to come straight up to her suite.

He arrived at the door a few minutes later.

Pity he's such a bastard, she thought, as she let him in, *because he is extraordinarily handsome, in an arrogant kind of way. And under other circumstances ...*

He brought her red roses, naturally. No imagination.

She took the sweet-smelling blooms from him and placed them on the hall table. 'How lovely!' she exclaimed. 'I'll call the maid to put them in a vase.'

'You look exquisite,' he said, touching her arm.

'I ordered champagne,' she said. 'Will you open it?'

He followed her into the living room where the bottle was sitting in an ice-bucket on the table. 'Ah . . . Cristal,' he said, picking it up. 'Excellent choice.'

'And there's caviar over there.'

'Brigette,' he said admiringly, 'for an American girl, you are very sophisticated.'

Yes, she thought. *So sophisticated that I fell for your little trick of slipping a knock-out pill in my drink. How clever is that?*

She couldn't help wondering why he had to drug women, anyway, since he could probably take his pick. He was tall, blond and handsome with a title – what more could any man possibly need? Lina would've jumped into bed with him in a flash. So would a hundred other girls.

'How long have you lived in London?' she asked, moving over to the fireplace.

'Eighteen months,' he answered, popping the champagne cork. 'I do not like it here, the English are too cold. I'm Italian. We Italians are more warm-blooded.' He gave her one of his long, lingering looks, obviously a Carlo speciality. 'You know what I mean?'

'I hope I'll find out tonight,' she murmured seductively.

He continued to look at her with lust in his eyes. Not only was this delicious blonde due to become one of the richest women in the world, she was also one of the most desirable.

He revelled in the thought that soon she would be all his. *He* would be in control of the Stanislopoulos fortune. He, Carlo, who'd never been in control of anything in his entire life, would be in charge of a billion-dollar fortune. Watch people kiss his ass when *that* happened.

'Come over here, my little angel,' he said, beckoning her towards him.

She walked over and allowed him to kiss her. He had a most insistent tongue that darted in and out of her mouth in a practised way as his hands began moving over her body, coming to rest on her breasts.

After a few moments she gently pushed him away. 'I'd like to make a toast,' she said, slightly out of breath.

'Please, allow *me*,' he said, moving over to the champagne bottle, filling two glasses, and handing one to her. 'To the most beautiful girl in the world,' he said, raising his glass to her.

Another corny line. Didn't he have anything original to say?

They clinked glasses, and he twisted his arm through hers as they drank.

Better make sure he doesn't slip another pill in my drink. Got to watch him every moment.

'You must miss Italy,' she said, taking a small sip of champagne.

'I do,' he said. 'Only it seems that when I am with you, I do not miss anything.'

Oh, God, his lines were getting cornier all the time.

He moved in to kiss her again. Over his shoulder she glanced at her watch, this had to be timed perfectly. 'Shall we go in the other room?' she suggested.

'It will be my pleasure,' he said, delighted that the evening was progressing so well.

'Come,' she said, taking his hand and leading him into the bedroom, where – very slowly – she stepped out of her silver dress, revealing that all she had on underneath was a flesh-coloured thong.

'*Bellissima!*' he murmured, thinking this was moving faster than he'd anticipated. 'So beautiful!'

'Take off your clothes, Carlo,' she said invitingly.

He didn't need asking twice. Without further ado he quickly threw everything off until he stood before her in his black briefs, erection bulging.

She lay back on the bed, and he got on top of her. Even though she felt incredibly vulnerable, she knew that any moment now she was going to feel triumphant, because any moment now revenge would be hers.

As he started to kiss her again, the doorbell rang.

Saved by the bell! Timing was everything.

'Ignore it,' he commanded.

'It'll be the maid to arrange the flowers,' she said, struggling to sit up.

'She'll come back later.'

'No, get it – please, darling. Those roses are so beautiful, let's have them in here while we make love.'

Hey, if he can be corny, so can I.

'Very well,' he said, reluctantly getting up. Clad only in his underwear, he went to the door and opened it.

It wasn't the maid, it was Fiona.

'Carlo?' she said, her eyes widening with shock and surprise as she took in his lack of clothes and saw past him to the bed. 'Carlo. I don't understand . . .'

Next to her stood her father. 'Carlo!' Leopold bellowed, immediately understanding. 'What the bloody hell is going on here?'

Brigette knelt on the bed, holding up the sheet to cover herself. 'I . . . I'm so sorry, Fiona,' she said, meaning it, because she had nothing against the poor girl. 'I . . . I thought Carlo had told you about us.'

Fiona was in shock. 'You cow!' she exclaimed, her eyes filling with tears. 'You unbearable little cow!' And with that she turned and ran off down the corridor.

Leopold glared at Carlo. 'I will *ruin* you in this town,' he roared, before turning and chasing after his distressed daughter.

Carlo shook his head, obviously stunned. 'This is impossible,' he said, a dull red flush covering his face. 'How could they possibly know I was here?'

'Maybe they had you followed,' Brigette said, surprised that her feeling of triumph was so hollow. 'You were breaking it off anyway, you shouldn't feel *too* bad.'

'I never expected her to find out like this,' he said. 'Never.'

'You have to go,' Brigette said, getting off the bed and slipping on her dress.

'Why would I go?' he said, puzzled.

'Because I'm too upset for you to stay.'

'Don't be ridiculous.'

'I have feelings, Carlo. What happened is very disturbing.'

'We will sit quietly and talk about this,' he said, taking her arm.

'No,' she said, shaking free and going into the living room.

'Brigette,' he said, right behind her, 'you are leaving tomorrow, we must talk.'

'I don't think so,' she said, finally turning to face him.

'What do you mean?'

'Here's the deal, Carlo,' she said, savouring every word because this was the moment she'd been waiting for and standing up to him felt good. 'You just got yourself set up.'

His ice blue eyes clouded over. 'Excuse me?'

'*I* invited Fiona and her father here,' she announced

triumphantly. 'I know what you did to me in New York. You drugged me so you could sleep with me. And, if you thought I was going to sit back and take that kind of behaviour, then you picked the wrong girl.'

His face darkened with fury as her words sank in. 'You set me up?'

'Yes.'

'You set *me*, Carlo Vittorio Vitti, up?' he repeated.

'Yes, Carlo, I did,' she said. 'Now kindly put your clothes on and get out. And *never* try to contact me again. This game is over.'

'You fucking American bitch!' he snarled, and without warning, swung his arm back and hit her so hard across the face that she stumbled and almost fell.

She could not believe that he'd struck her. It was totally unexpected.

He went to hit her again.

'Stop it!' she yelled. She hadn't reckoned on his violent temper. 'You'd better get out of here before I call Security.'

'Shut the fuck up, American bitch!' he screamed, his handsome face a twisted mask of fury.

She backed away, suddenly scared.

He went after her, grabbed her in a lock from behind, placed his hand over her mouth and slapped her again. Then he dragged her into the bedroom and threw her down on the bed.

'One word out of your mouth and I'll kill you,' he threatened, a wild look in his eyes. 'Nobody treats Carlo this way and gets away with it. Do you hear me, bitch? Nobody. DO YOU HEAR ME?'

44

Price did not go for conventional, he preferred his look to be more cutting edge: for Venus and Cooper's party he chose a black tuxedo with a black shirt, and instead of a satin stripe down the sides of his pants, the stripe was black leather. With his bald head and smooth, dark-chocolate skin, he knew that he looked pretty damn hot. And he felt good too, for that afternoon his agent had sent over the final contracts for his first starring role in a movie. Price Washington: soon to add movie star to his long list of achievements.

He was psyched.

His date for the evening, whom he'd be picking up shortly, was Krissie, the no-brain model. He'd decided to take her because she was the best-looking armpiece of all, and as long as she kept her mouth shut he'd be the envy of every man there.

He checked himself out in the mirror one more time, rubbed a touch of oil on his head to make it gleam, and doused himself in Christian Dior's Eau Sauvage. Finally ready, he went downstairs.

As usual, Irena was busy in the kitchen. 'I'm leaving now,' he said.

She didn't turn around, which irritated him. The woman had spent the night in his bed, the least she could do was pay him some attention and tell him how fine he looked. But no. She was too goddamn busy polishing a silver coffee jug.

'I said, I'm leaving now,' he repeated.

This time she turned her head. He threw out his arms expecting a compliment. 'Like the outfit?'

'You look nice, Mr Washington,' she said, her face impassive as usual.

Nice? Fuck that shit. 'Yeah, well, a man's gotta try,' he said.

You smell like a whorehouse, she wanted to say, but she bit her lip. It wouldn't do to be truthful, there were certain boundaries she never dared cross.

Mila wandered into the kitchen and let forth a low wolf whistle. 'Wow, Mr W – lookin' *good*!'

He nodded in her direction. Truth was he couldn't stand the girl: everything she said was insincere. He reminded himself to tell Teddy he didn't want him hanging with her now that they were back in LA. Lately he'd noticed Teddy sniffing around the girl again, and it was best to discourage him before it went any further. Now that Mila had a job, there was no reason for him to spend any more time with her.

Mila threw him a cold hint of a smile. 'Going somewhere special, Mr W?'

Irena shot her daughter a look. She did not approve of her talking to the boss.

'A party,' Price said.

'Someone famous?' Mila persisted.

Irena shot her another furious look.

'Venus Maria and Cooper Turner's,' Price said, annoyed with himself for bothering to reply.

'Oooh, big stars,' Mila said, a faintly mocking tone in her voice. 'Maybe I should give you my autograph book.'

Maybe I should give you a sharp slap across the face, he thought. And what was with the badly dyed blonde hair? 'Where's Teddy?' he asked abruptly.

Mila shrugged. 'Dunno.'

'In his room,' Irena said.

Price went to the bottom of the stairs and called his son. 'Teddy!'

Teddy appeared at the top of the stairs. 'Whass up, Dad?'

'I'm leavin' now. You home tonight?'

Teddy nodded, noticing that Mila was downstairs. If they could only get rid of Irena, they'd have the house to themselves and maybe they could take up where they'd left off.

'So ... uh ... behave yourself,' Price said, waiting for a comment on how he looked. Teddy didn't say a word. 'See you later, then,' Price said, walking out to the garage and getting into his black Ferrari – a recent purchase.

Settling behind the wheel, he started the car and set off to pick up Miss No Brains.

☆

'It's rude to question Mr Washington about where he's going,' Irena said, glaring at her daughter. 'You're fortunate he allows you to stay here now that you're grown.'

'Aren't *I* the lucky one?' Mila said sarcastically. 'Suppose I should learn to kiss his big black ass – like you.'

Irena's eyes signalled anger. '*What* did you say?'

'Nothing,' Mila murmured, beating a quick retreat. She never stopped hating her mother. Hating her for many reasons, the main one being that Irena had never been truthful about the identity of Mila's father. She did not believe it was some old boyfriend from Russia. If that was the case, then why couldn't she know his identity?

Irena was full of lies and mystery about her life in Russia before coming to America. She'd informed Mila that her entire family had perished in a train wreck. According to Irena, there

were just the two of them. Oh, yes, and Mr Big Star Price Washington and his wimpy son, the jerk with the pussy balls. Mila hated Teddy, too.

For the last few days she'd been trying to figure out a way she could nail Teddy for the shooting *and* pick up the reward. One hundred thousand dollars. An astronomical amount. A fortune. The entrée to a new, much improved life. She'd called the cops to make sure the reward existed, now all she had to do was figure out a way to claim it.

It was a tricky problem, of course, because *she'd* been the shooter and, apart from Teddy – who didn't matter – there was only one other person who could finger her and that was Lennie Golden, the survivor. So even though she had Teddy's prints on the gun, Lennie Golden would identify *her*, and that simply couldn't happen.

How to stop it? That was the question.

She'd finally come up with an off-the-wall solution.

Kill Lennie Golden.

Oh, yes, and how was she supposed to do that?

For one hundred thousand dollars, she'd come up with something.

45

The Hollywood Hills mansion of Venus Maria and Cooper Turner was alive with lights and hidden security as the guests began arriving. There was also plenty of security on show – guards at the gate holding clipboards with lists of invited guests, off-duty cops with dogs patrolling the enormous grounds, a few chosen detectives who mingled looking like guests.

No press. Cooper had been adamant about that, and over the six years they'd been married, Venus had learned to go along with what he wanted. It made life so much easier. After all, she was married to a catch, a confirmed playboy bachelor whom everyone had assured her would *never* get married.

Oh, yes? She'd soon changed *that* misconception. And, after a shaky start, they were now as happy as two people could be, living in the Hollywood fish-bowl. Because it *was* a fish-bowl. Everything Venus and Cooper did was scrutinized

Jackie Collins

and written about. Once a month the tabloids came out with scandalous stories about how Cooper had fallen in love with his current co-star, or how Venus was sleeping with the latest stud around town. It made a change from the reports that she was supposedly suffering from anorexia, bulimia, or having a nervous breakdown. Or the stories that Cooper had been caught with three strippers in Tijuana – that is, when he wasn't conducting a secret affair with Madonna, Venus's biggest rival.

All the outlandish headlines were pure fantasy, of course. They'd settled for laughing about them – suing cost too much and took too long.

For their party, Venus had chosen to wear a gold strapless dress that skimmed her incredible body like a second skin. She worked hard at keeping the best body in town; it was a tough daily grind, but worth it.

Cooper was in his bathroom putting the finishing touches to his bow-tie when she walked up behind him. He studied her reflection in the mirror. 'You look great, baby,' he said.

'So do you,' she answered, knowing that Cooper got off on compliments as much as any woman did. After all, he was an actor and, however famous, all actors were insecure and needed constant reassurance.

'Thanks,' he said. 'Are we ready to go downstairs?'

'If you think it's cool to be the first guests at our own party.'

'I do,' he said. 'Oh, and before we go, I've got a little something for you.'

'Not *now*, Cooper,' she said, with a dirty laugh. '*Please*. You're insatiable. We'll do it later.'

'Get your mind out of my pants,' he joked.

'Why? I like it there!'

He reached in his pocket and handed her a small leather jewellery box. She opened it. Inside nestled a perfect square-cut emerald and diamond ring.

'Happy anniversary,' he said.

'Wow!' she exclaimed, taking it out of the box. 'It's fantastic!'

'Does it fit?'

She slid the ring on her finger. 'Perfectly.'

'Then, my sweetheart,' he said, taking her arm, 'let us go downstairs and enjoy our party.'

☆

'You're late,' Lucky said crisply, looking strikingly beautiful in a black Richard Tyler evening suit with nothing underneath.

'I don't even know why I'm here,' Steven said.

'You're here because Carioca wants to go to the party, and therefore it'll be fun for you. It also means you can leave early.'

'Isn't she staying the night with you?'

'*No*, Steven. Tonight Carioca is going home with you. I don't know how many times I have to tell you this but your little girl lost her mother, and it would be tragic if she lost her father, too. By the way, you look extremely handsome.'

'Thanks,' he said dourly. 'I don't feel it.'

'Can I fix you a drink before we go?' she asked, walking over to the bar.

'No,' he said. 'Where are the girls?'

'Upstairs, finishing getting dressed,' she answered, pouring herself a shot of vodka. 'You should see how excited they are. I'm so glad you changed your mind and decided to come.'

'Venus sat in my office and changed it for me.'

'You should be very flattered that she went to all that trouble.'

'Yeah, it was nice of her to bother.'

'Your friends all love you, Steven. Never forget that.'

Before he could answer, Lennie entered the room. 'Good to see you, Steven,' he said.

Steven nodded. 'You too, Lennie.'

Lucky knew how strained things had been between them, but she was hopeful that tonight would change everything.

A few minutes later, Maria and Carioca came running downstairs, all dressed up and extremely giggly.

'You two little monkeys look fantastic!' Lucky said, grabbing her Nikon camera. 'Come on, get together. Photo time!'

Maria threw an arm around Carioca's shoulders, stuck out her leg and tilted her head, posing like a *Vogue* model.

I'm going to have my hands full with this one, Lucky thought. *She's exactly like I was at her age. A true mind of her own.*

'Steven,' she instructed, 'get in the photo. Stand between the girls.'

'No photos,' he said, shaking his head.

'Come on, it's an adorable picture.'

'Yes, c'mon, Daddy,' Carioca pleaded. 'Please! Please! Please!'

'Uncle Steven, do it!' Maria commanded.

Reluctantly Steven obliged. Lucky took the shot.

'Okay,' she said. 'Enough. It's time to party!'

☆

'I'm overdressed, aren't I?' Lina said, sounding unsure for once.

'You look sensational,' Max answered, helping her into his Maserati.

'No, I went too far,' she said, wishing she'd chosen the sleek, black Versace instead of the shocking pink Betsey Johnson.

'Lina, you're gonna knock everybody on their *ass*!'

'You think so?'

'I know so,' he said, throwing her a sideways glance. Personally he thought she'd gone over the top with her dress. It was a shocking pink number, with ruffles and frills, short in the front and long in the back. She resembled an overdressed bridesmaid. Fortunately he knew enough about women not to voice his opinion.

'Can I tell people I'm in the new Charlie Dollar movie?' she asked, extracting a pot of lip gloss from her purse.

'No. Never mention anything until a deal is signed.'

'Got it,' she said, dabbing more gloss on her lips with her finger.

'What do you care anyway?' Max said. 'Everybody knows who you are. It's the year of the supermodel – and, baby, you're it!'

She grinned happily. 'That's true.'

'I spoke to Charlie before he left,' Max said, steering his Maserati into the fast lane.

'Oh, yeah,' Lina said casually. 'Mention me, did 'e?'

'Thinks you're enchanting.'

'Enchanting, huh?' she said, with a pleased smile.

'You *do* know he has a girlfriend?'

'Yes. He mumbled something about her busting in an' shooting me.'

'Don't think she wouldn't,' Max said, imagining the headlines. 'Dahlia's a tough lady, and I *mean* lady. She's not one of those pretty little things he takes to bed on occasion.'

'Who is she?' Lina asked curiously.

'Dahlia Summers is a serious actress. She and Charlie have been on and off for years. They have a two-year-old son together, Sport.'

'That's 'is name?'

'Chosen by Charlie himself.'

'Figures. Anyway,' she added, 'I wasn't planning on *marrying* him.'

Max laughed. 'I'm relieved to hear that, 'cause *I*'m not into sleeping with married women.'

'What makes you think you're sleeping with me tonight?' she said, teasing him with a slow, sexy look.

'Because . . . you remind me of myself. We're both predators. We both get off on stalking the prey.'

'Yes?' she said.

'Yes,' he said.

Lina smiled. For an agent Max Steele was pretty damn smart. And she liked that in a man. Brains and a great butt. Two major assets.

Tonight, if he kept up the dialogue, Mr Max Steele might get extraordinarily lucky.

46

Slowly Brigette regained consciousness. As she began to come to and remembered what had happened, she was gripped with fear.

She was lying on the bed in the bedroom of her hotel suite, with Carlo hovering over her holding a damp towel to her forehead. He was fully dressed. She wasn't. 'You fainted,' he said.

'I didn't faint,' she managed, wincing with pain because it felt as if someone had hit her across the face with a sledgehammer.

'Yes, you did,' he said, in a soothing voice, his patrician features calm and composed. 'I was worried about you.'

This was unbelievable! He'd beaten her into unconsciousness and now he was sitting on the edge of the bed acting as if nothing had happened.

She attempted to move.

'Stay where you are,' he said. 'We don't want you fainting again, *cara*.'

Oh, God! This was crazy. He'd beaten her up and now he was acting like a concerned boyfriend.

She lay very still, trying to collect her thoughts. What would Lucky do? Probably shoot his balls off and run. Lucky lived by her own rules.

She reached up and touched her face, her cheek felt tender and swollen where he'd hit her. Maybe she was marked for life. Should she start screaming? Or now that he seemed calm, should she simply work on getting him out of there? Some night of revenge this was turning out to be.

'Carlo,' she said, in a cool, even tone, 'I think it would be best if you left.'

'Why?' he said, frowning.

Why? Was he kidding? Didn't he know what he'd done?

'Because I'm tired and I want to sleep. We can talk in the morning.'

'I can't leave you, Brigette,' he said. 'I never want to leave you again.'

'I know,' she said, playing along with this bizarre game. 'I feel the same way. But right now I'm exhausted.'

'I hit you, didn't I?' he said.

'Well . . . yes.'

'I didn't mean to,' he said, 'but you made me so mad.' He got up and began pacing around the room. 'You treated me badly, Brigette. I can't stand it when people treat me badly.'

She was smart enough not to get into it with him. She did not want him losing control again, he was obviously unbalanced.

'I'm sorry if you think I treated you badly,' she said slowly.

'You accused me of things,' he said heatedly. 'Things that are not true.'

'Maybe I was mistaken,' she said, struggling to sit up.

Without warning, he leaned over and hugged her. She felt his shoulders begin to shake. Oh, God! He was actually crying.

'Brigette,' he sobbed, 'you must forgive me. Sometimes I don't know what I do. Please – forgive me.'

'I need to sleep, Carlo,' she said, asserting herself.

'No, no, I can't be alone,' he said. 'Come home with me to my apartment.'

'That's impossible.'

'Why?'

'Because I'm uh . . . expecting some important phone calls,' she said, thinking fast. 'If I'm not here, people will worry.'

'You can phone *them*.'

'Well . . . yes.'

'Put some things in a bag and come with me.'

'No, Carlo, I can't.'

His eyes flashed sudden danger. 'Yes, Brigette, you can, and you will.'

'Okay,' she said, forming a plan. Once they were in the lobby she would be able to scream for help and escape from him. 'If you really want me to.'

'I do,' he said, helping her off the bed. 'I have to make this up to you, my angel.'

She grabbed her dress from the foot of the bed and slipped into it. The bastard must have taken it off her when she was out. She wondered what else he'd done . . .

She was desperate to peek in a mirror, see how damaged her face was. 'I need to use the bathroom,' she said.

'I'll come with you.'

'No, Carlo. You wait outside.'

'I don't trust you, Brigette.'

'Trust me to what?' she said lightly, although inside she was shaking. Why did she always find herself in these impossible situations. Why? Why? Why?

Her legs felt weak as he escorted her to the bathroom. He came in with her and stood by the door, blocking the wall phone.

'Go,' he said. 'Hurry.'

'I don't need to go now,' she said, trying to catch a glimpse of herself in the mirror.

He blocked her there too.

They returned to the bedroom. He went to the closet and flung it open.

'What are you doing?' she asked, wondering if she could make a run for it.

No. Impossible. He was between her and the door, and she didn't care to risk being beaten again.

'You need something to cover you,' he said, pulling out a long purple Armani scarf. 'Put that over your head. Where are your sunglasses?'

'It's dark outside,' she said.

'I know,' he said. 'Now, where are they?'

She pointed to a drawer. He opened it and found the opaque glasses.

Do something, a voice screamed in her head. *Get the fuck away from him.*

How can I? He's got me trapped.

He searched through the closet, found her long raincoat and handed it to her. She put it on.

'We're leaving,' he said, taking her arm. 'Is there anything you wish to bring?'

She shook her head, no, thinking that the moment they hit the lobby she would be free. It wasn't as if he had a gun on her or anything. And he could hardly beat her up in front of people.

He went to the door, opened it a few inches, and peered out. 'Okay,' he said, 'let's go.'

The long corridor was empty.

Damn! She had hoped to see a maid or a room-service waiter, someone who could help her.

Carlo gripped her arm firmly as they headed for the elevators. When they got there, he bypassed them and headed through another door.

'Where are we going?' she asked, starting to panic.

'The service entrance,' he said.

She stopped abruptly. 'No!' she said. 'Take me back to my room.'

'If that's what you want, my angel.'

And then he socked her so hard on the jaw that once more she fell into a deep hole, and everything faded to black.

☆

47

Lucky circled the party searching for Venus and Cooper. People kept trying to stop her and talk but, over the years she'd spent in Hollywood in a position of power, she had become extremely adept at moving on. Lennie had vanished into the throng of guests, Maria holding tightly on to his hand. Steven and Carioca had gone with them.

An overly familiar hand on her shoulder. 'What's going on, Lucky?'

She spun around, coming face to face with Alex. 'What's going on with *you*, Alex?' she retorted, not even sure if she was glad to see him because he was becoming a complication she didn't need.

'How was the rest of your weekend?' he asked.

'Pretty good,' she said noncommittally. 'And yours?'

'It would have been better if—'

'Now don't start, Alex,' she interrupted, giving him a warning look, for she knew exactly what he was about to say.

'I take it the reconciliation went well.'

'It wasn't a reconciliation. We were only apart one night.'

'Yeah, but that one night could be the start of something.'

'Don't get your hopes up.'

His eyes searched the room. 'Where *is* the missing husband?'

'He's here. And the good news is he's getting back to work.'

'Doing what?'

'Writing a script about violence,' she said, extracting a cigarette from her purse.

'Violence isn't Lennie's genre,' Alex said, producing a light. 'He's known for comedy.'

'Well, now he wants to write something more serious,' she said, drawing deeply on her cigarette.

'Really?' Alex said, holding her eyes with a more than best-friends look.

'Yes, really,' she answered, wishing he wasn't so damn attractive.

'Let's go to the bar,' he suggested, taking her arm.

'I was actually looking for Venus. Have you seen her?'

He gestured across the room. 'She's in the middle of those ten guys over there.'

'Guess she's enjoying *that*.'

'I'm sure she is,' Alex agreed.

'Are you ever going to put her in another movie?'

'If I find the right project.'

'I know it's what she wants. She loved working with you.'

'Venus is a very underrated actress,' he said, steering Lucky to the bar. 'What'll you have?'

'Vodka martini.'

'Make that two,' he instructed the barman.

'Didn't figure you for a martini drinker,' she remarked.

'I'm not. But tequila always gets us in trouble, remember?'

He was determined to bring up the past, and she was equally determined to bury it. 'No, I don't,' she said shortly.

The bartender expertly mixed their drinks and handed over two chilled martinis.

'Did you give any thought to that discussion we had?' Alex enquired, as he led her over to a quiet corner.

'What discussion was that?' she asked, sipping her drink.

'The one about you producing.'

'Haven't had time to think about it,' she lied, because she wasn't about to tell him that Lennie had been less than enthusiastic.

'How about the *three* of us working together?' he suggested. 'You, me and Venus? What a combination that'd be. We could *really* kick ass.'

'You're very persistent.'

'That's 'cause it's not much fun seeing you out of work. You're not the housewife type.'

She couldn't help smiling. 'You sound like Lennie. I had to make him a sandwich today because he informed me that's what stay-at-home wives do.'

'Bet you loved *that*.'

She rolled her eyes. 'You can imagine.'

'I've got a couple of interesting things in development,' Alex said. 'How about I send you the scripts, see what you think?'

'Are they good?'

'No, Lucky,' he deadpanned. 'I only develop projects that stink.'

'Okay,' she said, laughing. Hey – if Lennie didn't want to work with her, how could he possibly object to her doing something with Alex?

Only she knew that he would. No doubt on *that* score.

☆

'That's Dahlia,' Max said, nudging Lina, who was gobbling small toast squares loaded with caviar from the hors d'oeuvres table.

'Where?' Lina said, continuing to stuff her mouth.

'Over there. The woman in the green dress.'

'Oooh!' Lina said, checking out a tall, thin woman in her forties with a sweep of long dark hair and prominent features. 'Scary!'

'She's actually very nice,' Max said. 'If Charlie was smart, he'd marry her.'

'And she's, like, got no clue 'e fucks around?'

'I'm sure she knows. But Dahlia's a wise woman, she chooses to ignore it.'

'What's so wise about *that*?' Lina asked, cramming more caviar into her mouth.

'As long as no one threatens her territory, she's happy.'

'What's 'er territory?'

'The public Charlie,' Max explained. 'The one that goes to benefits, award ceremonies, industry events and sits at the top tables. Dahlia is *always* his date on those occasions.'

Damn! Lina thought. *There goes my chance of being photographed with him.* She'd envisaged walking into a première with Charlie, arm in arm, flashbulbs popping and everyone oohing and aahing. Her mum would've creamed over *that*.

'Hold the eating for a minute,' Max instructed. 'My partner, Freddie Leon, is on his way over. Be nice. Freddie takes care of most of the major talent in this town.'

'Am I supposed to be impressed?'

'Yes. And do *not* come on to him. Freddie is very happily married.'

'Sure,' Lina snorted disbelievingly. 'Aren't they all!'

'Hey there, Freddie,' Max said, as his partner approached. 'I want you to meet Lina, she's with the agency.'

'Hello, Lina,' Freddie said. He was a poker-faced man with flat brown eyes and an expressionless demeanour.

'Guess I'm with your better 'alf,' Lina said cheerfully. ''Ope 'e's as good as you.'

'Max'll look after you,' Freddie said smoothly. 'I hear we've got you into the new Charlie Dollar film. Congratulations.'

'I'm not supposed to say anything until it's signed.'

'That's all right,' he said. 'We represent you.'

'Oh, yes, so you do,' she said, attempting a quick flirt.

Freddie was unresponsive. 'Pleasure to meet you, Lina,' he said, and quickly moved on.

'He's a cold one,' Lina remarked, returning to the caviar.

'That's Freddie,' Max said, with a glimmer of a smile. 'There's one thing you have to remember in this town. *Never* cross Freddie Leon.'

'I wasn't planning to. Oh, Christ!' she said. 'Look who's comin' our way *now*!'

'Who?'

'Flick Fonda.'

'You know Flick?' Max said, wondering who the legendary rock star's agent was, and if Flick was stealable. 'I've never met him. Introduce me.'

'He's with that boring wife of 'is,' Lina said, pulling a disgusted face. 'Quick, let's make a run for it!'

'Don't be crazy,' Max said. 'It's too late anyway.'

'Hello, darlin',' Flick said, bearing down on them, looking suitably rock star-ish in sprayed-on leather pants and a floppy white shirt, diamond studs in both ears. 'How ya doin'?'

'Nice to see you, Flick,' Lina said, giving him a perfunctory kiss on each cheek, leaving full lipstick imprints. 'You know Max Steele, the agent? *My* agent, actually.'

'Hello, Max,' Flick said, bloodshot eyes checking out the room to see if there were any women he'd missed out on.

'My pleasure, Flick,' Max said, suddenly oozing bullshit agent charm. 'I'm a big, big fan.'

'Always happy to hear that,' Flick said. 'That'll sell me a few more CDs, huh? This is my wife, Pamela. Pammy, say hello to everyone.'

Pamela stepped forward, an angry expression on her long-suffering face. Once a beauty, she was now suspicious of every woman her husband talked to, and considering he'd been to bed with most of them, her suspicions were usually justified.

'Hi, Pam,' Lina said, with a lackadaisical wave. ''Aven't run into *you* in a while.'

'I see *you* everywhere,' Pamela retorted. 'Aren't you frightened of overexposure?'

'Nah,' Lina replied, tossing back her long black hair while giving Flick 'the look'. 'The more you give 'em, the more they want. Right, Flick?'

Flick, sensing trouble ahead, grabbed his wife's hand and said, 'C'mon, darlin', I spy Rod and Rachel. Let's go say hello.'

'Nice dress,' Pamela said, unable to resist a parting shot. 'Left over from Mardi Gras?'

'What a cow!' Lina muttered, as the two of them moved off.

'I see his wife is a fan,' Max remarked.

'Can't win 'em all.' Lina sniffed, once again returning her attention to the caviar.

☆

Miss No Brains wore a dress that had to be seen to be believed. Price had wanted to be the envy of every man there, but the dress Krissie almost had on was ridiculous. The orange material was cut down to the cheeks of her ass in the back, plunged all the way to Cuba in the front, and up the sides were see-through zigzags revealing even more skin.

Price was embarrassed. She looked like she belonged on the cover of an X-rated video. 'Krissie,' he'd said, when he'd picked her up, 'you wearing that?'

'Price,' she'd retorted, quite sassy for a dumb blonde, 'you wearing *that*?'

Their evening did not get off to a great start.

As soon as they arrived at the party, Price found a corner couch, placed Krissie there with a drink and took off, assuring her he'd be right back. No way was he cruising around with *her* by his side.

Truth was, he hadn't needed to bring a date, the party was full of glamorous women of all shapes and sizes. He even spotted supermodel Lina across the room – someone he *definitely* wanted to meet, although the dress she had on was another disaster. What was wrong with these women tonight? One big party and their clothes sense ricocheted out of control.

He searched around for Venus. They'd been friends for a while, ever since they'd gotten together at a couple of charity events. He'd taken Teddy to her last concert at the Hollywood Bowl, and Teddy had loved it, even though the only music he claimed to be into was gangsta rap.

'Price,' Venus said, sneaking up behind him, 'don't tell me *you're* responsible for bringing the tart in the orange dress?'

'Shh, girl,' he said, holding a finger to his lips, 'she's a mistake.'

'I was under the impression you had better taste,' Venus said tartly.

'I do,' he said.

'We'll have to find someone to palm her off on.'

'Like who?'

'There's a bunch of Cooper's old producer friends here,' Venus said. 'I'm sure one of them would be thrilled to get a quick grope in the back of a limo.'

'Arrange it,' Price begged. 'I need help.'

'You certainly do,' Venus said, pursing her luscious lips, looking every inch the superstar.

'Oh, yeah,' Price added. 'On the way in I got an eyeful of that model, Lina. She's unfuckin' believable! You gonna set me up?'

'Any time, baby. You're a star, it's arrangeable.'

'I love it when you talk up to me!'

'How's about down and dirty?' she said, mildly coming on to him.

'Don't even go there.'

'If you insist. Now, how's that cute little son of yours?'

'Kid's doin' okay,' Price said.

'I bet half your girlfriends are younger than him,' Venus said, grabbing a glass of champagne from an attentive waiter. 'Anyway, no need to sweat it – the two of you look like brothers.'

'Will you *stop*, woman?' he said, loving every compliment that came his way.

'Let's go find that little model babe,' she said, linking her arm through his. 'I haven't met her myself yet. Gotta hunch she's here with Max Steele.' A sly laugh. 'Rumour has it that

Max hangs out at airports picking off the girls as they leave the plane!'

Price winked. 'Sounds like my kinda guy!'

☆

Venus and Cooper's five-year-old daughter, Chyna, was holding court at her own table. She was precocious, but in a likeable way. She wanted to act, just like Mommy and Daddy, and had already appeared in one of Cooper's movies.

'Daddy, Daddy, I gotta go to the bathroom,' Carioca announced, pulling on her father's sleeve.

Steven, who was busy wishing he wasn't there, was only too happy to take her. He felt completely out of place and couldn't wait to go home.

'I'm coming back,' Carioca informed Chyna.

'Hurry!' Chyna said, bouncing up and down in her seat. 'Gonna have big huge cake!'

Steven led his daughter through the crowded room. He hardly knew any of the guests, which didn't bother him at all because he wasn't interested in the movie crowd. Carioca clung to his hand, a mirror image of her mother.

'Daddy,' she said, her pretty little face twisted into a serious expression.

'Yes, baby-girl?' he asked, sad because she would never see her mother again, and that wasn't right.

'I'm glad you came to Palm Springs. It was so so *fun*! *This* is fun. And, Daddy, I am *not* a baby.'

'Okay, big girl.'

'Daddy, now that Mommy's not here, can we do stuff together?'

'Of course we can, honey,' he said, squeezing her hand.

'I like staying at Lucky's, but being with you is *best*!'

'That's nice to know, Carrie,' he said, using his mother's name as her nickname, 'and I promise you, we'll spend a lot more time together.'

When they reached the guest bathroom it was occupied. Carioca waited outside, hopping from one foot to the other. 'Daddy, Daddy, I *gotta* go *now*!' she squealed.

'Okay, honey,' he answered, tapping on the bathroom door. 'Can you hurry it up?' he called out. 'I've got a desperate child out here.'

A few seconds later the door was flung open, and there stood a vision in a shocking pink dress. 'Sorry,' Lina said, staring directly at him. 'Was I in there too long?'

'Uh, no, that's okay,' he said, somewhat taken aback by the woman's exotic beauty. 'My little girl here was getting out of control.'

'Daddy!' Carioca scolded. 'I wasn't *desperate*. I just gotta *go*.'

'That's what I meant, honeybun.'

'It's all yours, cutie,' Lina said, patting Carioca on the shoulder. 'In you go.'

Carioca raced into the bathroom, pushing the door shut behind her. Lina turned to Steven with a dazzling smile. He was the best-looking man she'd seen in a long while – giving new meaning to the phrase 'Black is beautiful'. 'Your little girl's adorable. What's 'er name?'

'Carioca.'

'Now *that*'s what I call a name,' she said, staring at this incredibly handsome man, wondering if he was an actor. Then it suddenly occurred to her who he was. 'Hey, wait a minute,' she exclaimed. 'You must be Steven.'

'Do I know you?' he asked politely.

'I'm Lina.'

He frowned, embarrassed because it seemed she expected him to know who she was and he didn't. 'Lina?' he questioned.

'Don't you recognize me?' she said, almost teasingly.

'Should I?' he asked tentatively.

'I'm Brigette's friend,' she said, as if that would explain everything. 'Y' know, Lucky's goddaughter, Brigette Stanislopoulos? God, that's a mouthful, wonder 'ow she struggled through childhood with a name like *that*.'

'Of course . . .' Steven said. 'Brigette's a model in New York. What do *you* do?'

Lina started to laugh. 'You honestly *don't* recognize me, do you?'

'I'm really bad at recognizing people. Are you an actress? My wife was an actress.'

'I was ever so sorry to 'ear about your wife,' Lina said, suddenly serious. 'Brigette told me 'ow beautiful the funeral was.'

'Thank you.'

'Your wife was lovely,' Lina continued, talking too fast, but quite mesmerized by this delicious-looking man. 'I used to watch 'er on TV. It's difficult to find words, but I'm really, really sorry for you. Um . . . I mean, y' know, for your loss.'

'I appreciate it,' he said.

'That's okay.'

'So, where *is* Brigette tonight?'

'In London with Lucky,' Lina said, imagining this green-eyed man without his clothes.

'She can't be,' he said. 'Lucky's here with me.'

'You mean she's back?'

'She hasn't been anywhere.'

'Hmm . . . Brigette must've been telling little white lies. Maybe she got herself a fellow and didn't want me to know.'

'Are you two close?'

'Best mates. We live in the same building in New York. By the way, for your information we're *both* models.'

'Interesting.'

'You're a lawyer, right?'

'Guilty.'

'I'd love to *meet* Lucky. Will you introduce me?'

'When I can find her. Who are you here with?'

'My agent. It's strictly business. Actually,' she said, leaning towards him, 'can you keep a secret?'

'Lawyers are good at keeping secrets.'

'I flew out to LA to see Charlie Dollar. Now I'm gonna be in his new movie. My agent said I mustn't tell anyone.'

'Your secret's safe with me,' he said, intrigued by this exotic creature with the oddball accent. 'Then you *are* an actress?'

'Model slash actress.'

'An *English* model slash actress, right?'

''Ow did you guess?'

'Beats me,' he said, smiling.

She giggled. 'Gotta take some speech lessons if I'm gonna be a movie star.'

'I think you sound charming.'

'Thanks.'

'I lived in London for a couple of years,' Steven said.

'Really? Whereabouts?'

'Hampstead.'

'Very posh.'

Carioca emerged from the bathroom. 'Come along, Daddy,' she said impatiently, tugging on his sleeve. 'We gotta go now.'

'Okay, sweetie.'

'See you later,' Lina said, giving him a lingering look.

'It was nice meeting you,' Steven said.

'You too. Brigette 'as talked about you a lot.' A pause. 'Although she forgot to tell me 'ow handsome you are.'

'No need to flatter me,' he said, half smiling.

'I know that,' she said, uncharacteristically shy.

'Daddy, come *on*!' Carioca said crossly, pulling his arm.

'Uh, if I find Lucky I'll let her know you want to meet her,' he said.

Lina dazzled him with a smile. 'Thanks.'

☆

'Are we having fun?' Lucky said, finally locating Lennie, who was sitting at the kiddies' table next to Maria.

'The kids are having a great time,' he said. 'We've had balloons, a magician, watched a clown show. What've *you* been doing?'

'Circulating. Missing you.'

He pulled her close. 'Come here, wife.'

'Yes, husband.'

'Can we go home soon?'

'I can't desert Venus so early.'

'Then would you mind if I took Maria home and sent the limo back for you?'

'Well . . .'

'Please, babe, I'm not feeling social yet. I just want to be . . . you know, at home.'

'If that's what you want,' she said, sighing, 'but I *have* to stay.'

'Understood.'

'Okay, but when you go, do *not* say goodbye. There's nothing worse than guests saying goodbye too early. Slip out quietly, and I'll be home as soon as I can.'

'You're the best.'

'No, Lennie,' she said, mock-serious. 'I am *not* making you another sandwich.'

'It wasn't a sandwich I had in mind.'

'Later, you sex-crazed homebody!'

'Love you, babe.'

'You, too.'

'Sure you'll be all right without me?'

'Somehow I think I'll manage.'

And she kissed Maria, hugged her husband and slipped back into the heart of the party.

48

And so the nightmare continued. Once more Brigette regained consciousness, and this time she found herself in a strange bed in a dark, unfamiliar room. The drapes were pulled tightly over the windows, and when she got unsteadily out of bed and tried the door, she discovered it was locked.

It came to her in a horrible flash – Carlo had kidnapped her.

She felt as if she were caught in the middle of some insane TV soap opera. This kind of thing didn't happen in real life, it simply didn't.

I will not panic, she told herself. *I will stay calm and talk myself out of this mess.*

But there was no one to talk to. Carlo was not around.

She got up and went to the window, pulling back the drapes. The window overlooked an alley and was probably ten or eleven storeys up, too dangerous to attempt an escape.

'Damn!' she muttered. Now her jaw hurt, too, where he'd hit her. Gingerly she opened and closed her mouth, finding that, fortunately, nothing seemed to be broken.

She returned to the door and tried it again. Still locked. She rattled the handle and yelled his name.

Nobody came.

After a while she went back to the bed and lay down. There was no point in using up all her energy. She felt like crying, but she didn't. She'd shed too many tears in the past to keep on repeating the same old pattern.

Instead she began chanting a mantra in her head.

You will be strong.

You will survive.

You will be strong.
You will survive.
And eventually she drifted off into a fitful sleep.

She awoke a few hours later to an even worse nightmare. Standing over her were Carlo and a strange man. The man was in his thirties, tall and gangly, with tufts of hair growing out of his ears, and long, greasy sideburns. He was dressed in brown pants and a stained sweatshirt. A small gold ring protruded from one of his nostrils.

Carlo was holding her down, while the stranger was tightening a leather belt around her left arm, searching for a big fat vein. In his other hand he held a syringe.

The horror of what they were about to do struck her too late. As she began to scream, the man plunged the needle into her arm.

'You sure this is what the bitch wants?' she heard him say.

'Yes,' Carlo replied, 'but it doesn't matter, does it? You're getting paid. That's all that should concern you.'

And then everything started spinning, and a wave of euphoria came over her.

She lay quietly watching the shadows on the ceiling, feeling kind of peaceful and happy.

And soon she drifted off into a long drug-induced sleep.

49

Irena had gone to bed early, and since Price was at a party, Teddy realized that he and Mila had the house to themselves.

He found her in the kitchen watching a game show on television. 'Whass up?' he said.

'Nothing,' she answered, not in the mood to hang with him. He was boring, and she had too much on her mind to bother with him.

But he was all over her and, since she couldn't risk him turning against her at this crucial stage, she let him have a quick grope or two. Then they went upstairs to his room where she unzipped his pants and took it out for some air.

He was certainly well hung – better than her current boyfriend at work: he had a long, thin johnson that didn't get her off at all. It was a shame. Teddy had the equipment, not the brains.

She wondered if he took after his father in the goodies department. Hmm ... maybe she should give Mr W a test drive, simply to prove that she could.

In the meantime, she'd keep Teddy happy and try to work out how she was going to eliminate Lennie Golden. One hundred thousand dollars was the jackpot she'd been dreaming of all her life. One way or another it was going to be hers.

She pushed Teddy down on his bed and gave him a little mouth action. When he was satisfied, she told him she wanted to see Price's room.

'He gets mad if I go in there,' Teddy said nervously. 'My dad's got a thing about privacy.'

'Crap!' Mila said. 'Like, you can't show *me*?'

Teddy was ready to show Mila anything she wanted. She had taken him to heaven and back, and even though she hadn't let him touch her *there*, he felt like a man at last. And for once he'd stopped thinking about that fateful night. Mila was right, he had to forget about it and move on.

Price's bedroom was a fantasy of deep brown leather and black lacquer furniture. Masculine and sexy, one of LA's top designers had put it together. The platform bed was positioned in front of a large-screen TV. And it was covered in a luxurious fur throw. Mila flopped on to it, grabbed the remote and clicked on the TV.

'Better not mess with anything,' Teddy warned.

'Oooh, is this you?' Mila said, picking up a silver frame next to the bed and staring at a picture of a cute little four-year-old boy balanced on Price's shoulders.

'Don't touch,' he said, attempting to grab it from her.

She wouldn't give it up. He fell across the bed on top of her, and before he realized what was happening, she was unzipping his pants again and pulling up her skirt.

Man! He was on his freaking father's bed and she wanted him to do it to her! This was *so* bad it was good. Especially since he was hard as a bat and ready for the home run.

She began wriggling out of her panties. 'You ever done this before, Teddy?'

'Sure,' he gasped.

'Liar,' she jeered. 'I know you haven't.'

It didn't matter what came out of her mouth, because once he got an eyeful of the mound of black hair between her legs, he wanted in. The fact that they were on his dad's bed in his very private bedroom made it all the more forbidden and exciting.

Her skirt was bunched up around her waist, her panties around her ankles. She kicked them across the room and spread her legs. 'If you're gonna do it, get started,' she said.

He knew he should wear a rubber, take precautions just as his dad had warned him to do if he ever had sex. But what was one more risk? This was happening now, and nothing was going to stop him.

He rolled on top of her, dipping into a sticky, welcoming paradise. And then he was brought up short by the resounding buzz of the front gate.

Both of them froze. Teddy's pride and joy shrivelled like a collapsible umbrella.

'Shit!' Mila said. 'The buzzer's gonna wake my mom and she'll come nosying around. *You*'d better get it fast.'

Teddy crawled across the bed, grabbing the phone and pressing the button that connected him to the gate. 'Who's there?' he yelled, shouting, because the thought of Irena catching him with his pants down, rolling around with *her* daughter in the middle of his dad's bed, was enough to panic anyone.

'The police,' said a disembodied voice. 'We'd like to talk to the owner of the black jeep.'

50

'Finally!' Lina exclaimed, tapping Lucky on the shoulder.

'Excuse me?' Lucky said, turning around.

'I'm Lina. Brigette never stops talking about you. Says you're the greatest thing since fried bread.'

'Fried bread?!' Lucky said, amused at the girl's off-the-wall accent. 'Is that English flattery?'

''Spect she's told you all about me,' Lina said confidently. 'Only you mustn't believe a word. She's a raging liar!'

'Actually,' Lucky said, recognizing the famous model, but

not remembering Brigette ever mentioning her, 'she's always spoken very highly of you.'

'I must admit I'm confused,' Lina said. 'Brigette told me she was going to London with you, only when I spoke to Steven earlier, 'e said you weren't with her. So I don't get it.'

'She told *me* she was flying to Milan,' Lucky said.

'No, no, she cancelled out Italy,' Lina said, 'which kind of pissed me off, 'cause we always go there together. Y' know, run riot on the runways, 'ave a wild time.'

'Hmmm ... I wonder what she's up to,' Lucky mused. 'Maybe I should give her a call.'

'Could be she's got herself a secret boyfriend,' Lina said. 'Although if she 'as, I'm pissed she didn't confide in me.'

'Does she tell you everything?' Lucky asked, amused.

'Usually. Only I guess she didn't want me knowing about this one.'

'I was under the impression that Brigette had given up on dating for a while – at least, that's what she told me last time we spoke.'

'Well, yes. Then she had that 'orrible experience in New York.'

'What horrible experience?'

'Uh-oh,' Lina said, clapping a hand over her mouth. 'I'm givin' away secrets.'

'Too late now, keep going.'

'Some jerk slipped a pill in her drink – y' know, one of those date rape drugs. And Brig is under the impression that the bastard might've raped her. I promised not to tell anyone – especially *you* – 'cause Brig says she always 'as to run to you to get 'er out of trouble.'

'When did this happen?' Lucky asked, frowning.

'A coupla months ago,' Lina said. 'She was furious, but she got over it. Me – I would've chopped off 'is ding-dong with a blunt knife!'

Lucky couldn't help smiling. 'Lina, Lina, you're my kind of girl.'

Lina grinned back. 'That's what Brig always says.'

'So who is this guy?' Lucky asked.

'Some Italian arsehole we 'ad dinner with. I mean 'e was an attractive bloke – I would 'ave given 'im one in a flash. It beats me why 'e 'ad t' do it.'

'Men are a problem for Brigette. She's always had bad luck with them,' Lucky said. 'I'm sure you've heard things.'

'Yeah. Brutal,' Lina said. 'Thought *I*'d met every prick in town until I 'eard *her* war stories.'

'What are you doing in LA?' Lucky asked.

'Actually, I'm leaving tomorrow, going to Milan for fashion week. I came out here to meet with Charlie Dollar for his new film.'

'Charlie's a good guy,' Lucky said. 'You'll love him.'

'I know,' Lina said, with a secretive smirk.

'You do?'

'Well,' Lina said. 'I know 'e's great in the sack. I've already 'ad 'im.'

'I advise you not to advertise,' Lucky said drily. 'Charlie has a very steady relationship with Dahlia.'

'Guess I'm not being exactly discreet,' Lina admitted. 'It's just that it was *sooo* exciting. Me mum loves him.'

'Here comes Venus,' Lucky said. 'Have you two met?'

'No. I've met Cooper, though,' Lina said, refraining from adding that she'd had him, too. Somehow she didn't think Lucky would appreciate the information, even though it had been way before he married the blonde superstar.

'Venus,' Lucky said, 'this is Lina. She's a good friend of Brigette's.'

'Of *course* I know who Lina is,' Venus said. 'Watched you kick ass in Paris at the Chanel show. You *killed* 'em on the catwalk. Loved it!'

'Thanks,' Lina said, quite intimidated for once.

'Oh, and this is Price Washington,' Venus added, as Lucky drifted off. 'He's been dying to meet you all night.'

''Ello, Price,' Lina said, giving him the lowering-of-the-eyes look. Sexy and demure. An unbeatable combination.

'Hey—' Price said, checking her out and liking what he saw. 'Noticed your African safari in *Vogue* last month. Those were *some* pictures.'

'What were *you* doing reading *Vogue*?' she teased.

'One of my girlfriends left it at the house.'

'*One* of your girlfriends?' she said, flirting outrageously. ''Ow many d'you 'ave?'

'A guy's gotta go for variety, huh?'

'Oh, so *that*'s what you're into?'

'Could be.'

'Lordy, Lordy,' Venus said, fanning herself with her hand. 'Lust is in the air. I'm tracking down my husband. See you all later.'

☆

Somehow or other, Max Steele found himself deep in conversation with Price Washington's girlfriend, Krissie. He was unamused at getting trapped.

'So, you see,' Krissie said, huge breasts jiggling with indignation, 'after I did the *Playboy* shoot, I thought it was all going to happen. Everybody *told* me it would. I mean, if you do the full spread, you expect results – right?'

'Right,' he said, searching for an escape.

'Now I've got this agent who tells me I have to be *seen*. He chose this dress for me 'cause he wanted everyone to notice me tonight. But Price is not being very nice to me. He should be nicer to me, wouldn't you say?' Max nodded. 'And I know you're a very important agent, 'cause someone told me. So I hope you don't mind me coming up and talking to you, but I need a new agent, and I think you'd be the man for me.'

'Have you had any film experience?' he asked, still looking around for someone to rescue him.

'No, except I did do a kind of . . . Well, it was really *soft* core. And if Traci Lords can make it in legit movies, *anybody* can, don't you think?'

'Traci Lords is a passable actress,' Max said. 'She did pornos when she was a teenager. After that she studied her craft and now she's not bad.'

'I can study my craft, too,' Krissie said excitedly, forty-inch double Ds heaving with emotion.

Christ! Max thought. *Where's Lina when I need her?*

☆

Lina was sharing a joint with Price Washington on the terrace. And although he was black and a star and very sexy, she couldn't help wondering what had happened to Steven Berkeley – him being one of the best-looking men she'd ever seen, black *or* white. And he was nice with it: he hadn't even come on to her, although she'd certainly given him every opportunity.

She was dying to ask Brigette more about him, but who knew where Brigette had run off to, the secretive little brat? Lina hated being left out. If Brigette had a boyfriend, she wanted to know about it, and how.

In the meantime, here she was in LA, surrounded by eligible black men – and that was quite unusual, because she usually only came across white dudes. White, rich and horny. The story of Lina, supermodel.

It wasn't that she didn't like men of colour, it was simply that she never got to meet any. There were a couple of gorgeous black models she often ran into on the circuit – both gay. And she'd briefly dated rapper Big TMF, who'd treated her like some hot little honey on a star trip. *Thank you, no.* Especially when all he'd wanted her to do was go down on him while he listened to his own CDs! What a cheek!

'So, Lina,' Price said, taking a healthy drag on the joint before handing it back to her, 'how long are you in LA?'

'Only a few more hours,' she said.

'Goin' to spend them with me?' he said, giving her the heavy-lidded sexy stare for which he was famous.

'You don't believe in wastin' time, do you?' she said archly.

'My mama taught me a moment wasted is a moment lost.'

Another city. Another night. And he might have been in with a chance. But LA was getting too crowded. Lina wanted to go back to her hotel and think about Steven. And she also had to let Max down. Gently, of course. After all, he *was* her agent.

'Sorry,' she said to Price, with a dazzling smile. 'Me dance card is full.'

☆

Lina's story about Brigette had worried Lucky. Basically Brigette was sweet and vulnerable, not the kind of girl to get caught up in the whole modelling scene of parties, drugs and money. Fortunately she'd made it to the top fast, like lightning in fact. And that had saved her from the seamier side of the business. Lucky knew all about the predatory men who preyed on gorgeous young girls with endless ambition; the agents who pursued them with phoney promises; and the designers who used them until they were finished.

Brigette had yearned for a career, something she could

achieve on her own and, like an answered prayer, it had come to her, for if Brigette had nothing except her vast inheritance, it would have destroyed her. As it was, Lucky could weep when she thought of all the things Brigette had suffered through.

Early in the morning, she decided she'd call Brigette's agent and find out exactly where she was and who she was with. If Brigette needed any kind of help, she'd be there.

Glancing across the room, she observed Alex talking with Pia. This one was lasting longer than the others, perhaps because she was a smart girl, a lawyer.

Why are you thinking about Alex, she asked herself, *when you should be getting home to Lennie and your children?*

Ah . . . domesticity. She loved and adored her family, but sometimes the thought of freedom was so damn tempting!

Maybe Alex was the wise one. No family. No ties. Only his work – about which he was passionate – and the occasional lover.

Ah, yes, but Alex would never feel the whispered kiss of a child, a baby's soft warm cuddle, or hear a little voice calling, 'Daddy, I love you,' in the middle of the night.

She took another look at him. Damn! He was whispering in Pia's ear.

Wasn't it about time he traded her in?

☆

'Good night, Steven,' Venus said, kissing him on both cheeks. 'I hope you're glad you came.'

Carioca was asleep in his arms, her innocent little face pressed tightly against his shoulder. '*Somebody* had a great time,' he said, with a trace of a smile.

'Good,' Venus said. 'We want to see more of you.'

'You will,' he said, thinking of Brigette's friend with the appalling dress and crazy accent. There was something about her . . .

'We'll call you next week,' Venus said. 'I'll set something up with Lucky and Lennie.'

He nodded. 'I'd like that.'

☆

And so the party wound down, and everyone went home. Venus grinned at Cooper and said, 'It was a *huge* success.'

Cooper agreed, and they went upstairs and made love under the stars in the Jacuzzi on their bedroom terrace.

And somewhere in a far-off tree, a paparazzo, balancing precariously on a high branch, took unbelievably intimate pictures with his telephoto lens.

And the caterers left.

And most of the security left.

And soon it would be just another balmy day in Hollywood.

BOOK THREE

Two Months Later

51

Teddy had left it too late to run. Too freakin' late. The last few weeks had been his worst nightmare come true, starting with two detectives turning up at the house, *questioning* him about the jeep – with Mila skulking upstairs in his bedroom, frightened to come down in case they recognized her from the computer likeness.

They'd questioned him for ten minutes before Irena had appeared, bundled into a long brown robe, her face scrubbed of makeup. 'What going on?' she demanded, glaring at everyone in a most unfriendly way.

For once, Teddy was thrilled to see her.

'We're investigating an incident involving a jeep with several of the same licence-plate numbers as the jeep registered to this address,' Detective Johnson said.

Irena pulled herself up to her full five feet six inches. 'Do you realize whose house this is?' she asked imperiously.

'Excuse me, ma'am,' the second detective, a heavy-set Hispanic man, enquired, 'who are *you*?'

'Who am *I*?' Irena said, putting on a good show of indignation. '*I* am Mr Price Washington's personal assistant, and I am sure Mr Washington's lawyer would be most disturbed if he knew you were speaking to Mr Washington's *son* without him present. You must leave immediately.'

Teddy was impressed. Irena could kick it *good*.

'Thank you, ma'am,' Detective Johnson replied, recognizing a pain in the ass when it stared him in the face. He was well aware that dealing with so-called celebrities was always trouble, and this uptight woman was definitely on protection duty. 'Hopefully we won't need to bother you again.'

'What was *that* about?' Irena asked, as soon as the two detectives had left.

Teddy shrugged, attempting to appear unconcerned, although inside he was shaking. 'Dunno. Somethin' about a jeep involved in a robbery.'

'There are thousands of jeeps in Los Angeles,' Irena said crossly. 'Why they come here?'

Teddy shrugged again and turned away. He didn't want her to see his face, which probably had 'Guilty' written all over it. 'Beats me,' he said.

'Where's Mila?' Irena snapped.

'Haven't seen her,' Teddy lied.

'Do not answer the door again,' Irena said sternly. 'It is *my* job to look after this house. *My* job, not yours.' She shot him a suspicious look. 'You have something to hide, Teddy?'

'Don't be stupid,' he mumbled.

Once rid of Irena, Teddy raced upstairs where he and Mila conferred way into the night.

'Whatever happens,' Mila insisted, her pointed face agitated and angry, 'deny everything. Understand, Teddy? Or, I promise you, you'll regret it big time.'

A week later the same two detectives were back. This time they requested to see the jeep.

Once again, Irena stonewalled them.

'How about we come back with a search warrant?' Detective Johnson said, with a weary sigh. He'd spent too much time and energy on this case. All he wanted to do was solve it so he could get the Santangelo woman off his back. She was bugging the shit out of him, completely unaware of the many other homicides that needed solving.

'Yes,' Irena said, glaring at him. 'Perhaps that's what you should do.'

'If that's what the miserable witch wants,' Detective Johnson muttered to his partner as the two men returned to their car, 'that's what she'll get.'

The more he thought about it, the more he was convinced that the jumpy black kid they'd talked to a week ago looked a lot like the artist's rendition of one of the suspects. That, combined with the jeep having some of the same numbers, was giving him cause to think they may have hit pay dirt.

Twenty-four hours later they returned with a warrant to inspect the jeep.

Irena, who on principle detested the police, almost pan-

icked. Price was in Vegas and she didn't wish to bother him with such nonsense, so she made the two detectives wait at the door while she contacted Price's lawyer, who yelled at her for not alerting him the first time they'd come to the house.

'*Podonki!*' she snapped, reverting to her mother tongue as she slammed down the phone. Police. Lawyers. All figures of authority made her sick. They thought they could march in anywhere and do whatever they wanted. But not in Price Washington's house they couldn't. Not while she was there to protect him.

The detectives with their precious warrant were out of luck, because Teddy was not home, so the jeep wasn't there.

'When will he be back?' the Hispanic detective asked.

'I not know,' she said, guarding the front door like a sentinel.

'We'll wait,' Detective Johnson said.

'Outside,' she said.

'What was your name again?' he said.

'Irena Kopistani,' she said. And felt fear, because if anyone discovered her true identity it was quite possible she would be deported, considering she'd entered the country under an assumed identity.

'Miss Kopistano,' Detective Johnson said, mispronouncing her name, 'do either of these people look familiar to you?' He held up the two computer-generated photographs.

Irena's stomach flipped. The girl in the photo resembled Mila. And the boy could certainly be Teddy.

'No,' she said, staring straight ahead.

'No?' Detective Johnson said, observing that her pinched face had flushed a dull red. 'Doesn't the boy look like that kid we spoke to the other day?'

'No,' Irena repeated.

'That boy was Price Washington's son, right?'

She nodded, reluctant to tell them anything.

'Does he have a white girlfriend?'

'Excuse me?'

'A white girlfriend,' Detective Johnson repeated, wondering what kind of bee she had up *her* ass, because she was definitely suffering an attack of the guilts.

'No,' Irena said flatly.

'Where are you from, Miss Koposta?'

Her face was stony. 'Do I have to answer your questions?'

Oh, yeah, she *definitely* had something to hide. 'It's up to you,' he answered mildly, playing good cop.

She threw him a filthy look. 'By *law* do I have to answer them?'

Detective Johnson's gut feeling told him he'd come across a vein of gold. He'd got a search warrant for the jeep, now he was turning around and getting one for the house. Pronto. This old bag knew more than she was saying.

Forty-eight hours later they were back with a warrant to search the house.

This time the surly housekeeper couldn't stop them. She got on the phone to Price Washington's lawyer again, but it was too late: they were all over the house, concentrating on Teddy's room. And when they picked up his mattress and discovered the many press clippings about the murder and Mary Lou Berkeley Detective Johnson knew for sure that this was it. They had suspect number one. And his experience told him that, once Teddy Washington was in custody, the boy would give it up within the first few hours, and they would have the name of his partner in crime.

☆

'Who's the girl?' Detective Johnson asked, waving the computer likeness of Mila in front of Teddy's face.

'Dunno,' he mumbled, terrified, because when Price found out he'd been arrested and hauled down to the police station, his life would turn to pure garbage.

'No good protecting her,' Detective Johnson said, ''cause the moment we get her in custody she'll give you up like the school tramp on prom night. And you seem like a nice kid – in fact, from what I understand you didn't participate.' He gave Teddy a moment to think about *that*. Then he said, 'Of course, being there makes you an accessory, and a sharp lawyer can turn this case around, and before you know it, you'll find yourself doing time for murder. Ever seen those prison movies, Teddy?' He paused to let that sink in. ''Cause if you have, then you know what goes on inside. So I strongly suggest you co-operate and tell us who the girl is, 'cause we'll find out anyway. An' if you're trying to protect her, it'll blow up in your face.'

Teddy shuddered. Murder. *He* hadn't murdered anyone, he'd just been along for the ride – that was all. And if they *did* find Mila, she'd *tell* them he was innocent, then they'd *have* to let him go. Yeah. Mila knew the truth better than anyone.

'So . . .' Detective Johnson continued. 'Who is she? And where can we find her?'

Teddy kept his silence, but they found her anyway. They discovered that Irena had a daughter, and when they saw her and noted her resemblance to the computer photo, she was arrested at her place of work in front of everyone.

Mila did not go to the police station quietly, she informed anyone who would listen that Teddy had *forced* her to go on the ride that fateful night; that he'd plied her with cocaine and booze; that he'd been carrying his father's gun, and that *he*'d shot Mary Lou. 'He raped me, too,' she added, for good measure, frustrated and angry that she hadn't been able to find anyone prepared to put a hit on Lennie Golden, therefore she had not been able to claim the reward. Now she was in deep shit and what the hell could she do about it? Exactly nothing.

Detective Johnson sat her down in the interrogation room and questioned her for three long hours.

She stuck to her story.

'Teddy says it was *you* who fired the gun,' he said, regarding her carefully. 'He says it was *you* calling all the shots.'

'Liar!' she snapped.

'Wanna tell us about it?'

'Teddy's in denial,' she said stubbornly. 'He's not thinking straight. I *told* you, *he* did the shooting. What would *I* be doing with his dad's gun?'

'Why didn't you come forward after it happened?'

'I was scared,' she lied, lowering her eyes. 'Teddy threatened to kill me if I talked.'

Detective Johnson sighed. Nothing was ever simple.

By the time Price Washington's lawyer arrived, both Mila and Teddy were locked away for the night. Teddy in juvenile hall, and Mila in jail.

'Too late for bail. Come back tomorrow morning,' Detective Johnson said, hardly looking at the Beverly Hills lawyer, whom he disliked on sight.

Howard Greenspan, a smooth-looking man with a tan, a

two-thousand-dollar suit and plenty of attitude, bristled. 'Price Washington won't like this,' he warned.

'I said tomorrow,' Detective Johnson repeated, refusing to be intimidated by the fat-cat lawyer in his expensive suit, reeking of costly aftershave.

'Mr Washington has friends in high places.'

'Congratulations,' Detective Johnson growled.

The two men locked eyeballs.

'What's the charge?' Howard demanded.

'Accessory to murder,' Detective Johnson said.

Howard G. Greenspan nodded. Price was out of town anyway. He'd spring Teddy in the morning, and then they'd see who had the clout in this town.

52

As soon as Lucky received word of the two arrests, she felt a deep sense of satisfaction. Lennie felt it too. 'This is exactly what I needed, closure,' he said. 'I'll never forget the hate in that girl's voice, or the cold-blooded way she went ahead and shot Mary Lou like it didn't mean a goddamn thing. When I see her put away for life that'll do it for me.'

'This is California,' Lucky pointed out. 'She might not get life.'

'By the time *I* get out of the witness box,' he said fiercely, 'it'll be life.'

Lucky nodded, although she wasn't so sure. California law was a strange and laughable thing. Criminal justice, more often than not, meant 'justice' for the criminal.

Steven felt the same way. 'When it comes to the trial we have to be there every day,' he said. 'It's *imperative* that the jury sees the victim's family as a united and ever present unit.'

'I'm in,' Lennie said.

'Me too,' Lucky said.

Although she was happy about the arrests, she was still worried about Brigette, who was due to arrive in LA any day. After talking to Lina at Venus' party, she'd immediately called Brigette's agent in New York, who'd informed her the agency had no idea where Brigette was. So Lucky had tracked her down to the Dorchester in London, where the reception desk confirmed that Brigette had been staying there but had checked out and left no forwarding address. Lucky was alarmed. It wasn't like Brigette to take off without telling anyone her whereabouts. 'I'm flying to London,' she'd informed Lennie. 'I've got a feeling something's wrong.'

'You're crazy,' Lennie had said. 'Brigette's a grown woman grabbing some privacy, you can't begrudge her that.'

'Brigette's an heiress,' Lucky had reminded him, 'due to inherit a billion-dollar fortune. *Someone* has to look out for her.'

Before she'd made up her mind whether to go or not, they'd received a postcard from Brigette with no return address, saying she'd met someone special and would be travelling around Europe for a while.

This did not satisfy Lucky, although Lennie seemed to think it was okay. 'Hey, listen,' he'd said, 'the kid's had all those bad experiences with guys. She wants to have fun. I'm glad she's found herself a guy.'

'Yes, but who is he?' Lucky had said, worried. 'For all we know he could be some fortune hunter in it for her money.'

They heard from her again the next week. Another postcard. 'Touring around Tuscany, having a fantastic time! Love Brigette.'

And so it went on for the next few weeks, Brigette communicating by postcards with no return address, until finally she'd phoned.

'Where have you *been?*' Lucky had demanded. 'And who's this guy you're with?'

'Take it easy,' Brigette had said. 'I'm having a great time travelling around Europe. I'll get in touch again soon.'

In the meantime, while Lennie worked on his computer all day, Lucky busied herself reading the scripts sent over from Alex's office. After several duds, she'd found one she liked in particular, a sharp romantic comedy about a very rich divorcee and a sexy male stripper, kind of a *Pretty Woman* in reverse. After reading it through twice, she'd messengered it to Venus, who'd immediately fallen in love with the female lead. 'I've got to play her,' Venus had said. 'She's me in another life.'

Lucky called Alex to tell him, and two days later the three of them had sat down over lunch at the Grill to discuss it. Venus wanted several changes, Lucky had her own ideas and Alex was simply delighted that he and Lucky might get a chance to work together.

'Have you told Lennie?' he'd asked, over coffee.

'No,' Lucky said, waving at James Woods as he sauntered out of the restaurant with a pretty teenager. Probably his niece. Or maybe not. Who could tell with actors? 'I'll tell him when we're closer to a deal.'

Alex had smiled his lazy crocodile smile. 'Really?' he'd said, liking the fact that Lennie wasn't in on this.

'No big thing, Alex,' Lucky had said crossly. 'Lennie won't mind.' But, deep down, she'd known that he would.

After thinking it over, she'd decided not to tell Lennie until the deal was set because the thought of producing a film *and* working with her two best friends was too exciting a prospect even to contemplate giving up.

A few weeks after Brigette's phone call, they'd received a glossy ten-by-eight wedding photo of her with a tall, handsome, blond man. Brigette had scrawled across it in her own handwriting, *'Count and Countess Carlo Vittorio Vitti!!'*

Lucky had raced straight into Lennie's study. 'You're not going to believe this one,' she'd said, waving the photo in front of him. 'She *married* the guy. No pre-nup, nothing. This is insanity!'

'Still no address?' Lennie had asked, checking out the photo.

'Nope. I can't believe it, we don't even know who he is. If it had been up to me I would've tracked her down weeks ago and found out all about him.'

'I hate to keep telling you, sweetheart,' Lennie had said, more interested in getting back to his computer than anything else, 'it's none of our business.'

Oh, yes, it is, Lucky had thought. *Somebody has to look out for her. And I guess that somebody is going to be me.*

She'd immediately phoned Lina, who'd just checked into the Bel Air Hotel ready to start shooting her movie with Charlie Dollar.

Lina had no idea what Brigette was up to either. Like

Lucky and Lennie, she'd received the occasional postcard with no real information.

'Did Brigette send you a photo?' Lucky asked.

'No ... but I've been in Paris for the collections,' Lina explained. 'Flew directly to LA.'

'Do you happen to be free for lunch?'

'For you, Lucky. Yes.'

'Good. It's important that we talk.'

☆

They met in the garden of the Bel Air Hotel, a leafy paradise with attentive waiters and delicious food. Lucky sat down, ordered a Perrier, lit a cigarette, and as soon as Lina arrived, got straight to the point. 'She married the guy.'

'*What?*' Lina exclaimed. 'Who *is* 'e?'

'See if *you* know him,' Lucky said, handing her the photo. 'This arrived today.'

'Bleedin' 'ell!' Lina squealed, peering at the photo. 'It's the Italian bloke she thought raped her.'

Lucky stubbed out her cigarette. 'You've *got* to be kidding?'

'No, that's 'im all right,' Lina said, still studying the photograph.

'Obviously she must have been mistaken about the rape.'

'Obviously,' Lina agreed. 'Oh, boy ... ain't love grand? I know 'is cousin – shall I talk to 'im, see what 'e knows?'

'Good idea,' Lucky said. 'Maybe at the same time you can find out where she is.'

As soon as she got back to her room, Lina called Fredo, who was as shocked as everyone else.

'I will telephone Italy and get back to you,' he'd promised.

'Not a word about the whole drugged-drink thing,' Lina said. 'It can't 'ave happened if she's married 'im, can it?'

'I understand,' Fredo said, obviously anxious to get off the phone and find out the real story.

He phoned back twenty minutes later. 'It is true,' he said, in shock. 'They were married at the Palace.'

'Are Brigette an' Carlo still there?' Lina asked.

'No. They left on a honeymoon.'

Lina reported in to Lucky, who immediately decided she'd better have Count Carlo Vittorio Vitti investigated. She contacted the private detective agency she used, and they immediately went to work.

Finally, Brigette phoned. 'We're coming to LA,' she announced over the phone from Portofino. 'Carlo wants to meet everyone.'

'And about time!' Lucky exclaimed. 'I'm so mad at you for running off the way you did and marrying in secret. I wanted to be at your wedding. So did Lennie and the kids. Not to mention you not conferring with your lawyers before you did it. Brigette, you have to realize, you are *not* an ordinary girl, you have big responsibilities. As soon as you get here, we must sit down and go over everything.'

'You're not my mother, Lucky,' Brigette said, in a flat voice. 'I'm aware of my responsibilities, so is Carlo. In fact, *he*'s the one who wants to meet with my lawyers. We're stopping in New York on our way to LA.'

Lucky was shocked at Brigette's unfriendly tone. 'What's the matter with you?'

'I resent being told what to do.'

'I'm merely pointing out that you'll be inheriting a vast amount of money, and you have to be careful.'

'I *know*,' Brigette said impatiently. 'Carlo and I will be there next week. We're staying at the Four Seasons.'

'We'd like to throw a party for you,' Lucky said. 'So we can all celebrate.'

'I . . . I don't know,' Brigette answered tentatively. 'I'll have to check with Carlo.'

'Does Carlo make all your decisions now?' Lucky asked, unable to keep a sharp edge out of her voice.

'No, Lucky, he doesn't,' Brigette snapped. 'Why would you think that?'

'The way you're talking . . .'

'Anyway, you'll like him. He's a count, very handsome. And Italian. Gino will be pleased about that.'

'There's more to a person than good looks.'

'Don't be mad at me, Lucky,' Brigette pleaded, suddenly sounding like her old self. 'I can't stand it when you're mad at me.'

'What about your career?' Lucky said, knowing how much Brigette's success meant to her. 'Your agent's not exactly thrilled about you running off. You'd better call in and tell her where you are.'

'Carlo doesn't want me to work,' Brigette said.

'*What?*'

'He says it's not necessary.'

'Why? Is he jealous?' Silence. 'Oh, God! Don't tell me you've married a *jealous* Italian, the worst kind.'

'He loves me,' Brigette said. 'That's all that matters, isn't it?'

How naïve and sweet. Typical Brigette. Her judgement of men was irreparably damaged; she always trusted the wrong ones.

Lucky hung up, hoping and praying that Brigette hadn't got caught up in another bad scene.

Shortly after their conversation, the detective agency delivered a report on Carlo. According to their research he was from a good but impoverished family, had been a playboy around Rome before going to London to work in a bank, and had been engaged to an English heiress. They had parted abruptly on a sour note shortly after he met Brigette.

Lucky feared the worst, that he'd homed in on Brigette for her money.

Not that her goddaughter wasn't beautiful – she was totally gorgeous *and* sweet *and* successful. But Lucky's gut instinct told her it was the Stanislopoulos fortune Carlo was after. And control. Italian men got off on control.

Oh, well, soon Brigette would be in LA, and there was nothing Lucky could do now except simply wait and see.

And watch . . . very, very carefully.

53

'**Surely you are not** wearing that?' Carlo said, his voice filled with criticism. They were standing in the living room of Brigette's New York apartment.

'What's wrong with it?' she asked, smoothing down the waistline of her long-sleeved dress.

'Makes you look fat.'

'I *am* fat,' she said flatly. 'I'm almost four months pregnant.'

Actually, she wasn't fat at all, she was painfully thin. Only her stomach protruded. The heroin Carlo had been feeding her on a regular basis had sucked the energy out of her. She was still beautiful, but not the glowing beauty she'd been two months ago. Now she was deathly pale, with sunken cheeks and huge, bright blue staring eyes. She personified the currently popular heroin-chic look – but in her case it had become the real thing.

'I'll change,' she said dully, realizing that whatever she changed into she had better keep her arms covered. The telltale tracks were becoming a problem. 'If you're sure you don't like this dress.'

'I suggest that you do change,' Carlo said, sipping a martini as he continued staring at her critically. 'Now that you are a contessa, Brigette, I would appreciate it if you would make an effort to look the part. Right now you look like a *puttana.*'

Sometimes he could be mean and cruel, other times kind and loving. She was never sure *what* sort of mood he'd be in.

There were moments she considered him to be the most wonderful man in the world. Other times she hated him with a deep, dark loathing.

Despite the mood, however, whatever he said, she did. It wasn't worth upsetting him: his temper tantrums were too violent to endure.

She sighed. Carlo was her life. He supplied the drugs that kept her happy, and the insidious heroin was all she cared about. She'd never known such euphoria, such a feeling of peace and joy each time after she shot up. Every trouble she'd ever experienced vanished – it was as if she were floating on a gossamer cloud of pure pleasure. She lived for the shots that Carlo's acquaintance had taught her to administer to herself.

The events of the last couple of months were more or less a blur. She vaguely remembered Carlo taking her to his apartment in London, where she'd been injected with drugs on a twice-daily basis, until eventually she'd been unable to function without them. And by the time he'd told her she was free to go, she'd had no desire to go anywhere. Carlo was the keeper of her heroin supply, and she had no intention of trying to stop using it, since it was the first time she'd felt free and alive and totally happy. Especially when Carlo made love to her, which he did frequently.

She depended on Carlo for everything, conveniently forgetting that it was he who'd forced her into such a position, because when he was sure she was truly hooked, he'd lured her with his charm, constantly telling her how much he adored her, making love to her with a fiery passion that left her breathless.

After a while they'd said goodbye to London and started travelling around Europe. Carlo was with her day and night, never letting her out of his sight.

One morning, after a night of passionate lovemaking, he'd informed her they should get married, for surely it was as obvious to her as it was to him that they were destined to be together for ever. Somehow she'd agreed, and later that day he'd driven her to his parents' palace outside Rome, where a priest had performed the simple ceremony in the garden, with only Carlo's family and a few servants present.

She was too out of it to understand what she was getting into. Besides, it seemed like the right thing to do, for Carlo was constantly telling her that he loved her more than any man had ever loved her before, so why *shouldn't* they be married?

After the brief ceremony they'd stayed in Rome only one night, then they'd set off on a honeymoon trip around Europe.

When they'd arrived at the first hotel, Carlo had handed her one of her chequebooks, instructing her to pre-sign dozens of cheques. 'I'm waiting for some money from England,' he'd said vaguely. 'In the meantime . . .'

She didn't care, money meant nothing to her.

A week later Carlo informed her that he thought it was best if she gave up her modelling career. She agreed readily. Who gave a damn about work? All *she* cared about was getting high.

One night in Paris they bumped into Kyra Kattleman at a disco. 'Oh my God!' Kyra squeaked, in her incongruous baby voice. 'I hardly recognized you, Brig. You must've lost thirty pounds.'

'This is my husband,' Brigette said, a blank expression on her face. 'Count Carlo Vittorio Vitti.'

'I know you!' Kyra exclaimed. '*You*'re the guy from the restaurant in London. You two got *married*! Way cool. Are you doing the Paris shows this year?'

Brigette had shaken her head. 'Not me. I've given up working.'

'Wow!' Kyra exclaimed. 'Maybe that's what I should do.'

After a while, Carlo decided they should go to America and meet with her lawyers. 'I must see exactly how your money is handled,' he told her. 'How do we know they're looking after it properly? I am the only one who has your best interests at heart, Brigette, the only person you can trust. All your life you've had people leeching off you. Now *I* will oversee everything.'

'My lawyers handle my trust and all of my investments,' she'd said. 'I'm sure they do a good job.'

'It might be prudent for you to give me power of attorney,' he'd suggested. 'That way I can make *sure* nobody steals from you.'

So far New York had been a nightmare. Her team of lawyers were concerned and angry that Carlo was attempting to interfere and take over. They'd tried to pull her aside and warn her that giving any kind of control to her husband was not a good idea. But Carlo had made sure they did not get her alone for more than a few brief moments.

'I liked it better in Europe,' she complained to Carlo, 'where people left us alone.'

'I know, *cara*,' he answered, in one of his caring moods, 'but we must get this settled so you and I can enjoy our lives. I was thinking that we should buy a house outside Rome. You could live there quietly with the baby, while I travel and take care of business. Would that please you, my sweet?'

As long as I have what I need every day, she wanted to say. But she didn't. She merely smiled, high as usual.

Sometimes she thought about the moment she'd told him she was pregnant. At first he'd been furious. 'Whose baby is it?' he'd demanded. 'What bastard did this to you? Slut! Whore! Who did you sleep with?'

'It's *your* baby, Carlo,' she'd assured him. 'I haven't slept with anyone else. It happened that night in New York.'

When he'd realized she was speaking the truth, he was pleased. 'It had better be a boy,' he kept on repeating. 'A boy who looks like me.'

Doctors were not on her agenda. She was scared to have

the test that would tell her the sex of the baby. She was also smart enough to know that doctors would try to stop the drugs that allowed her to get through each day.

Carlo had found a doctor in New York who did not ask awkward questions. They went to see him together and, after examining her, the doctor warned her that she had to give up drugs, otherwise her baby would be born addicted.

'Oh, yes, Doctor,' she'd lied sweetly. 'I intend to.'

'I can help you,' he'd said. 'There's a methadone programme we can put you on. You have to do this, Brigette.'

'I'll be back,' she'd said. 'Maybe then.'

'You've got to get off that shit soon,' Carlo had said, when they left the man's office. 'It would not do for our baby to be born addicted.'

'You got me on it,' she'd pointed out. 'I don't want to stop.'

'Of course not,' he'd spat in disgust. 'Because deep down you're a drug whore – exactly like your mother.'

She knew she should never have confided in him about Olympia, but in moments of intimacy she'd told him everything because when he was in a loving mood there was no one as sweet as her Carlo.

Now they were preparing to go out to dinner with Fredo, something she had no desire to do. She fumbled through her closet, muttering to herself. She hated it when Carlo was mad at her. All she asked for was peace and harmony and to be left alone. And to have her drugs.

After a while she pulled out a simple black Calvin Klein dress and a tuxedo jacket that hid her slightly protruding stomach. She changed quickly, pinning up her long blonde hair and adding jet drop earrings. The result was stunning.

When she returned to the living room, Carlo grunted his approval. 'That's better,' he said.

Fredo met them at Coco Pazzo with red roses and champagne on ice. He was with Lina's favourite model, Didi, who stared at Brigette rudely and said, 'What in hell happened to *you*? You're positively *skinny*!'

Fredo gave Didi a sharp nudge in the ribs, and she shut up. He, too, was wondering what had happened to the once glowing Brigette. She was pale and agitated and far too thin. She was still a knock-out, but in a different way.

Whereas Carlo, in an expensive Brioni suit with flashing gold and sapphire cufflinks that matched his piercing blue eyes, was even more handsome, if that was possible.

Fredo was not happy. Brigette was a true prize in every way, and somehow or other Carlo had won her. Fredo remembered going over to Lina's apartment the morning after the dinner they'd all had together. Brigette had accused Carlo of rape. Now she was married to him. It didn't make sense.

He wondered what Lina had to say about it, and if she'd seen them together.

As the evening progressed, Fredo noticed that Brigette did not seem like her normal self. If he hadn't known better, he would've sworn she was on drugs. But no, not Brigette – the girl he knew wouldn't so much as pop an aspirin.

After dinner he suggested they all go on to a club. Carlo said no, explaining that they were leaving for LA in the morning and had to be up early. Brigette said nothing, her expression dreamy.

'Have you seen Lina?' Fredo asked.

'Haven't had time to call her,' Brigette answered vaguely. And that was that.

The next morning they were on a plane to LA. Brigette leafed through a copy of *Vanity Fair*. Her latest fear was facing Lucky.

'Who is this Lucky woman anyway?' Carlo said irritably. 'She's not your mother or a blood relative. Why are you so influenced by her?'

'She's my godmother,' Brigette answered, watching the pretty stewardess flirt with Carlo as she leaned over and served him another drink. 'Lucky was married to my grand-father.'

'Ha!' Carlo said. 'She must be some gold-digger.'

'She's not,' Brigette said simply. 'Lucky's wonderful. I'm sure you'll get along with her.'

'*I*'ll be the judge of that,' Carlo said ominously.

She didn't like his tone. It would be impossible if he started trouble with Lucky, she simply couldn't stand it. 'Lucky's very smart, Carlo,' she said, 'so please, *don't* upset her.'

'Are you telling *me* not to upset *her*?' he said imperiously. 'I suggest you tell *her* not to upset *me*, otherwise I will make sure that you never see her again.'

Brigette was silent. She'd learned that when Carlo had a certain look in his eye, it was best to stay quiet.

☆

Shooting a movie with Charlie Dollar was like one long enjoyable party. Lina could not get over how much fun it was. She'd had two acting jobs before, both of them absolutely boring. Now here was Charlie, racing around the set, laughing, joking, encouraging everyone to do their best work. And when the cameras started to roll, his performance was so right-on that the entire crew was totally mesmerized. Charlie Dollar always delivered.

'How was Africa?' she asked, one day between takes.

He threw her one of his famous quizzical looks. '*You*'re asking *me*?'

She rubbed the tip of her nose and laughed. 'I might be black, but we're not *all* out of Africa. I'm from London, as a matter of fact. The Elephant and Castle, if that means anything to you.'

'I got a yen for English girls,' Charlie ruminated, with a beatific smile. 'Spent several months in London making a flick. Hung my hat at Tramp every night. Had myself many a page-three beauty.'

'I'd hardly call 'em beauties,' Lina snorted. 'More like scrubbers.'

'Scrubbers?' Charlie said, with a wild chuckle. 'Now *that*'s a word.'

'It's what we call 'em.'

'And it means?'

'Some cheapo bimbo babe who'll flash her tits an' sleep with anybody.'

'You wouldn't be calling *me* anybody, would you?'

Lina wagged a long finger at him. 'You'd better watch out, Charlie. Those little dolly birds'll sell their story to a newspaper soon as look at you!'

'Thanks for the warning. In the future I'll make sure I give them something juicy to write about.'

On the days that Dahlia visited the set, Charlie acted like a different person. It was as if one moment he was a naughty schoolboy up to no good, and then Mommy arrived, and he immediately turned into the opposite.

Jackie Collins

'Gee!' Lina exclaimed, after one of Dahlia's surprise appearances. 'Has *she* got your balls in a vice! Must be dead painful.'

'Dahlia's a lady,' Charlie said sonorously. 'And a talented one at that.'

'Do you two fuck?' Lina asked boldly.

'We did,' Charlie said. 'Hence, our son, Sport. However, now I have too much respect for Dahlia to give her the old one two three.'

'Oh, I see. You got a Madonna-complex thing going, huh?'

'You think you're very smart, Lina, don't you?'

'I *am* smart.'

'I suppose you are,' Charlie said, nodding to himself. 'You agree with my shrink. According to him, there is absolutely nothing wrong with a healthy Madonna complex. Y' see, my dear little English girl, I can't get it up for somebody I respect.'

'Guess that says a lot about me,' Lina said, getting in a quick dig.

'We did the dirty deed once,' Charlie said. 'And please take note that I have *not* invited you into my trailer since we've been shooting.'

'*Oooh*, should I be insulted?' she drawled sarcastically.

'Depends on your insult threshold.'

'I was going to ask you,' Lina said, changing track. 'Lucky's throwing a party for her goddaughter, Brigette, my friend. Can you take me?'

'If Dahlia's out of town.'

'The party's in two days'.'

'Hmm . . . I do believe Dahlia will be visiting her father on location in Arizona at that time.'

'How convenient,' Lina said, well pleased. 'So now you've got *no* excuse.'

Charlie executed an extravagant bow. 'Delighted, my dear.'

54

When Price returned from several weeks on the road and discovered that his son had been arrested and actually spent the night in juvenile hall, he flew into a foul rage.

'What the *fuck* am I payin' you a retainer for?' he yelled at

232

his lawyer, as he paced furiously around his living room. 'How come nobody contacted me? Why did you allow *my* son to spend the night locked up? You should've sprung him immediately.'

'They couldn't set bail until the next morning,' Howard explained, trying to placate one of his most high-profile clients. 'Teddy had to appear before a judge and, believe me, it wasn't easy springing him without you there. I had to call in some very big favours.'

'What the fuck is this anyway?' Price steamed, getting even angrier. 'I wanna know *why* they arrested him.' An ominous pause, then, 'Could it be 'cause he happens t' be *black*?'

'Calm down, Price,' Howard said, using his best soothing voice. 'The cops have an idea it was Teddy's jeep used in the Mary Lou Berkeley shooting.'

'What kind of bullshit is *that*?' Price yelled. 'That murder happened months ago.'

'There's a girl involved, too,' Howard continued. 'The daughter of your housekeeper.'

'Mila?'

'Yes. She was arrested with Teddy. Since she's eighteen they took her to jail. It seems Lennie Golden identified her as the shooter, but *she*'s telling the cops it was Teddy who did it. And here's the bad news. Apparently he used *your* gun.'

Price's eyes bulged. '*My* fucking gun?' he said, outraged.

'I suggest you check out where you keep it, see if it's still there.'

'*My* fucking gun?' Price repeated. 'Man, this is some bad joke.' He marched over to the bar and poured himself a hefty shot of Scotch. 'Where's Teddy now?'

'Out, in your custody. I figured school's the safest place for him to be – so that's where he is. I instructed him to continue to conduct his life as if nothing is happening.'

'Have the press gotten hold of this?' Price demanded.

'Not yet,' Howard replied, wondering if Price was going to offer *him* a drink. Not that he wanted one, but it was damn bad manners not to make the offer. 'It's only a matter of time.'

'Jesus!' Price said, slamming his glass down on the coffee table. 'I go away for a few fuckin' weeks, and come back to *this* shit storm. Who'd believe it?'

'Believe it,' Howard said. 'In my opinion they have a case.'

'Yeah? What kinda case?'

'Lennie Golden came up with the licence plate of the jeep. It's Teddy's jeep, no doubt about it.'

'Then it must've bin stolen.'

'Unfortunately not. The description of the two perpetrators matches Mila and Teddy. Besides, she's talking.'

'*Who*'s talkin'?'

'Mila. As I mentioned before, she's told the police Teddy did it. She's also said that he forced her along for the ride. Oh, yes, and she's accusing him of plying her with drugs and raping her.'

'Rape? Are you shittin' me?'

'This is most unfortunate, Price,' Howard continued. 'When the tabloids get hold of it, you won't like it.'

'What does Teddy say?'

'That it was all her.'

'Shit!' Price exclaimed. 'Where *is* the bitch?'

'I told you, she's in jail. I didn't imagine you'd want me posting her bail, considering what's going on.'

'Right,' Price said, thinking of Irena and what must be going through *her* head. She hadn't mentioned a word to him when he'd gotten home an hour ago. She'd merely said his lawyer had to see him immediately, so he'd instructed her to call Howard and tell him to get over to the house. Now this.

'What's the plan?' he said.

'I've already arranged an appointment with one of the best criminal defence attorneys in the state,' Howard said. 'He's prepared to meet with you and Teddy tomorrow. I figured that would give you a chance to talk to Teddy first, hear his side of it.'

'Can't *wait* to do that,' Price fumed. 'I don't get it – I gave the dumb shit everythin' *I* never had, an' what does he do? Pisses all over me. Like I need *this*.'

'I have a suggestion,' Howard said.

'What?'

'Bring his mother in on this as soon as possible. When we go before a jury it'll mean a lot. A boy with a concerned mother sitting in court is a more sympathetic figure than one without.'

'You *gotta* be taggin' my ass!' Price yelled. 'Ginee's an out-and-out coke whore.'

'When did you last see her?'

'What the fuck does *that* matter?'

'Maybe she's straightened out.'

'Not Ginee,' he said grimly.

'So we'll clean up her image for the occasion,' Howard said. 'Dress her in sensible clothes. Pull her hair back, instruct her not to wear makeup.'

'Ha!' Price exclaimed. 'Ginee wouldn't go t' the fuckin' john without stickin' on false eyelashes. Besides, she don't give a shit about Teddy. She hasn't seen him in years.'

'We'll see what your criminal attorney has to say. In the meantime I recommend that you start thinking about it.'

'Maybe *you* should start thinking about *this*,' Price said, almost spitting his fury. 'Your job is gettin' my boy off, an' keepin' the press outta my goddamn face.'

As soon as Howard left, Price summoned Irena into the living room. They exchanged a long, silent look.

'Why didn't you tell me?' he said, at last.

Irena's expression was pure stone. 'I don't understand what is going on,' she said. 'Mila is in jail – I must have money to bail her out.'

'Have you heard what she's saying?'

'Nobody's told me anything.'

'She's tellin' anyone who'll listen that *Teddy* shot the woman.'

'This is difficult to believe,' Irena said.

'Then why the fuck believe it?' Price shouted. 'The witness says it was *Mila* who pulled the trigger. You understand what I'm tellin' you? *She* had the fuckin' gun, an' *she* shot Mary Lou Berkeley.' A vein throbbed in his temple. 'Now she's tryin' t' shift the blame to Teddy.'

'Mila doesn't own a gun,' Irena said.

'Nor does Teddy,' Price shouted. 'But *I* do. And, according to your fuckin' kid, it's *my* gun they used.'

'Where is your gun?'

'Like *you* don't know,' Price sneered. 'You know where I keep everythin', from my grass to my rubbers. You know more about what goes on in this fuckin' house than *I* do. Now go check an' see if my gun is where it should be.'

Irena let out a long, deep sigh. 'I already have,' she said. 'It is not there.'

'Jesus!' Price yelled, punching his fist in the air.

'Mila could not have taken it. I do not allow her free access to the main house.'

'Mila has all the access she wants. She wanders around here whenever I'm out. I *know* she's been in my bedroom.'

'I would never let Mila do that.'

'This is shit!' Price said, thinking aloud. 'An' it'll affect me 'cause it'll be all over the fuckin' tabloids. An' it won't be about Teddy or Mila, it'll be about *me*, Price Washington, the black superstar with the big bad drug habit.' He marched back to the bar and poured himself another shot. 'Thank God Mary Lou was black,' he said, still thinking aloud. 'If she'd bin a white chick, Teddy's black ass would be fuckin' *lynched*!'

'What about Mila?' Irena said. 'She needs a lawyer.'

'Fuck Mila,' Price snapped. 'I gotta speak to Teddy. Go to the school an' bring the fool home. We'll talk about Mila later, after I've heard Teddy's story.'

☆

Teddy arrived back at the house with a lead weight in his stomach – or, at least, that's how it felt. Price was home, so he knew he could expect the worst.

The sad truth was that Mila had betrayed him. Not only had she betrayed him, but she was coming out with a bunch of damaging lies. He was confused and frightened. How was he going to convince people that *she* was the killer, not him?

Howard Greenspan had warned him to talk to no one about the case, so he hadn't. Now he was forced to face his father alone.

Price was in the living room drinking a large tumbler of Scotch, which Teddy knew was a bad sign: since cleaning up his drug addiction, Price rarely drank unless he was under pressure.

'Hi, Dad,' Teddy managed, as he sidled into the room.

Price greeted his son calmly. 'Sit down, Teddy,' he said.

'Yes, Dad,' he muttered, finding a place on the couch.

There was an uncomfortable silence, finally broken by Price who stood in front of his son, glaring at him accusingly. 'Now I want you t' give it to me straight, boy,' Price said. 'An' don'tcha go handin' me no bullshit story. You understand what I'm sayin' here?'

Teddy was flooded with shame. His dad had trusted him and he'd let him down. 'Mila did it,' he blurted. 'I didn't do nothin'. It was horrible, Dad.'

'So horrible you couldn't go to the cops an' tell 'em everything?' Price demanded. ''Cause if you'd done that, you wouldn't be in this mess today.'

'I know,' Teddy muttered.

'You'd better tell me, boy, what the fuck happened here?'

Teddy began to relate his miserable story. All about how he and Mila had gone for a drive, stolen CDs, drunk beer, snorted coke. And when he came to the bit about Mary Lou, he suddenly lost it and could barely speak.

Price turned away from him. 'Mila grabbed her jewellery, an' *you* put it in your pocket,' he said, in a low, angry voice. 'Is that what I'm hearin'?'

Teddy nodded, too ashamed to look his father in the eye.

'Where's the jewellery now?'

'Mila's got it.'

'And where the fuck's my gun?'

'Didn't know it was your gun,' Teddy mumbled. 'She must've taken it.'

'Jesus!' Price said. 'This is a tough one.' A long beat. '*I'm* gonna believe you, 'cause *I* know what kinda girl Mila is. But whaddya think the jury's gonna do, you bein' a black boy an' all, an' she bein' a white girl? That's one big mark against you. An' if Mila gets herself a smart lawyer, they'll dress her up like Little Mary Sunshine, an' make *you* out to be this bad motherfuckin' black asshole influencing this innocent white girl – feedin' her drugs an' shit. *Rapin'* her. You *do* know that's what she's sayin'?'

Teddy's eyes bugged. 'That I raped her?'

'Right on.'

'No way, Dad,' he shouted indignantly. 'She *wanted* me to do it to her. She was all over me.'

'So 'cause she was comin' on to you, you couldn't help fuckin' the little bitch? That your story?'

Teddy nodded miserably.

'Oh, I get it,' Price said sarcastically. 'You go out with her, she screws with your head, *shoots* somebody. Then later you find you gotta fuck her for good measure. That the way this went down?'

Teddy stared at the floor. 'I . . . I . . . thought she liked me,' he muttered. 'Didn't know it was gonna turn into this.'

'You didn't know, huh?' Price said harshly. 'You were with her when she *killed* somebody, boy. You stood back and *watched* it happen. An' you never came to me, never went to the cops. Are you fuckin' *insane*?' He marched back to the bar and refilled his glass. Then he came back and stood in front of Teddy, his eyes glittering with anger. 'I raised you to be a good upstandin' citizen, an' whaddya do? You shit all over everythin' I taught you. Fool!' He shook his bald head disparagingly. 'I can't save you, Teddy. I'll get you the best lawyers I can, but I can't save you. An' don't think *I*'m not gonna be dragged through the mud. Oh, yeah, they're gonna rake it up about me – Price Washington, ex drug addict. Let's hope it don't reflect on my career. Let's get down an' pray you haven't fucked *that* up, too.'

'I'm sorry, Dad . . .'

' "Sorry" don't cut it, boy. You'd better get your black ass up to your room an' stay there, 'cause I can't stomach lookin' at you no more.'

'I gotta talk to Mila,' Teddy said desperately. 'I know I can get her to tell the truth.'

Price gave a hollow laugh. 'Stupid, too, huh?'

Irena, who'd been listening outside the door, took a step back. She felt the same way Price did. She'd given Mila everything she could, and the girl had betrayed her. Mila was a bad girl, she'd bring Irena down, for how could Mr Washington keep her as his housekeeper if Mila and Teddy were up against each other?

If only she could persuade Price to bail her daughter out, then maybe she could talk some sense into her, because if Mila confessed everything, then Teddy would be free.

Irena waited until Teddy pushed past her and ran upstairs to his room, then she knocked tentatively on the door. Price did not answer.

Very slowly she opened the door and peered inside.

Price was sitting at the table, his head buried in his hands. She could be mistaken, but she thought he might be sobbing.

This was no time to disturb him. Very slowly she backed out of the room and closed the door.

Tomorrow she would ask him about Mila.

55

Lucky suggested to Brigette that they get together before the party, but her goddaughter demurred, saying she had a thousand things to take care of. Lucky had asked her whom she wanted invited, and all Brigette said was, 'I'd love to see Gino and the kids, I don't care about anybody else.'

'Fine,' Lucky said. 'I'll put together a list of interesting people.' She didn't mention that Lina was in town; she thought it would be a nice surprise.

Lucky fervently hoped she was wrong about Brigette's new husband, that maybe he'd turn out to be a great guy. She reasoned that if he was making Brigette happy, that was all that mattered. Although, when she'd spoken to Brigette's lawyers in New York, they'd seemed to think that Carlo was on a mission to take control of Brigette's fortune, and they were quite disturbed. 'As you know, Lucky,' one of the lawyers had told her, 'the way things are set up, nobody can touch the bulk of Brigette's inheritance until she's thirty. That means it's secure for another five years.'

'Perfect,' Lucky had said. 'Because if the marriage lasts five years, then it proves she's really in love. And if it doesn't she'll be well rid of him.'

After she'd finished dressing for the party, Lucky had the barman fix her a vodka martini before she strolled casually into Lennie's study. She'd decided that now was as good a time as any to tell him she was producing a movie with Alex. Although he knew she'd been reading scripts, he wasn't aware of where they'd been coming from.

'Hey, babe,' she said, standing behind him, 'time to get dressed. Guests will be arriving soon.'

He was barely able to drag his eyes away from his computer, but eventually he did. 'Don't *you* look beautiful?' he said, letting out a long, low whistle as he checked her out. 'Love your hair that way.'

She'd worn her hair long and wild and curly, the way she knew he preferred it. And she'd slithered into a long red dress, his favourite colour.

'Sweetheart,' she said, massaging his shoulders, 'remember I told you I'm looking to produce a movie?'

'Uh-huh.'

'Well . . . I think I've found the right property,' she said, continuing to knead his back. 'And here's the good news. I've got my co-producer, my director, *and* my star. So I'm considering making an announcement in the trades next week. Naturally I wanted you to hear it first.'

'Sounds good to me,' he said. 'How come you haven't mentioned it before?'

She stopped massaging his shoulders and perched on the edge of his desk. 'Because you've been so totally immersed in your script that I didn't want to disturb you.'

'Yeah, I do get kinda carried away,' he said, smiling ruefully. 'I like what I'm working on. It's a different deal from anything I've done before. Of course, I'll probably never get a studio to put up the money. And since you're not at Panther any more . . .' A big grin. 'Hey, maybe you can slide in a good word for me.'

'If you're very nice to me, maybe I will,' she said, smiling back at him.

'So,' he said, switching off his computer. 'Tell me about *your* movie. What's the story?'

'It's kind of an edgy black comedy with a feminist twist. And, uh . . . Venus has agreed to star in it.'

'Venus, huh? The two of you together will be a trip. Who's the brave man who's agreed to direct this project?'

A short pause before she gave him the zinger. 'Alex,' she said casually.

'Alex,' he repeated, the smile sliding from his face.

'That's right,' she said, speaking fast. 'It was one of the scripts he had in development, and he thought it might be a good vehicle for Venus. So, since he knew I wanted to work with her, he sent it my way.'

'Alex Woods is going to direct your movie,' Lennie said slowly. 'Is that what I'm hearing here?'

'You don't sound thrilled.'

'Should I be?'

'Why not? If I'm doing this, it has to be with the best, and you *know* Alex is one of the most talented directors in town.'

'Alex Woods is a raving egomaniac,' Lennie said sourly.

'He does everything *his* way. You'll be at each other's throats before you can turn around.'

'I think I can handle him,' she said, annoyed that Lennie didn't trust her judgement.

'Yeah,' Lennie said. 'I'm sure you can.'

'What does *that* mean?' she said, her black eyes giving forth major danger signals.

'I'm not happy about you working with Alex.'

'Why?'

'Hey – news flash – the man has a gigantic crush on you.'

'Lennie,' she said, curbing her anger, 'Alex was very good to me when you were kidnapped. He was always there for me whenever I needed support. I love him as a friend, nothing more, so please don't spoil this for me because of some petty jealousy.'

'What would you do if I said I *didn't* want you working with him?' Lennie said, getting up abruptly.

'I don't like people telling me what I can and can't do.'

'Uh-huh, that figures,' he said, walking into their bedroom.

'Are you mad at me?' she said, following him.

'I'd better take a shower or I'll be late for the party.'

'I repeat, are you mad at me?'

He headed into his bathroom. 'I'm not mad, Lucky. You can do what you want. You always have and I guess you always will.'

And before she could say anything else, he slammed the bathroom door in her face.

Why do I have to go through this? she thought, angry and frustrated. *I don't want to have to ask for permission to do anything. I love Lennie. I'm faithful to him. What more can he possibly want?*

And yet, deep down, she knew that if the situation was reversed she'd probably be pissed, too.

☆

Steven stood in front of his bathroom mirror, shaving carefully. He was in a reflective mood. Two people being arrested for Mary Lou's murder had brought back every detail of that fateful night. And now that they'd caught the perpetrators, there would be a trial ahead, which meant that the publicity machine would start again, wrecking his privacy, bringing back all the painful memories.

It was going to be difficult to forget and move on when the story of Mary Lou's senseless murder would be all over the news media every day. And, of course, it would be, all the more so because the boy they'd arrested was the son of Price Washington.

Steven was well aware that he would have to be there during the trial, sitting in the front row of the courtroom every day. He'd told Lucky it was important they present a united front along with Mary Lou's family, who were still totally devastated. Carioca would have to be there too.

God! How could he possibly put his little daughter through such a painful process? Yes, her presence would definitely sway the jury, but there was no way he wanted her to hear the details of that awful night.

Life without Mary Lou did not get any easier. He'd tried to compensate by throwing himself into his heavy caseload of work, but nothing took away the loneliness he felt. At night, in bed, there was nobody lying next to him, nobody to fight over the remote control with; nobody to share a hot dog or a tunafish sandwich with on a Saturday afternoon while he sat in front of the TV watching football. Nobody . . . nobody . . . nobody.

And the sad fact was that he didn't want anybody. Because there wasn't a woman in the world who could possibly replace Mary Lou.

'I'm very, very happy, Daddy,' Carioca Jade announced, bouncing into his bathroom, all dressed up in her best party dress.

'Why's that, honeybunch?' Steven asked, glancing down at his daughter.

'I'm happy 'cause we're going to a party and *I'm* your date.' She tilted her head, gazing up at him, her big brown eyes filled with love. 'Can I *always* be your date, Daddy?'

'You always *are*,' Steven assured her. '*You* are the most important girl in my life.'

'*I* get to spend the night with Maria,' Carioca said.

'Yeah, you haven't done that in a while.'

'She's great, Daddy,' Carioca said seriously. 'She's like my sister.'

He finished shaving and put down his razor. 'She's your sister all right. And don't you two girls go getting into any trouble.'

'CeeCee's taking us to Disneyland tomorrow,' Carioca informed him.

'Disneyland, huh?' he said, reaching for a clean white shirt.

'Daddy?'

'Yes, honey.'

'Where's Mommy?'

He felt the pain as he always did whenever she mentioned Mary Lou. 'You know where she is,' he said quietly. 'Mommy's sleeping with God.'

'Does God have a very big bed?'

'Yes, he does. And all his favourite children curl up in it every night.'

'I wish Mommy could come home now,' Carioca said, her lower lip trembling. 'I wish she could sleep in *our* bed with you.'

'We'd both like that, but it's not going to happen. Mommy was taken because she's so special. You know that, baby, I've told you before.'

Carioca gave a big sigh. 'I know, I know. Sometimes I get sad, though, 'cause I miss Mommy so much.'

'Yes, honey,' he said, sadly. 'Everyone does.'

'Everyone,' Carioca repeated. 'Everyone in the world.'

'And who looks pretty tonight?' Steven asked, quickly changing the subject.

'Me!' she said, giggling.

'And why is that?'

''Cause *I* get to see Brigette,' Carioca said. 'An' *she*'s really pretty.'

'Not as pretty as you.'

'Silly Daddy,' Carioca said, beaming.

Steven reached for his watch. 'I'd better get a move on,' he said. 'We're picking up my friend at the Beverly Hills Hotel, and we shouldn't be late.'

'Who?'

'Uncle Jerry, my partner from New York.'

'Will he have a present for me?'

'I'll be *very* surprised if he doesn't.'

'Okay, Daddy, but hurry *up*!'

'I gotta finish getting dressed first.'

'Okay, I'll wait.'

☆

'I'm, like, *so* honoured!' Lina exclaimed, dazzlingly sleek and sexy in a bias-cut Versace burnt-sienna silk dress.

'You are?' Charlie said, eyebrows shooting up above his tinted glasses as they strolled through the gardens of the Bel Air Hotel.

'Well, of course,' she said, linking her arm cosily through his. 'The great Charlie Dollar picking up little old me. I'm flattered.'

'The doll is flattered,' Charlie said, as if addressing an audience. 'I'm ten degrees away from a freakin' heart attack, and *she*'s flattered.'

'Are you sick?'

'Only mentally.'

'Charlie,' she giggled, 'stop teasing me.'

'What I'm trying to tell you, kiddo, is that I'm an old fart movie star who could drop at any moment.' He sighed despairingly. 'I'm freakin' *old*.'

'Not too old for me,' she said quickly. 'Or anyone else you fancy.'

'I'm thinkin' of marryin' Dahlia,' he said mournfully. 'She's under the impression it's time we walked that thin red line to Dullsville.'

'Oh,' Lina said, not even trying to hide her disappointment. 'Does that mean I shouldn't try seducing you tonight?'

'I'm *thinkin'* of marryin' her,' he said, with an affable grin. 'Not *doin'* it.'

'So sex *is* a possibility?' she teased.

A raunchy chuckle. 'Thought you only slept with me t' get the part?'

'I did. But the sex was *sooo* good, I've decided I want more.'

'Sassy *and* smart,' he said, raising his glasses for a moment. 'I like that in a woman.'

'I *do* 'ave an ego, you know,' Lina said, quite indignant. 'Since we've been making the movie, you 'aven't looked twice in my direction – 'cept as a friend.'

'It's safer being friends with me,' Charlie said. 'I might be carrying all kinds of unspeakable diseases.'

'This is a twist!' Lina exclaimed. 'Usually it's *me* beatin' 'em off with a stick!'

He threw her a quizzical look. 'Are you by any chance chasing me, my dear?'

'Well,' she answered cheekily, 'I wouldn't mind another slice.'

'You English girls,' he said, with a wild chuckle. 'You and your funny language.'

'What's *wrong* with our language?'

'Nothing that a nice fat joint won't cure. Follow me,' he said, leading her down a path to the serene lake where several magnificent swans made their home.

'Oooh,' she said, '*now* you're talking. Got any coke?'

'Don't do coke,' he answered calmly, as if it was a perfectly normal question – which, in the film and modelling worlds, it was. 'A joint takes the edge off, makes me nice and mellow.'

'A joint'll do,' she said.

'You don't wanna get into that whole coke scene,' he lectured. 'Snorting it up your pretty little nose – it ain't lady-like.'

'Ha!' Lina said. 'Lady-like is the *last* thing I am!'

'I never argue with a female,' Charlie said, producing a joint from his pocket and lighting up.

'Good!' Lina said, accepting a toke.

Then they strolled companionably by the side of the lake, sharing the cigarette, taking turns inhaling deeply.

When they were finished, Charlie said, '*Now* I'm ready to party.'

'So am I,' Lina said, winking at him. 'Ready to rock 'n' roll the night away!'

56

'You look like shit,' Carlo said, inspecting Brigette in an arrogant way. 'Surely you can pull yourself together better than this?'

Lately he never had a good word to say. When they were

first together he'd often told her how beautiful she was, especially after they'd made love and were lying relaxed in each other's arms. Now, whenever he opened his mouth, it was to spew forth criticism.

'I can't help being pregnant,' she said defensively. 'Clothes don't hang on me the way they used to.'

'You're an embarrassment,' he grumbled, his handsome face full of disdain.

'I'm doing my best,' she said, fighting back tears, although she really couldn't care less *what* she looked like. All she cared about was the comfort of drugs.

'I can assure you,' he said pointedly, 'your best is not good enough.'

'Carlo,' she said restlessly, 'before we go tonight I need . . . a shot.' She glared at him accusingly. 'You promised you'd get me something.'

'I told you, Brigette,' he said irritably, 'you have to stop depending on that stuff so much.'

'*You* introduced me to it and I like the feeling, so don't try to cut me off because you'll . . . you'll regret it.'

'Are you threatening me?' he said, turning on her.

'Yes,' she answered bravely. 'I am.'

'You're nothing but an uppity bitch!' he said. And before she saw it coming he slapped her hard across the face.

It had been a while since he'd hit her, so she was taken by surprise. She fell back on the bed and before she could stop herself, started crying, engulfed in her own pitiful misery. 'Can't you see I need something?' she sobbed. 'And you'd better give it to me, or I'm not going anywhere tonight.'

'Whiny bitch,' Carlo sneered. 'And to think that *I*, Carlo Vittorio Vitti, married someone like you. It seems impossible.'

'You begged me to marry you,' she cried.

'Don't make me regret it,' he said warningly. 'Now that you are my wife, it is about time you started living up to the title I've bestowed on you. *Not* that you deserve it.'

'Just get me something,' she moaned.

He marched out of the room. Brigette lay on the bed, pulling her knees up and hugging them to her stomach.

I have a baby growing inside me, she thought. *And what am I doing? I'm feeding it heroin, not eating properly, allowing this man to beat me. And yet . . . I don't care, because all I crave is the drugs.*

And she knew she was spiralling downwards, but there was absolutely no way she could stop herself.

☆

Gino had flown in from Palm Springs accompanied by his wife, Paige.

'Whatever you're doing to him, it works,' Lucky said, drawing her stepmother to one side. 'He looks sensational.'

'Gino is in excellent health,' Paige said briskly. She was quite a woman, with her mass of red hair, compact curves, and genuine love for her much older husband. 'He's planning a European tour for us next year. I told him I can't keep up with him.'

Lucky smiled. 'Yeah, my old man's something, isn't he?'

'He certainly is,' Paige agreed. 'And I wouldn't trade him for Mel Gibson!'

Lucky knew that her father and Paige had a checkered past. At one point in their relationship, before they were married, Gino had caught Paige with another woman – the other woman being Susan Martino, his wife at the time. That particular incident had nearly been the end, but somehow or other they'd got through it, and now they were happy in their Palm Springs house, playing golf and poker, and hanging out with their friends.

'Where's Lennie?' Paige asked. 'I haven't seen him.'

'Sulking somewhere,' Lucky said, with a shrug.

'Oh?' Paige said. 'Anything you want to talk about?'

'Not really,' Lucky said offhandedly. 'It's just that I can't be told what to do. It drives me crazy, and Lennie knows it.'

'Hmmm . . .' Paige said knowingly. 'You're exactly like your father. You look like him, you sound like him, you *are* him.'

'I'll take that as a compliment,' Lucky said, grinning. 'Although I'm not too sure about the looking like him.'

'Tell me, dear,' Paige said, always one for a quick gossip, 'what *exactly* is Lennie sulking about?'

'Oh, something stupid,' Lucky said casually, not wanting to make a big deal out of it. 'I'm planning on producing a movie with Alex Woods, and Lennie's under the mistaken impression that Alex will immediately jump my bones. It's quite ridiculous.'

'Well, won't he?' Page drawled, giving her another knowing look.

'Don't *you* start,' Lucky said, with a weary sigh. 'Alex and I are the best of friends. Can't anyone understand that?'

'Maybe you protest too much,' Paige ventured.

'*What?*' Lucky said.

'Nothing,' Paige said, suddenly distracted as she glanced over towards the bar. 'I've got to go rescue your father. He still attracts the women. Look at that silicone blonde draping herself all over him. It's disgusting what these girls will do to get a man.'

'He's eighty-seven, for God's sake!' Lucky exclaimed, quite amused. 'You can't possibly be *jealous.*'

'I've always found it prudent to keep a beady eye on my territory,' Paige said, smoothing down her short dress. 'If you're smart, Lucky, you'll do the same.'

'Right,' Lucky murmured, irritated because Lennie had not yet emerged to join the party, and she hated having to greet all the guests by herself. God! He could be a pain. And yet, she understood him, because in some ways they were exactly alike. Stubborn, stubborn, stubborn.

Still, there was no way she was giving in to him. She'd never objected when he was an actor and had to perform steamy love scenes with sexy actresses. After all, it wasn't as if she was planning a love scene with Alex. They were simply going to work together as friends. What was wrong with that?

Just as she was thinking about him, she spotted Alex coming through the door accompanied by Pia. *Hmm . . .* Lucky thought. *This one is definitely lasting longer than any of the others.*

'Hi, Pia,' she said, lukewarm as the girl came towards her. 'Welcome to our house.'

'We've driven past it on many occasions,' Pia said, pretty and petite in a Vera Wang cocktail dress, her shiny black hair worn in a straight, shoulder-length bob with a fringe. 'Alex always points it out. Last time I said to him, "Alex, if you tell me one more time this is Lucky Santangelo's house, I'll throw myself out of the car screaming."'

'Very funny,' Lucky said. 'I guess Alex feels I'm some kind of a tourist attraction.'

'Leave out the tourist and you've got it,' Pia said succinctly, her almond-shaped eyes never leaving Lucky's face.

Oh, God, what *was* this? Pick-on-Lucky-and-Alex Night? Did *everyone* think they were all set to have a raging affair?

'Where's the happy couple?' Alex asked, walking up to join them. 'I brought them a wedding present.'

'That's nice of you,' Lucky said.

'This *is* their wedding celebration, isn't it?'

'I suppose so. What did you get them?'

'A set of knives.'

'Excuse me?'

'One of those wooden block things where you keep ten lethal knives. It's my standard wedding gift. I figure one of these days somebody'll turn around and stab their partner, then *I* can take the credit. Maybe even make the movie.'

'Alex,' Lucky said, shaking her head and smiling, 'you *do* know you're a little off.'

'You only just realizing that?' he questioned.

Pia studied both of them then, seemingly bored by their conversation, she wandered off to the bar.

'What's up with *this* long-lasting romance?' Lucky asked, nodding after the pretty Asian woman.

'Jealous?' Alex said, grinning.

'*Pleeze!*' Lucky responded scornfully.

'I like it when you get into my love life.'

'Who's getting into your love life?' she said, unamused that he should think she cared.

'You are.'

'Don't flatter yourself, Alex,' she said coolly. 'Oh, and by the way, not a word to Lennie about our movie.'

'How come?'

'Because . . . well, I kind of mentioned it to him earlier and he's not exactly dancing.'

'That's pretty stupid,' he said, plucking a canapé from a tray held by a passing waiter.

'I know, but do me a favour and don't bring it up. Unless, of course, he does. In which case, sort of dismiss it. Tell him it's one of many movies you're involved with, and you probably won't be able to spend much time on it.'

Alex gave her a long, sardonic look. 'Never thought I'd hear *you* talking like this.'

'Like what?' she asked irritably.

'A nervous married woman.'

'Bullshit.'

'Truth.'

'It's merely polite in a marriage to keep your partner happy.'

'Oh, really?' he said, teasing her. 'The only things I've heard about marriage is that once you sign those papers, sex goes out the window.'

'I can assure you, Alex,' she said haughtily, 'that is *not* the case with *my* marriage.'

'I can assure *you*, Lucky,' he said, still grinning because he loved it when he could get to her, 'I believe you.'

They locked eyeballs, challenging each other.

'Where the hell's Brigette?' Lucky said, breaking the look and glancing at her watch. 'I throw a party in her honour and she's not even here.'

'Have you met the husband?'

'I wanted to take them for a quiet dinner last night. However, she informed me they were busy. I have a gut feeling he's going to be a money-hungry prick.'

'What's worse?' Alex asked. 'A plain prick, or a money-hungry one?'

She laughed. 'A prick is a prick is a prick.'

'So eloquent.'

'But of course.'

'I love you,' he said lightly.

'Right back at you,' she said, without taking a beat.

57

Much as he hated doing it, Price contacted his ex-wife, Ginee, with an eye to bringing her into the loop before the press jumped on the story.

'We have a crisis with Teddy,' he said, over the phone. 'I need to see you immediately.'

'Who's this?' Ginee wanted to know – as if she didn't.

It crossed his mind to say, 'Hey, this is the dude who's been paying you all that alimony you sure as hell don't deserve for the last twelve years.' But he held back: he needed something from her, so the deal was to play it like a gentleman. Not that Ginee was any kind of lady – she was a coked-out nightmare, always had been. He'd married her when he was equally out of his head, and the moment he'd stopped doing drugs he'd realized his mistake. By that time they had a kid – Teddy – and a nightmare of a marriage.

Extracting Ginee from his life had taken a long time, for she had not gone without a vicious, dragged-out battle. And when he'd married his second wife – the ten-month mistake – even though it was four years later, Ginee had *really* freaked.

He'd been paying ever since.

'Don't fuck with me,' he said sharply. 'This happens t' be important shit concernin' both of us. Can you come over?'

'Why should *I* come there?' she sneered.

''Cause it's about *your* son.'

'Oh,' she said sarcastically. 'Do you mean the son *you* insisted on having custody of? *That* son?'

Once a bitch always a bitch. 'Quit breakin' my balls, Ginee.' He sighed, hating the fact that he had to talk to her again after all these years.

Her voice curled with sarcasm. 'Still got 'em, have you?'

With great difficulty he kept his cool. 'If it's easier for you, I'll come there.'

'Have your ass here in ten minutes,' she said shortly. 'I havta go out.' And, true to form, she hung up without waiting for his answer.

Swearing to himself, he grabbed a jacket and hurried out to his car, because if he knew Ginee she wouldn't wait.

On the drive over to her apartment on Wilshire he listened to some vintage Al Green, attempting to get his head in a better place. Nothing worked. By the time he got there he was ready to explode. He needed a joint and a drink. And he needed them like an hour ago.

Ginee met him at the door clutching a miniature French poodle in her arms. The surprise was that his once gorgeous ex-wife must have piled on over a hundred pounds. She was now a big fat mama with dyed strawberry blonde hair and an even more belligerent attitude than he remembered.

Mountains of flesh came towards him, clad in patterned leggings and a purple knit top. Huge jiggling breasts, wobbly thighs, and incongruously thin calves balanced on red patent hooker heels. What a sight!

He pretended not to notice her tremendous weight gain.

She knew that he did and it infuriated her. 'S'pose you think I put on a pound or two,' she said, challenging him to say yes.

A pound or two! Was the woman nuts? She was a walking, talking mountain for Chrissakes.

'Can I come in?' he said.

'Ha!' she snorted. 'Too goddamn famous to stand out in the corridor.' She spun around, and he followed her mammoth ass into the apartment.

Her taste level was the same as when they'd parted company. Pink, pink, and more pink. Oversized pink couches, fancy pink cushions and rugs – even a large shell-shaped pink coffee table. Above the fireplace hung an enormous oil painting of a much thinner Ginee wearing a diaphanous gown and leaning on a grand piano. The outrageously vulgar portrait dominated the room.

'You, Price Washington, are a motherfuckin' bastard,' she announced, before he had time to take a breath. 'You ruined my goddamn life, my gorgeous figure, my everything!'

Bad-assed, foul-mouthed drama queen. Nothing had changed about Ginee – except her weight.

'Teddy's in trouble,' he said dourly, sitting down on one of her overstuffed pink couches.

'What kinda trouble?' she demanded, heavy false eyelashes fluttering above her small eyes like a series of trapped birds.

'He's bin involved in a shooting.'

'I knew you could never be a decent father to that poor boy,' she shrieked. 'You got him runnin' around in gangs shootin' people. It ain't right!'

'He's not in a gang.'

'Then what in hell was it? A drive-by?'

'Ginee, I repeat, he is *not* in a gang. This has to do with some girl gettin' hold of him an' leadin' him astray.'

'*What* girl?' she asked suspiciously.

'Mila.'

'Who's she?'

'My housekeeper's daughter.'

'*Jeez!*' Ginee exclaimed. '*That* Russian witch. I coulda told you her brat would turn out no good. You shoulda fired her skinny ass years ago.'

'Well, I didn't,' he answered patiently. 'An' it's not Irena's fault.'

'Nothin' was *ever* that cow's fault,' Ginee muttered, double chins quivering with indignation as the dog struggled to escape from her suffocating embrace. 'She musta bin blowin' you stupid with all the shit you let *her* get away with.'

He focused on the reason he was there. 'Can we concentrate on Teddy?' he said gruffly.

'Sure, honey,' she replied, with a sugary smile. 'All you gotta do is tell me what you want, an' then I'll tell *you* exactly how much it's gonna cost you.'

Money. Oh, yeah, he'd almost forgotten: with Ginee, nothing was ever free.

58

Carlo gave Brigette what she needed, and after a while she felt ready to face the world. She changed her dress, touched up her makeup, piled her hair on top of her head, and after she'd done all that, they left for the party.

'*Now* you look like my adorable Brigette,' Carlo said, taking her hand in his and squeezing it reassuringly as they walked outside to the waiting limo. 'Come, my darling, you must be looking forward to showing me off to all your friends.'

When he was nice it was almost as if she imagined his bad moods. She smiled dreamily. Everything was peaceful. Everything was good ... except that soon she would have to face Lucky and, much as she loved her, in a way she was dreading it, because Lucky was the only person who could see right into the depths of her soul.

You're a big girl, a voice said in her head. *Lucky doesn't control you. You control your own destiny.*

No, another voice argued. *Carlo controls everything you do. You are completely under his influence.*

'Carlo,' she said, settling into the plush leather seat in the back of the limo.

'Yes, my dear?'

'I want you to promise me that you'll be nice to Lucky. It's important to me. She and Lennie, their kids and Gino are my only family.'

'Brigette, Brigette,' Carlo said, shaking his head in a pitying way. '*I* am your family now. You've told me how you were treated when you were growing up. You had a mother who was never around. Your father was long gone, and you were raised by a series of nannies. *I* am the one who will look after you now, Brigette. *I* am closest to you. This Lucky woman is nothing more than a friend.'

'She's my godmother, Carlo.'

'That means nothing – trust me. She will see you are fine with me, and if she doesn't,' he gestured with his hands, 'too bad.'

'Promise you'll be nice,' Brigette said anxiously, dreading the evening ahead.

'Of course, my contessa, I am nice to everyone.' And he smiled his superior smile and patted her reassuringly on the knee.

☆

Lennie finally put in an appearance. By the time he did, Lucky was simmering. First of all, Brigette was unforgivably late for her own party, and Lennie, leaving Lucky to cope with all the guests by herself, had infuriated her.

'Nice of you to join us,' she hissed, as he passed by. 'Sure it's not too much trouble?'

'I've had it with you making all your own decisions without including me,' he said, in a low, angry voice. 'We're *married*, in case you forgot.'

'I *told* you, Lennie, I do not require permission to do what I want.' And she turned her back on him and hurried over to the bar, where Gino was surrounded by an admiring group listening to him tell tales of his early days in Vegas.

'Everyone having a good time?' she asked, falsely cheerful. It was almost nine o'clock. The party had started at seven thirty. The caterers kept badgering her about what time she wanted them to serve dinner. Normally she would've had them start at nine, but since the guest of honour had not yet arrived, she instructed them to try to hold off.

'Where's Brigette?' Gino demanded. 'I'm waitin' to see the kid.'

'She'll be here any minute,' Lucky assured him, thinking that it wasn't like Brigette to be so rude.

Lina strolled over, hand in hand with Charlie Dollar. They looked like a couple.

'Well, well, well,' Lucky said. 'What's this? A new you two?'

Charlie chuckled. 'Do *not* tell Dahlia,' he said, like a naughty little boy caught sneaking candy.

'As if I would,' Lucky said.

'Lina's in my movie,' Charlie explained. 'And she's pretty damn sensational.'

'Oooh!' Lina squealed, thrilled. 'Do you really think so?'

'Wouldn't say it if I didn't, doll.'

Lucky shook her head. 'Charlie, Charlie . . .' she murmured.

'Yes?' he said, with a big, wide, shit-eating grin.

She shook her head again. 'Nothing.' It was no use warning Charlie that Dahlia would not be pleased if he was photographed with Lina. Dahlia suffered the little unknowns who shared his bed for a night or two, but there was no way she'd accept Lina, who was far too high-profile.

'So, where's Brig?' Lina asked. 'I'm dyin' t' see 'er.'

'*You* tell *me*,' Lucky said.

'Hmm . . . she's not usually late,' Lina said. 'Did you tell 'er *I* was 'ere?'

'No, you're the big surprise.'

'I think you'll find *Carlo* is the big surprise,' Lina said, rolling her eyes. 'Can't wait to see 'im again. He's absolutely gorgeous, if you like that type, but I gotta feelin' 'e's a bit of a bastard. I dunno . . . you'd better form your own opinion.'

'Oh, I will,' Lucky said. 'I certainly will.'

☆

Steven's partner, Jerry Myerson, was delighted to be in Los Angeles – even more delighted to be at a genuine Hollywood party filled with glamorous women. Recently divorced for the third time, Jerry was acting like a horny teenager let loose in the girls' locker room. Steven was embarrassed: age did not slow good old Jerry down – he was after action with a vengeance.

'Who's that?' he kept asking, every time an attractive woman walked by.

'Hey, slow down,' Steven said, thinking there was nothing worse than a fifty-something divorced man with a permanent hard-on. 'You've got the rest of the night in front of you.'

'Jesus!' Jerry exclaimed. 'How can you live here? The women are too fucking much.'

'You get used to it,' Steven said calmly.

'Nothing fazes you, does it?' Jerry said, winking at an over-endowed redhead. 'But, then, pussy has never been your burning passion.'

Steven threw him a cold look. He did not think it appropriate that Jerry was discussing women with him so soon after Mary Lou's death.

Carioca had run off to play with Maria. He wished she hadn't, he would sooner have spent the evening with his daughter rather than talking about women with Jerry. Sure, Jerry was his friend and partner, but he didn't need this crap.

'Holy shit!' Jerry exclaimed, eyes popping. 'Now *that*'s what I call a sexy broad.'

'You're giving away your age,' Steven remarked. 'Broad is not a politically correct term any more.'

'Who gives a shit?' Jerry said. 'Look at her – it's that supermodel, Lina. What a body!'

The name sounded vaguely familiar. Steven followed Jerry's rapt gaze, and immediately recognized the girl Jerry was staring at. He'd met her at Venus's party when he'd been standing outside the guest bathroom with Carioca.

'Yes, that *is* Lina,' he said.

'Don't tell me you fucking know her?' Jerry asked, practically salivating.

'Sure, I know her,' Steven answered casually.

'I think she's with Charlie Dollar,' Jerry said. 'Jesus! You can't turn around here without bumping into a star.'

'That's Hollywood for you,' Steven said.

'So if you know her, introduce me,' Jerry said, gulping straight bourbon.

'I'm not about to go over there and interrupt her.'

'You don't have to,' Jerry said, smoothing back his reddish hair. 'She's on her way over here.'

And before Jerry could say another word, Lina was upon them. ''Ello,' she said, with a huge smile directed at Steven. 'Fancy bumping into *you* again.'

Jerry edged forward, dying to be introduced, while Lina gave Steven the famous Hollywood kiss on each cheek. She smelt exotic and womanly. For a moment Steven thought about Mary Lou and the way she'd smelled – sweet like spring flowers. It was a painful memory.

Lina was obviously waiting for him to say something. 'Uh . . . nice to see you again,' he managed. Jerry gave him a sharp dig in the ribs, his somewhat bloodshot eyes begging for an introduction. 'This is my friend and partner, Jerry Myerson, he's visiting from New York.'

'Hi, Jerry,' Lina said, without much interest.

'I'm a big fan,' Jerry said, standing tall. 'Big big fan.'

'Thanks,' Lina said casually, barely looking at him.

'Saw your photos in a *Victoria's Secret* catalogue. My God, they were sensational. You're the best.'

Steven threw him a why-don't-you-shut-up? look, but Jerry was on a roll and kept going. Steven moved away: he'd spotted Venus across the room and was anxious to talk to her.

'You're a bad boy, Steven,' Venus scolded, when he came over. 'You never answer my phone calls.'

'Sorry,' he said. 'I've been so busy at the office, then on weekends Carioca and I usually take off.'

'I'm glad to hear you're spending more time with her,' Venus said, licking her succulent bright red lips. 'You should bring her over to spend the night with Chyna.'

'Can we talk about Price Washington and his son?'

'God!' she said. 'When Lucky told me the boy was involved, I was completely shocked.'

'It'll hit the news any moment,' Steven said. 'I don't see how they can keep it quiet much longer.'

'Oh, yeah, the tabs'll go all the way with this one.'

'Do you *know* his son?'

'Met him once. Price brought him to one of my concerts. He seemed like a nice enough kid.'

'Did he look like a gang member?'

'A gang member? No, why would you say that?'

'I'm confused. Lennie insists it was the girl who pulled the trigger, while the boy stood there watching. Which makes him an accessory. But what I'm hearing from Lucky is that the girl's accusing *him* of doing the shooting.'

'I feel sorry for Price,' Venus said. 'He's a nice guy. This must be such a downer for him. Can you imagine?'

'It might be bad for him,' Steven said harshly, 'but think about what happened to Mary Lou . . .'

'I know, Steven,' Venus said softly. 'We all know.'

59

The woman was young and voluptuous, perhaps in her mid-twenties, and although quite beautiful in a raw and natural way, she was cheaply dressed and nervous-looking. Hanging on to her hand was a five-year-old child – a boy – with dirty-blond hair and green eyes.

The two of them hovered across the street from the valet parking area of Lucky and Lennie's house at the beach. Nobody took any notice of them – if anybody *had* noticed them, they would have dismissed them as a couple of fans trying to get a glimpse of the parade of famous people arriving at the house in the Malibu Colony.

The boy was tired and hungry, he kept indicating to his mother that he wanted a drink. She shushed him. She was tired and hungry herself, for it had been a long day and she had not expected to get to the house and find a big party in progress.

They'd arrived that afternoon on a flight from Rome. Neither of them had ever been on a plane before, and the boy had been sick, throwing up all over her dress. She'd cleaned up as well as she could, but she knew she was not looking her best.

It had taken a while to get through Customs, until eventually she'd convinced the official sitting behind his high desk that they were staying with her aunt in Bel Air and would only be in the country for a few weeks.

He'd nodded and stamped their passports, imagining what it would be like to make love to such an earthy-looking woman. Her smouldering eyes alone would keep him happy for the rest of the day.

She'd felt lost at the airport – it was so big and crowded and noisy. Her son had clung to her leg while she'd tried to discover how they could get to a place called Malibu. She'd had no idea if it was near or far. Fortunately, her English was passable and her looks so appealing that she was able to find out the cheapest way to get there by asking around.

A friendly black porter had given them a lift into the city, dropping them off on Wilshire. From there they'd got on a bus to Santa Monica.

Once off the bus, she'd stopped at a fast-food place and bought a hamburger, which she and her son had shared, then they'd got on another bus, which took them along the Pacific Coast Highway.

As the bus progressed, she'd gazed out of the window, filled with wonderment at the odd array of houses lining the edge of the ocean and the tall cliffs towering over the other side of the road. Her stomach was churning with the daring of this adventure she had embarked on – an adventure she had dreamed about for five years.

America. She was in America.

The thought made her weak with excitement.

60

'Hi, Lucky,' Brigette said, finally arriving at the house.

'And about time too!' Lucky exclaimed. 'I was beginning to think you'd flown back to Europe!'

It was meant as a joke, but Brigette didn't seem to get it. Neither did she apologize for arriving so late, which pissed Lucky off.

'This is my husband, Carlo,' Brigette said, her normally exuberant tone strangely flat.

'Where's my hug?' Lucky said, sussing out the situation. She'd immediately observed that Brigette was thin and jumpy, with blank eyes and a slack expression, whereas Carlo, a tall, good-looking man with arrogant features and long, blondish hair, was glowing with health.

Brigette gave her a perfunctory hug.

You're too damn skinny, Lucky immediately wanted to say. But she didn't, since obviously this was neither the time nor the place. 'Nice to meet you, Carlo,' she said, with a pleasant smile. 'We've all been looking forward to this.'

He took her hand, brought it to his lips and gave it one of those barely there kisses.

A bullshit artist, she thought. *I can recognize 'em a mile off. A bullshit artist, wearing a five-thousand-dollar suit and a twenty-thousand-dollar Patek Philippe watch. Damn! He was spending pretty good.*

'Where's Bobby?' Brigette asked.

Lucky took another close look at her goddaughter. The once vivacious and adorable Brigette was a shadow of her former self. Something was definitely not right.

'He's gone to see your mutual relatives in Greece,' she said. 'Something you might think about doing in the future.'

'Maybe,' Brigette said vaguely.

'We have no plans to visit Greece,' Carlo said.

Who asked you? Lucky thought, as she looked around for Lennie. Where was he now? She couldn't wait to get *his* take on the situation.

'So,' she said cheerily, 'what's with the sneaking off and getting married bit? You *know* we would have given you a sensational wedding. Everyone's disappointed.'

'Brigette and I did not require one of those lavish Hollywood weddings,' Carlo said, with a touch of disdain. 'We preferred to be married at the palace. It has been in my family for hundreds of years.'

'How nice,' Lucky said, with an edge. 'If we'd known, we would've flown over.'

'Sorry,' Brigette said, a touch sheepishly. 'We didn't plan it . . . we just did it.'

'And what exactly is it that you *do*, Carlo?' Lucky asked.

'Investments,' he replied, staring at the exotically beautiful dark-haired woman with the dangerous black eyes. She was not to be charmed, he knew that instinctively. He had to tread carefully with this one.

'Sounds interesting,' Lucky said, deciding that he was an arrogant prick.

'It is,' he replied.

By the time Lennie came over, there was simmering animosity in the air. 'Lennie, meet Carlo, Brigette's husband,' Lucky said.

'Congratulations,' Lennie said, sweeping Brigette up in a big bear hug. 'How's my favourite golden girl?'

'Married.' She giggled, feeling somewhat light-headed.

'Oh, yeah, we know that,' he said, with an affectionate grin.

'Where's Maria and little Gino?' she enquired.

'They've gone to bed,' Lucky said, 'but Steven's around somewhere. And I know big Gino is longing to see you, so why don't we go find him?'

'I'll be right back,' Brigette said to Carlo.

'I'll come with you,' he said quickly.

'I think she's safe with me,' Lucky interrupted, leading Brigette away from her husband. 'So,' she said, as soon as they were out of earshot, 'how *are* you?'

'I'm fine, Lucky. I told you on the phone.'

'You look a little pale to me.'

'I do?' Brigette said, filled with guilt, because if Lucky knew the real truth . . .

'Yes, you do.'

'Too much travelling,' Brigette explained. 'I have *major* jet lag. It's a killer.'

'How about just you and I have lunch tomorrow?' Lucky suggested. 'That way we'll get to talk.'

'We can talk now.'

'Not with your husband hovering a foot away,' Lucky said. 'I *know* what Italian men are like – possessive isn't the word for it!'

'Carlo's not possessive,' Brigette said, springing to his defence.

'Oh, yes, he is,' Lucky said. 'I can tell.'

'No, he's *not*,' Brigette repeated.

'Ah, there's Gino,' Lucky said, refusing to argue with her goddaughter. 'Eighty-seven and still kicking butt.'

Gino jumped to his feet as they approached. 'Hey, kiddo!' he said to Brigette, tapping his cheek for a kiss. 'You went an' got yourself married, huh? An' I was lookin' forward to bein' best man.'

Brigette kissed him on both cheeks, she'd always had special feelings for Gino. 'You're my best man anyway,' she said, adding a warm hug.

'Yeah, yeah, sure,' he said, chuckling. 'Betcha say that to all the guys.'

'Of course I don't.'

Suddenly Lina crept up behind Brigette, placing her hands over Brigette's eyes. 'Surprise!' she yelled.

'Oh, wow!' Brigette said, wriggling free. 'What are *you* doing here?'

'*Bitch!*' Lina said, with a happy grin. 'How come you ran off an' got hitched without me? I thought we were planning a *double* wedding?'

'Sorry!' Brigette said, laughing.

'An' *look* at you,' Lina added. 'You must've dropped twenty bleedin' pounds. What's up with *that*?'

'It's the new me,' Brigette explained. 'I decided it was time to dump my puppy fat.'

'Puppy fat, my ass,' Lina shrieked. 'You're thinner than a stick. Jeez, what's your agent gonna say?'

'Nothing, because I've given up work.'

'*You've* given up work?' Lina exclaimed. '*You?*'

'Yes, me.'

'I don't get it. Why? Are you pregnant?'

She hadn't planned on telling anyone, but this seemed like the perfect opportunity. She took a long deep breath and plunged right in. 'As a matter of fact I am.'

Once again Lucky was shocked. If Brigette was pregnant, how come she didn't look more healthy?

'How pregnant are you?' she asked quickly.

'Only a couple of months,' Brigette replied vaguely.

'Way t' go, girl!' Lina hooted, obviously delighted for her friend. 'Bags I'll be the godmother. Y' know, the *black* godmother. I like it!'

'So do I,' Brigette said, and suddenly she felt like bursting into tears. She didn't know why, but seeing her friends and family seemed to bring back only good memories. Carlo had kept her isolated for so long that she'd forgotten what it was like to be with people she genuinely loved.

I'm doing heroin, she thought. *I'm in a drugged-out haze most of the time. That's how he keeps me under control. I've got to get away from him. He's sucking the life out of me.*

Oh, God, what had happened to her? Was she repeating her mother's pattern?

Before she could think about it any further, Carlo strolled over, placing a possessive arm around her shoulders.

'Well,' Lina said, wagging a finger at him, 'aren't *you* the sneaky one? *Daddy!*'

'Ah,' Carlo said, with a satisfied smirk. 'So Brigette has told you.'

'It's fantastic news!' Lina said enthusiastically. 'Does Fredo know? He'll freak!'

'No, this is the first time we have told anyone,' Carlo said. 'It is indeed wonderful news. I wanted Brigette to share it with the people she is close to.'

Lucky watched him as he spoke. There was something very devious and cold within those icy blue eyes, something she didn't trust. Abruptly she walked away and sought out Lennie to ask him what he thought.

'It's not good,' Lennie said, frowning.

'Why do you say that?'

'I gotta tell you, Lucky, I think she's doing drugs.'

'You mean smoking a joint? What?'

'No. She's on something. Take a look at her eyes. Then notice how thin she is. This isn't our Brigette.'

'Well, here's the big news,' Lucky said, hoping Lennie was wrong. 'She just announced she's pregnant.'

'You'd better have a serious talk with her.'

'We're having lunch tomorrow. I'll find out everything.'

'That's good.'

'What's your take on *him*?' Lucky asked.

'He's not exactly Mr Warmth. What do *you* think?'

'A good-looking con man with a big dick,' she said flatly. 'I can smell 'em at twenty feet.'

Lennie nodded. 'So, Lucky,' he said, trying to appear casual, but obviously bothered, 'have you made a decision about Alex?'

'What decision?' she asked innocently, although she knew exactly what he meant.

'You're not doing the movie with him, right?' he said, obviously uptight.

'Why are you on about Alex?' she said, exasperated. 'We're friends, that's all.'

'Friends, my ass.'

'Don't push me in a corner, Lennie. If I say we're friends, you'd better believe me.'

'Who's pushing? I'm merely asking you not to work with him.'

'That's totally unreasonable,' she said angrily. 'I have a project I want to do, and it happens to be attached to Alex. Big fucking deal. Get over it, Lennie.'

'So you're telling me that, if there's a choice here,' he responded heatedly, 'you'd choose Alex?'

'Are you *forcing* me to make a choice?'

'Jesus! You're *really* starting to piss me off.'

'Oh, like you're not pissing *me* off?'

'I never do anything to piss you off. I'm the perfect faithful husband, and I ask you one little thing—'

'Lennie, can we talk about this later? Now's hardly the time.'

'Whatever,' he said. 'As usual, it's *you* calling all the shots.'

☆

Over dinner Brigette was quite animated. Lucky had surrounded her with the people she was closest to, including Lina, who was all over Steven.

Watching the action, Lucky noticed that the more lively Brigette became, the more withdrawn Carlo seemed to be. She made an attempt to engage him in conversation. 'Where are you two planning to live?' she asked.

'Perhaps we buy a house outside Rome,' he answered restlessly, one eye on Brigette.

'Wouldn't that be lonely for Brigette?' Lucky said. 'Y' know, her being in a strange country where she doesn't speak the language. Stuck outside the city with a baby to look after.'

'Brigette does not need people around her,' Carlo said shortly.

'I think it's very touching that you seem to know so much about her, when in point of fact you've only known each other for – what? Three months?'

'Lucky,' he said, fixing her with a malevolent gaze, 'I realize you have Brigette's best interests at heart, but it is time for you to let go. She is *not* your daughter. She is *my* wife. And I will see that she is happy.'

'I'm sure you will,' Lucky murmured. 'There's only one small thing – she doesn't *look* happy.'

'You are ridiculous,' Carlo snapped. 'And rude.'

'Really?' Lucky said, thinking what a pompous asshole he was. 'I was Brigette's mother's closest friend, and since Olympia is no longer with us, I look out for Brigette. So you'd better treat her right, Carlo, otherwise you'll have *me* to answer to.'

'Is that a threat?' he said, arching an aristocratic eyebrow.

'No threat, Carlo,' Lucky replied calmly. 'I'm merely telling you the way it is. You might have had her to yourself for the last few months, but in future I shall be watching what's going on. Oh, and by the way, I spoke to Brigette's lawyers in New York. There's no necessity for you to interfere in the way her trust is being run. She does not inherit the bulk of her estate for another five years, so I suggest you lie back. In five years, if you're still married, then I'm sure Brigette will be only too happy for you to take over.'

'I resent the way you talk to me.' He bristled, livid that she would have such nerve.

'I'm sorry, Carlo, but that's the way it is. So here's what I suggest.' Her black eyes hardened. 'Get used to it.'

☆

'What kind of music are you into?' Lina asked, toying with the stem of her champagne glass as they sat at one of the round dining-tables set out next to the pool.

'Al Green, the Temptations, Aretha. Y' know, classic soul,' Steven said. 'How 'bout you?'

'Soul's cool,' she said quickly. 'Keith Sweat, Jamiroquai . . .'

He smiled. 'You like to dance, don't you?'

'How can you tell?'

' 'Cause you've been jiggling around in your chair all night.'

She grinned. 'I have?'

'You have.'

She took a sip of champagne. 'Y' know, Steven, you're a *really* nice guy.'

'What makes you say that?'

'Well, I mean, take that friend of yours, Jerry whatever his name is, the one from New York. Every time I speak to him the guy is leering all over me like I'm naked or something. But you, you're just a regular guy. And you *could* be a prick, 'cause you're major good-looking.'

'Don't say that,' he mumbled, embarrassed. 'I'm not an actor. No need to build *my* ego.'

'You're better-looking than any actor I've ever seen,' she said, meaning it. 'You've got that Denzel Washington charisma thing going.'

He roared with laughter.

'An' you got great teeth,' she added with a cheeky grin.

'Y' know,' he said thoughtfully, 'this is the first time I've laughed since Mary Lou died.'

'I told you when I met you before 'ow sorry I was to 'ear about your wife,' Lina said. 'It must've been tough for you.'

'It's beyond tough, it's impossible. Nobody realizes what it's like unless they've lost somebody close to them,' he said gravely. 'There are mornings you barely make it out of bed. All you want to do is pull the covers over your head and stay there for ever. It's the nightmare that never goes away.'

'I can imagine,' she murmured sympathetically.

'Sometimes, when I walk into my house, I almost expect to find her waiting for me.'

'I'm sorry, Steven. What else can I say?'

'Thank you, Lina. I hope you never have to go through it.'

☆

'We're leaving,' Alex told Lucky shortly after dinner was finished.

'Why so early?' she asked, disappointed.

'You know parties aren't my favourite thing,' he said. 'Let's meet tomorrow and talk about the script.'

She hesitated a moment. 'Uh . . . I'm having a slight problem with Lennie.'

'What problem?' Alex said, giving her a penetrating look.

'He doesn't want me to do it.'

'That's crazy!'

'I know. And I'll work it out. But in the meantime, don't call me, I'll call you.'

'What does *that* mean?'

'It means I'm playing good little wife.'

'Bullshit!'

'I promise I'll get back to you in the next couple of days.'

'Are you saying we might *not* work together?'

'Of course we will. I simply have to handle it my way.'

'You know, Lucky,' he said, staring at her intently, 'I'm only going to tell you once—'

'Oh,' she said, challenging him with her eyes. 'What are you going to tell me, Alex?'

'Sure you love Lennie, and he's a great guy. But he's too moody for you. You need somebody more in sync with your lifestyle.'

'Somebody like you, I suppose.'

'You could do worse.'

'Only one problem.'

'And what would that be?'

'I'm a nice Italian American girl – well, actually, leave off the nice. But here's the thing. It's a well-known fact that you only go for Asians.'

'You kill me, Lucky. Call me when you've sorted things out with your husband.'

'Bet on it.'

☆

'So tell me, Princess, am I getting the royal English dump?' Charlie enquired, not sounding too disappointed because he already had his eye on a replacement – a scrubbed-faced TV star with big boobs and trouble in her eyes.

'What?' Lina said, all girlish innocence.

'You've been talking to that lawyer dude all night. The old fart movie star is beginning to feel like a spare prick at a wedding.'

'Oh, Charlie,' she giggled, leaning back in her chair, 'can I help it if I'm in lust?'

'So I *am* getting the good old English dump?' he said triumphantly.

'No,' Lina insisted. 'Me and 'im were just 'aving a very interesting conversation about the environment, that's all.'

'Like, *you* know about the environment.' Charlie snorted.

'I do,' she said indignantly. 'I used to walk in the park in London when I was a kid. I love trees and stuff like that.'

Charlie squinted at her. 'I'm not used to getting the old heave-ho, doll.'

'You've got a girlfriend, Charlie,' she pointed out. 'You're hardly marriage material.'

'Is that what you're looking for? To get hitched 'cause Brigette did the dastardly deed?'

'Not at all,' she said, glancing across the table at Steven, who was now conferring with his friend from New York. 'You've got to admit, 'e *is* cute. And – 'ere's the biggie – 'e's *my* bleedin' colour. We match.'

Charlie jumped on that one. 'Ha!' he said. 'Are you tellin' me I'm too white for you? Is that your current complaint?'

'You're *scary* white, Charlie. Don't you ever go in the sun?'

'Sunbathing's for movie stars who've got nothing else to do.'

Lina clinked her wine-glass with his. 'Anyway, it's not like 'e's asked me out or anything.'

'Oh,' Charlie said. 'And if he did? What would that make me? Second choice?'

She giggled again. 'Better than not being in the running at all, huh?'

☆

Pia was waiting for Alex by the door. 'Sorry, honey,' he said. 'Had to take care of business.'

'You like Lucky Santangelo, don't you?' she said, as they walked out to the parking area.

'She happens to be my best friend,' he replied, handing his ticket to the valet.

'No,' Pia said softly. 'I mean you like her as a man likes a woman.'

'Where do you come up with this crap?' he said, irritated that she knew so much.

'A woman's intuition.'

'I'm with *you*, aren't I?' he said, thinking of what he would do to her later in bed.

'If you had a choice, Alex . . .' she murmured.

'You're full of shit.'

'Am I?' she said. Then, because she was smart, she briskly changed the subject. 'See those two people across the street? They were here when we arrived. They look like gypsies. A child shouldn't be out this late at night.'

'Maybe they're lost,' Alex said, hardly glancing over.

'Do people get lost on the Pacific Coast Highway, and wander down to the Malibu Colony?'

'If you're so concerned, go ask them.'

'I think I will,' she said, crossing the narrow road. The woman stood up from the kerb as Pia approached. 'Excuse me,' Pia said. 'I couldn't help being concerned, seeing you out here all night with your child. Are you all right?'

The woman nodded, clutching her thin sweater across her dress. 'I – I wait to see Mr Golden,' she said tentatively. 'Is he in house?'

'Yes,' Pia said. 'Would you like me to ask someone to fetch him?'

'Please,' the woman said, shivering.

Pia returned to Alex. 'She's apparently waiting to see Lennie Golden.'

'Is she a fan?'

'I hardly think so. She's quite beautiful, and speaks English with an Italian accent.'

'Maybe *I* should talk to her,' he said, 'see what she wants.'

'Go ahead.'

He walked across the road.

The woman stared at him as he approached. He took a good look back and was quite startled by her smouldering beauty. She reminded him of a young Sophia Loren in the movie *Two Women*. Full breasts, long legs, ample hips and a swirl of long, wavy chestnut hair. He wondered if she was an actress – she was certainly lovely enough in a very raw, womanly way.

'You're waiting to see Lennie Golden, right?'

'That is right,' she said, her lilting accented voice barely more than a whisper. 'If I can see him, it would be good.'

'Do you *know* Mr Golden?'

'Five years ago . . . we knew each other in Sicily.'

'You did, huh?'

She nodded.

'What's your name?'

'Claudia. I think he remember me.'

'Oh, yes, Claudia,' Alex said, as it all came together. 'I've got a feeling he'll remember you very well indeed.'

☆

61

'**I wish to leave,**' Carlo said imperiously. 'I wish to leave soon.'

'We can't,' Brigette answered. 'The party's for me, and I'm having a nice time.'

'If *I* say I want to go,' Carlo snapped, 'then we will leave. That Lucky Santangelo woman is a bitch. Make the most of her tonight, Brigette, for I will not allow you to see her again.'

'Don't tell me that, Carlo,' Brigette said, starting to get distressed. 'I love Lucky. I'll see her whenever I want.'

'If we were at the hotel now,' he said ominously, 'you would not dare talk to me like that.'

It was at that exact moment that she realized how desperately she needed help, and right now she was in the only place she was likely to get it.

Perhaps Carlo realized it too, for he was certainly anxious to get her out of there.

Her mind was running in different directions. She had to tell someone what was going on. Maybe Lina. Yes, that was it – tell Lina, who'd alert Lucky, who would come once more to her rescue.

But how could she ask Lucky for help again? She was supposed to be all grown-up. She had a career, a baby growing inside her, and a husband.

No, she couldn't humiliate herself again.

And yet . . . she knew she had to escape, or was she doomed to be under Carlo's evil spell for ever?

'I have to go to the bathroom,' she said.

'Do so,' he said. 'Then we must leave. You will tell them you are not feeling well.'

Her blue eyes searched the party for Lina.

Gotta tell her, gotta tell her, gotta tell her, she thought.

But Lina was nowhere to be seen. Damn!

Outside the bathroom, she ran into Lennie.

'How's my favourite ex-stepdaughter?' he asked.

'I'm great, Lennie,' she said, still looking around for Lina.

'Enjoying the party?'

'It's great.'

'So . . .' he said. 'Little Brigette is having a baby.'

'I certainly am.'

'I was thinking how sad it is that Olympia isn't here to see it – she would have been very proud of you.'

'She would?' Brigette said, reacting immediately. 'My mother never noticed anything I did. I was simply there, Lennie. I was a child accessory.'

'That's where you're wrong, sweetheart,' he said, watching her closely. 'Olympia was *always* talking about you.'

'How could she?' Brigette said. 'She never even *knew* me.'

'You know, Brig, in her own way, she loved you very much. I *know*,' he added. 'I was married to her.'

'Well . . . I suppose she might have been excited about the baby,' Brigette admitted. 'Although she would've hated being called Grandma, right?'

'Oh, yeah,' he said. 'She would've hated *that*.' They both laughed at the thought. 'So, tell me,' he continued. 'How *is* married life?'

'Wonderful,' Brigette said, falsely cheerful.

'You like it, huh?'

'Of course I do. Carlo's very . . .' She searched for the right word. 'Uh . . . special.'

'Wanna snort some coke?'

'Excuse me?' she said, startled, her eyes widening.

'Y' know,' he said casually. 'You an' me – do a little of the white stuff?'

Now she was really disturbed. 'Lennie, what *are* you *talking* about?' she asked agitatedly.

'I know it's what you like to do, Brig,' he said gently. 'I can see it in your eyes.'

'You're wrong,' she said, flushing a dull red. 'Why would you even think that?'

''Cause I used to be into that whole scene.'

'I resent you assuming such a thing.'

'Take a look in the mirror, sweetheart. It's written all over your face.'

'How can you say that?' she mumbled, close to tears.

'Because I'm right. And, since you're pregnant, I was figuring you might need some help.' He took a long beat. 'Is Carlo involved?'

She shook her head. 'Carlo doesn't do drugs.'

'Then why do you?'

Her eyes filled with tears. She wanted to tell him everything, but Lennie wasn't Lucky, he would not be able to save
her. 'I don't understand why you're saying such things to me,'
she cried, pushing past him into the bathroom, slamming the
door behind her.

She stood in front of the marble sink staring hopelessly
into the mirror. Blonde Brigette with the huge blue eyes and
pathetic little face.

Brigette Stanislopoulos – heiress.

Brigette – supermodel.

Lennie was right: all anyone had to do was look at her and
they could see she was nothing but a drug addict.

She was disgusted with herself. Why *was* she doing drugs?

Because Carlo had hooked her up. Gotten her addicted so
that she couldn't stop.

Then she'd embarked on a relationship with him – which,
if she was truthful with herself, was totally sick.

Sometimes he loved her.

Sometimes he treated her as if he hated her.

Mostly he controlled her.

How had she ever gotten into such a mess? This made all
the other dramas in her life pale in comparison.

'Lucky, Lucky, please save me,' she murmured.

No, a voice answered in her head. *You cannot run to Lucky
every time. No! This time you must do it by yourself.*

She splashed water on her face and touched up her
makeup. Then she stood up very straight.

I can handle it, she told herself. *I can handle anything.*

☆

'Steven, can I spend the night with you?' Lina murmured
provocatively.

'What?' he said, not sure he'd heard correctly.

'It's not that I'm forward or anything,' she said, in a low
husky voice, 'it's just that I really want to be with you.'

He took a long, steady beat. 'I thought you came with
Charlie Dollar?' he said at last.

'I did. But I'd sooner be with you.'

He was silent. He hadn't felt like this in a long time. The
excitement of something new. That pounding-heart thing.
Sweaty palms. A feeling of recklessness.

And yet it was ridiculous. He wasn't a young stud looking to get laid. He was a fifty-something widower with a pain in his soul that was too deep ever to go away.

And then there was Lina ... so indescribably lovely. Skin with a dark satin sheen, long luscious black hair, a mouth to die for ...

Who could blame him if he fell?

'Well, can I?' she asked insistently.

'I ... uh ... don't know.' *Yeah, right. Sound like the biggest fool in the world.*

'*What* don't you know?' she asked, leaning into him. And there came that smell again. Warm, exotic, intoxicating.

'I don't know if it's the right thing to do.'

'There is no *right* thing, Steven. We're here, Mary Lou's gone. She wouldn't want you turnin' into a monk or anything.'

No. Mary Lou wouldn't want that. She'd expect him to start living again as soon as possible. And why not? He was so goddamn lonely he could die.

'If you ... would like to,' he finally managed.

''Course I would, otherwise I wouldn't've asked.'

'Then ... all right.'

'All right, 'e says,' Lina crowed, with a big grin. 'Don'tcha know that most men would cut off their right ball for a night with me?'

She was not very modest, but that was okay – he wasn't planning on spending the rest of his life with her. Just one night of pure, unadulterated pleasure. He deserved that, didn't he?

☆

'I told her I thought she's doing drugs,' Lennie offered, catching Lucky on her way out of the dining room.

'What?' Lucky said. 'Why did you do that? I'm seeing her for lunch tomorrow, now you've probably frightened her off.'

'I did it in a very laid-back way.'

'How laid-back can it be when you tell somebody you think they're doing drugs?' Lucky said, exasperated. 'What was her reaction?'

'Naturally she denied it.'

'You should've asked me first.'

'I needed your permission?'

'No . . . but—'

'Why does everything have to be a fight with us?' he said angrily. 'Why is it always a fucking battle?'

'There's no battle. It's you. I thought you'd recovered from the whole shooting incident, but I guess I was wrong.'

'Incident?' he said, outraged. 'Is that how you regard it? A fucking *incident*?'

'You know what I mean, Lennie,' she responded, regretting her choice of words.

'Anyway,' he said stiffly, 'I thought I should warn you.'

'Where is she now?'

'In the bathroom.'

'I'll try to catch her when she comes out, make sure she's not freaked.'

'I'm sure you can do it, Lucky. Let's face it, you always get your own way.'

'I'm getting a little tired of your snide remarks.'

'And *I'*m getting tired of always jumping to your tune.'

'Hey, if you don't like it . . .'

They locked eyeballs, both angry, both refusing to back down.

'. . . I know what I can do,' Lennie said, finishing the sentence for her.

'Fuck you, Lennie. Just fuck you!'

'Thanks. Now I know how you really feel.'

☆

'It's like this,' Steven said.

'Like what?' Jerry replied.

'Well . . .' Steven said, frantically trying to think of a good enough excuse. 'You'll have to get a ride back to your hotel. There's plenty of people who'll be driving to town. Or you can call a cab.'

'Are you shitting me?' Jerry said. 'Why would I need a ride?'

'Because uh . . . I have to leave soon, and I know you want to hang out.'

'Of course I do. It's a Hollywood party, isn't it? There's broads a-plenty, and I don't plan on missing a thing.'

'Exactly,' Steven said. 'I have to meet with the district attorney early in the morning, she's trying to get the case put on an accelerated schedule, so I'm sure you'll understand if I split.'

'You can't stay for another hour?' Jerry said, sounding disappointed.

'You'll get along fine without me,' Steven assured him.

'What am I supposed to do? Walk up to somebody and request a ride?'

'Ask Gino. You know him.'

'Gino's eighty-seven years old. He'll be staggering out of here any moment.'

'Don't bet on it. He's a Santangelo.'

'I forgot about the freaking Santangelos,' Jerry said, raising his bushy eyebrows. 'They can walk on water, right?'

'Only Lucky,' Steven said, straight-faced.

'Yeah, yeah,' Jerry said. 'Okay, get lost, leave your friend here all by himself. See if I care.'

☆

While Steven was talking to Jerry, Lucky grabbed Lina. 'What do you think?' she asked.

'I think I'm leaving any moment with *the* most gorgeous man,' Lina said breathlessly, perfectly happy.

'I'm not talking about your sex life,' Lucky said. 'And, anyway, since when was Charlie Dollar so gorgeous?'

'Not Charlie,' Lina said. 'Steven.'

'*My* Steven?'

'Oh, yeah, *your* Steven. I forgot – he's your half-bro, right?'

'Exactly.'

'I don't quite get it,' Lina said, cocking her head on one side. ''Ow come 'e's black an' you're white?'

'Steven's mother was a beautiful black society woman with whom Gino had an affair many years ago,' Lucky explained. 'It took Steven a long time to track down his family roots, and when he did – we stuck.'

'Holy cow!' Lina exclaimed. 'Life's always stranger than fiction, in't it?'

'You could say that. Especially *this* situation. Now, what's your take on Brigette's husband?'

'What's yours?' Lina countered.

'I think he's after her money,' Lucky said bluntly. 'Can't you see that?'

'I wasn't exactly looking, but now that you mention it I can't help remembering what happened in New York when she thought 'e raped her.'

'Lennie thinks she might be into drugs.'

'Who? Brig?' Lina hooted. 'She won't even smoke a joint!'

'Things change.'

'All I know is that when we girls used to get together on a shoot, y' know, when everyone was doin' blow an' 'aving fun, Brig *never* got involved. Although, now that you mention it, she *does* look kind of zonked tonight.'

'We're having lunch tomorrow. Can you come?'

'If I'm not on call.'

'Good,' Lucky said. 'I've got a hunch Brigette needs us.'

☆

Brigette ventured out of the bathroom, hoping not to bump into Lennie again. He'd unnerved her with his accurate assessment of what she was doing. How did he know?

She wished she could shoot up right now. She needed the feeling of peace and calm it gave her.

Occasionally, in moments of lucidity, she thought about quitting. Only, when she was straight she felt so empty and alone – it was as if she was nobody, nothing, like she didn't even exist. And that Carlo was the only man who would have her because she was so worthless.

Ah, Carlo . . . when he was nice, he was very, very nice . . .

And when he was bad, he was horrid.

'Hey,' Lina said, racing up to her. 'We 'aven't 'ad a chance to get together all night.'

'Oh, hi,' Brigette said.

'Did you get an eyeful of Steven?' Lina said excitedly. 'What a babe!'

'I certainly noticed you lusting after him all through dinner.'

'Was it that obvious?' Lina said, delighted.

'Very.'

'Anyway,' Lina confided, 'he and I are making a discreet exit. And since *you* an' I 'aven't had any time together, I'm coming to lunch tomorrow. I've *sooo* much to tell you. You must've heard I'm making a movie with Charlie Dollar? Is that cool or *what*?'

'I'd love to see you, Lina,' Brigette said wistfully. 'I miss you.'

'You, too, sweetie. I miss working with you, 'aving you disapprove of all the things I get up to. An' I *certainly* miss not telling you all the good stuff. Have I got gossip!'

'I guess I was busy getting married.' Brigette sighed.

'Do you love 'im?' Lina asked. 'Do you really, really love 'im? 'Cause if you don't, get out now, girl. Make a run for it.'

'Of course I love him,' she said defensively.

'He 'asn't got you doing stuff you don't want to, 'as he?'

'What do you mean?'

'You seem kind of – I dunno . . . distracted.'

'I'm not distracted, I'm pregnant.'

'Yeah, well, I guess that'll do it every time.'

Brigette nodded.

'I'm outta here,' Lina said. 'Lucky will set a time and place so I'll see you tomorrow.' She gave Brigette a big hug. 'It's cool about the baby, but listen to me, girl, you *gotta* put on a pound or two.'

'I will,' Brigette promised.

'God!' Lina said. 'Now I gotta deal with dear old Charlie.'

'I shouldn't think he'll mind too much,' Brigette said, gesturing towards the terrace. 'He's making out with that TV actress by the pool.'

'What am I gonna *do* with that boy?' Lina said, rolling her eyes. 'He's, like, *unbelievable*. Oh, well,' she added, 'at least I don't have to say goodbye to him.' And with that she made her way to the front door, where Steven was waiting.

They walked outside, almost bumping into Alex, who was entering the house accompanied by a young woman and a small boy.

'Seen Lennie?' Alex asked.

Lina shook her head. 'He's around somewhere.'

'Thanks,' he said. 'Wait here,' he instructed the woman, stationing her by the door. She stood very still, the small boy clinging to her skirt while her huge eyes darted nervously around the spacious hallway.

'Don't move,' Alex warned. 'I'll be right back.'

He found Lennie drinking at the bar. 'There's somebody here to see you,' he said.

'Who?' Lennie said dourly.

'Come with me and check it out.'

'Y' know, Alex,' Lennie said aggressively, 'I want you to stay away from my wife. I know what's going on, and I don't fucking like it.'

'Well,' Alex said, 'it's not really *your* decision whether I see Lucky or not. It's hers.'

'Fuck you,' Lennie said. 'You're the cause of nothing but trouble between us.'

'I thought you and I were friends,' Alex said.

'That's the way Lucky would like it,' Lennie responded, half drunk. 'But I *know* what you're trying to do.'

'Yeah, well, maybe you'd like to see what *you*'ve been doing. Follow me.'

'What the fuck is this shit?' Lennie muttered belligerently.

Spotting Lucky, Alex waved her over. 'You might want to be along for this,' he said.

'For what?' she asked.

'You'll see.'

The two of them followed Alex to the front door.

Claudia was standing where he'd left her, the child still clinging to her dress. When she saw Lennie, her face brightened. 'Lennie!' she exclaimed excitedly. 'I have prayed for this moment so long.'

'Claudia?' he said, hardly able to believe she was standing in front of him.

'Yes, it is me,' she said.

'Jesus!' he said. 'What are you *doing* here?'

'I came to America to find you,' she said. 'And now that I have, I am the happiest woman in the world.'

62

'I suppose you are satisfied,' Carlo said, his face grim.

Brigette slid along the leather seat in the back of the limo, moving as far away from him as she could. She sensed the mood he was in and did not care to be the recipient of his anger.

'The party was nice,' she said noncommittally.

'Nice for *you*,' he said, steaming. '*You* did not have to sit around and be insulted by that bitch!'

'What bitch?' she asked, with a sigh, for now it would start, the nagging and the screaming and the cold-blooded fury that somehow he'd been slighted.

'Lucky Santangelo.'

'She's not a bitch, Carlo,' Brigette said patiently. 'She's merely looking out for me.'

'Do you *realize* how badly she insulted me?' he said, his voice becoming loud and accusing.

'No, what did she do?'

He reached up and pressed the switch for the tinted privacy glass, cutting them off from the driver. 'She implied that I, Count Carlo Vittorio Vitti, am after your money.' A glowering pause. 'I do not need your money, Brigette, I have plenty of my own. My family goes back hundreds of years. Who are *you*? You're nothing.'

'My grandfather was a very well-respected Greek billionaire,' she pointed out. 'He was a friend of kings and presidents.'

'Pity that your mother turned out to be such a piece-of-shit whore,' Carlo sneered.

'Don't say that,' she cried out. 'My mother might have had her problems, but she was *not* a whore.'

'I abhor your attitude,' he said. 'Try to behave like the wife of a count. I gave you that honour, and you spit on it.'

'Perhaps getting married was a mistake,' she ventured bravely.

'*My* mistake,' he said harshly.

'Then what shall we do about it?' she said, trying to keep her composure.

The thought crossed his mind that if they were to divorce, he would certainly be able to claim millions. But why claim millions when he could control an unbelievable fortune?

'You used to be such a beauty,' he said spitefully. 'Now look at you.'

'What do you want from me, Carlo?' She sighed, tired and dispirited. 'What do you really want?'

'For you to respect me as a proper wife should.'

'I try,' she said wearily.

'Tonight you did nothing to support me.'

'What do you mean?'

'You *allowed* that Santangelo bitch to insult me.'

'I have no idea what she said.'

'I can assure you, Brigette, I will *never* allow you to see her again.'

And he determined that as soon as they got back to the hotel, he would call the airlines and book them on an early-morning flight to Europe, away from the people who dared to threaten his future.

☆

'Slow down,' Steven said.

'What?' Lina said, half-way out of her Versace dress.

'You're moving too fast.'

'For what?' she asked, genuinely confused.

'For me.'

'I thought—'

'Don't think. Slow it down.'

Lina was puzzled. The first thing guys wanted to do was to get her out of her clothes. So what was with Steven and his request for her to slow down? She knew what she was doing. Oh, yes, and so she should, she'd been doing it since she was fourteen.

They'd walked into his house five minutes ago. 'Would you like a drink?' he'd asked.

'Champagne,' she'd answered. And when he'd gone over to the small bar in the corner of the living room, she'd started to remove her dress, thinking he'd be totally turned on. Instead of which he was asking her to slow down. Talk about being embarrassed!

She quickly pulled the top of her dress up, insecure for once.

'I have no champagne,' Steven said, still at the bar. 'Only white wine.'

'That'll do,' she said, feeling awkward, for she really liked this man, and now he probably thought she was the world's worst tramp out for a quick fuck.

He poured her a glass of wine, took a Diet Coke for himself, came over and sat beside her on the couch.

'Lina,' he said gently.

'Yes, Steven?' she said, switching from wild party girl to demure good listener.

'Always let the guy set the pace.'

'Huh?'

'You're young, famous, extremely sexy – not to mention beautiful. I'm sure you're rich, too. So, lay back.'

'I don't think—'

'Listen to me,' he interrupted. 'When was your last serious relationship?'

Her mind started racing, ticking off a list of conquests that included rich playboys, rock stars, media moguls, sports personalities, trust-fund babes – she'd had 'em all.

'I'm not into getting serious,' she said defensively. 'Doesn't interest me.'

'Why?'

Why? Why? Why? Good question. She was twenty-six years old and the longest time she'd spent with any one man was a seven-week fling with an extremely wealthy New York business tycoon who'd used her to irritate his wife, a jaded society woman who was busy screwing their Puerto Rican chauffeur.

'Me mum was always by herself,' she said at last, 'an' she did all right. Brought me up, didn't she? No bloody man 'anging round *'er* neck tellin' 'er what t'do.'

'A relationship is not telling someone what to do,' Steven explained. 'A relationship is being with someone you love, having fun together, caring through good times and bad.'

'Oh,' she said, wondering how she was going to get him into bed, because the more he talked, the more she wanted him. And getting everything she wanted was one of the main perks of being a supermodel.

'All I'm saying,' Steven continued, 'is take it easy.'

'Yes, Steven,' she said obediently, and waited for him to kiss her.

☆

'Claudia, what are you *doing* here?' Lennie said, in total shock.

Claudia smiled at him, a dazzling smile filled with warmth and raw love. 'You said if I ever needed anything . . .' she murmured, her words trailing off as Lucky stepped forward and stared at Lennie questioningly.

'Uh . . . sweetheart,' he said, highly uncomfortable because who in a million years would imagine that this situation could occur? 'This is Claudia. She's the uh . . . person who helped me escape when I was kidnapped. I uh . . . guess I owe her my life.'

'I guess you do,' Lucky said, checking out the curvaceous combination of Salma Hayek and a young Sophia Loren. Lennie had failed to mention how gorgeous his rescuer was. In fact, when questioned, he'd mumbled something about her being a dog.

'This is my *wife*, Claudia,' Lennie said, with a strong emphasis on wife.

'Oh.' Claudia's face clouded over with disappointment – something Lucky did not miss.

Neither did Alex, who was still standing there, an avid observer.

'Where did you come from?' Lennie asked, noting her somewhat exhausted appearance.

'Italy,' she said.

'Italy?' Lucky repeated. 'You mean you arrived today?'

Claudia nodded. 'This is so,' she said. 'We arrive by plane from Roma. Then a kind man drove us to a place where we could get a bus to come here. All I had was your address, Lennie. I was hoping you would still be here. It has been five years . . .'

'I know,' he said, utterly confused. 'So you got on a plane and came here – with the hope of finding me?'

Her eyes shone with sincerity. 'You told me if I ever needed help . . .' she said again.

'Well, yeah, but you should've called or something.'

'Is this your son?' Lucky asked, gesturing towards the little boy. 'He looks exhausted.'

'Yes,' Claudia said. 'He is tired and very hungry.'

'What's his name?' Lucky asked, feeling sorry for the child, who hadn't uttered a word.

Claudia glanced at Lennie, before dropping her gaze to the floor. 'Leonardo,' she murmured.

'Leonardo,' Lucky repeated. And then, even though she knew the answer just by looking at the boy, she couldn't help asking the question, 'Who's his father?'

Claudia's eyes met Lennie's. 'He is *our* son, Lennie,' she

said, her voice barely more than a whisper. 'Leonardo is the reason I am here.'

'Oh, God!' Lucky cried, turning to her husband. 'Your *son*?'

'I – I don't know anything about this,' Lennie muttered, shocked and surprised.

Lucky's expression was icy. 'Why don't we go somewhere where Claudia can explain properly, without half the party listening?' she said coldly, shooting Alex a look. 'Good night, Alex,' she added abruptly.

'Hey, it's not my fault,' Alex said, shrugging. 'She was hanging around outside asking for Lennie. I was only doing my good deed for the day.'

Lucky turned on her heel, furious that on top of everything Alex was a witness to her humiliation. 'Bring Claudia into the library,' she said to Lennie.

Once they were settled in the library, Claudia started to talk, her words directed at Lennie. 'The day we made love I became pregnant,' she said, clasping her hands together. 'After you escaped, my brothers and the rest of my family became very angry. When they discovered it was *I* who helped you I was beaten. Then later, when my baby started to show, I was sent to live with relatives in a distant village.' She hesitated for a moment, overcome with emotion. 'They said I was a disgrace to my family. After my son was born, nobody would talk to me, so one day we fled to Roma, where I got a job. But the money was not enough to make things work. After years of hardship, I realized my son should be with his father, so I brought Leonardo to you, Lennie, in America, where I know he will be well looked after.'

Lennie swallowed hard as the world he knew crumbled around him. He had a child he hadn't been aware of until now. A son. And he knew it would change everything.

Yes, it was true, he *had* made love to Claudia – once. He should've told Lucky as soon as he'd gotten home, asked for her forgiveness.

But he hadn't. He'd figured it was something she need never find out.

Wrong. Because if he knew Lucky at all, he knew that she would never forgive him. Never.

He'd lied to her about another woman, and in her eyes that was about as bad as it could get.

63

When the news hit, it exploded with a vengeance, becoming the lead news story on all three TV networks. Not to mention headlines in the *LA Times* and *USA Today*, even making the third page of the *New York Times*. The tabloids came out in force with a slew of lurid stories about Price's former drug addiction and Mary Lou's long-ago nude photos – as if either of those things had anything to do with the murder.

Price Washington had not realized what big news he was. *Fuck!* This was not the way he'd wanted to make the headlines. If his mother knew – Teddy's grandma – she'd climb out of her grave and beat up on both of them.

Outside his house, news crews and reporters gathered, clamouring for a quote or a soundbite.

This was shit! He forbade Teddy to leave the premises. 'An' don't look out any windows,' he added. 'They're everywhere with their goddamn cameras.'

Mila was still in jail, even though Irena had begged Price to put up bail if it was granted.

'No fuckin' way,' he'd growled. 'She's the one that got Teddy into this shit storm. Let her stay there.'

'If I can see her, I'll make her tell the truth,' she'd said.

'Yeah, sure,' Price had answered disbelievingly. 'You'll let your daughter take the rap so Teddy can go free? Not on my time. You'd better pack your bags an' split, Irena, it's over.'

'I cannot understand how, after all these years, you would tell me to go,' she'd said, in a muffled voice.

'What the fuck am I *supposed* to do?' he'd yelled, filled with frustration. 'How can I keep you with what's goin' on?'

Irena had gone to her room and brooded.

☆

The day the news broke, Howard Greenspan smuggled Ginee in through the back of the house for a reunion with her son. Once inside, she strutted her enormous bulk around the living room like she owned it, which of course she once had – in a way. 'Place is lookin' good,' she said grudgingly, fingering the plush velvet-covered couch. 'I see you redecorated.'

'Be careful what you say to Teddy,' Price warned, hating the fact that she was back in his house, her very presence invading his personal space. 'He's real down.'

'Shit! *I*'m down,' Ginee announced, double chins quivering. '*I*'m the goddamn *mother* of the criminal. You think *that*'s the kinda reputation gonna get me the best table in a restaurant?'

'We made a bargain, Ginee,' Price said evenly. 'You keep your side of it and I'll keep mine.'

'Now, now,' Howard said, playing good lawyer. 'It's important that you two get along, *especially* in front of the boy.'

Price nodded his agreement.

'Price an' I always get along good,' Ginee said, sticking out her mammoth bosom. 'An' I got the cheques to prove it!'

Price glared at her. He was trying to stay calm, even though he was heading for a black funk. His agent had been on the phone that morning claiming the studio wanted to push the start date back on his upcoming movie. 'What kinda bullshit is *that*?' he'd screamed.

'It's a stalling technique,' his agent had explained. 'They're waiting to see which way the case'll go before committing. If you attract the public's sympathy, it'll mean big box office. If you don't, it's disaster time, so they're hedging.'

'Fuck the studio,' Price had steamed.

'Yeah,' his agent had said. 'Like I haven't heard *that* before.'

'What does a girl havta do t' get a drink around here?' Ginee asked coyly.

Price buzzed Irena, who arrived instantly, as if she'd been listening outside the door.

'Christ!' Ginee said, her lip curling in disgust when she saw Irena. '*You*'re still here. What a freakin' joke *that* is.'

Irena avoided eye contact, although it didn't cause her grief to notice that Ginee had put on a hundred pounds.

'Get me a black coffee with a shot of Sambuca,' Ginee ordered, then turning to Howard she added – 'This Teddy crap is upsetting. I gotta get me a lift.'

Howard nodded, wondering how on earth Price had ever been married to this large piece of blubber.

Irena glided from the room. The only lift Ginee needed was around her face.

☆

Teddy combed his hair yet again and pulled a pose in the mirror. He had a definite look. Oh, yeah, Will Smith mixed with a touch of Tiger Woods.

Today he was seeing his mom for the first time in twelve years, and his stomach was turning upside down with fear and anticipation. Would she still love him with all this shit going on? Had she *ever* loved him? Was it true what his father said about her? *Was* she a whore?

Price had taken him to one side last night and warned him, 'Your mom's put on a few pounds. Don't mention it, 'cause she could get nasty.'

Did that mean she was *fat*? It didn't bother Teddy if she was. What *did* bother him was that she hadn't wanted to see him in all these years.

Still . . . seeing her now was better than nothing, because he sure as hell couldn't communicate with his dad. Price's fury was a scary thing.

The news was full of Mary Lou again. Her picture stared out at him from the front of every newspaper. That heart-shaped face and sweet, sweet smile reminding him of that fateful night. Every image of her filled him with grief, self-loathing and a fearsome guilt.

He hated himself all over again. Hated Mila even more. She was a witch. *She'd* done it. *She'd* shot down Mary Lou like a dog. And he'd stood and watched. Done nothing to stop her.

He deserved to be punished – even if it meant being locked away with gang-bangers and thieves and murderers. He deserved the worst.

His dad was right, he should've gone to the cops when he'd had a chance.

But he hadn't. Now it was time to pay the price.

☆

Locked away with a bunch of other females, Mila didn't like it one bit. She especially didn't like the unflattering uniform and the prison guards who seemed incapable of cracking a smile. Bunch of ugly old dykes. She'd be out before they could screw with *her*.

On her second night in jail she got into a verbal battle with a puny brunette, and ended up beating the crap out of the girl. Twenty-four hours in solitary confinement went a long way to raising her status with the bad-ass contingent.

Shortly after she got out of solitary she bonded with her cell-mate, Maybelline Browning. Maybelline was slight and pretty with a baby face and quite an appealing overbite.

'What did *you* do?' Maybelline asked, chewing on a strand of her own wispy pale red hair, a disgusting habit Mila soon got used to watching.

'Shot some black bitch who was getting in my way,' Mila replied, full of bravado. 'How 'bout you?'

'Stabbed my step-grandma with a bread-knife while she was sleeping,' Maybelline said, an angelic smile on her baby face. 'Unfortunately the old cunt didn't die. But that's okay, I'll get her another time. Me or my brother will finish her off.'

'Did your brother help you last time?'

'No. Duke was away, otherwise the miserable old cow would've been dead meat.'

'What did she do to piss you off?' Mila asked curiously.

'Stayed alive after my grand-daddy died. Bitch!'

Mila appreciated Maybelline's style, although her street smarts warned her that Maybelline was a girl to be careful around.

As the days passed, Mila waited for Irena to arrange bail. It didn't happen.

She also waited for Price's expensive Beverly Hills attorney to arrive. That didn't happen either. Instead, a court-appointed public defender came to see her. Willard Hock-smith, a seedy-looking jerk with yellow teeth and bad breath. He was dressed in a mud-brown suit and a frayed-at-the-collar white shirt. She didn't trust him on sight.

'I want out,' she said, glaring at him balefully, as if it was *his* fault she was locked up. 'I didn't do it. Teddy Washington did it. And I can prove it.'

'How?'

'You'll see.'

'Give me whatever you can.'

'When the time is right.'

'I'll see what I can do,' he said. And then she didn't hear from him.

As the days passed, a deep fury started to build within her. It appeared that everyone was against her – even her own mother, who had not come to see her. Surely Irena realized IT WASN'T HER FAULT.

She didn't care, because they'd all pay, Teddy and Price *and* Irena. She had her secret weapon. She had Price Washington's gun with Teddy's prints on. It was hidden away and she didn't want to mention it until she was sure it would get into the right hands. Because cops could be bought, and it would be easy enough for Price to pay someone off.

So she would wait. Until the right moment.

And then, oh, yes, by the time she was finished, they'd all pay big time. Every single one of them.

☆

'Say hello t' your mom,' Price growled, lurking by the door, rubbing his bald head – a sure sign that he was uptight.

Teddy stood in the doorway, frozen for a moment. What was he supposed to do? Run towards her yelling, 'Mommy! Mommy!'

Who was this woman anyway? Nobody *he* remembered. This woman was huge. A mountain. A mountain he had no desire to hug.

'How ya doin', Teddy?' she asked, chewing gum like a cow chewing the cud, lipstick smeared liberally across her front teeth.

'Okay,' he mumbled, unable to match this woman with the picture he had of his mother holding him on her lap when he was two years old. The woman in the picture was a beauty. This other woman was a big fat freak with clown makeup.

'We'll leave you two alone,' Howard said, steering Price out of the room and shutting the door behind them.

There was an awkward silence.

'Got yourself into some trouble, huh, kid?' Ginee said at last, picking up one of Price's TV awards and examining it.

'Guess so,' he said, staring at the carpet, focusing on her low-cut-at-the-front red shoes, from which her toes bulged like a row of fat black maggots.

'It's your fuckin' father's fault,' she said, putting the award down with a bang. 'Bad fuckin' genes. Guess you inherited 'em.' She sighed and fluttered her hand in front of her face. Her painted nails were so long that they curved under at the tips. He wondered how she ever did anything with nails of that length. 'So you wanna tell me about it?' she continued. 'This girl grabbed you by the short an' hairies an' you got all hot 'n' horny, that it?'

'She . . . she influenced me,' Teddy said carefully.

'Course she did,' Ginee said, plopping her heavy frame on to the couch. The springs creaked. 'Any sixteen-year-old hot-rod with a hard-on is gonna get himself influenced by some little honey. Anyway,' she added, twirling one of her large gold earrings, 'here's the thing – ya gotta learn to think with your brain, not your ding-dong. Get it?'

He was embarrassed that she was talking to him this way. Was that how mothers talked to their sons? He had no point of reference.

'I suppose Price has told you the DA's gonna prosecute,' she continued. 'Which means *I*'ll havta be in court every day, sittin' there bored outta my goddamn skull. Course, your father's compensatin' me – an' so he should.'

'How come I never saw you all these years, Mom?' Teddy asked, determined to get some answers. 'Didn't you *wanna* see me?'

'Oh, *pul-ease*. Don't go givin' me that poor-little-boy-lost bit,' she said, irritated. 'Your daddy wouldn't *let* me see you. Only thing *he*'s got on his poor excuse for a mind is makin' money an' gettin' laid.' She tapped her long nails on the table. 'He's a *bad* motherfucker. Paid me to skedaddle, so I went. Couldn't fight him in court.'

'Why?' Teddy wanted to ask. But he didn't.

'You could've come to visit me if you'd wanted,' she added lamely.

'Didn't think you'd see me,' he muttered.

'Anyway, it's old news,' she said, yawning, bored by having to deal with her son after all these years. 'An' I'm gonna havta buy myself a whole new wardrobe.' She glanced at her watch, embedded deep in the folds of her fleshy wrist. 'So *I* gotta get goin',' she said, hauling her massive bulk off the couch, happy to be on her way. 'See ya in court, Teddy-bear.'

Was that it? Was this the meeting he'd dreamed about?

His father was right about her. She was a money-hungry whore with her bright red lipstick, fake eyelashes and maggoty toes.

At least his dad seemed to care about him. This woman didn't give a rat's ass.

BOOK FOUR

Six Weeks Later

64

'**So what** do *you* think?' Alex said.

They were sitting around a big conference table at his offices. Alex and several of his assistants, Venus with her production partner, Sylvia – a gay woman with plenty of attitude – and Lucky, who'd come to the meeting by herself.

'Are you talking to me?' Lucky said, suddenly realizing that everyone was looking at her.

'No,' Alex said sarcastically. 'I'm talking to the fucking man in the moon.'

Her lips tightened. Alex sure turned into a different person when he was working. 'Sorry, Alex,' she said coolly. 'I must have lost my concentration for a moment.' She threw him a long hard look. 'No crime? Right?'

Everyone at the table sensed the tension. 'Hey,' Alex said, 'either you're into this meeting or you're not.'

'I'm into it,' she said, glaring at him.

This was the first production meeting on their movie, working title *Seduction*. Everything had come together fast, Lucky had worked hard to make sure of that. So had Alex. Between the two of them they'd made it happen.

Six weeks had passed since Claudia's arrival on her doorstep. Claudia – armed with Lennie's child.

Naturally, once the story was out, she and Lennie had become involved in a big battle. He'd lied to her, told her nothing had gone on between him and the Sicilian girl. And now, five years later, here she was with his goddamn kid.

'Why weren't you truthful with me?' she'd demanded, hurt and angry.

'I was fighting for my life,' he'd answered, obviously as shocked as she was. 'Claudia was my only way out.'

'I see,' she'd responded coldly. 'You were *forced* to fuck her to get out of there – is that it?'

'Oh, God! Try to understand, Lucky.'

'Maybe I'd be more understanding if you'd told me,' she'd said unsmilingly. 'Why didn't you *fucking tell me*?'

'It didn't seem important enough to risk hurting you.'

'And I suppose some Sicilian hooker turning up with your kid – that *doesn't* hurt me?'

'Claudia's not a hooker,' he'd said curtly.

That's all she'd needed, Lennie defending the girl. 'You know, Lennie,' she'd said icily. 'As far as I'm concerned, you can take off and check into a hotel with your new family. Because I don't care to have either of them anywhere near my children.'

'You're not being fair,' he'd argued. 'I'm trying to tell you, I didn't know anything about the boy.'

'Hey, now you do. *You* fucked her, take the consequences.'

She knew she was being hard-nosed about it, but the one thing she refused to accept was lying, and he'd lied about the most important thing of all. Fidelity.

Maybe she'd have been more forgiving if he'd told her the truth when he'd first gotten back from his ordeal. But he hadn't. He'd insisted that nothing had happened between him and the girl.

Timing was everything. She could kill him. Kill the cheating son-of-a-bitch. He'd ruined their lives.

The day after the party Alex had called, wanting to know everything. She'd refused to discuss it with him or anyone else. It was private.

On top of everything, the court case was coming up and Steven was getting real edgy. The DA had put it on an accelerated schedule on account of all the publicity. This was good, it meant they could get it over and done with.

The other thing on Lucky's mind was Brigette. By the time she'd called the hotel the day after the party, she'd been informed that Count and Countess Vitti had checked out, news that stunned her. She'd immediately called Lina, who knew nothing.

'As soon as I can get away, I'm tracking them down,' she'd said to Lina. 'That bastard has her under some kind of spell and I'm *breaking* that spell – along with his fucking Italian balls.'

Most nights she lay in bed, filled with unrest and confusion about Lennie, remembering the time she'd caught her second husband, Dimitri, with his former lover, flamboyant opera star Francesca Fern. That was shortly before Lucky had had her second encounter with Lennie in the South of France. After that memorable day everything had changed. Their passion was on fire. Nothing and no one could stop their affair.

Alex called a break in the meeting. Grabbing Lucky by the arm, he pulled her roughly to one side. 'Are you planning to concentrate on this project or not?' he demanded. 'I can't work with someone whose mind is elsewhere.'

'I'm *here*, aren't I?' she said stubbornly.

'*You*'re here, your mind isn't.'

'Oh, please, Alex. Sometimes you talk such crap.'

'Producing a movie has to become your life,' he lectured. 'Can you allow that to happen, Lucky? Or are you going to spend all your time brooding about Lennie and his new-found kid?'

'I don't brood,' she answered coldly. 'Lennie's history. We had a few good years together, now he's free to go his way and I'll go mine.'

'You're not very forgiving,' Alex said. 'So he screwed the girl. So what?'

'You don't get it.'

'Did you tell him about us?' Alex said, lowering his voice.

'I've asked you never to mention that,' she said, furious that he was bringing it up.

'I know. But you can't deny it happened.'

'I thought Lennie was dead,' she said flatly. 'It didn't count.'

'Listen,' he said. 'I'd like nothing better than for you to dump the guy, but you gotta think about it carefully 'cause I don't want you dumping him then wishing you hadn't.'

'I hate to tell you this, Alex,' she said, thoroughly fed up with him, 'but what I choose to do has absolutely *nothing* to do with you.'

'Yes,' he said forcefully, 'it does. Because if you're available, so am I.'

'Meaning?'

'You and I should be together. That's where we belong.'

She knew he was mad that the only contact she'd had with him since her split with Lennie was business-related. But, hey, the last thing she needed was an involvement. Besides, he was still with Pia.

Venus came over with Sylvia, interrupting them. 'Y' know,' Sylvia said, somewhat officiously, 'there's still some changes Venus requires in the script.'

'Yes,' Venus agreed. 'The scene where my character's in the swimming-pool. Why does it take place in a pool? A sauna's sexier.'

'Pools are over,' Sylvia added, in case they hadn't got the message.

'You've got to get it visually,' Alex said, irritated that he had to explain. 'I'm not using just any fucking pool. I see a black-bottomed infinity pool perched precariously on the edge of a mountain. That way there's a real element of danger. The audience doesn't know if he's going to push her over the side or not. They simply have an uneasy feeling that he *might*.'

'Or that *she* might,' Venus interrupted. 'I plan to play her as a dangerous woman.'

'I can go with that.'

'Dangerous like Lucky,' Venus said, teasing him, because she knew how he felt about her friend. 'Lucky's my role model, you know.'

'Really?' Alex said.

'Uh-huh,' Venus said. 'Lucky taught me everything about being a real strong woman. And believe me, Alex, some of it would blow even *your* mind.'

'Nothing would blow *my* mind, Venus,' he said shortly. 'I've seen it all and done it all. I'm a weary warrior.'

'And a poetic one, too,' she said slyly.

'Can we get back to work?' Lucky questioned. 'There are decisions to be made.'

☆

Living in a large hotel suite at the Chateau Marmont with Claudia and Leonardo was freaking Lennie out. He hadn't touched Claudia since she'd reappeared in his life, wasn't even tempted. She was unsophisticated and vulnerable, almost childlike in a way. And she was so grateful for every little thing he did.

He slept in one bedroom, Claudia and Leonardo in another.

All he could think about was getting back with Lucky. The problem was that his strong-willed wife refused to have anything to do with him. As far as she was concerned, she'd thrown him out and that was that.

'I have to see the kids,' he'd told her over the phone.

'Get a court order,' she'd replied curtly.

'Is that what you want me to do?'

'Yes.'

Lucky could be a hard woman.

He'd driven to Palm Springs and appealed to Gino. Gino had shrugged and said, 'Hey, you think I can tell my daughter anythin'? She's a Santangelo, for Chrissakes. She does whatever she wants t' do.'

Lennie knew what *that* meant. Lucky made all her own decisions, and whether they were right or wrong, she followed them through to the end.

Claudia, meanwhile, was filled with wonderment at her new surroundings. She ran around the hotel suite touching the furnishings, inspecting the kitchen, staring at the television. America was all new and exciting to her, and she was entranced.

Lennie soon found out that Leonardo had a problem. The boy was hearing-impaired. Claudia's eyes had filled with tears when she'd revealed that such was her brothers' anger at her for betraying the family, that while Leonardo was growing up, he'd endured numerous beatings. 'They punished him for what I did,' she'd explained.

Lennie was filled with guilt. If he hadn't slept with her she'd have led a completely different life.

But he *had* slept with her. Temptation had gotten the better of him, and he'd made love to her and given her a child. Now he had to take the responsibility.

As each day passed, Claudia was there to smile and comfort him, never uttering a cross word. And Leonardo seemed like a good kid. He didn't speak English; in fact, he barely spoke at all because of his hearing problem.

Lennie often found himself staring at the boy. Leonardo

had ocean-green eyes and longish dirty-blond hair. Lennie found the resemblance to him at the same age unmistakable.

He was looking to rent a house to put them both in. He'd also fixed Leonardo appointments with some first-rate doctors, to find out if there was anything they could do. In the meantime, he kept working on his script, but it was not easy to concentrate, especially with the court case coming up in which he would be the key witness.

The media had run with the story as everyone knew they would. Along with Lucky and Mary Lou and Gino, he was also a favourite of the tabloids. Lennie Golden: former movie star, former comedian, son of Jack Golden and a Las Vegas stripper. Once married to the fabulously wealthy heiress, Olympia Stanislopoulos, who'd died of a drug overdose in a hotel room with Flash, a famous rock star. They dragged it all up. Pictures too. Lennie's life flashed before him.

Lucky was also getting her fair share of unwanted publicity. According to the press, she was the gangster's daughter who'd made good. The studio head with the shady past. The woman who'd killed a man and pleaded self-defence.

He knew she must be devastated by all the publicity. Lucky's preference was for staying *out* of the spotlight. He wished he was with her so he could protect her from all this crap. But every time he called and tried to see her, she wanted nothing to do with him.

The last time he'd called she'd been quite even-tempered. 'I understand that you didn't know she was pregnant, Lennie,' she'd said calmly, 'but I'm afraid you betrayed me, so therefore I feel I can never trust you again. And if I can't trust you, I can't be with you. So, please, stop calling.'

Lucky's logic. Sometimes it defied reality.

He'd heard she was forging ahead with her movie with Alex, and that drove him crazy. All Alex wanted was an opportunity to get close to her, then the bastard would move in and cement the deal. Alex was not to be trusted.

Lennie called him up one night when he'd had too much vodka, and Claudia and Leonardo were asleep in the other room. 'Stay away from my wife,' he warned.

'Aren't you separated?' Alex said.

'Stay away from my wife,' he repeated.

'Go fuck yourself,' Alex said.

This situation made Lennie even more uneasy. What was he supposed to do? How was he going to win her back?

The day before he was due to appear in court, he decided to take them both to Disneyland. The day trip was as much for him as for them. He desperately needed to chill out, put things in perspective.

Claudia was excited, Leonardo too. First he took them to the Gap, where they fell in love with everything.

Their excitement made Lennie feel good. If only Lucky could accept the situation. Claudia was a beauty, but she meant nothing to him. He'd clung to her in a time of fear and desperation. She'd been his only hope.

Why couldn't Lucky understand?

65

Mila made a short court appearance where, due to the severity of the charge against her, she was refused bail. The public defender in his mud-brown suit tried to argue on her behalf, but the judge dismissed him with a wave of his hand.

Irena, sitting in the front row, was unable to help, even though she'd gone to the bank and withdrawn every penny of her precious savings to assist her daughter in case they allowed bail.

It was probably just as well that they didn't, for if she'd been allowed to take Mila home, Price would more than likely have kept his threat and thrown them both out. As things stood now, he hadn't mentioned again her leaving.

Mila spotted Irena and bounced a quick look off her. Why wasn't her mother doing anything to get her out? Teddy was free because of his rich fucking daddy. She was locked up because her mother had no damn clout. It wasn't fair.

Irena was torn between wanting to help her daughter and being loyal to the love of her life. For although she'd never told him, Price *was* the love of her life.

Often, from the age of four, Mila had demanded to know who her father was. Irena had always lied, making up some story about an old boyfriend from Russia.

It was not the truth. The truth was too awful for anyone to hear. The truth was Irena's dirty little secret.

She would never forget that fateful night. Price and Ginee were upstairs in the bedroom, stoned out of their minds . . .

They'd kept on buzzing the kitchen with outrageous demands, summoning her, telling her what to do, bossing her around. This was between house calls from two different drug-dealers.

Ginee was Price's girlfriend then, an extraordinarily beautiful woman, with waist-length hair and a devastatingly sexy body.

Irena was in awe of the beautiful black woman, but at the same time she loathed her. She loathed the fact that she and Price were both out of their heads on drugs all the time, and that Ginee was the one who encouraged him to get wasted.

This one particular night they were both completely out of control, and on a twenty-four-hour binge. The third time they summoned Irena to the room, Ginee staggered out of bed wearing nothing at all, waved her inside and locked the bedroom door behind her.

Irena, who was twenty-nine at the time, and quite well versed in the ways of the world, having been a prostitute in Russia for several years, did not think anything of it. However, when Ginee refused to let her out, she began to be concerned. There she was, trapped in a room with her employer and his girlfriend, both naked, laughing, joking and stoned, and she was their prisoner.

'Tell us about Russia,' Ginee said, sprawling on the bed, legs spread. 'You ever get fucked in the good ole mother country? You ever taken it up the ass?'

Price was lying on the bed snorting, smoking, mainlining. He was not really listening to any of this. It was Ginee's idea to torment her.

'I'm sorry?' Irena said, staring at the woman with loathing in her eyes.

'Cut the crap, Irena, we're all girls together,' Ginee said. 'You ever get *laid*? You look like you never get any. You look *real* uptight.'

Price surfaced from his drug haze long enough to say, 'Hey, babe, what's goin' on here? Thought we was gettin' another girl for tonight. You promised me.'

'Irena was supposed t' arrange it,' Ginee slurred, 'but seems she got a soft spot for you herself, Pricey hon. She wants your *fine* black body. An' your fine black ass. Oh, yeah, an' that *fine oversized* black cock.'

Irena backed towards the door, immediately realizing that she couldn't get out because Ginee had taken the key.

'Step outta your clothes, honey,' Ginee instructed. 'An' stop bein' so goddamn uptight. You *know* you're *creamin'* for some action.'

Irena glanced over at Price to see what *he* wanted her to do.

'Yeah, yeah, go ahead,' he mumbled, his eyes glazing over. 'Chill out.'

'Mebbe she needs a drink,' Ginee suggested. 'Loosen up, for Chrissakes, you're not a bad-lookin' fox. Take it all off an' chug a little drinkie.'

Irena shook her head, which infuriated Ginee. 'Whassamatta? You too good for us? You come over from freakin' Moscow or wherever, an' now you're too freakin' *good* for us? You wanna work for this guy, you better get with it. Anyway, 's too late to find us another girl. You're it, hon.'

And with that, Ginee pounced, pulling at Irena's clothes like a madwoman.

Irena didn't know whether to fight back or not. She needed to keep her job, losing it was unthinkable. Would it be such a terrible hardship to sleep with Price? Not if Ginee wasn't around.

Ginee had already ripped off her bra and sweater, now she was dragging on her skirt. Irena did nothing to stop her.

Price attempted to sit up. 'Hey, babe, nice tits,' he said, reaching for them. 'Real nice.'

She decided that if she was going to do it, she may as well make it memorable. She reached up, removing the pin that held her hair in a tight bun. It came tumbling down around her shoulders. Long brown wavy hair complementing her thin face and porcelain skin – a complete contrast to Ginee, whose skin had a dark black sheen.

Then she picked up the vodka bottle beside the bed and took a long swig, thinking, *Why not? Why shouldn't I have some fun? It isn't like I haven't done this before.*

Then she was into it. And Ginee was pawing her, hungry hands everywhere, and Price was watching them, cheering the two women on.

As the night continued, she allowed herself to be used by both of them, soon realizing that the thrill of making love to Price was something she'd dreamed about since coming to work for him.

Later, when Ginee and Price fell into a drug-induced sleep, she'd found the key, let herself out, gone back to her room, and hugged herself to sleep, comforting herself because she knew that nobody would remember except her. Tomorrow she'd be just the housekeeper again, someone for Ginee to boss around.

Six weeks later she discovered she was pregnant. She didn't tell anyone because she *wanted* to have his baby. If she had his baby, he'd *have* to take notice of her.

While she waited to give birth, she made up a story, told him she was pregnant by an old boyfriend, and Price allowed her to stay on. 'You wanna have a kid, go ahead,' he said, in spite of Ginee's extremely vocal objections. Ginee kept insisting that he fire her. Price refused.

When she gave birth, the baby was white, which shocked her, because since arriving in America, Price was the only man she'd slept with.

Because of the baby's skin colour, she knew there was no way she could convince Price he was the father, and yet she also knew that, without a doubt, he was.

She had no choice but to keep her silence. If she said anything, nobody would believe her, and Ginee would force him to get rid of her.

Eighteen months later *Ginee* became pregnant, and because of this she managed to nag Price into marrying her. A few months after that Ginee gave birth to Teddy. It took four tumultuous years for Price to decide he'd had enough. He divorced Ginee, which as far as Irena was concerned was a good thing: she was convinced that if Price didn't clean up his excessive drugging and drinking, he'd be finished.

She'd never told anyone the identity of Mila's real father.

Today there were DNA tests that were extremely accurate. If Mila and Price were tested, they'd be able to tell without a doubt whose daughter she was.

But how could she reveal the truth to him now? How could she tell him, when she suspected that Teddy had been sleeping with his own half-sister?

Oh, God, what was she going to do?

For a brief moment she thought about confiding in Price's lawyer, but instinctively she knew Howard Greenspan would be no help.

There must be somebody out there who could advise her. But until she found them, the only thing she could do was keep her silence.

66

Brigette tossed and turned in her sleep before waking with a start, her cheeks flushed.

She was experiencing the same old nightmare – the nightmare that had haunted her for years.

Tim Wealth.

Smiling.

Happy.

Saying, 'How ya doin', little girl?'

His dead body lying in his apartment, while Santino Bonnatti stripped off her clothes and did his degrading deeds, abusing her and Bobby.

The gun.

Santino's gun.

Lying on the table.

Santino, molesting Bobby, his filthy face a smirking mask.

It was up to her to stop him . . .

She'd crawled across the bed, reaching the weapon, Bobby's screams of terror spurring her on.

With shaking hands she'd picked up the gun.

Santino's gun.

She'd pointed it at him. Squeezed the trigger.

Santino. Blood splattering everywhere. Surprise and fury spilling from every pore.

She'd pulled the trigger two more times, and he had fallen to the floor without another word.

The memories of that fateful day floated around her brain in vivid technicolour and terrifying detail. Now she had an extension to the nightmare.

Locked in a room.

Carlo and another man coming at her with a syringe.

Days.

Weeks.

Maybe even months.

The pure rush of heaven as the heroin hit her system.

Oh, God! What had happened to her? She was pregnant and desperate to get off heroin. But there was no way she could do it by herself. She needed help.

While they were in America she'd planned on telling Lucky, but Carlo had rushed her out of the country before she'd had a chance. She'd argued with him all the way to the airport to no avail. He'd hustled her on a plane to Europe, far away from anyone who could help her. And when they'd arrived in Rome, he'd taken her straight to his parents' palace outside the city, where they'd moved into a suite of rooms at the back. He'd kept her away from everyone, although occasionally she bumped into his mother, a granite-faced woman who looked upon her with disapproval.

What a cruel and thoughtless son-of-a-bitch Carlo was. He'd raped her, forced a powerful addiction on her, and trapped her into marriage. Now he thought he had her exactly where he wanted her. And maybe he did.

She knew that, for the baby's sake, she had to do something about her three-times-a-day habit.

She remembered the doctor in New York who'd told her he could help her, something about putting her on a methadone programme.

'I have to quit,' she told Carlo. 'I know it'll be tough, but I must do it for our baby's sake. I need help. I'm not strong enough to do it on my own.'

'I cannot send you to a clinic,' Carlo grumbled. 'People would know, and they would blame me. If this comes out you would be an embarrassment to the entire family.'

'Carlo,' she said, pleading with him, 'you *have* to get me help. How about that doctor in New York? He can put me in a methadone programme like he said. Can we go back to him?'

It occurred to him that if Brigette was *not* hooked on heroin, she might try to leave him. But then he thought, How could she? They were married, she was pregnant. There was no way she could leave him now, so he might as well help her, because who needed a drug addict for a wife? Especially as one day she would be the mother of his child.

'You are right,' he said. 'I will think of a plan.'

She nodded, relieved. She was prepared to go through anything to get straight.

A few days later he told her to pack a small suitcase and be ready to leave in an hour.

'Where are we going?' she asked.

'To get the help you asked for,' he said.

She was flooded with relief, hopeful that they were returning to New York.

Instead he drove her to the family hunting lodge several hours away in the middle of sparsely populated countryside.

It was a large, overgrown place, deserted and unused because the Vitti family did not have the money for its upkeep.

'Where are we?' Brigette asked, when they arrived. 'This doesn't look like a clinic.'

'That's because it isn't,' Carlo said, unloading canned foods and bottled water into the kitchen. 'You will be fine here.'

'Is there a nurse coming? A doctor?'

'Of course,' he said, his face expressionless. 'I have everything arranged.'

'When will they arrive?'

'I have to meet them tomorrow, bring them here myself. This place is too isolated for them to find without me to guide them. There is no other house for thirty miles.'

She looked at him with hope in her eyes, anxious for the well-being of her baby. 'Are you sure this will work?'

'Yes, Brigette. You wanted help, and I am giving it to you.'

'Thank you, Carlo,' she whispered. 'Thank you so very much.'

67

The first day of the trial, Steven was up at five thirty a.m. After taking a shower he called Lina in the Caribbean where she was working on a modelling job.

'Hello, you,' she said affectionately, taking the call in her room. 'This is telepathy. I was just about to pick up the phone, only I thought it was too early in LA and you'd be snoring.'

'You know I don't snore,' he said, delighted to hear her quirky voice.

'I've 'eard a peep or two,' she said, laughing.

'What were you going to say to me?'

'Oh, y' know, wish you good luck an' all. An' tell you I'm on a plane out of here and back to LA this afternoon.'

'That's great,' he said. 'Only you *do* know that you can't come to court with me. The publicity on this trial is outrageous. If they even get a sniff that you and I are seeing each other . . .'

'Right,' she agreed. 'I 'aven't told a soul.'

'Somebody showed me one of the tabloids last week,' he said casually, trying not to sound as if he cared. 'You and Charlie Dollar walking around the lake at the Bel Air Hotel smoking grass. How do they get those pictures?'

'Some schmuck lurkin' in the bushes with a telephoto lens,' she said, matter-of-factly. 'Anyway, that was before you. I've got a new motto now.'

'And what would that be?'

'BS. An' I *don't* mean bullshit.' She giggled. 'BS stands for Before Steven. Nothing mattered Before Steven.'

'You're a very impulsive woman.' A beat. 'When are you coming?'

'Now, if I could,' she said with a dirty laugh.

'Don't talk like that, Lina,' he admonished.

'Oh, yeah, right. That's how I *used* to talk BS.' She giggled again. 'You're really a big old handsome prude, aren't you?'

'Enough with the big.'

'You should be flattered. I was referring to your dick!'

'Have you got the key I gave you?' he said, choosing to ignore her ribald comment.

'I wear it around my neck when I sleep. It sort of reminds me of you.'

'She's a romantic too.'

'Aren't *you*?'

'I used to be.' He sighed.

'Do you realize I 'aven't even *looked* at another guy since you an' I got together? It's the first time I'm not into eyeballing other men.'

'That's encouraging.'

''Ow about you?'

'I *never* look at other guys,' he said, mock-serious.

'Glad you 'aven't lost your sense of humour.'

'I'll probably lose it today, sitting there staring at that girl's face. Jesus! I'm going to be facing the person who murdered my wife – shot her for no reason. What kind of monster *is* she?'

'At least they caught her. That's *gotta* make you feel good.'

'Nothing's good about this whole mess, Lina. Except now, when I wake up in the morning, I thank God I found you. You've managed to put a little bit of happiness back in my life.'

''Ave you told Carioca I'm comin' t' stay?' she asked curiously, because above all else she wanted his daughter to like her.

'Yes. She's excited. Thinks you're the best thing since fried chicken.'

'*Oooh*, did I ever tell you I can *make* fried chicken?' Lina said proudly, for she was not known for her culinary skills. 'I was 'anging with this rap star, and 'e was, like, into cooking. So he taught me.'

'I do not care to hear what any other man taught you – okay?'

'Okay,' she said, laughing. 'See you tonight. Keep the bed warm. Oh, and, Steven, don't forget, I'll be thinking of you.'

He hung up with a thoughtful expression. He hadn't intended to embark on an affair so soon after Mary Lou's death, but Lina was something else. She was unique, and once he'd calmed her down, and got her to realize that liking somebody did not mean immediately jumping into bed with them, then they'd been able to take the time to get to know each other.

They'd gone out on three dates before anything had happened. On their second date he'd presented her with an AIDS test certificate, and asked if she'd mind doing the same. 'Bloody 'ell,' she'd commented, all haughty and pissed off. 'Nobody ever asked me t' do *that* before.'

'Which is exactly why I'm asking you,' he'd said. 'I have responsibilities. A wonderful little daughter. Not that I'm casting any doubts, Lina, but you don't exactly come across like a vestal virgin.'

'Ooh,' she'd said, grinning, liking him too much to stay angry. 'What's a vestal virgin?'

She made him smile, which was a good thing. And once Carioca got used to seeing another woman around the house, she was crazy about her, too. Not that Lina had moved in, she stayed with them when she was in LA. Most of the time she travelled around the world on modelling assignments.

When they'd first got together, he'd reasoned with her exactly the same way he'd reasoned with Mary Lou at the beginning of *their* relationship. 'There's a big age difference,' he'd warned her. 'You live a different kind of lifestyle. I have a young daughter, responsibilities. We're not a good match.'

She'd held his face in her hands and kissed him very, very slowly, her tongue snaking in and out of his mouth. And suddenly none of the differences had mattered.

He reached for the phone and called Lucky. 'Should I pick you up?' he asked.

'No, I'm taking my own car,' she answered, as she finished getting dressed. 'At lunch recess I'm planning to drive over to the production offices. We start principal photography in a few weeks, I need to see what's going on.'

'What will you do when you see Lennie?'

'Don't worry,' she said calmly. 'I'm sure we'll be polite to each other.'

'That's a relief.'

'The thing I'm really pissed about is the way everyone's being dragged through the tabloids,' she said, putting on a pair of silver hoop earrings. 'Jesus, Steven, I've *tried* to live in a very private way, now they're digging up any kind of dirt simply to sell papers. They're vultures.'

'Mary Lou realized that,' Steven said. 'She's an innocent victim, and look at all the trash they're writing about her.'

'Yes, *and* they're dredging up crap about Gino being a former Mafia boss – which is total bullshit. And me shooting Enzio Bonnatti all those years ago. It was self-defence for Chrissakes. What does it have to do with anything?'

'Self-defence?' Steven questioned, his tone quizzical. 'I was there – remember?'

'Hey,' Lucky said indignantly. 'He tried to rape me. He deserved what he got.'

'And it had nothing to do with the fact that he was the man who ordered a hit on your mother, brother and boyfriend?'

'Steven,' she said, her black eyes glittering dangerously as she cradled the phone under her chin, 'Enzio Bonnatti got his. Santangelo justice works its own way.'

'So I found out.'

'Well, you should know, you were the DA at the time. Talk about fate.'

'Right. I'll never forget *that* day.'

'Neither will I, Steven.' She sighed. 'Neither will I.'

68

Flanked by his publicist, bodyguard and lawyer, Price attempted to enter the courthouse. The media, gathered outside, flew into a frenzy. This was *the* story of the moment, and they were out to capture every single detail. Several helicopters hovered overhead as the press rushed Price. 'We have no comment,' Howard said, as the bodyguard pushed a path through the crush.

Teddy had been smuggled into the courtroom earlier. Price had not wanted his son subjected to the glare of the media. As it was, Price had read things about himself that even *he* couldn't begin to believe.

Howard had suggested that Ginee arrive with him. 'No way,' Price had argued. 'I'm not gettin' photographed with that greedy user.'

'It's good for your image,' Howard had said. 'She's a big fat mama. Every fat woman across America will identify with her.'

'Bullshit,' Price had responded. 'Nobody wants to identify themselves with Ginee. They all wanna look like Whitney Houston. I am *not* being photographed with her. Don't even think about it.'

'You have to sit next to her in the courtroom,' Howard pointed out.

'Fine. I'll do that. Shit! I'm payin' her to be there.'

The criminal defence attorney they'd hired, Mason Dimaggio, was one of the best in Los Angeles. Price was more than satisfied. A large, imposing man with florid features, Mason was a character. He was always a sartorial delight in a three-piece, pinstriped suit, and a large cowboy hat. The suit and the hat made for an incongruous combination, but Mason seemed to know what he was doing, and he had an impeccable reputation. He'd gotten off twin sisters who'd shot their uncle just so they could borrow the uncle's Ferrari for the night. He'd also pleaded the case of a female serial killer, who'd murdered three rich old husbands. Somehow or other, he'd made it look like they'd asked for it, and his client had walked.

'Don't worry about a thing,' Mason had informed Price at their first meeting. 'It'll cost you, but I can assure you your boy will be walking.'

'The sooner this is over and done with, the better,' he'd responded.

'We got the case on an accelerated schedule,' Mason had said with an expansive smile. 'Can't do more than that.'

'What about the girl?'

'Mila Kopistani has a court-appointed lawyer. He takes care of *her*, and *I* take care of Teddy.' A confident smile. 'Now, I ask you, Mr Washington, who do *you* think will come out of this smelling like Madonna on a good day?'

☆

Teddy knew he must look like the geek of all time. They had him in some kind of Brooks Brothers button-down white shirt and a dark blue suit. They'd also insisted that he get a real short haircut. And Mason Dimaggio had forced him to wear glasses, giving him the studious, serious image they were obviously going for.

'When you're on that witness stand,' Mason had informed him, in his loud, booming voice, 'you make sure you talk nicely at all times. No jive talk, no slang.' A long meaningful pause. 'And no black talk.'

'What's black talk?' Teddy had asked rudely, not sure if he liked the overbearing, bossy attorney.

'I think you know what I mean,' Mason had answered. 'If

you listen to me at all times, you'll walk away, Teddy, and the girl will stay in jail. But you start screwing with what I tell you, boy, and it could be *you* who ends up in jail. Remember, initially their sympathy will be with her.'

'Why's it gonna be with her?' he'd asked. '*She*'s the one who did it.'

'That's what *you* say. And, fortunately, so does Lennie Golden. But it's just you and him against this poor little white girl who'll come into court looking as innocent as apple pie. And never forget – you're black and this is America.'

Teddy, who'd never experienced racism, had no real idea what Mason was getting at. But he was prepared to obey him, because Price had impressed upon him that he was fighting for his life, and therefore he realized the seriousness of the situation.

There were times, though, when he couldn't help wondering what was going through Mila's head. She'd been locked up in jail for a while. Was she frightened like he was? Or was she braving it out in her usual sassy way? He'd been dying to ask Irena how she was doing, but Price had forbidden him to talk to Irena about anything.

'I really shouldn't keep her,' Price had griped, 'but my life would fall apart without her.'

After his one meeting with his mother, Teddy had expected her to call, or at least ask to see him again before they landed up in court. She didn't do either. That one visit was it.

Out of the corner of his eye he saw Price enter the courtroom. He was grateful his father was there, for he knew what an ordeal it must be for him to brave the photographers and news crews milling around outside.

Shortly after Price arrived, Ginee made her own flamboyant entrance. She had ignored Mason and Howard's advice about how she should look, and was all done up in a leopard-skin jumpsuit, an outfit that emphasized every one of her overly ample curves. Over it she wore a shaggy red shawl, huge red plastic earrings, and a this-is-my-moment-in-the-sun smile on her overly made-up face.

Teddy heard Mason mutter curses under his breath. Then Mason and Howard huddled in a furious discussion.

Oblivious to the fuss her entrance had caused, Ginee settled in next to Price. 'I was gonna bring my little doggy,' she confided to her uninterested ex-husband, 'only some dunce told me dogs aren't allowed in here. Asshole!'

Price threw her a glare. 'Didn't the lawyers instruct you to dress down?'

'You think I wanna look like some kinda *skank* for all those photographers outside?' she countered. 'This could be a big moment for my career.'

'*What* career?'

'You're not the only one with a goddamn career, Price. After we split I took up singing. An' I have quite a voice.'

'Singing?' he said, choking back his amazement. 'You can't even carry a tune.'

'That's what *you* think,' she replied smugly. 'Truth is, I got a real Diana Ross thing goin', an' plenty of people know it.'

'The whole point of you being here,' Price said, curbing his irritation, 'is to give Teddy a united family image. Right now you look like you wandered in off Hollywood Boulevard.'

'Screw you!' Ginee snapped. 'I'm here, ain't I?'

'You're here 'cause I'm *payin'* you to be here,' he muttered. 'Dress down tomorrow, or don't bother comin'.'

'Screw you!' she repeated.

Price clenched his jaw. Last night he'd heard from his agent that his upcoming movie had been put on hold indefinitely. Fuck the movies! Who needed to be a movie star? He made his living with on-the-edge comedy. There should be plenty of material from this little adventure by the time they were finished.

☆

Sitting in the van on the way to the courthouse, Mila was thinking about Maybelline and what they'd agreed.

'Consider this,' Maybelline had said a few days earlier. 'You got one witness *saw* you do it. And then you got Teddy. Now, if that one witness wasn't around, who've you got? Just Teddy. It'll be you against him. White girl, black boy. Who do *you* think'll win?'

'I thought of that,' Mila said. 'When they posted the big reward, I was planning on hiring someone to put a hit on Lennie Golden. My bad luck I left it too late.'

'You should've known me then,' Maybelline said slyly. 'I could've helped out.'

'Yeah, well, now there's no more reward.'

'You got money?' Maybelline asked, sucking on her hair.

'Me? I'm broke.'

'Can you get any?'

'What do you mean?'

'Your mom works for Price Washington. His house is probably full of stuff. He must have a safe filled with jewellery and cash. Y' know black dudes always keep a lotta cash around, it's kind of their thing 'cause they're raised in the ghetto with no money.'

'There *is* plenty of stuff around the house,' Mila said, thinking about it. 'Price has an expensive watch collection and, yeah, there's a safe in his dressing room.'

'Well, then,' Maybelline said. 'So if you were free, you could get your hands on plenty. Y' know, steal his crap an' make a run for it. Hang out in Mexico until everything cools down.'

'Right,' Mila agreed.

'Or, even better, you could draw *me* a map of the house and tell me how to work the alarm. And you could share with me exactly where the safe is.'

'So you could—'

'Have someone break in.'

'What would be in it for me?'

'I've got this great plan,' Maybelline said. 'My brother will whack Lennie Golden for you.'

There was a short silence while Mila digested this information.

'It'd be cool,' Maybelline continued. 'My brother knows what he's doing.' Another pause. 'You into it?'

Mila's mind was spinning. Only Lennie Golden could finger her. Teddy didn't count. She nodded wordlessly, excited and sick all at the same time.

'I'll ask Duke,' Maybelline said, as casually as if she was asking him to stop by the supermarket. 'He'll go down to the courthouse when the trial starts, follow Lennie home an' blow him away. It's that simple.'

'I like it,' Mila said, a chill coursing through her veins. 'Do you think your brother will do it?'

'Why not? He's got nothing else going for him right now. And Duke'll do anything for me. Did I tell you we're twins?'

'No, you didn't tell me that.'

'We think alike, look alike. This'll be a blast.'

And then, because it seemed that Maybelline was the only person on her side, she told her about the gun with Teddy's prints on it.

'What?' Maybelline said, eyes bugging. 'You've got evidence like that and you haven't told your lawyer?'

'I don't trust him,' Mila said. 'But if Duke can get the gun, and keep it until I'm sure, that'd work for me.'

'Oh, yes,' Maybelline said, deciding that this current scenario could work in their favour. 'He can do that. All you've got to do is tell me where it's hidden . . .'

So Mila had told her. Then she'd drawn a map of the house, pinpointing the alarm system and the safe. She'd also given Maybelline the alarm code.

Now, sitting in the van on her way to court, she wasn't sure if Maybelline wasn't all talk.

Maybe.

Maybe not.

She'd soon see.

69

Brigette thought she was going insane. She'd never known a feeling like this in her life. It was as if her entire body had been taken over by a million demons, and every inch of her screamed aloud for relief.

Carlo had left her in the middle of nowhere. A pregnant woman hooked on heroin.

'I'll be back in a few hours with a doctor and a nurse,' he'd promised, the day after they'd arrived at the lodge.

'Why are you leaving me?' she'd asked, nervous about being by herself in the deserted house with no heating or electricity.

'Because, as I told you before, I have to bring them here myself. This place is impossible to find.'

Now it was a week later and she'd gone through a living hell.

At first she'd been calm, not realizing what lay ahead.

She'd wandered around the ramshackle house, and after a while she'd curled up on a bed and tried to take a nap.

When she awoke she was horrified to find it was early morning and Carlo had still not returned. She'd immediately panicked, for she had already begun to crave the drugs that saw her through each day.

She felt nauseous – nothing new about that, for it was the same feeling she experienced every morning before getting her first shot.

Later in the day the pains started to come. Shooting pains that racked her body, followed by excruciating cramps, diarrhoea, sweating and even more nausea.

By the next day she was screaming aloud, even though there was nobody around to hear her.

Weak and faint, her skin crawling, she'd yelled curses at Carlo for failing to return, realizing the bastard had tricked her. There was no doctor or nurse on their way to help her through this. She was on her own.

As each day passed, she'd wanted to die. But because of the baby growing inside her, she'd forced herself to stay sane.

On the fourth day, racked with agonizing cramps, weak and dehydrated, she'd begun to haemorrhage. Hours later she'd lost the baby.

The pain of the miscarriage was indescribable. Dazed and bloodied, she'd lain on the floor, too weak to move, and thought she was dying. In fact, death would've been a welcome relief.

After a long while she'd managed to crawl into the kitchen and grab a bottle of water to take a few sips.

I will live, she vowed. *I will survive.*

And after that she'd slowly started to regain her strength and sanity.

The baby was a boy. She'd buried him under an olive tree in the garden and said a little prayer.

She wondered how many days or weeks Carlo would leave her alone in the lodge. He'd probably checked into it, discovered how long it would take before she was even vaguely normal.

Allowing her to go through this withdrawal by herself was the lowest thing he could have done.

What if she'd died? Would it matter to him?

No. Why should it? He was her legal husband, and as such he'd inherit plenty.

That's when she started thinking that maybe he had no intention of ever coming back.

Then she thought, *No, he's too smart to do that. He might be accused of murder.*

One thing she knew above all else, Carlo was capable of anything. And it was imperative that she get away from him, otherwise her life was over.

70

Lucky arrived outside the courthouse to be greeted by a blinding barrage of flashbulbs. To her horror she was becoming the tabloids' favourite. Journalists were digging into her life like maggots feasting on a rotting carcass.

Their latest story was all about her teenage marriage to Craven Richmond, son of Senator Peter Richmond. Since Craven himself was now a senator in Washington, Lucky could just imagine his embarrassment at this revelation. Not to mention hers – Craven was a major jerk.

She had nothing to hide. She'd always lived her life in a very upfront, honest way. Unlike Lennie, who was really pissing her off with the way he was carrying on. It was driving her crazy that he'd set up housekeeping with the Sicilian girl in the Chateau Marmont. She had her spies, she knew exactly what was going on, and it didn't please her.

What was Lennie *thinking*? This was no way to win her back. Claudia had come looking for him. Did that mean he'd had to move in with her?

Was he sleeping with the girl? Lucky couldn't believe he'd be so blatant.

He kept on calling, insisting that he wanted her back.

If he wanted her back so badly, why didn't he get rid of Claudia? He could give her money, and put her on a plane back to Italy where she and the kid belonged.

Then, of course, there was the Sicilian girl's identity to take into consideration. Lucky had found out that she was Dona-tella Bonnatti's niece, which made her part of the Bonnatti

family. Surely Lennie *realized* this? Wasn't that enough to tell him *something*?

Now Lennie had a son who was connected to the Bonnattis. It didn't bear thinking about.

Their own children missed him, they asked about him every day. Lucky had told them he was on location, and that they'd have to get used to the fact that Daddy wasn't coming home any time in the near future.

She wanted a divorce. She'd made up her mind. There was no going back, she was too hurt by his behaviour.

Alex was being a real pain. He kept trying to remind her that they'd slept together once. How often did she have to tell him that at the time she'd truly believed Lennie was dead? Plus the fact that she'd been completely drunk and barely remembered the entire episode.

Alex was causing other problems. On the movie he was treating her like someone he could boss around. If this was how he behaved when involved in production, it was no wonder he had such a terrible reputation for being an ogre on the set.

Alex Woods. Troubled genius. Well, he needn't try his little Star Director tricks with her, because she refused to take it.

Casting on *Seduction* was in full swing, and although she hated missing a moment of the action, Steven needed her support in court, and naturally she was there for him.

She also had Brigette on her mind. There was something very troubling about her situation. Why had she and Carlo left LA so abruptly? What was the deal with the way Brigette looked?

After thinking it over, Lucky had contacted her former bodyguard, Boogie, who now lived on a farm in Oregon, and persuaded him to track down Brigette and find out exactly what was going on. 'It's important, Boog,' she'd said, luring him out of retirement. 'You have to take care of it for me.'

Over the years Boogie had been a friend and confidant and she trusted him implicitly. He'd left for Europe several days ago.

Her handsome brother was waiting when she arrived.

'Hey, babe,' she said, kissing him on the cheek. 'Are we holding up?'

Steven nodded. 'We're holding up.'

Lately she'd noticed a new ease about him, which made her think he might have a woman in his life. It was just a hunch, because he certainly hadn't said a word. 'Don't rush into anything,' she wanted to warn him. 'Take your time.'

But who was she to give lectures on relationships?

☆

The deputy DA was a woman, Penelope McKay, early forties, attractive and business-like. Steven liked her, because although she presented a cool, calm exterior he knew her to be a tough one.

She nodded at Steven when he entered the courtroom. He nodded back. He knew he would not be called as a witness today because the first day of the trial was a settling-in period when both sides presented their opening statements.

He noticed Mary Lou's family sitting together in the middle of the courtroom, her mother, aunt and various cousins. He hadn't brought Carioca with him, because although he knew it was a good move as far as the jury was concerned, it was also bad for Carioca. He didn't want her exposed to the media circus this early on. In fact, he was seriously considering not bringing her at all.

Jury selection had taken place the previous week. There were two sets of jurors, one for Mila and one for Teddy. Steven took a seat near the front, and waited for them to file in so he could check them out. He had an eye for jurors: experience usually told him which way they'd go.

Penelope McKay had informed him that they'd selected an interesting mixed group. Teddy's jury was a perfect balance of six men and six women. Three of the women were black, as were two of the men. There was also an Asian woman and two Hispanic men. The rest of the jurors were white. Mila's jury was mostly women, with only two men included.

Steven was well aware that when it was his time to get on the witness stand he should play to the women. He didn't fool himself: his appeal to the opposite sex had been one of his greatest assets as a successful lawyer. Women always fell for his looks. At first he'd tried not to use it – it had seemed like a cheap ploy – but now, he thought, *what the hell*? Jerry had taught him to go with what he had, and he planned to.

Before the judge arrived, Steven got up and went over to

Mary Lou's family, greeting them all. Her mother had tears in her eyes. 'Why?' she said to Steven, desperately clutching a framed photo of Mary Lou on her lap. 'Why?'

It was a question he had asked himself on many a sleepless night.

☆

When Mila was brought into the courtroom there was a hush. Everyone wanted to get a look at the girl at the centre of this drama. She was dressed in a plain white blouse, below-the-knee blue skirt and penny loafers. Her hair, recently white blonde, was back to its natural shade of brown. She wore little makeup and no jewellery. Her expression was as demure as she could make it.

Maybelline had given her advice on how to come across. 'I know it's a drag,' she'd said, 'but you gotta play to the stupid jury. Get their sympathy.'

So Mila had followed her advice, although she'd have preferred to tell them all to go fuck themselves. Mila did not care to be judged by anyone.

Her narrow eyes raked the courtroom. Bunch of wankers come to watch.

Willard Hocksmith, her lawyer, touched her arm. His suit smelt of mothballs, he gave her the creeps. 'What?' she snapped, pulling away.

'Put a pleasant expression on your face,' Willard whispered, his bad breath disgusting her.

'Why?' she whispered back. 'They all hate me. I'll never get a fair trial.'

She didn't look at Teddy, even though he was only a few feet away.

Teddy. What a pathetic dork.

Soon she'd finish him off for good.

☆

Penelope McKay had attitude and style, all of which impressed Lucky, and she listened carefully as the deputy DA presented the case for the prosecution.

As Penelope spoke, Lucky inspected the jurors. Steven had taught her plenty about reading people's faces, and she was good at it. She imagined being one of them, sitting in their place and listening to the case. Who would have their sympathy? Teddy Washington, rich son of a famous superstar? Mila Kopistani, an ordinary-looking girl of Russian descent, arrogant and pinch-faced?

Or Mary Lou Berkeley, a gorgeous young black actress murdered in her prime, and Lennie Golden, also shot?

Lucky studied the defendants. Teddy, the boy, looked scared shitless. And Mila Kopistani, yes, definitely guilty. Lucky didn't need to sit through the trial to realize *that*. Lennie's word was enough. He'd told her all about the hate in the girl's voice and the way she'd lifted her gun and shot Mary Lou without giving it a second thought.

Lucky did not feel sorry for either of them. Play with guns and you get hurt. This girl had shot Mary Lou in cold blood, and for that she deserved to be locked away for a long, long time.

And if she wasn't . . .

Santangelo justice was not a bad thing.

71

Duke Browning was twenty-five and a psychopath. Baby-faced, of medium height, slim and well dressed in grey pants and a preppie sweater, he sat in a stolen car across the street from Price Washington's house, watching and waiting.

He observed Price's exit early in the morning, thinking to himself that this was one stylish dude. Black guys, when they possessed style, had it going for them. As far as Duke was concerned, black guys had always known how to have a better time than their white brothers. They were better dancers, better dressers and, from what his ladyfriends had told him, certainly better in the sack.

Duke reached in his pocket, removing a small bottle of Binaca spray. He opened his mouth and took a couple of hits. Keeping fresh was important to Duke. He sweetened his breath every hour, and carried a toothbrush, which he always tried to use after meals. First thing every morning he took a shower; if he happened to be home at lunch, he jumped in another time; before going out at night, shower number three; and finally, before bed, one last wash-down.

Cleanliness was next to godliness. Duke Browning knew that only too well.

Shortly after Price left his house, a woman appeared. Obviously the Russian housekeeper: he'd had a description of her from his sister.

Poor Maybelline, stuck in jail awaiting trial. At least she seemed to be making the best of it. *Making connections*, that's what Grandpa Harry had always taught them. *Making connections*, according to Grandpa Harry, was the most important thing a man or a woman could do.

Grandpa Harry had been a highly respected con man, and fortunately he'd done very well at it. He'd taught Duke and his sister a thing or two when they were growing up. Oh, yes, Duke and Maybelline had had quite an education.

Their parents had been killed in a car crash when they were eight. A somewhat eccentric couple, they'd named *him* after the famous jazz musician Duke Ellington, and Maybelline after a makeup company. She wasn't thrilled with her name. He loved his.

After the demise of their parents, they'd been sent to live with Grandpa Harry, the only sour note being Harry's second wife, step-grandma Renee, a bitch on roller skates with an insatiable appetite for money. Maybelline loathed Renee, and Renee loathed her back.

Since Harry's unfortunate death – he'd died choking on a piece of undercooked liver – they'd all lived together in a rambling Hollywood Hills house, left to the three of them by Harry.

Not any more. Maybelline had ruined that cushy set-up with her vicious, unpredictable moods. One day he'd have to teach her how to control that nasty little temper. It got her into more trouble . . .

Duke was sad that his sister was languishing in jail. He missed her. They'd done everything together. Of course, if Maybelline had exhibited more sense she would've waited for *him* before stabbing Renee with the stupid bread-knife. What a *dumb* thing to do. What was she *thinking*?

If he'd been there – instead of doing time in Florida for a series of rapes – he would have come up with a far better way to get rid of Renee. And he certainly wouldn't've gotten caught.

He waited five minutes after the Russian woman's departure before alighting from the car and slowly crossing the street. Then he strolled casually up to the front door and rang the bell.

Consuella answered. Consuella was Hispanic and pretty with a round ass and big belly.

'Good morning,' Duke said politely, flashing a phoney identification card. 'I'm from the DA's office. I've been sent to collect some items from Teddy Washington's room. Is it all right if I come in? Or would you prefer me to return later?'

Consuella regarded the well-dressed, nice-looking man and decided it was perfectly okay to let him in. After all, if he was from the DA's office, what could be wrong about it?

'Come in, please,' she said, holding open the front door.

And Duke entered the house. An invited guest.

72

Lucky spent the entire morning in court. As soon as they called lunch recess, she hurried off to join the group at Alex's production office.

When she arrived, his Asian assistant, Lili, stopped her outside the conference room. 'They've already seen seventeen actors this morning,' Lili confided, 'every one of them quite gorgeous. Right now they have a young TV actor in there.'

'Has Alex liked any of them?' Lucky asked.

'No,' Lili replied. 'However, Venus is perfectly happy. At the last moment she decided to come in and read with all of them.'

'Hmm . . . I wonder how Cooper will feel about *that*,' Lucky said, thinking of Venus's movie star husband, who had a definite jealous streak.

'Not too happy,' Lili said, with an enigmatic smile.

Lucky snuck into the conference room and took a seat next to Mary, the casting director, with whom Alex had worked on five movies and whom he trusted implicitly. Venus was reading through a scene with a young, good-looking actor.

Alex glanced up. 'Everything okay?' he mouthed.

She nodded.

When the TV actor had done his stuff, and everyone had

told him how excellent he was, and Mary had said that they'd contact his agent, Alex stood up and announced, 'Time for a break. I've got actor phobia. They're all too goddamn eager.'

'Interesting morning?' Lucky asked.

'You missed it,' he said, giving her a quick kiss on the cheek.

'Oh, boy, did you miss it!' Venus said, joining in. 'There sure are some hot and horny guys in this town. I can't wait to get home and tell Cooper how old and decrepit he is!'

'That'll be good for your marriage,' Lucky remarked drily, groping in her purse for a cigarette.

'It'll do him good to know about all the studly competition floating about.'

'Competition? Or great butts?'

Alex shook his head. 'You girls! Is this the way you talk about guys?'

'Yes, when we're being *clean*,' Venus said, fluffing out her platinum hair.

'Was there anyone *really* exciting?' Lucky asked.

'A couple of possibles,' Alex said. 'Nobody special. How about you, Venus? See anything big in the talent department?'

'I thought that Jack Something guy was kind of great. He had intense eyes and great shoulders.'

'Too old,' Alex said, dismissing him instantly.

'Oh, right,' Venus responded sarcastically. 'He must've been all of twenty-five, *definitely* too old.'

'Hey, c'mon, you know what I mean. The character in the script is twenty. Kind of a young Richard Gere.'

Sylvia put in her two cents. 'I liked the second actor we saw today,' she said. 'He had a lot of sexual energy.'

'Bad skin,' Venus said. 'I saw a guy on TV the other night. He had a small role in one of those sitcoms but, boy, he really buzzed the screen.'

'So tell Mary, and she'll get him in,' Alex said.

'Dunno his name,' Venus said vaguely.

'Find out what show it was and when it aired. Mary'll do the rest. All it takes is a little detective work.' A beat. 'Now, can I take you ladies to lunch?'

'Oh, wow, Alex, you're getting so formal,' Venus said, teasing him. 'Lucky shows up and all of a sudden you turn into Mr Nice.'

'Something wrong with that?' he said, putting his arm around Lucky's shoulders. 'How was it?' he asked.

'Pretty harrowing,' she said. 'I didn't see Lennie. They're keeping him outside because he's their key witness. Steven was there, of course. And all of Mary Lou's family.' She took a long drag on her cigarette. 'You know what really blew my mind?'

'What?'

'Watching that girl. Her name's Mila Kopistani. She's a bad one.'

'Nothing wrong with bad girls,' Alex said, being flippant.

'Don't even joke about it,' Lucky snapped, her eyes flashing. 'You know exactly what I mean.'

The three of them went to lunch at Alex's favourite Chinese restaurant around the corner. He invited Sylvia to join them, but she informed him she was meeting her girlfriend.

'Don't you think it looks a little odd, your production associate being a dyke?' he mentioned to Venus as they settled into a corner booth.

'You know, Alex,' Venus said, dazzling the hovering proprietor with her famous smile, 'for someone so hip, you really are an old-fashioned guy.'

'People might think you're gay,' he said, ordering three large bottles of Evian for the table.

'Why would they think that?'

'Well, if *I* had a fag by my side at all times—'

'You probably have and you don't even know it,' Venus said. 'And I might remind you that *fag* is not a politically correct term.'

'I can see you two are getting along great,' Lucky interrupted. 'What am I? The outsider.'

'No, as a matter of fact,' Alex said. 'Venus and I have discussed it.'

'Discussed what?'

'We want to do an intervention.'

'Excuse me?' she said, frowning.

'An intervention,' Alex repeated, wondering why he'd allowed Venus to talk him into this.

'I hate to tell you guys this, but I hardly ever drink,' Lucky said, thinking they'd both gone a little bit crazy.

'It's not *about* your drinking,' Venus said, leaning across the table. 'It's about your marital status.'

'My marital status is nobody's business but mine,' Lucky said irritably.

Alex summoned a waiter and quickly ordered an obscene amount of food.

'Don't we get a choice?' Lucky asked.

'I know what's good here,' he said.

'So you're saying our tastes don't count?'

'What do you want that I haven't ordered?'

'Seaweed.'

'Seaweed?'

'Yes.'

'The lady wants an order of seaweed,' he said to the waiter, who added it to the order pad and departed. Alex turned back to Lucky. 'Venus knows how I feel about you,' he said. 'She's your best friend, so I'm sure there're no secrets between you. In fact, you probably even told her about that one crazy night.'

'*What* one crazy night?' Venus asked, jumping in.

'He doesn't know what he's talking about,' Lucky said, throwing him an angry shut-the-fuck-up look.

'Anyway, here's the thing,' Alex continued. 'Venus and I have been talking and, for your own peace of mind, we've decided that you've got to give Lennie another chance.'

She couldn't believe these words were coming out of *Alex*'s mouth. 'Excuse me?' she said.

'Yes,' Venus said, joining in. 'You and Lennie are fantastic together. Everyone knows it.'

'The jerk made a mistake,' Alex said. 'Which is understandable, because the poor bastard was trapped in a fucking cave for three months with no chance of escape, and along came this girl who gave him an opportunity to get out.'

'He was lonely and frightened,' Venus continued, 'so he went for it. He's destroyed, Lucky. All he wants is a chance to get you back.'

'If he wants me back so much, how come he's living in a hotel with that – that woman?'

'He's there because of his kid,' Alex said. 'People make mistakes. How did he know she'd get knocked up? The kid is deaf or something, Lennie's trying to help.'

'He's renting a house for them to live in,' Venus added. 'He spoke to Cooper the other night and told him. He certainly doesn't want to live with them himself.'

'Then why is he?'

'They're in a huge suite at the Chateau Marmont, separate bedrooms.'

'It's not that I'm jealous of her,' Lucky explained, feeling like a fool, because maybe if she was honest with herself she'd admit that she *was* jealous. 'I mean, look at her, she's just some kind of peasant girl.'

'Now, now,' Venus admonished, 'don't get bitchy. It doesn't suit you.'

'Yeah,' Alex said. 'You're usually so supportive of women, it's not like you to put them down.'

'I guess I'm upset.' Lucky sighed. 'You know, her being Bonnatti's niece and all.'

'She's not *really* Bonnatti's niece,' Venus said.

'Think about it,' Alex said. 'Donatella was married to Santino, so Claudia's only his niece by marriage. It's not as if she has Bonnatti blood running through her veins.'

'She got him out of that cave,' Venus said. 'If she hadn't, you'd probably never have seen him again.'

'And y' know, Lucky,' Alex said, 'I'm the *last* person who wants to see you back with Lennie, but you gotta give the guy a break. If you don't, you could spend the rest of your life regretting it. And that I do *not* want to see.'

'I don't know . . .' she said unsurely.

'Go back to him, Lucky, before it's too late,' Venus urged.

'Yes,' Alex said. 'Take him back, and although it pains me to say so, it could be the right thing for you to do.'

73

Perhaps the first day in court was the worst. Teddy didn't know. All he knew was that every eye was on him. It was quite unnerving. He saw his dad sitting near the front, and his mom next to him. He noticed people, probably journalists, scribbling in notebooks, and a handsome man whom he recognized from the pictures in the newspapers as Mary Lou's husband.

'Try to sit very still,' Mason whispered in his ear. 'And don't make eye contact with any of the jurors. It's too early to try to win them over.'

So he sat and listened as both sides presented their opening statements, listened to Mason Dimaggio talk about him as if he wasn't even there. Occasionally he glanced over at Mila. She refused to acknowledge his presence, her expression blank as she stared straight ahead.

Late in the afternoon, when he was allowed to leave, there was no escaping the media onslaught. The TV news cameras and reporters made a frantic dash in his direction, yelling his name, thrusting microphones under his nose. Fortunately the judge had refused to allow TV cameras in the courtroom, so it was only outside that he was set upon.

His father had slipped out a few minutes earlier. 'It'll be less of a party that way,' Price had said.

Yeah, sure, Teddy had thought. *Like the press is going to ignore Mr Major Star.*

Ginee was hanging around outside, waiting for him to emerge. As soon as she saw him, she grabbed his arm and clung to it, urging him to pose for pictures with her.

'No,' Howard said brusquely. He and Mason had discussed it earlier, and they'd decided that in view of Ginee's unsuitable appearance, they should keep Teddy well away from her. She was not the comforting mother figure they'd envisioned.

'Dad said I mustn't pose for pictures,' Teddy mumbled, shaking his head.

'Oh, *c'mon*,' Ginee crowed, basking in the limelight. 'I'm your *mommy*, for Chrissakes. C'mere an' cuddle up for a photo op. It'll make all the front pages.'

Teddy backed away. The press, sensing dissension, began to yell. 'C'mon, Teddy, let's have a picture with your mom. Teddy! Teddy! This way, this way. Smile! Wave! *Do* something.'

Howard hustled him through the rabid throng, leaving Ginee to pose all by herself.

She was happy. She was a woman *finally* getting what she wanted after all these years of being shoved in the background.

Eat your heart out, Price Washington. I'm a star, too.

And she beamed for the cameras.

☆

While Ginee posed, Irena sidled quietly from the court, unnoticed. She'd slipped out of the house directly after Price, leaving Consuella in charge. She and Price had not discussed the case, it was such an awkward situation, and at this point in the proceedings it was probably just as well not to get into it.

When she'd entered the courtroom she'd made sure Price had not seen her sitting at the back. Even if he spotted her, there was no way she was going to miss being there, she was just as entitled as anyone else to watch what happened.

Mila had not noticed her either, so all day long she'd sat there, staring at her and Price's daughter, thinking to herself that maybe she was mistaken, because there was nothing to remind anyone of Price in Mila's looks. In fact, she was the image of Irena at the same age.

The truth was, it didn't matter who Mila looked like, she *was* Price Washington's daughter. That was a fact.

As Irena left the courtroom she was more confused than ever because apparently Mila had been saying such terrible things – accusing Teddy of plying her with drugs and raping her. If it came out that she was his half-sister, the scandal would be too much for anyone to bear. It would also cast Irena into the spotlight, which she feared because of her nefarious past.

Besides, she could never do it to Price.

She could never ruin his career.

Because if she revealed the truth – the scandal surely would.

☆

Steven needed a drink. On the way home he had a strong desire to stop at a bar, but he knew that if he did one drink would not be enough.

Being in court all day had left him numb. Listening to the two sides present their opening statements had completely stunned him. He'd known what had happened to Mary Lou, but hearing it in so many words was beyond his comprehension. And the Russian girl sitting there, her pointed face blank and expressionless. No remorse there.

He'd wanted to stand up, go over and beat her senseless. She'd taken away the love of his life, and he hated her for it.

He, who'd always been so liberal, wanted to see her die for what she'd done.

God, what was happening to him? He drove home filled with a mix of emotions.

It wasn't until he got into the house and Carioca ran to greet him, throwing herself into his arms, that he started to feel even slightly normal.

'Hey, cutie,' he said, hugging her close.

'How was it today, Daddy?' Carioca asked, all big eyes and sticky hands, for she was in the middle of eating a peanut butter and jelly sandwich.

'Not much fun,' Steven said, glancing over at his English au pair, Jennifer. She was a bright girl, and nice too. He was fortunate that she'd been there for him and Carioca all the way.

'You know, Jen, I've got an idea,' he said.

'Yes, Mr Berkeley?'

'How about you take Carioca to London for a few weeks? You know, just while the case is going on.'

'Sounds like a brilliant idea to me,' Jennifer said cheerfully. 'Carioca will love London. We can stay with my parents in St John's Wood. When would you like us to go?'

'As soon as possible,' he said, grateful that Jennifer was so together.

'Super! I'll organize it.'

'Hey, cutie,' he said to his daughter, 'what d'*you* think?'

'Do I get to ride on a plane?' Carioca asked excitedly.

'You certainly do.'

'Then I wanna do it, Daddy. It'll be *cool*!'

When Carioca went off to bed, Steven wandered into the den, put on the television, and fell asleep in his favourite leather chair. The next thing he knew, Lina was standing behind him with her hands over his eyes.

'Surprise, surprise,' she said. 'It's your trusty FedEx lady delivering a package from the Bahamas.'

'Oh, baby,' he said, pulling her around the chair and on to his lap. 'You're a sight for very tired old eyes.'

'Was it tough today?' she asked, settling on his knee and cuddling up.

'It was.'

'Wish I could've been there with you.'

'I know.'

'Listen to *this*,' she said. 'I've cancelled all my gigs for the next two weeks. This girl ain't goin' nowhere!'

'You can't do that because of me.'

'Already done,' she said firmly. 'I want you to 'ave someone t' come 'ome to.'

He couldn't believe how sweet she was. To look at her, most people would imagine she ate guys up and spat 'em out. Maybe she did that to other men. To him she was an angel. A very sexy angel who'd come along to help him through this painful ordeal.

'How did the shoot go?' he asked.

'Same old boring thongs.'

He summoned a smile. '*You* might find them boring.'

'Can you imagine if your mate from New York, Jerry whatsisname, was there?' she said, with a ribald laugh. ''E'd 'ave bin drooling from 'ere to Sin City.'

'You got *his* number.'

'You eaten anything?' she asked, climbing off his knee.

'I'm not hungry.'

'*I* am,' she said forcefully. 'They served *the* most disgusting 'amburger on the plane. I refused to 'ave anythin' t' do with it.'

'Not a Fatburger, huh?'

''Ow about we go out somewhere cosy an' grab a bite?' she suggested.

'This is LA, Lina,' he said, standing up and stretching. 'There's nowhere cosy. Besides, you'll be spotted everywhere we go.'

'Then let's send out,' she said. 'I'm 'appy to stay right 'ere.'

'I don't want to turn you into a hermit.'

'We can stay 'ome as much as you want until this is over. That 'ardly makes us 'ermits.'

'You're very sweet.'

'Ooooh.' She giggled. 'Never been called sweet before.'

'There's always a first with you, isn't there?'

'Yup. An' you're my first soul brother. An' you know what, Steven?'

'What?'

'I like it.'

'So do I, sweetheart, so do I.'

Somehow Lina always managed to make him a little less sad.

74

By the time Lennie left the courtroom to go home, he had the headache from hell. Being in a small, stuffy room all day, not knowing what was going on, except for occasional reports from Brett, the other deputy DA who was working the case with Penelope McKay, did not make for a pleasant day.

He felt totally out of it and alone, especially as he knew Lucky was in there somewhere. He hadn't seen her in weeks, and the truth was that he needed her. She might be gone from his life for now, but he was determined that it was only on a temporary basis. There had to be some way of winning her back. Only how?

Flowers didn't work with Lucky. She wasn't into roses and heartfelt speeches, so how could he prove to her that he loved her above all else? How could he make it up to her?

He'd sat in the little room for hours, developing a major headache, trying to work things out.

Shortly before he left, he'd called the hotel and spoken to Claudia. 'What's going on?'

'A lady phoned,' she'd said. 'I am to tell you she's found the perfect house.'

'Good. Call her back, say I'll go see it tonight.'

He wondered how Claudia would manage without him once he had settled them in a house. He'd been thinking about *buying* her the house as opposed to renting: it was the least he could do under the circumstances.

Yes. He'd buy them a house, find her a job – if that's what she wanted – and hopefully get the kid some help with his hearing difficulties. What more could she expect from him?

There was no way he could abandon them. He'd ruined her life, and she'd *saved* his. Why couldn't Lucky understand that?

'Do you think I'll be called tomorrow?' he asked Brett before leaving.

'No,' the young man said. 'It'll take a few days. There's a huge amount of interest in this case, so both sides will take their time. You're our star witness. We're saving you.'

'How are the lawyers on the other side?'

'Naturally Teddy Washington has the *crème de la crème*, Mason Dimaggio. And the girl, Mila, she's stuck with an ambulance-chaser.'

'Is that good or bad?'

'The good news is that they're up against each other. The bad news is that it could work against us.'

'How come?'

'We might end up with one of the juries being split.'

'What do *you* think?'

'It's a tough call. Mary Lou was a public figure with a clean reputation. You're famous. In my experience, celebrities usually come out on top. Unless you're Kim Basinger and the opposing lawyer gets the jury to turn against you. I think we're in pretty good shape.'

Lennie was able to leave before the session was over. He'd parked several blocks away on purpose, so he ducked out of a back entrance and strode down the street, managing to avoid the crowds of media people milling around out front.

His mind was buzzing. If he could only put this case behind him, he could concentrate on getting Lucky back.

☆

The press might have missed Lennie Golden's exit through the back, but Duke Browning didn't. He'd known exactly where Lennie would emerge. Duke had a knack for getting inside people's heads and figuring out what they'd do. Lennie Golden would leave by the back entrance, and he would leave early. That was a fact.

Duke had spent a most enjoyable day, even finding time for a midday shower – not in his own home, but sometimes one had to make do with what was available.

He was in a different car from the one he'd stolen that morning. Now, instead of a 1990 Ford, he was in a '92 green Chevy. He pressed a cassette into the tape deck to see what kind of musical taste his latest victim had. Joe Cocker. Duke was not pleased, his preference was classical.

He sat in the car allowing Lennie to get ahead of him as he

walked along the street. Duke idled the engine, barely keeping up.

When Lennie finally reached his car, Duke pulled the Chevy into the kerb, stopped the car and emptied the centre ashtray out on to the road. If there was one thing he could not abide, it was the smell of stale smoke.

As soon as Lennie set off, Duke slid into the traffic behind him, humming softly to himself. The sound of his own voice pleased him far more than the annoying rasp of Joe Cocker.

This was an interesting assignment. Maybelline had come up trumps – she knew how he liked his juices tickled. And this morning he'd had more than his juices tickled.

He would never forget the look on the maid's face when he'd turned on her. She was so trusting, so secure that he was a good person simply because he'd flashed some phoney ID that she'd hardly bothered looking at.

Why were these women so dumb? They deserved everything they got for not having plain common sense. They should all learn from his sister.

Nobody was more street smart than Maybelline. Which made it so irritating that she'd got herself caught. And not only caught, she hadn't even finished the job. Step-grandma Renee was alive and well and living in *their* house.

He would have to take care of it himself at a later date. Now was not the time because it wouldn't do to draw suspicion, considering he'd only recently been released from a Florida jail.

Yes, he mused. *A little time, a good alibi, and then he could go in and finish Renee off.*

A truck slid between his car and Lennie's, annoying him. He honked his horn. The truck driver gave him the finger.

Ah! If only he had more time, the man behind the wheel would regret that little move. Duke did not appreciate rude gestures. Too bad that he had other things on his mind.

He was considering whether he should hit Lennie Golden now, or wait until he got out of his car. An interesting choice.

Or maybe he wouldn't even do it today, because sometimes watching and waiting was the most fun of all.

Prolonged foreplay.

Prolonged foreplay to . . . murder.

75

Price couldn't find his key so he rang the doorbell, expecting Irena to answer immediately. She didn't, which annoyed him.

He had to do something about Irena. Keeping her on as his housekeeper was a big problem, considering that his son was in court accused of being an accessory to a murder, with Mila right next to him, pointing an accusing finger in the boy's direction.

The fact that Irena was still living in his house wasn't right. 'You've got to fire her,' Howard had told him repeatedly.

'You don't get it,' Price had answered. 'She organizes everything I do.'

'So you'll get somebody else to iron your shirts,' Howard had said sarcastically. 'It's imperative you fire her, Price. If the press finds out . . .'

'Yeah, yeah, I will,' he'd promised.

But deep down he had no intention of doing so. Irena was part of his life, he couldn't manage without her. Over the years she'd done so much for him, including helping him to conquer a fierce drug addiction, then keeping him more or less straight. The truth was that he owed her.

He rang the doorbell again, waiting impatiently for a response. Nobody came.

Goddamn Irena! The press could be here any minute, and he wanted to get safely inside before they arrived. He rang a third time. Still no answer. He searched his pockets, finally coming up with the elusive key. He let himself in quickly.

The first thing he noticed as he entered the house was a strange smell – kind of a musky, pungent odour.

'Irena!' he called out. 'Where the hell are you?'

Throwing off his jacket, he started upstairs. Things were turning to shit. He had a son being tried for murder, an ex-wife who was the joke of the century, and his career was going to pot. Plus he had no time to work on new material, and his movie had been put on hold. Fuck! What else could go wrong?

What was it with kids today? Didn't they have any conscience? He'd raised Teddy so carefully, giving him all the guidance he'd never had himself. And even if Teddy *hadn't* pulled the trigger, he'd been there, watching, while that little Russian witch had blown Mary Lou Berkeley away. And Teddy, the dumb shit, hadn't done a thing to stop her.

Price shook his head. Right now he needed some pleasure. He needed to get high.

One joint. Was that such a terrible thing? One joint and a woman.

Hey – not a bad idea. One joint, one woman, and a good steak dinner. He'd take the fortunate lady to Dan Tana's.

Yes. That's exactly what he needed. One long night of mindless sex.

Naturally Krissie came to mind. He hadn't spoken to her since he'd dumped her at Venus's party, but she was the sort of woman who was always available to a star. And he wouldn't mind burying his head in those huge silicone boobs and forgetting about everything.

He walked into his bedroom and was startled to see that his bed was unmade. Then he heard the sound of running water coming from the bathroom. It sounded like someone was in there taking a shower.

'Irena!' he called out again. 'You there?'

No answer.

The smell he'd detected in the hall was even stronger now, a weird mix of scents.

God! he thought. *Don't tell me a fan has broken in and is taking a shower in my bathroom.* Stranger things had happened.

Tentatively he entered his bathroom. The shower was indeed running, but the cubicle was empty, the etched-glass door swinging open, water starting to spill out on to the marble floor.

Every bottle of aftershave he possessed was open and lying around the black porcelain sink, the contents splashed all over the room. And sitting in the middle of the bathroom floor, tied to a stool, was Consuella – her mouth taped, hands and ankles bound to the chair. She was naked.

He stared at her.

She stared back at him, a hysterical whimper emerging from the back of her throat.

'Jesus!' he yelled. 'What the *fuck* . . .'

Then he called 911.

☆

Lucky was confused, she, who was usually so together. Lunch with Alex and Venus had thrown her. She wasn't an idiot, she was well aware how Alex felt about her, and even though he was still with Pia, she knew he'd drop his girlfriend in a minute if she gave him any encouragement at all. So the fact that even *Alex* was trying to persuade her to take Lennie back made her think about it very carefully.

On her way home she called Gino from the car. 'How'ya doin', old man?' she asked.

'Who the fuck you callin' old man?' he grumbled, feisty as ever.

'The kids are coming to stay with you again this weekend,' she informed him. 'I'm starting to think they're spending more time with you than with me.'

'And *I*'m startin' to think you should let 'em see their father,' he responded gruffly.

Why was everyone ganging up on her at the same time?

'Has Lennie been phoning you?' she asked suspiciously.

'You gotta let him see the kids, Lucky,' Gino said. 'It ain't fair.'

'Why?' she demanded, more than a little irritated.

''Cause if you don't, he'll get a fuckin' lawyer to make *sure* he does. Tell him he can drive to Palm Springs this weekend.'

'You mean you'd have Lennie stay at the house?' she said furiously. 'Maybe he should bring the Bonnatti girl? Would you like that too?'

'Don't get cunty with me, kiddo. He can come an' stay, an' if he wants he can bring the other kid.'

'Fuck you, Gino!' she yelled, and slammed down the phone, almost rear-ending a truck.

What was going on here? Didn't anyone *get* it? Didn't anyone understand how Lennie had betrayed her?

She was mad as hell. Yet . . . she knew she wasn't being fair to little Gino and Maria. They *should* see their father, she had no right to deprive them of that.

Feeling guilty, she called Gino back. 'Okay,' she said guardedly. 'If you want to see him so much, *you* call him. He's shacked up at the Chateau Marmont with the Sicilian. Invite him down, I don't care. But you'd better not invite her.'

'Calm down,' Gino said. 'It don't suit you to be hysterical.'

'And it doesn't suit *you* to be on his side,' she retorted sharply. 'And, for the record – I am *not* hysterical.'

'Hey, what's right is right.'

'I hear you, Gino. And if you think what Lennie did was right, then your opinion is *crap*!'

'Well, anyway, kid,' he said, ignoring her outburst, 'I'm lookin' forward to seeing the little ones. An' since it's okay with you, I'll give Lennie a buzz.'

'I repeat. As long as he doesn't drag along that – that woman.'

'Okay, okay, I got the message. Is it all right with you if he brings the kid?'

'Why not?' she drawled sarcastically. 'You can all have a nice time with the little Bonnatti brat. I'm sure it'll be wonderful.'

She slammed down the phone again, immediately regretting she'd told Gino it was okay. How could she allow little Gino and Maria to meet Leonardo, or whatever the stupid boy's name was? They might even *like* him. This was impossible.

She imagined the situation in reverse. What if *she*'d got pregnant after her one night with Alex? What if *she*'d said to Lennie, 'Oh, here's a little Alex Woods junior for you.' Would he have accepted *that*? No freaking way! He didn't like Alex as it was.

Ha! He *should* like Alex. Alex was the one trying to persuade her to take him back.

God, she was so furious! And, on top of everything else, she'd had to sit in court all day listening to the lawyers' opening statements, and watching the girl with the thin pointed face and the black boy with his rich fat-cat white Beverly Hills lawyers, who were so sure they were going to get him off just because his daddy was a famous person.

If it was up to her, she would've hauled Mila Kopistani and Teddy Washington outside, and given them both a taste of what they'd given Mary Lou.

She called her service. There were several messages, the most important one from Boogie in Rome. She had no desire to hear more bad news but, then again, she needed to know what was going on with Brigette.

She called him back, even though it was three in the morning in Italy.

'Hey,' Boogie answered, sounding alert. 'Knew it was you.'

'How did you know that?'

'Other people are thoughtful, Lucky. They'd wait until six at least.'

'Don't criticize me, Boog.' She sighed. 'I've had it with criticism today. What have you found out?'

'It's not good, not bad.'

'Tell me.'

'Carlo flew back here with Brigette and took her to live at the family home – some kind of rundown palace just outside Rome. They holed up there for a while, and when I went looking for them, Carlo's mother, who barely speaks English, informed me they'd gone.'

'Gone where?'

'That's what I'm trying to find out.'

'I'm worried about her, Boog. You didn't see her when she was here, it wasn't our Brigette.'

'I've made a solid connection so hang in there. You'll hear from me as soon as I have something.'

'I'd get on the next plane if I could, but I'm in court every day and my movie starts shooting in four weeks.'

'If I need you, I'll call.'

'Yes, and if it's an emergency I can be there immediately.'

'I'll be in touch.'

At least Boogie knew what he was doing. Lucky felt confident that if anything was going on with Brigette, *he* would find out. She drove home with a lighter heart.

☆

'How do you feel it went today?' Howard asked, driving his maroon Bentley along Wilshire.

Sitting next to Howard in his fancy car, Teddy wondered how Price's stuffy lawyer had become his new guardian. Why couldn't he come and go with his dad every day? What was so terrible about that? ''S all right,' he said carefully, although it wasn't all right at all. He'd had a terrible day, listening to the attorneys present their case, painting him as some drunken jerk who'd aided and abetted Mila on her bloodthirsty mission.

'You like Mason, huh? He's a good man?'

He's white. You're white, Teddy thought. *What's not to like?* Both of them were working for his dad. Both of them were highly overpaid. This whole deal must be costing Price a shitload of money.

'Yes,' he lied, although the truth was he considered Mason Dimaggio to be a bossy asshole. What was with the ridiculous suits and hats he wore? And why were they forcing *him*, Teddy Washington, to look like such a geek?

'Your mother's something else,' Howard remarked, a derogatory sneer on his smug, pampered face.

'She used t' be beautiful,' Teddy said defensively.

'Price showed me the wedding pictures the other day,' Howard said, checking out his appearance in the rear-view mirror. 'She was a beauty, all right. Shocking how people let themselves go.'

'Do I havta drive to court with you every day?' Teddy asked, fiddling with the radio control.

'It's the way your father wants it,' Howard replied, swatting Teddy's hand away.

Sure, Teddy thought. *It's what my dad's paying for. That's the only reason you're doin' it.*

As they proceeded down Wilshire, two police cars raced up behind them. Howard drew into the kerb, allowing the two cars to scream their way past. 'This will not be a pleasant experience for the next few weeks, Teddy, but you'll come through it,' he remarked. 'All the wiser I hope.'

''S'pose so,' Teddy mumbled, staring out the window at a girl on a bicycle wearing red shorts and a tight tank. She reminded him of Mila.

'Remember to be yourself,' Howard lectured. 'You're a nice boy, not a wild kid. You were led astray. That's our case and we're sticking with it. But you have to back us up. Your demeanour in that courtroom means everything.'

Teddy shifted in his seat. Driving to and from court every day with Howard Greenspan was going to be torture. Fortunately, they were almost home.

As they neared the house, Teddy noticed the two police cars that had roared past them a few minutes ago were now parked outside. 'Why're *they* here?' he asked.

Howard slowed his Bentley, took a look out the window and groaned. 'It's probably something to do with the press,' he said shortly. 'I've *told* Price to control his temper. Let's hope he hasn't hit anybody.'

'Why'd he do that?'

'Because your dad is angry about all the publicity,' Howard said, pulling up behind the second police car. 'He's angry and frustrated. Have you any idea what this is doing to him?'

What about me? Teddy thought. *I'm the one sitting in that courtroom getting accused of all kinds of shit.*

They got out of the gleaming Bentley. Howard locked it and hurried over to a uniformed cop standing outside the house. 'I'm Mr Washington's lawyer,' he said officiously. 'What's happening here?'

The cop shrugged. 'You'd better go inside,' he said.

'Was Mr Washington involved in a fight?'

'There's been a robbery,' the cop said. 'And a rape.'

'Christ!' Howard exclaimed heatedly. 'More bad publicity! This is *all* we need.'

76

The realtor was a petite bottle blonde clad in an expensive Escada suit, diamond-stud earrings, and extremely high heels. In her fifties, she had a permanent smile and an overly friendly manner.

'Mr Golden,' she gushed, as he got out of his car, 'or can I call you Lennie?'

'Sure,' he said, walking up to the front door of the house she was about to show him.

'This is a *most* delightful house,' she said, inserting a key and letting them in. 'It's up for rent, but the owner has said that because it's you he might be prepared to sell, furnishings and all. The house was once rented by Raquel Welch. And last year a very famous young television star lived here for several months.' The woman lowered her voice. 'She insists we protect her privacy, so I'm not allowed to reveal her name.'

Big deal, Lennie thought, checking out the spacious front hallway.

'*Do* look around,' the realtor continued. 'I think you'll find this is an excellent house for you, with the added advantage of a panoramic view of the city. And, of course, all the rooms offer a terrific flow for entertaining.'

He followed her around the one-storey house located high up on Loma Vista. It had three bedrooms, all with bathrooms *en suite*, three entertainment rooms, a large country-style kitchen, a pool, and a tennis court. It was really too big and fancy for what he wanted.

'How much is the owner asking?' he enquired.

'Three million,' she said, as if this was a bargain price. 'However, I'm sure we can get it for less.'

'And the rental is?'

'Twelve thousand per month.'

'I told you over the phone I was looking for something in the six to eight thousand range,' he said, annoyed that she was wasting his time.

'Yes, indeed you did, Mr Golden – Lennie. But when I saw this house, it seemed *so* perfect. You mentioned wanting three bedrooms and a view, and after all, Suzanne Sommers *did* live here.'

He threw her a quizzical look. 'I thought you said Raquel Welch.'

'They *both* lived here,' she said, not batting an eyelash at her obvious lie.

This woman was beginning to irritate him. He'd clearly told her over the phone that eight thousand was his limit, which to his way of thinking was far too much anyway. However, he did not want to spend all his time searching for houses for months on end. His priority was getting Claudia and Leonardo settled and out of his life.

'How about making the owner an offer?' he suggested, checking out the kitchen.

'What kind of offer?' she retaliated, dollar signs lighting her eyes.

'Seven thousand a month.'

She laughed politely. 'Mr Golden – Lennie – they're asking *twelve*.'

'I know,' he said, wandering into the dining room. 'How about compromising at nine?'

'I can put in the offer.'

'I suggest that you do that.'

'And shall we make a provision that if you wish to buy?'

'Yeah, throw that in. Although for three million they don't stand a chance.'

'Property values are rising all the time, Mr Golden,' she lectured. 'I sold three houses this month, all of them fetched over four million.'

'I'm sure,' he said impatiently. 'Anything else you want to show me?'

'No. I'll put in your offer and let you know.'

He felt like he was being taken because he was a celebrity. Shit! Twelve thousand a month! Who was she kidding?

When Lennie arrived back at the hotel, Leonardo was already in bed, and Claudia was in the kitchen fixing pasta. He wasn't hungry, but what the hell? He sat down anyway.

One thing about Claudia, she was a fantastic cook, her Bolognese sauce was beyond delicious and he found himself stuffing down two heaped bowls of pasta without even thinking.

She didn't eat. She hovered, making sure he had everything he needed. Thick crusty garlic bread; a mixed green salad; a cold beer.

Hey, living with Claudia he'd grow fat as a hog. Especially as he wasn't working out because all his equipment – Stair-master, weights, et cetera – were at the beach-house. Along with Lucky.

His Lucky. The one love of his life.

And what was he doing to get her back? Because if he didn't move fast, he knew that Alex Woods was ready and waiting. The bastard.

☆

Duke awoke with a start. He'd fallen asleep behind the wheel of the comfortable green Chevy, parked on the street near the entrance to the garage of the Chateau Marmont. And who could blame him? He'd had a tough day. Stealing two cars. Ransacking the Price Washington mansion. Raping the maid.

He allowed his mind to focus on the maid for a moment. A juicy little piece. She'd squealed like a baby pig at the moment of rear entry. He'd liked that.

A faint smile flitted across his face at the memory. He got off on fear. Other people's. Especially women's.

The truth was he'd done enough for one day and he was genuinely tired. Too tired even to consider offing Lennie Golden. There was always tomorrow. And, besides, he had to think this thing through in a more business-like way.

Maybelline had made a deal with Mila, her cell-mate. The deal was that he got to rob the Washingtons' house in exchange for whacking Lennie Golden. Mila had given Maybelline details about the house – alarm code, safe location, layout – which Maybelline had passed on to him during his last visit.

So what? He could've got in without any of that information. And once he was in, he could've persuaded Consuella to tell him anything he wanted. Especially when he'd had her bent doggie-style over the bathroom stool, and was dousing her big juicy ass with various aftershaves and colognes.

That had been some kick. *Especially* when the mixed scents had hit the tip of his cock, stinging the shit out of him.

Ah . . . but he'd liked the pain. It added to the adventure, and every gig was a new adventure.

So . . . this was not a fair deal. Why should he risk jail-time – not that he'd ever allow himself to get caught again – for such small rewards?

Jesus Christ. Was Maybelline getting soft? He could score big for putting a hit on someone.

Full of these thoughts, he consulted his watch and decided it was way past time to dump the Chevy. Removing a small chamois cloth from his pocket, he dusted every surface he'd touched, then left the car and made his way down the hill on foot, heading for home.

Since Maybelline had screwed their chance of living in the big house with step-grandma Renee, home was now a one-bedroom apartment situated off Hollywood Boulevard. It was not Duke's ideal choice. He knew where his rightful place was – back in the house their grandfather had left them.

Damn Maybelline and her vicious temper.

If only she'd waited for him to come home, it could have all been so easy.

☆

Irena sensed trouble long before it happened – she'd always had an antenna for such things. So when she saw the police cars parked outside the house, her first thought was that they'd finally come to arrest her. They'd discovered she'd entered the country with false papers, and were preparing to deport her. She wasn't Irena Kopistani. She was Ludmilla Lamara, a known criminal in Russia.

She'd been waiting twenty years for this to happen.

She walked up to the front door dragging her feet.

A uniformed cop blocked her way. 'Yes?' he said, in a none-too-friendly voice.

'I live here,' she said, studying his broad, beefy face for clues regarding her imminent arrest.

'Your name?'

She hesitated a moment. 'Irena Kopistani,' she said, rubbing her hands together. 'I'm Mr Washington's housekeeper.'

'You'd better go inside.'

'What's happening?' she asked tentatively.

'Detective Solo will fill you in.'

'Where's Mr Washington? Is he all right?'

'He's in the house, ma'am.'

Sometimes she had nightmares that something bad might happen to Price before she could tell him how much he meant to her. She couldn't bear it if he was hurt in any way. He was her only reason for living. The one true love of her life.

Her heart was beating much too fast. She walked through the door into the front hallway, where there was a gathering of unknown faces. She saw Howard Greenspan talking to a tall, haggard-looking man with greasy hair.

'Who's this woman?' the haggard-looking man asked, as she came into view.

'It's all right,' Price said, emerging from the living room. 'Irena's my housekeeper.'

'Good,' the detective said. 'She's the one I want to speak to.'

Irena's heart sank. Irene Kopistani. Ludmilla Lamara. Who did he think she was?

77

When the news flashed across the TV screen, Mila was sitting with a couple of Puerto Rican hookers whom she found quite entertaining. Anything to take her mind off her day in court. They were teaching her all kinds of things she hadn't learned in school. Like how to give the mother of all blow-jobs in the back of a moving car, and how to recognize a vice cop when he tried to entrap a girl. Obviously they weren't too good at the second one, because they'd both been arrested during a recent vice bust.

Pandora, one of the hookers, was busy telling stories about her famous clients, when the news broke.

The newscaster, a dour-faced man wearing too much makeup and a bad rug, began relating the story. 'Sometime this afternoon there was an invasion of Price Washington's home in the Hancock Park area of the Wilshire district. Mr Washington was in court at the time, where his son is accused of being involved in a hold-up and the subsequent shooting of TV star Mary Lou Berkeley. An Hispanic maid – alone in the house – was raped and tied up while the house was robbed of jewellery, clothes, and cash. The estimated loss could be in the millions. Police are looking for a white male, early twenties . . .'

'Price Washington,' Pandora purred, stroking her own thigh. 'That dude's about as sexy as they get.'

'I had an NBA player once,' her friend confided. 'All he wanted was a hand job in the alley. He must've liked it, 'cause he came back three nights in a row. Guess I was doin' *somethin'* right.'

Both girls cackled.

Mila got up and returned to her cell where Maybelline was lying on her bunk sucking her hair and staring into space.

'It's all over the news,' Mila announced excitedly.

'What is?' Maybelline said.

'The goddamn robbery. I didn't think Price Washington was *that* important.'

'He's a big star,' Maybelline said.

'You didn't tell me your brother was gonna rape the maid,' Mila said accusingly.

'Oh, that's Duke,' Maybelline said, not at all surprised. 'He has these little . . . habits. Can't break him of them.'

'Rape is a little habit?' Mila said, raising her eyebrows. 'He shouldn't've done that. Now *I* feel responsible.'

'Listen to *you*,' Maybelline snorted, turning nasty. 'You shot some bitch in a car, but you can't stomach my brother raping the stupid maid. What the fuck does it matter to you?'

'I hope he found my gun,' Mila muttered, backing down, because she sensed it was not pretty when Maybelline got pissed.

'If it was where you said it was, he'll have it.'

'How about Lennie Golden? Has he done it yet?'

'Knowing my brother, he's done enough for one day. He'll take care of it tomorrow.'

'Yeah, but if Lennie's called as a witness . . .'

'They won't call him for another few days. There's plenty of time.'

'How do *you* know?'

''Cause the courts drag things out for ever. Don't worry, it'll be taken care of. Duke's a pro.'

Mila was steaming. She wasn't so sure about Duke. The fact that he'd stopped and taken the time to rape the maid infuriated her. What if Irena had been in the house? Would he have raped her too?

Not that she cared about her mother, because Irena sure as hell didn't give a shit about her. Still . . . she hadn't reckoned on her being physically harmed.

Maybe she should get the gun to her lawyer.

Yes, she decided, she'd tell him about it in the morning, then she'd have Maybelline instruct Duke to deliver it.

Right now her trust level was sinking fast. Duke was obviously a maniac, and Maybelline didn't seem to care.

They'd made a deal. And if Maybelline and her crazy brother didn't keep their side of it, they'd both be way sorry.

☆

78

Lucky caught the story on the ten o'clock news. She was shocked. She immediately called Venus, knowing that Venus was friendly with Price Washington.

'What in hell's going on? Has this got anything to do with the case?'

'How do I know?' Venus replied. 'I haven't spoken to Price in weeks.'

'Isn't it kind of weird?' Lucky said. 'His house getting broken into?'

'Not really. Somebody knew he was in court and took advantage of the situation.'

'There's something not quite right about it,' Lucky said. 'Why don't you phone him, see what he has to say?'

'I'm not calling him to find out,' Venus objected. 'That's like *ghoulish*.'

'No, it's not,' Lucky insisted.

'Okay, maybe later.'

Lucky reached for a cigarette. 'How did everything go after I left?' she asked.

'Great. Seven more actors came in to read. One of them was pretty damn hot.'

'Did Alex like him?'

'*Nooo.*'

'He's hard to please.'

'Right. Hard to please and *very* particular.'

'Which is what makes him such a great director.'

'And a huge pain in the ass at times,' Venus said with a dry laugh. 'Although, don't get me wrong, I love working with him. Alex inspires me. He has soul.'

Lucky inhaled deeply, thinking that yes, he did, which was why she was so attracted to him – as a friend, nothing more. 'Now,' she said, 'perhaps you'd like to tell me about ganging up on me today? What was *that* about?'

'It's because Alex and I see what's going on,' Venus explained. 'You're too close to it.' She took a deep breath. 'The deal is this. Alex wants to be with you – no surprise, you've known *that* for the last five years. But he understands that if he's with you, you *cannot* be thinking about Lennie. So until

Lennie's history – which we both know he's *not* – Alex realizes he has no chance.'

'Is that why you're both trying to *force* me back with Lennie? It doesn't make sense.'

'What does?' A beat. 'So . . . what d'you think?'

'About what?'

'About Lennie, of course,' Venus said, exasperated. 'You've got to call him, go out, talk things over.'

'I . . . I don't know any more,' Lucky said unsurely. 'I've always felt that the biggest betrayal of all was sleeping with somebody else when you've made the big commitment. I slept around as much as I wanted before I was married, but once you're married that should be it. It's like being on a diet and seeing this incredible chocolate cake, and you're a chocolate freak, so all you want to do is have a bite of that cake. But you know that if you have one small slice, you'll end up eating the whole thing. I know it sounds crazy, but to me that's what fidelity is about.'

'I can dig it,' Venus said. 'You and I both lived our lives like guys. We ran around doing whatever we wanted, and we married guys who'd done the same. Which makes for a real been-there-done-that situation, so nobody's looking around to see what they missed 'cause nobody missed anything!'

'Exactly,' Lucky agreed. 'So when that woman showed up at my door with Lennie's child, how do you think I felt?'

'I know I keep on repeating myself,' Venus said, 'but it's not as if he ran off and had an affair. He was desperate – you've got to take that into consideration.'

'Why?' Lucky said stubbornly.

''Cause it's only fair. And Alex agrees with me. What you need is closure.'

'I guess you could be right.' Lucky sighed. 'Maybe I *will* call him.'

'Best thing you can do,' Venus said. 'Dinner. The two of you. No outside interference. Make sure it's on neutral ground.'

'Good thinking.'

'By the way,' Venus added curiously, 'what *did* Alex mean when he mentioned your one crazy night together?'

'Nothing,' Lucky said quickly.

'You sound guilty,' Venus said gleefully. 'Did something happen between the two of you?'

'If it did – and I'm not *saying* it did – then it would've happened while I thought Lennie was dead.'

'Oh, you *bad* girl,' Venus admonished, loving every moment. 'You *slept* with Alex, didn't you?'

'No, I didn't.'

'Yes, you did!'

'Okay, Venus, enough. I've got to go. Let's talk tomorrow.'

She hung up the phone. Something was bothering her. Price Washington's house getting broken into and the maid getting raped. Could it possibly be connected to the case?

She called Detective Johnson. 'Any connection?' she asked.

'I'm studying the reports now,' he said.

'How about any leads on who did it?'

'Not yet. However, a neighbour did see a man arriving at the house this morning. I'll keep you informed.'

'Thanks,' she said, finally getting off the phone and going into her children's room, where she found little Gino and Maria in the middle of a fierce pillow fight. 'And how're my two little scamps?' she asked, hugging them both.

'Hi, Mommy,' they chorused, out of breath and giggling.

'Hello, you two naughty little rug-rats.'

'Where's Daddy?' Maria demanded.

'I keep on telling you, Daddy's working.'

'Wanna see him,' little Gino chanted. 'Wanna see him! Wanna see him! Wanna see him!'

'You will. You're going to Grand-daddy's this weekend, and Daddy'll be there, too.'

'Supercool!' Maria said, her favourite new word. 'Can we all go swimming together?'

'I'm not coming this weekend, sweetheart,' she explained. 'I've too much work to do here.'

'Oh, Mommy, c'mon,' Maria pleaded. 'I *like* you and Daddy in the pool. You look so pretty together.'

Lucky couldn't help laughing. 'People aren't *pretty* together, darling. They're *nice* together.'

'No, Mommy, you and Daddy are pretty.'

'Well, thank you. I'm glad you think that.'

After reading them a bedtime story, she kissed them both,

tucked them into bed, and went back to her bedroom, where she stared at the phone for a while.

Maybe Venus was right. Closure. She needed closure.

☆

'That was good,' Lennie said, pushing his plate away.

'I'm glad you enjoyed it,' Claudia said, gazing at him with adoring eyes.

He had a horrible feeling she had a crush on him. Of course he knew why. It was because he was there for her, and she'd obviously never had anyone care about her before. He'd been thinking that it was definitely time for her to get out and meet new people.

'I think I've found a house,' he said, standing up from the table.

'A house for us, Lennie?' she asked eagerly.

'No, a house for you and Leonardo.'

'Where will you be?' she asked, disappointed.

'I'll stay here.'

'Why can't you live with *us*?'

'Because, Claudia,' he said patiently, 'I've tried to explain this to you before. I have a wife whom I love very much, and she's not very happy about you turning up here with a child. Now, I understand it's not your fault, but I have to get my life back together. And it's not helping matters that I'm living here with you.'

'I'm sorry, Lennie,' she said, lowering her eyes. 'I have tried to be no trouble. I could not stay in Italy. Leonardo is your son and he needed help.'

'I know, Claudia, I know,' he said, trying to be patient and nice and all the things he didn't feel like being, 'and we're getting him help. I'll speak to the doctors in a day or two, see what their tests have come up with.'

'Thank you, Lennie.'

'This is what I've decided,' he said. 'I'm moving you and Leonardo into the house I've found. Then maybe you should get a job. Your English is pretty good, you shouldn't have any problems. You could be an interpreter, or work at the Italian Embassy.'

'Whatever you say.'

'I say you can have a good life here, Claudia, but you have to realize that it's not going to be with me.'

'I understand,' she murmured, not understanding at all.

'Now I gotta take a shower,' he said, pleased that he'd told her the way it was going to be. 'If the phone rings, pick up, it could be the realtor.'

'Yes, Lennie.'

He went into the bathroom and ran the shower. Tomorrow he would make a concentrated effort to talk to Lucky. This had gone on long enough. As each day passed, they were growing further and further apart, and he couldn't take it any more.

The moment he stepped into the shower, the phone rang.

Claudia picked up. 'Hello?' she said.

On the other end of the line Lucky hesitated for a moment. 'Put Lennie on,' she said at last.

'I'm sorry,' Claudia purred, 'Lennie is in the shower.'

Lucky slammed the phone down.

This was not going to work out.

79

One thing Brigette had tried to learn from Lucky was how to be strong. Obviously she hadn't done such a good job, because if she had, she wouldn't have got into such a devastating predicament.

If only she'd taken Lucky's advice and had the strength of character not to get involved with Carlo. After her previous dismal experiences with men, Lucky had warned her to take great care when entering a new relationship. She should've taken heed of Lucky's philosophy – *fight back or get trampled.* It was a good one.

But Carlo hadn't given her a choice. She'd gone to London to track him down, all set on punishing him. And what had happened? He'd kidnapped her and forced her into becoming a heroin addict. Then, when she was totally addicted and depended on him for everything, he'd *married* her.

She'd really had no choice in the matter because heroin took away the decision-making process. You got up in the morning, took your first shot, and then it was like, okay, here comes another great day – lie back and enjoy it . . . whatever.

So, yes, her life had become a series of dream sequences. And Carlo made sure she always had what she wanted, never depriving her.

And, in some sick way, because of her dependency on heroin, she'd grown totally dependent on *him*, putting up with his verbal abuse, black rages and sometime physical abuse.

It was only now that she could see the picture clearly. Only now that she realized what he'd done to her, and what an unconscionable monster he was.

Perhaps he'd done her a favour by abandoning her . . . leaving her in the middle of nowhere . . .

He would be punished, for she'd lost his baby, his son. And now that she was no longer pregnant there was nothing to tie them together except a marriage certificate, and her lawyers would soon take care of that. She didn't care how much she had to pay to get rid of him. It would be worth it.

She was doing her best to regain her physical strength, and even though she was still weak with stomach cramps, aching bones and a permanent headache, she was determined to walk out of this place as soon as possible. She knew for sure that she had to get out before Carlo returned.

Who knew what he would do? She would put nothing past him. He might even try to hook her up again. Then once more she'd be trapped. It would be an easy enough task for him to accomplish, because although she hadn't had heroin in a week, it was an addiction she knew she'd probably have to spend the rest of her life fighting.

When she was high, even Carlo being the biggest bastard in the world didn't matter.

Every morning she walked outside and sat by her baby's grave. Her son. Being near him gave her a sense of peace. The poor little soul would have been born addicted, and she could not have taken the pain and suffering the baby would've had to go through.

After a while she began exploring the big old house and the surrounding grounds, eventually discovering a barn in the back, where she found a rusty old bicycle with flat tyres. After more searching, she came across a pump. It was an exciting discovery, and although she was not mechanically minded, she set about getting the bike into working order.

She had no idea where she was. Carlo had mentioned that they were in the middle of nowhere. But she was sure that if she took a supply of water and cans of food, and followed the road, eventually she'd reach another house or someone who could help her.

She formed a plan in her mind. Two more days of guarding her strength, drinking plenty of nourishing cans of soup from the fast-dwindling supply in the kitchen, and building herself up.

Then she was getting on the bike and leaving.

☆

People were drawn towards Boogie. A Vietnam vet with a laid-back attitude, tall and lanky, he never presented a threat. Somehow, wherever he was, he always managed to fit in. So when he started hanging out with a group of old men in the village square near the Vitti palace, they accepted him as an American writer, studying other cultures, and allowed him to join in their daily game of boules, and sit around afterwards, drinking bitter black coffee and puffing on strong cigarettes.

Boogie had his eye on one old man in particular, Loren zo Tiglitali, the houseman from the Vitti family palace. Lorenzo was a gregarious character, short and stocky, with a shock of silver hair, tanned, wrinkled skin, and a wooden leg – a souvenir from the war. He was seventy-two and proud of it, boasting that he'd never had one sick day in forty years of working for the Vitti family.

Lorenzo loved telling tales, and fortunately he spoke very good English. Boogie soon became his best listener.

It was an easy job eliciting information from Lorenzo. He never stopped talking, carrying on about everything from the price of bread, to how tight his boss was with money.

It didn't take Boogie long to get on to the subject of Carlo.

'That boy!' Lorenzo spat in disgust. 'He's spoiled. No good. Even now he has the American wife he's *still* no good.'

'An American wife, huh?' Boogie asked quietly. 'Do they live at the palace?'

'They did,' Lorenzo said, chugging down a brandy, bought

for him by Boogie. 'Now he go to Sardinia with another woman. And the wife . . .' The old man suddenly stopped talking, aware that he might be saying too much.

'What about the wife?' Boogie urged. 'Where is she?'

Lorenzo shrugged, draining his glass of Cognac.

'Another?' Boogie offered.

'I shouldn't . . .'

'Go ahead.'

'Just one more.'

The 'just one more' loosened Lorenzo's tongue. 'His American wife is pregnant, you know. And very rich. Carlo has promised to get the family a few million dollars by the end of the year.'

'No!' Boogie said, feigning surprise.

'Oh, yes,' the old man assured him.

'Tell me about the American girl. Is she happy to be left behind while her husband goes off with other women?'

Lorenzo chuckled. 'She doesn't know about it. He took her to the family hunting lodge in the country.'

'Really? Where's that?'

Lorenzo screwed up his eyes and peered at Boogie. 'Why you so interested?'

'Sometimes I dabble in real estate. I have a friend who might be interested in purchasing a property outside Rome.'

The old man wheezed with laughter. 'Not this place. It's run-down and deserted. The family has no money for upkeep. Maybe when the millions of dollars come they restore it.'

'If it's so run-down and deserted, why would Carlo take his wife there?'

'I heard him telling his mama she would be happy there.'

'Really?' Boogie said, buying the old man yet another Cognac. 'About my friend. Perhaps I should look at this hunting lodge. If you go to your boss with a big enough offer, you could score yourself a healthy commission.'

'I could?' Lorenzo said, his rheumy old eyes popping at the thought.

'Yes,' Boogie said casually. 'Tell me where it is, and I'll go take a look. If I run into the American woman, I'll say I'm a potential buyer. I'm sure she won't object.'

'You'll never find the place,' Lorenzo said.

'If I can find my way through the jungles of Vietnam,' Boogie said, 'I'm sure I can find my way to this house. Here,' he added, pulling out a wad of money, 'let me give you five hundred dollars as good-faith money. If I like the place, you'll get more. If I don't, nothing lost, and you'll be a richer man.'

Lorenzo stared at the money, a greedy expression on his wrinkled old face. His salary had been the same for the last ten years, and he could certainly use something extra. His daughter wanted to go to Milan to be a teacher; his wife was desperate for a new winter coat; his son was married with two children and needed many things.

He grabbed the pile of notes, quickly stuffing them in his pocket. 'Tomorrow I will draw you a map.'

'Good,' Boogie said, sensing it would not do to rush him. 'We have a deal.'

80

Duke reviewed his stash. He knew he'd done well at the Washington house, but he had not taken the time to ascertain exactly how well. Now he was checking out his spoils.

The safe, which he'd been able to crack – having been taught by a master safe-cracker in jail in Florida – had revealed plenty of treasures. A leather pouch containing twelve expensive Patek Philippe watches, bundles of cash totalling over fifty thousand dollars, some important-looking papers that he would read at a later date, and a leather box full of assorted gold and diamond rings and cufflinks.

He'd also packed a Vuitton suitcase with several custom-made suits, shirts and ties. Even though Price Washington was obviously a much bigger man than he was, Duke liked the idea of hanging these clothes in his closet. Nothing like a three-thousand-dollar suit to give a man a buzz – even if it was just to look at.

He'd also found the shoebox Maybelline had told him to collect. It was exactly where she'd said it would be, hidden in a cupboard above the fridge in the kitchen, unreachable except by step-ladder.

He stared at the shoebox. Maybelline had said not to open

it. Fuck that shit. He opened it and discovered a handgun wrapped in a towel. He was smart enough not to get his prints on it.

Very interesting, he thought. *Have to find out more.*

He removed the watches from their pouch and laid them out, admiring them *and* the assorted jewellery. Then he re-counted the money – just to make sure.

He wished he could speak to his sister right now, but she would not be allowed to make a collect call until morning.

Damn! He missed Maybelline. He was miserable without her. They had such a strong connection, and that connection suffered when they were apart.

Maybe he should think about getting her out . . .

☆

Mila didn't sleep well. She was disturbed by Maybelline's couldn't-give-a-damn attitude and Duke's rape of the maid. How dare he! How fucking dare he!

Early in the morning she grabbed Maybelline by the arm and said, 'You'd better talk to your brother. I need him to deliver my package today.'

'He's not a delivery boy,' Maybelline snapped, confirming Mila's suspicions that all was not right.

'I didn't say he was,' Mila said, trying to stay calm, 'but my information got him into the house. Now he has to get that package to my lawyer today. I'll give you the address.'

'I'm not sure I like your attitude,' Maybelline said. 'It's a shitty attitude, like we work for you or something.'

'And *I'm* not sure I like yours,' Mila retaliated.

The two girls glared at each other.

'Your brother was supposed to hit Lennie Golden *yester-day*,' Mila said, in a fierce whisper. 'I'd like to know why he didn't.'

'Fuck you,' Maybelline responded. 'Who do you think you're talking to?'

'I thought we were friends,' Mila said, realizing her pre-carious position, because now Maybelline's obviously unsta-ble brother had the gun with Teddy's prints on it, and that was a valuable piece of property.

'Don't be so sure of that,' Maybelline said.

'Listen to me,' Mila said, her pinched face darkening with

fury. 'If your brother doesn't do what I say, I'll go to the authorities and tell them it was *him* who broke into the house and raped the maid.'

'You can't do that,' Maybelline said, her baby face turning bright red. 'I'll bash your head in before you do that.'

'Let's not fight about it,' Mila said, backing off because all she really wanted was for things to go smoothly. 'We're supposed to be partners in this. The news story said he got a million dollars' worth of stuff. I'm happy for you. All I want is what you promised. He's got to deliver the gun and hit Lennie Golden today. If he does, then everything'll be cool.'

Maybelline didn't say a word.

Mila went off to court still furious. As soon as she saw her lawyer she filled him in about the gun.

'You mean you have a gun with Teddy Washington's prints on it and you're only telling me about it now?' Willard Hocksmith asked incredulously.

She took a step backwards: his foul breath was making her sick. 'Yes,' she said. 'I thought it was smart to save it for later in the trial, when we really needed it.'

'What makes you think there'd even *be* a trial if I had evidence like that?' Willard said, frowning at her stupidity.

'Well, anyway,' she said, 'it's being delivered to your office today.'

'By whom?'

'By this . . . person.'

'What person?'

'Just someone,' she said irritably. 'Don't question me.'

'I *have* to question you, I'm your lawyer. Can't you understand what's going on here? They've got a witness, Lennie Golden, who swears it was *you* shot the girl. *You*, not Teddy Washington. Now you're telling me you've got a gun with his prints on it? How did you get it?'

'It doesn't matter how I got it,' she said sullenly. 'He shot her. I told you that at the beginning. You should've believed me.'

'And *when* am I supposed to get this gun?'

'Sometime today. You'd better tell them in your office that nobody should open it. It'll be in a shoebox wrapped in a towel.'

'You're a very strange girl,' Willard said.
'Like you're normal,' she muttered.

81

Day two of the trial and the media interest was stronger than ever. Especially with the added attraction of the rape and robbery at Price Washington's house.

Price himself was in shock. He'd known this was going to be an ordeal, but he'd had no idea it would be anything like this. Headline news day after day, the intrusion into his house, the rape, the robbery, the loss of his precious collection of watches and other jewellery. Even worse was the way everybody was talking and writing about him as though they could say whatever they liked, however untrue. He felt used and abused.

And poor Consuella. She'd worked for him for several years and was a nice woman. The fact that the rape had happened to her in his house was devastating.

'You'd better watch out,' Howard said. 'She'll probably sue you.'

'What're you talking about?' Price said. 'I had nothing to do with it.'

'It happened on your premises,' Howard said. 'Some smart shyster will get hold of her and sue you for everything you've got. I hope your personal liability policy is up to date.'

Price was so furious that Teddy had brought all this attention on their family that he could hardly bring himself to speak to him. They'd spent the previous evening in silence – eating dinner, then going to their respective rooms – barely bidding each other good night.

Because of the interest in his household affairs, the media had now discovered that Irena was Mila's mother. Boy, were they getting off on that one. And Irena was freaked, hiding in her room like a wanted criminal.

Price felt under siege. Every time he attempted to leave the house, he was deluged with press. He'd hired four bodyguards, two for him, and two for Teddy. This fucking case was going to cost him a fortune. He'd already had to postpone several lucrative gigs to deal with it.

The whole thing was bad news. He'd been thinking that after it was over, maybe he'd take Teddy away somewhere – the Virgin Islands or the Bahamas. Somewhere they could chill out and get to know each other better.

He had a bad feeling about the house now. His house that he'd loved for all those years. The house where Teddy was born *and* Mila, and look what had happened to the two of them. Bad karma.

He couldn't get the image of a terrified Consuella, bound and gagged, out of his mind. Her image was haunting him.

He needed a break, and as soon as this was over he was taking one.

'You know, Teddy,' he said to his son before they left for court on the second day, 'I hope this has taught you a real tough lesson. Because I am so fuckin' pissed about this I can't even see straight. You did somethin' really bad. You've brought shame on this family.'

What family? Teddy wanted to say. *We're not a family. There's you, and there's my mom – and she's not family. She's just some fat old publicity-crazy cow.*

Teddy was crushed by his mother's behaviour. He'd hoped she'd be there for him. And she wasn't.

'Sorry, Dad,' he mumbled. But he knew being sorry would never be enough.

☆

Steven awoke with Lina cuddled in his arms, still asleep. 'Hey,' he said gently, trying to extract himself. 'I've gotta get up. You can sleep a little longer.'

'I wanna make you breakfast,' she murmured sleepily, clinging to him.

'Oh, no,' he said, laughing. 'I'm not eating fried chicken for breakfast.'

'Don't be mean,' she said, her hand snaking down between his legs. 'I wanna learn to cook for you, Steven. I wanna do all the things I've never done before. You're makin' me into a changed woman.'

'I am?' he said, removing her hand, because much as he was tempted, now was not the time.

'You am,' she said, stretching her long arms above her head. 'Oh, boy,' she sighed. 'Never thought I'd feel like this about anyone, but you're like ... so solid, you know. I feel safe with you.' As soon as the words escaped her lips, she knew she'd said the wrong thing.

'Mary Lou felt safe with me,' he muttered grimly, 'and look where it got her.' He jumped out of bed and went into his bathroom.

Lina, who found any kind of rejection hard to take, followed him. She was gloriously naked and determined to make him feel good. 'Sorry, sweetie,' she said. 'Didn't mean anything by that . . .'

He attempted to ignore her spectacular body – so sleek and black and perfect.

She rubbed up against him, and suddenly he was lost, hard as the proverbial rock and way past the point of no return. Lina had that immediate effect on him.

'Got five minutes to spare?' she asked provocatively.

'What makes you think I only need five minutes?' he joked.

Lina was something else.

☆

In view of all the publicity about the case, Lucky decided the children should go to Palm Springs earlier than planned. Thank God that Gino loved having them.

She saw them all safely into the station wagon with CeeCee, stood outside and waved them goodbye.

Once they were gone she almost picked up the phone to call Lennie again. But she didn't. If she had to listen to Claudia's lilting voice saying, 'Hello,' one more time, she'd throw up.

You're jealous, a little voice whispered in her head.

Sure I am. Why shouldn't I be? My husband slept with another woman, and that other woman gave birth to his child. I'm not only jealous, I'm furious!

She was still angry, although she'd decided that she *did* want to see him. Alex was right, she could never start another relationship until she had closure with Lennie. Their love affair was too passionate to end on a sour note.

Decisively she grabbed the phone and called him. Once more, Claudia answered.

She refused to give the girl the satisfaction of asking to speak to her own husband, so she hung up again.

Boogie phoned from Europe just as she was leaving the house. 'I've located Brigette,' he said. 'I'm hoping to see her tomorrow.'

'That's good news.'

'It's good and it's bad. Carlo has taken her to a deserted hunting lodge in the country and left her there alone.'

'Where is *he*?'

'I understand he's in Sardinia with a girl.'

'Oh, great.' Lucky sighed. 'Brigette is pregnant, could be doing drugs, and Carlo's running around with another woman. What a winner she found this time. I wish I could get on a plane and come over. I'd like to kick his balls from here to China.'

'Hey, hey, Lucky, tell me how you *really* feel.'

'What's your next move?'

'It's evening here, I'll find the house first thing in the morning.'

'And then?'

'I plan to check on Brigette, make sure she's okay. If she's doing drugs, I'll know.'

'Let's hope Carlo's not around, then maybe she'll tell you. I have a hunch she'll feel more comfortable confiding in you.'

'As soon as I have news I'll call you.'

'Boog, remember this. If she's in any kind of trouble, you've *got* to bring her back.'

'That's the plan.'

'I trust you, Boog.'

'I know you do, Lucky. We've been through a lot together, and I don't come out of retirement easily. But for you – any time.'

'Retirement! Listen to you, you sound like some old man.'

'There are times I feel old.'

'You know, Boog, you're talking far too much. I can remember when you used to be the strong silent type.'

'I'll report in to you later.'

'That's fine. I'll be in court all day, but I'll have my cell-phone on.'

'Then I'll keep you informed.'

'Thanks, Boog.'

☆

82

'**You didn't** happen to mention there was a toy in the box,' Duke said, on the phone to his sister.

Maybelline was allowed to make an occasional collect call. Duke was the only person she spoke to. They were both aware that their calls were sometimes taped, and that they had to be careful what they said. Because of this they'd developed a way of speaking in code.

'I didn't tell you 'cause I knew you'd look,' she said. 'I hope you didn't play with it.'

'Why?'

''Cause it's got patterns on it. Teddy Bear patterns.'

'Interesting.'

'Isn't it? Auntie wants you to deliver it to the charity people – the ones she's working with. I think we should keep it. But, in the meantime, take care of that other thing 'cause Auntie's throwing a fit. And you know how close she is to the board.'

'Got it.'

'When?'

'I'll drive by later.'

'Love you, brother.'

'See you Saturday.'

Duke hung up, thinking about Maybelline's hidden messages. She was telling him the gun had Teddy Washington's prints on it, and that he shouldn't deliver it to Mila's lawyer. She was also telling him to go ahead and whack Lennie Golden, otherwise Mila might cause trouble.

Fine with him. He had nothing else to do today. And it wouldn't be the first time he'd sent someone to swim with the fishes. In fact, he had quite a history. Funny that the cops would lock him away for a few lousy rapes, when they could've had him for so much more . . . But, then, nobody had ever said that cops were smart. *He* was smart. Maybelline was smart. The rest of the world were merely stumbling through the day.

He locked all his spoils in a special steel-lined closet he'd had installed in his apartment. It wouldn't do to get *robbed*.

Then he checked his gun and decided exactly how and when he'd take Mr Golden.

Killing someone was such an easy thing to do.

And as long as one didn't get caught, extremely satisfying.

83

How to navigate her way through the crush of press without hitting one of them, that was Lucky's problem. 'Get that fucking microphone out of my face,' she snapped at a vacuous blonde reporter, who jumped back in surprise.

'She used the F-word,' the blonde said to her cameraman, her pretty face shocked.

'She's in the mob,' the man muttered. 'Read it in *Truth and Fact* this week.'

'Far *out!*' the blonde said, her attention shifting towards Price Washington and his entourage of lawyers and bodyguards, who'd just arrived.

Safely inside, Lucky got hold of one of the deputies. 'I'd like to see Lennie Golden,' she said. 'Penelope McKay said it's okay.'

The deputy led her to a small room where Lennie sat at a table reading *Newsweek* and sipping coffee from a Starbucks container.

'Hi,' she said, standing in the doorway.

He looked up. 'Uh ... hi,' he said, surprised and quite delighted by her visit.

'Thought I'd drop by, wish you luck just in case they get to you today,' she said casually.

He put the magazine down and stared at his wife – his gorgeous wife with the jet hair and matching eyes, devastating body and sensual olive skin. His incredible smart, dangerous wife, whom he missed and loved with a passion.

'Come in,' he said.

She did so, shutting the door behind her. 'I hate this place,' she remarked. 'I'll be glad when this is over, won't you?'

'Can't wait.'

'Where did you get the coffee?'

'Round the corner. Want one? I can see if somebody'll go out.'

'It doesn't matter.'

'Have mine,' he said, thrusting it at her.

'Just a sip,' she said, tasting it. 'I didn't have time to make any this morning, what with getting the kids on their way.'

'Where to?'

'Gino's. They're better off in Palm Springs until this is over.' She took a beat. 'You heard about the break-in at Price Washington's?'

'Who didn't?'

Awkward silence.

Lucky opened her purse and removed a pack of cigarettes.

'Thought you were giving it up.'

'I was trying, then this came along,' she said, shaking one out of the pack. 'Did Gino call you?'

'No.'

'He will,' she said, lighting up. 'He's inviting you to spend the weekend. You and your . . . uh . . . other son.' She couldn't bring herself to utter the child's name. 'Just the two of you. Not—'

'I get it,' he interrupted.

'Good,' she said coldly, almost wishing she hadn't come, but glad to see him all the same.

'Yes, Lucky. I do get it. And I'm pleased you're here, because I have several things to tell you.'

'What?' she said, noticing dark circles under his eyes, which meant he hadn't been sleeping well, and neither had she. *I want to kiss him*, a little voice whispered in her head. *I want to hug him and kiss him right now.*

'It's about Claudia . . .'

Oh, Christ, what now? Was he going to tell her he'd fallen in love with the Sicilian girl and wanted to be with her for ever?

Oh, shit! *Here I come, Alex, complete with broken heart.*

'Yes?' she said carefully.

'About me and Claudia,' he said.

'We don't have to go over it again,' she said. 'Especially here.'

'We need to talk. I have to explain everything. I know how upset you are that we're all living at the Chateau Marmont, but I had no choice. What could I do with them? The kid's got a hearing problem, so I've been sending him to doctors. And they had nowhere to go.'

'It's not your responsibility.'

'Yes, it is. I got her pregnant.'

'You don't even know if it's your son or not. She has no proof.'

'Take a look at him, Lucky. He looks exactly like me.'

'Oh,' she said, crushed.

'Anyway, here's the plan,' he said, hoping she'd approve.

'What plan is that?' she said, exhaling smoke.

'I've found a house to put them in, and I want you to come and see it.'

'Why would *I* want to see it?'

'Because you've got to be part of this. It's not me and Claudia and Leonardo against you. It's *us* – you and me – trying to deal with a difficult situation.' He stared at her long and hard. 'I've missed you, sweetheart. I can't tell you how happy I am to see you today.'

'I tried calling you,' she said. 'Only every time I got through, your girlfriend picked up.'

'Will you quit with that girlfriend shit?'

'Just pissing you off. I like to see you rattled.'

She smiled, faintly, but it was enough to give him the encouragement he needed. 'Let's not get into it here,' he said. 'Can you meet me later?'

'Where?'

'At the house I'm renting for Claudia and the kid. The realtor's dropping off the keys at my hotel.'

'Well . . .' she said hesitantly.

'It's important to me that you're part of this, Lucky.'

What did she have to lose? 'Okay,' she said.

'Meet me there at seven. After, we'll go for dinner and talk. I don't know about you, but I can't go on like this – I love you too much to be away from you.' He took a long beat, studying her carefully. 'I know this has been a shock for both of us,' he continued, 'but we've got to face the fact that I *have* a kid, and there's no way I can abandon him.'

'I suppose so,' she said, not sure *how* she felt.

'I'll get you the address,' he said. 'We'll work everything out, trust me on this.'

'I always used to trust you.'

'And you will again. You know you can't shut me out of your life. We belong together. It'll always be that way.'

'Hmm . . .' she said. 'That's what everyone's been telling me.'

'Who's everyone?'

'Your friend, Alex.'

'Not *my* friend.'

'He's on your side. Between him and Venus, they railroaded me into seeing you. They said we either have to be together, or get some closure.'

'I'm here to tell you,' he said forcefully, 'closure ain't anywhere in our future. Not if *I* have anything to do with it. We'll get through this together, like we've gotten through everything else over the years. We have two incredible kids, and I'm not losing them *or* you.'

'I'd better go,' she said, standing up. 'Penelope McKay let me in as a favour. I'll see you at seven.'

'Do I get a kiss?'

'Don't get carried away,' she said.

He grinned. She couldn't help grinning back.

Both of them had a strong suspicion that everything was going to be all right.

☆

Venus and Alex ate breakfast downstairs in the coffee shop. Alex attacked a stack of blueberry pancakes, while Venus settled for strawberry yogurt and herbal tea.

'Mary tracked that actor you were carrying on about,' Alex said. 'He's coming in at noon. If he's as good as you say he is, I want Lucky to see him too.'

'I've got the eye,' Venus said, stealing one of his pancakes with her fingers. 'Just you wait until you see him. If he can act, we're in business.'

Alex squirted more syrup on his pancakes. 'How'd'you think Lucky's holding up?' he asked.

'Pretty good, considering what the tabloids are doing to her. Have you seen them?'

'She's pissed, huh?'

'Wouldn't *you* be pissed if you were called a mobster's daughter? Gino was never really a *mobster*, was he?'

'Who the fuck knows?' Alex said, gulping his coffee. 'I like the guy. Who gives a shit if he was connected way back? *I* certainly don't.'

'I think Lucky should sue 'em,' Venus said, sipping her tea.

'Who needs to sue 'em and all that crap?' Alex said. 'You ever had to give a deposition? It's the pits.'

'Yes, Alex, *I* have experienced everything.'

'No doubt about *that*,' he said, quickly getting back on to his favourite subject. 'So what is she doing about Lennie?'

'Taking our advice and meeting with him.'

'Yeah?' he said, not looking too thrilled.

'Hey, listen, we both thought it was a good idea to talk her into it,' Venus said. 'And you're right.'

'We did?' he said quizzically.

'Okay, okay, I *know* you're dying to get into her pants, but as long as she's still lusting after Lennie, it would be a losing proposition for you *and* you know it.'

'So now we'll see,' he said.

'Yes, now we'll see,' Venus repeated.

'What do *you* think's going to happen?' he asked.

'Who knows?' Venus said. 'I mean, Lennie and Lucky, they've always had this kind of love-hate simmering relationship. Very passionate. I'm sure she likes you a lot, Alex. In fact, I know she loves you as a friend. But while Lennie is around, baby, you got no shot.'

'Yeah,' he said ruefully. 'I guess the only way I'll get rid of Lennie is if I put a contract out on him.'

'Very funny,' Venus said. 'You're starting to believe your own scripts.'

Lili joined them at the table, clutching a stack of photographs. 'We have fifteen actors coming in today,' she said, placing the photos in front of Alex. 'The first one's due shortly.'

Alex turned to Venus. 'You sure you want to read with them all?'

'Of course,' she said. 'It's important to test the chemistry. Not that I don't trust your judgement, but me reading with them makes them feel good. It's tough being an actor – there's nothing worse than rejection, something they're facing all the time. You're a director, you sit there rejecting whoever you want, but can you imagine how *they* feel? *I* know what it's like. *I* had to struggle to get where I am today.'

'Yeah, yeah,' Alex said. 'It's so friggin' tough that when they make it they turn into the asshole pricks of the world, right?'

'It's their revenge for being treated like garbage on the way up,' Venus explained.

'Okay, I get it,' Alex said, calling for the check. 'Let's get this show on the road.'

☆

Lucky left the courtroom before the lunchbreak. She was anxious to see what was going on over at the production office. She was also thinking about seeing Lennie that morning, and how nice it had been.

Steven had wanted her to stay with him in the courtroom. 'I need to talk to you about something,' he'd said.

'Not now, Steven,' she'd told him. 'I'll be back later. I promise.'

He'd nodded, not very happy about her leaving.

When she arrived at the production office, Alex was standing outside smoking a cigarette.

'What're you doing out here?' she asked, parking her Ferrari in a convenient spot.

'Waiting for you,' he said.

'Waiting for me? I thought you had a line of actors coming in?'

'I think we've found the right one. It's the guy Venus spotted on TV. He's up there now. I don't want to audition anybody else until you've seen them read the scene together.'

'He's that good?'

'*You* tell me. I might be too close to it. It seems they've got chemistry.'

'I'll be happy to look.'

'And talking of chemistry . . .'

'Yes?'

'I hear you're getting together with Lennie.'

'As a matter of fact, I saw him this morning,' she said. 'We're meeting again tonight.'

'Uh-huh.'

'Thanks for talking me into it, Alex. I know you're right.'

He took her hand. 'Lucky, you're my best friend. I never want that to change.'

'It won't, Alex.'

'The only way it could is if you weren't with Lennie, and I've explained the way I feel about *that*. Now, if you and Lennie *do* get back together, I've made a decision.'

'What decision is that?'

'I'm gonna marry Pia. She's a good girl. Never gives me any crap, is always there, smiling, happy. She's an excellent conversationalist, intelligent, smart, beautiful . . .'

'Hey, I think I should marry her myself,' Lucky said jokingly.

'Seriously, what *do* you think?'

'Seriously?' she said, not sure how she felt at all. 'Uh . . . if that's what you want, then you *should* do it. Although I always thought that getting married had something to do with being in love.'

'How long do you think love lasts?' he asked.

'When you find the right person – for ever.'

☆

Upstairs, Venus was chatting away to her new discovery, Billy Melina, twenty years old, a very young combination of Brad Pitt and Johnny Depp.

'Hi, Billy,' Lucky said, entering the room, checking him out, and immediately liking what she saw.

'Nice t' meet you, ma'am,' Billy replied, six feet two, blond and polite with it.

'Billy only got into town six months ago,' Venus explained. 'From Texas.'

'Do you mind running through the scene again with Venus?' Lucky said, taking a seat. 'I'd love to see the two of you together.'

'Sure, ma'am,' Billy said. He had the bluest eyes she'd ever seen, but she wished he'd quit with the ma'am.

Mary leaned in to Lucky. 'We found him on a cancelled series. This kid's going to be big. He has a very special quality. Even Alex thinks so.'

'Really?'

Venus winked at her. 'Okay,' she said, walking over to Billy. 'We're reading the scene that takes place by the pool. Got a feeling you're going to like it a lot.'

'Read away,' Lucky said. 'I can't wait.'

84

Ginee arrived at court on the second day dressed in an orange jumpsuit with too much cleavage, fake diamonds dripping from her ears, wrists and fingers, and leopardskin mules on her feet – the only tiny thing about her. She was accompanied by a camera crew from *Hard Copy*.

Once there, she stood on the steps outside, giving *Hard Copy* an exclusive interview, while a scattering of paparazzi took her picture. She couldn't have been happier.

Price was outraged. So were his lawyers. The three of them huddled in a corner. 'She looks like a Vegas lounge act who's seen better days,' Price complained.

'I'm instructing her not to come here any more,' Howard said. 'This is a bad joke. She's going to turn people against Teddy. She's making a spectacle of herself.'

'I'm not so sure she'll stay away,' Price said. 'She's gettin' off on the attention.'

'We won't pay her,' Howard said. 'It's as easy as that.'

'Not so easy,' Price said. 'Knowin' Ginee, she's gettin' money from the TV show.'

'You're probably right,' Howard agreed. 'Which means we're stuck with her. I'd better talk to her again today.'

'Wish you would,' Price said. 'This is too humiliatin'. People are lookin' at her thinkin', What kind of taste has *he* got?'

'I'll try to slip a couple of your wedding pictures to the tabloids,' Howard said. 'That way they can see she used to be gorgeous.'

'No,' Price said, shaking his head. 'My ego don't need that kinda stroking. I'll survive.'

He'd already decided that he would talk to her himself.

Later in the day he got the opportunity. 'Hey, Ginee,' he said, 'you're supposed t' be lookin' like a mother figure. How about gettin' it together?'

'Why should I look like a goddamn *mother* when I'm on TV?' she demanded. 'They want glamour, pizzazz. *Hard Copy* love me. Tomorrow they're having me sing!'

'You're gonna do *what*?'

'Watch it tomorrow. They're doing one whole segment on little old me!' She smiled triumphantly. 'Now we got *two* stars in the family.'

'Jesus,' he muttered. 'You're really milkin' this. Your own son is in trouble an' all you can think about is yourself.'

'Why shouldn't I?' she said belligerently. 'After you threw me out, I never had a chance.'

'I *didn't* throw you out. We couldn't live together any more, and I paid you plenty over the years. You could've done whatever you wanted t' do.'

'Get it straight, Price. This is my big opportunity, and *nobody*'s stoppin' me.'

'Have you talked to your son today? Did you call him at home last night? Tell me this, have you comforted him in any way?'

'Comforted him?' she squealed. 'I hardly even *know* him. Only don't tell that to *Hard Copy*. They think me an' Teddy are real tight. They think I'll get 'em an interview with him. An' you know what? I can get 'em to *pay* for it.'

Price shook his head in disgust. 'Give it a rest, Ginee,' he said. 'Stay home. I don't want you here.'

'Too bad, Price. Teddy is *my* son, and I'll be here every single day.'

☆

By lunchtime Mila was getting nervous. 'Has the gun been delivered yet?' she kept on asking Willard.

'You've asked me ten times,' he said. 'I've called the office. Nothing. Who is supposed to be delivering it anyway?'

'A friend of mine,' she said.

'Where did they get it?'

'That's none of your business.'

'It *is* my business, Mila,' he said patiently. 'As your attorney, you're supposed to tell me everything.'

'Why should I?' she asked suspiciously.

'Because I am here to help you.'

'And what if I don't need your help?'

'Of course you need my help,' he said, losing it. 'You're accused of murder, for Chrissakes. Did *you* shoot Mary Lou Berkeley? Or did Teddy?'

'I told you, Teddy did it, and I've got the gun to prove it.'

'Then *get* me the gun.'

'I'm trying to, only it's not so easy when you're locked up in jail.'

Willard shook his head. He didn't know whether to believe her or not. If she'd had this proof all along, why hadn't she produced it before?

God, he wished he could get a job in a decent law firm instead of defending people who had no money.

He stared over at the two high-powered attorneys employed by Price Washington. One day he would like to be just like Mason Dimaggio. Now *that* was a star.

☆

Irena hadn't told Price she was coming back to the courtroom on the second day. But, then again, he hadn't questioned her as to why she wasn't in the house when Consuella had been attacked and the house robbed. She didn't care. She just knew that she had to be in court to watch what was going on.

Fortunately, the police being at the house had not been about her, although she'd worried about it all night. What she *didn't* like was the newspapers and tabloids dragging her name up. If they started to investigate . . . if they got a sniff of the real truth . . . she would be deported for sure.

Irena Kopistani had died long ago. If they found that out . . .

She shook her head and stared at the judge, a stern-looking man with white hair and a neat goatee. What if he sentenced Mila to a long jail term? Or even worse, what if he sentenced her to *death*? It was possible.

Irena took a deep breath. She'd made a decision. She was going to tell Price the truth about his daughter. Maybe then Mila would stand a chance.

☆

Later in the day, Duke Browning slid into the back of the courtroom, having paid a member of the public for their seat.

It had occurred to him that he should get a look at Mila Kopistani. He wanted to see this person who shared Maybelline's cell. He wanted to study this girl who was threatening his precious sister.

She wasn't as pretty as Maybelline, but he had to admit she had something. Kind of a tough, sexy quality that he found quite appealing.

He decided that when and if they called her to the stand, he wanted to be there. He was keeping his eye on this one.

Little did she know that the man sitting at the back of the courtroom was preparing to help her. Later that day, he would get rid of Lennie Golden for her, the prosecution's key witness.

And when he did, and she found herself free, he expected her to be suitably grateful.

85

Carlo had not expected Isabella to come back into his life. Ah . . . Isabella. Such an exciting beauty for one so young. Twenty-two years old, with delicate features and a ballerina's body, she was his one true love. She was also the reason he'd been banished from Italy, thanks to the death of her eighty-year-old husband. Every finger had pointed towards him because the husband had died under mysterious circumstances. But nobody had any way to prove he was involved.

However, instead of Isabella bonding with Carlo after her husband's death, she'd run off with an overweight opera star.

It had infuriated Carlo beyond control. He had wanted to punish her, but there was nothing he could do. And then he'd been banished to England.

Now, suddenly, Isabella was back in his life. One phone call and he was ready to do anything she wanted, for Isabella was the only woman who had power over him.

'I'm leaving Mario,' she'd told him over the phone. 'I hear that you are married.'

'It means nothing,' he'd said.

'We have much to discuss,' she'd said. 'When can I see you?'

Since Brigette was safely tucked away in the hunting lodge, he decided he would take a few days to visit Isabella at her vacation house in Sardinia.

'Where are you going?' his mother had demanded.

'I have business to attend to,' he'd said.

'What business?'

'It's personal.'

His mother had looked at him with disgust. She was furious that he had married a foreigner. Even more furious that the American girl was pregnant with his baby.

'You have married a cheap whore,' she'd said, at the time of his marriage.

'No, Mama,' he'd replied. 'I have married one of the richest women in the world. I will get us money for this place. We will live like kings again.'

'You never do anything right,' his mother had complained. 'You might be handsome, but you're useless.'

In all of his thirty-one years he had never heard a word of praise from his mother's lips.

Without giving a second thought to how Brigette was doing all by herself in the middle of the countryside, he got on a plane and flew to Sardinia. The few days he spent with Isabella convinced him that there was no other woman in the world for him.

'Why did you leave me?' he asked.

'I was foolish. Now it is time for us to be together.'

'I have a wife,' he said.

'Divorce her,' she said.

'I have a very rich wife.'

Isabella's interest had immediately perked up. 'A rich wife. This is good, because my inheritance is not as big as I thought.'

'Well,' Carlo said, 'if we play this right, and I stay with this woman perhaps a year or so, I should be able to come away with a fortune.'

'Or she could have an unfortunate ... accident,' Isabella said. 'Like my husband ...'

'Your husband was an old man.'

'We need to be together, Carlo,' she said, encouraging him, 'but we both know we cannot be together with no money. We have expensive tastes, and neither of us cares to be without the things that make us happy.'

Isabella had a point. 'Leave it to me,' he said. 'I will work on getting a sum of money that will keep us happy for ever.'

'Do that,' Isabella said. 'Because if you don't, I'll be forced to move on.'

☆

Brigette was exhausted. It seemed as though she'd been riding the bike for hours. Perhaps making her own way out of there was a stupid idea. Carlo was right: the hunting lodge was totally isolated and now she was lost. She'd followed the dirt road as far as she could, until eventually it had ended at the edge of a thickly wooded area. Obviously, somewhere along the way, she had taken a wrong turn.

She hadn't realized how weak she was. Two hours out and she was ready to collapse. After losing the baby she'd bled non-stop for twenty-four hours. Not only had it frightened her, it had weakened her even more than the excruciating pain she'd gone through with the drug withdrawal.

She was completely lost. There were no other houses in sight, nothing but bushes and trees and the mud road she was trapped on.

She got off the bike, leaned it against a tree, and sat on the damp ground. This didn't seem possible. It was like being in the wilderness. And on top of everything else the sky was darkening and a drizzle of rain was starting to fall.

She drank some bottled water, trying to decide what to do next. Without a cellphone, or any other means of communication, she was stranded.

After a while, she got up and climbed back on the bike. There was only one thing to do, and that was to head back in the direction she'd come from.

☆

Boogie decided that maybe he should have brought the old man with him, because Lorenzo was right, the Vittis' hunting lodge was impossible to find. He'd been driving for hours before locating the turn off the main highway that would eventually lead him to the dirt road that would take him to the hunting lodge. But it seemed there were more twists and turns and more side-roads that led nowhere.

Boogie stopped the car and studied the crudely drawn map again. He was determined to find the place before nightfall. It couldn't be *that* difficult.

86

In spite of herself, Lucky was excited. She'd been having all these crazy thoughts about Lennie – divorcing him, starting a new life, maybe even getting together with Alex. But if she was truthful with herself, she knew that Lennie and she were destined to be together for ever.

She smiled to herself. Later she would meet him at the house he planned to rent for Claudia and the boy. And that was a nice thing for him to do, a temporary solution. Lennie had good principles, and at least he was having *her* look at the house, making her part of his decision. Yes, if he put Claudia and the boy in a house of their own, it would certainly make things easier. She wasn't exactly ecstatic about it, but at least she was learning to accept it.

Maybe. She'd see. It would depend on his actions. Lennie was his own man, she'd always respected that about him. He'd never let her take control. Something she found quite easy to do.

She smiled to herself again. God, she'd missed him. She hadn't realized quite how much until she was with him.

Hmm, she thought. If they could get through this, they could get through anything.

☆

It was the second day of the trial and he still hadn't been called, so Lennie was able to slip away a few minutes early.

He called Claudia from the car. 'I'm taking you to see the house I've found for you and Leonardo,' he said. 'Be down-stairs.'

He had it all planned. He would show Claudia the house, drop her back at the hotel, and return to meet Lucky. That way everybody would be happy.

He felt good about Lucky coming to see him that morning.

He knew her doing that meant she was almost ready to forgive him. Not that she had anything to forgive him for. It was something that had happened long ago now. However, he couldn't blame her for being angry and upset that Claudia had turned up with his son. It wasn't exactly an everyday occurrence.

He stopped for a burger on his way to the hotel, suddenly finding himself ravenously hungry. Penelope McKay had told him that they would probably be calling him to the witness stand tomorrow. He was looking forward to telling his story, getting it out there for public consumption. The media were completely ridiculous. It was about time the truth was heard.

When he arrived at the Chateau Marmont, Claudia and Leonardo were waiting dutifully. He ran inside and picked up the house keys from the desk.

Claudia stood beside the car. She looked like she belonged in an old-fashioned Italian movie, with her voluptuous body, flowing chestnut hair and Mediterranean complexion. She shouldn't have any trouble at all finding a man.

Leonardo was wearing his new jeans and a Batman T-shirt. He grinned at Lennie. Lennie grinned back: he was getting fond of the kid. Maybe if he could talk Lucky into it Leonardo could spend some time with them.

Claudia jumped into the car. 'I'm so excited,' she said.

'You should be,' he said. 'This house is costing me a fortune. Wait till you see it.'

He felt good because at least he was doing something for her. He would make sure she was looked after, had enough money, and found a job.

Surely that couldn't piss Lucky off?

☆

Outside the hotel, Duke sat in his car watching and waiting. He had this thing about waiting, prolonging the moment. It was like great foreplay. Never rush anything. Always see how long you can string it out.

He'd watched Lennie devour a hamburger, then followed him to the hotel, where a woman and a small boy waited outside.

As soon as Duke set eyes on the woman, he knew he had to have her.

She was the most luscious-looking piece he'd ever seen.
And she would be his. For an hour or two.
He was entitled to *some* fun.

87

'There's been a big mistake,' Mila said, her pointed face
flushed with anger.

'What mistake is that?' Maybelline answered, chewing her
hair.

'Your fucking brother didn't deliver the gun today.'

Maybelline shrugged. 'Not my fault,' she said coolly.

'What do you mean, not your fault?' Mila exploded. 'We
had an agreement, a bargain. He broke into the Washington
house, raped the maid, stole everything he could get his hands
on, and now he hasn't delivered my gun. Nor have I heard
anything about Lennie Golden yet.'

'Don't worry,' Maybelline said, still calm. 'He's taking care
of Lennie Golden tonight.'

'I hope he does. Otherwise everyone will be sorry.'

'Don't threaten me,' Maybelline snapped, her baby face
contorted with anger.

'And what about my gun?' Mila said. 'My lawyer's been
waiting for it all day. He says that if he'd had the gun before,
I wouldn't even have to be locked up like this.'

'I'll speak to Duke,' Maybelline said.

'I thought you already did.'

'Didn't know the gun was so important.'

'Are you serious?' Mila said. '*Of course* you knew.'

'You're making me sorry I ever met you,' Maybelline said.

'What does *that* mean?'

'My brother doesn't have to jump for anybody, especially
not *you*.'

'You don't get it, do you?' Mila said. 'The reason your
brother got into Price Washington's house was *because* of me.'

'If I have to hear you say that one more time,' Maybelline
said, 'I'm gonna scream. He'll hit Lennie Golden tonight. So
shut the fuck up.'

'That's all very well,' Mila griped, 'but I need my gun, too.

And if he *doesn't* hit Lennie Golden tonight, and I *don't* get my fucking gun, I'm going to the authorities.'

Maybelline stared at her. 'Do you understand who you're fucking with?' she said. 'Do you understand?'

Mila turned her back and walked over to the corner of the cell. She'd had it with this baby-faced cow. Had it with her *and* her stupid brother. If nothing happened by tomorrow, she was telling her lawyer about the break-in.

Fuck *them*! They were screwing with the wrong person. She'd fix them both.

88

By Carlo's reckoning, Brigette would be over the worst. He'd left her alone because it really was her problem, and he wanted no scandal about his wife. This way there were no witnesses, no doctors or nurses saying what a bastard he was to have gotten her hooked in the first place. Who knew what she would have told them?

Now that she was straight, he'd still have control. She was his wife, his pregnant wife at that.

He knew how to tap into Brigette and what she needed. She was the original poor little rich girl with no mother to guide her, an absentee father, and a desperation to be loved.

The truth was that he, Count Carlo Vittorio Vitti, was her saviour. He was the only man who'd been able to give her what she wanted, which was discipline.

She'd probably be mad at him when he arrived back at the hunting lodge, but so what? There was nothing she could do about it.

Now that he had Isabella again, he was a different man. He had a goal to work towards – not just getting Brigette's money, but getting enough so that he and Isabella could be together, for she was the only woman who was his match.

He often thought about their first meeting. She with her elderly husband, he with one of the more desirable women in Rome. It had been at a party. They'd had sex in the bathroom. Frantic, anonymous sex. She'd laughed, and gone back to her husband's side and kissed him on the mouth, and winked at

Carlo behind her husband's back. It was then that he'd known they were two of a kind. So when she'd asked, he'd helped her get rid of the miserable old man. And where had that got him? Exactly nowhere. Two days after the funeral, Isabella had run off with the fat opera singer.

'I only did it to take suspicion away from us,' she'd explained, 'because if people saw us together, they would have surely known it was you who killed my husband.'

'I didn't kill him,' he'd said. 'I assisted *you*.'

Isabella had laughed. 'Whatever.' She had the most seductive laugh in the world.

As soon as he arrived back in Rome, he got in his car and set off to bring Brigette home.

He had a new plan now, and that plan was to travel with her to New York and get her to transfer ten million dollars into a Swiss bank account in his name.

And if she refused . . . she'd be very sorry indeed.

☆

Brigette was getting nowhere fast. Exhausted and weak, she navigated a series of dirt roads that led nowhere except into heavily wooded areas. The rain had turned from a drizzle to a steady downpour, and she was soaked through and freezing cold. She started to despair that she was ever going to find her way back to the hunting lodge.

It occurred to her that soon it would be dark, and then what?

She began to panic, pedalling her way to nowhere. Until suddenly she careened into a tree-trunk and was propelled off the bike, hitting her head on the ground.

She lay to the side of the mud road, unconscious.

And the rain poured down.

89

Claudia ran around the house like an excited child discovering Disneyland for the first time. 'It's wonderful, Lennie,' she gasped. 'Much too grand for Leonardo and me. We can't possibly live here.'

'Yes,' he said, pleased she was so thrilled. 'I've rented it for a year. By that time you will have decided what you want to do.'

'But, Lennie, it is so big.'

'I know,' he said. 'I was thinking . . . you talked about your relatives in Sicily . . . maybe somebody could come visit, a sister or something.'

'My family, they do not talk to me,' she said sadly. 'When I had the baby I was a black sheep . . . Is that how you say it in America?'

'Yeah.' He nodded. 'But if you call your mother, somebody – the circumstances are different now, you're in America. Surely they'd want to come?'

'I don't know. Lennie, I wish *you* could live here with us.'

'I told you, Claudia,' he said seriously, 'it's impossible. I have my wife, and my own children.'

'But Leonardo *is* your son, Lennie. He was born out of love. You and I, when we were together, it was so . . . special.'

'Claudia,' he said, trying to let her down gently, 'I'm taken. I *have* the woman for me.'

'I understand, Lennie. But sometimes I dream . . .'

'You'll meet somebody else,' he said, veering away from a dangerous subject. 'You're a beautiful woman. There's plenty of guys who'd give anything to be with a woman like you.'

'You think I am beautiful, Lennie?' she asked.

He looked into her glowing face. 'Oh, c'mon, Claudia, you know you are.'

'Thank you.' She put her arms around him and gave him a little hug.

He pushed her gently away and glanced at his watch. Lucky would be here soon. It would not be cool for her to find Claudia hugging him.

Leonardo had gone straight out by the pool, and was sitting on the edge, gazing into the water.

'I hope he can swim,' Lennie said.

Claudia shook her head vigorously. 'He does not swim. Will you teach him?'

'Sure,' he said easily. 'We can all be friends. Once you get to know Lucky you'll love her, and she'll love you. And the kids – well, the kids are something else. Gino and Maria will teach Leonardo to swim in a minute. He needs to spend time with other children.'

'He can't be with other children, Lennie. Because he doesn't hear them, they tease him, call him names.'

'I talked to the doctor. He thinks there's something they can do about his hearing.'

She clasped her hands together. 'Oh, Lennie, that would be so marvellous!'

'It would, wouldn't it?' he said, hoping that everything was going to work out.

☆

Duke had parked his car on the street near the house. It was not his car, it was another stolen one. This time he'd taken a Mercedes – striving for a more classy image.

He'd followed Lennie and the woman and the child from the hotel, wondering where they were leading him. And when they'd arrived and parked in the driveway of what seemed to be an empty house with a for-lease sign outside, he couldn't have been more delighted.

This meant he could achieve both of his objectives: do away with Lennie Golden *and* satisfy himself with the woman.

Of course, if the woman saw him shoot Lennie, he'd have to get rid of her too. But Duke didn't mind. There was nothing to connect him with either of them. He would *never* be caught.

He waited five minutes before leaving the Mercedes, locking it carefully behind him. Then he walked up to the house.

The front door was slightly ajar. What was wrong with these people? Didn't anyone consider that there were bad elements in the world who were out to do them harm?

He'd instructed Maybelline *never* to let her guard down. She carried mace, a lethal hunting knife and a stun gun. He'd even taught her some karate.

He pushed open the door and walked inside, straight into a spacious hallway that led through to a huge living room overlooking an azure lap pool.

The boy was sitting outside by the pool. Duke had forgotten about the child. He stared at the boy for a moment, wondering what he should do about him. Then he decided he would face that problem when the time came.

He could hear voices coming from the back of the house.

He took out his gun.

First he would rape the girl.

Then he would kill Lennie Golden.

An audience would make it all the more fun.

90

'**I can only** stay a minute,' Lucky said, running into the production office.

'Why?' Alex asked. 'Where are you rushing off to?'

'I told you, I'm meeting Lennie.'

He nodded. 'Okay, that's good – I guess. Will you call me later?'

'Will I call you later?' she said mockingly. 'I told you, I'm meeting Lennie. Hopefully I won't be calling anyone later. Where's Venus?'

'She went home. Cooper's getting edgy, says she's spending too much time here.'

'Ah . . . she's giving Coop a taste of what it's like. He was the biggest playboy of all time.'

'Nothing wrong with that,' Alex said.

'Anyway, I just wanted to drop by and go over a few things with you,' Lucky said. 'And to tell you that I definitely approve of Billy Melina. You're right. He's fantastic.'

'Yeah, Billy's got a quality,' Alex said. 'And this is just the beginning. Once I get *my* hands on him . . .'

'Oooh, I've heard what happens when you get your hands on actors. They become nervous wrecks and end up in the psychiatric ward.'

'Yeah, but do I get a performance out of them?'

'You certainly do, Alex.'

'Now listen,' he said, 'how about a drink before you go?'

'Do you think I need one?' she asked, amused.

'Wouldn't do any harm. C'mon, spend a few minutes with me.'

'I don't want to be late. Lennie is showing me the house he's renting for the Sicilian and the kid.'

'Now there's a title for a movie – *The Sicilian and the Kid*.'

'Don't make fun of me, Alex. I'm very vulnerable right now. I'm not used to feeling like this.'

'No, you're not, are you? Lucky Santangelo, mobster's daughter. Fearless in the face of anything.'

'Will you stop? I have a good mind to sue them.'

'Yeah?'

'Why should they be allowed to say whatever they want about people?'

''Cause they know they can get away with it. It'll cost you more money and more time to sue them, so forget about it, it's yesterday's newspaper. Somebody's using it to clean up the rat shit.'

'You're right.'

'How does Gino feel about it?'

'Oh, you know Gino. It's kind of given him a higher profile amongst his friends down in Palm Springs.'

They both laughed.

'Come into my office,' Alex said. 'I'll fix you a Scotch on the rocks, set you up for the night.'

'I guess I could do with a drink.'

'How'd it go this afternoon?'

'Things are plodding along. The media is there in full force. And those two kids are sitting up there like little superstars surrounded by their lawyers. And Steven – Oh, God, I forgot to call him. He wanted to talk to me about something, and we didn't get a chance in court. Can I use your phone?' she asked, following him into his office.

Alex was not the neatest person in the world. There were scripts and CDs, tapes and books stacked everywhere. At the centre of it all was his desk, a huge sprawling dark-wood affair, also piled high with scripts.

He passed her the phone, and opened a desk drawer.

'Somewhere in here I've got a bottle of Scotch,' he muttered. 'Don't keep it out in the open because everybody drinks it.'

'What're *you* – stingy?' she said, laughing.

'Naw, don't like to tempt people.'

She quickly reached Steven's number. A woman answered. 'Jen?' she said.

'No, who's this?'

'*Lina?*' she said. Lina's thick Cockney accent was unmistakable.

'Lucky, is that you?'

'Lina. What are *you* doing at Steven's house?'

'Oh . . . I think we're supposed to be a secret.'

'*What*'s supposed to be a secret?'

'Me and Steven.'

'I'm not quite following you here. Are you telling me that you and Steven are an *item*?'

'I guess so,' Lina said, with an embarrassed giggle. 'Never thought I'd get into this 'ole domestic bit, but I'm 'ere, supportin' him through 'is time of trouble. Making 'im scrambled eggs, massaging 'is feet, an' giving him anything 'e needs.'

'Who'd believe *this*?' Lucky exclaimed. '*You* and Steven.'

'What's so 'ard to believe?'

'Well . . . I mean I didn't think Steven was planning on getting involved with anyone.'

'I'm not just anyone, am I?' Lina said cockily.

'That's true,' Lucky said. 'I guess he was going to tell me, because in court he said he wanted to talk to me about something.'

'Probably me,' Lina said. 'I'm talkable about, aren't I?'

'You certainly are. Wow! This is a shock. But I'm real happy for the two of you. In fact, it's great! Is it *serious*?'

'I moved in,' Lina stated. 'Given up me modelling gigs for a while.'

'Let's have dinner, we should celebrate. Will you tell Steven I called?'

'I'd better not. I'm sure he wants to tell you about us 'imself. 'E should be 'ome soon. Give us a buzz later.'

'I'll do that.' She put down the phone, still in a state of shock. 'Guess what?' she said to Alex, who was busy pouring her an extra large tumbler of Scotch.

'What?' he said.

'My brother has a girlfriend.'

'Your brother Steven?'

'I only have one brother, Alex, and easy on the Scotch. I hardly want to stagger in to see Lennie.'

'Good for Steven,' Alex said.

'I didn't expect it to happen so soon,' Lucky said.

'It's not that soon. And I'm telling you, a man needs a warm body beside him in bed. Especially when you're not so young and horny any more.'

'Is that why you're thinking of marrying Pia? By the way, I meant to ask you, have you mentioned this marriage thing to her?'

'I'll tell her when I'm sure you're not coming back.'

'Very romantic.'

'Who *is* Steven's new girlfriend?'

'Even more peculiar. It's Lina. You know, the supermodel?'

'Holy shit!' Alex said. 'Steven and the supermodel. He seems so . . . kind of laid-back and quiet.'

'Before he was married, Steven was a big player. He settled down when he met Mary Lou. It *is* kind of a strange duo, but Lina's really nice, and a lot of fun.'

'Maybe it's exactly what he needs right now,' Alex said, handing her the drink.

She took a couple of gulps and almost gagged.

'Wow! This is strong,' she said. 'Don't you believe in adding water and ice?'

'What do you think this is? A bar?'

She laughed. 'I appreciate the drink, Alex, but I have to go now. Let me know what happens with you and Pia.'

'No, Lucky,' he said. 'You let *me* know what happens with you and Lennie.'

'I'll speak to you tomorrow,' she said. 'What are you doing tonight?'

'Pia is cooking me dinner.'

'There, you see – she *is* the right girl for you. Not only a warm body, but she cooks, too!'

'I'll see *you* in the morning.'

'You got it, Alex.'

91

It was almost dark, and the rain was pounding down. Boogie had been listening to the radio, the newscaster was predicting a big storm. Driving carefully, he noticed car lights up ahead of him on one of the many dirt roads he'd driven down over the last hour. It looked like a Maserati with a lone male driver. He wondered if he should flag the car down and ask directions. Or maybe he should just follow behind. The driver must be heading somewhere in this wilderness, and when he arrived, that would be the time to get directions.

This seemed like the best idea, because if he flashed his lights at the guy, it was highly unlikely he'd stop in this weather.

Boogie was angry with himself. He should have paid Lorenzo to come with him, guide him, but Christ, who'd have thought the place would be this hard to find? Although Lorenzo *had* warned him.

He had a feeling he must be getting near.

Up ahead of him, the Maserati was travelling too fast for the driving rain. Boogie found it easy to keep up – he hadn't taken a course in hazardous conditions for nothing.

It occurred to him that the man driving the car must notice he was being followed. How come he didn't stop and ask what Boogie wanted? Although, since this was Italy, perhaps he thought the car behind him might be driven by a kidnapper.

Boogie hung back, allowing the Maserati to race ahead. He didn't want the guy coming at him with a gun.

Suddenly the Maserati hit something, and for a few seconds the powerful car swerved out of control. The driver didn't stop.

Boogie slowed down to see what he'd hit. Checking it out, he spotted an old bicycle lying across the dirt road.

Something told him to stop. Like Lucky, he always followed his hunches, which is probably why the two of them got along so well.

He knew that if he stopped he'd probably lose the driver up ahead, but somehow he also knew that he had to.

He pulled over, turned off his engine, armed himself with a flashlight, and got out of the car.

The bike was dilapidated and rusty: it could've been lying there for months. Or maybe not.

Boogie began kicking it to the side so he wouldn't have to ride over it. He was surprised it hadn't torn up the Maserati's tyres.

As he was moving the bike, he noticed a flash of golden hair and an arm over to the right.

Christ! There was someone on the ground.

He ran over. A woman was lying there, semi-conscious. He immediately felt her pulse. Thank God she was still alive.

He shone his flashlight on her face and was horrified to discover it was an almost unrecognizable Brigette. She was shivering and shaking, her clothes saturated with rain and mud.

He scooped her up in his arms and carried her to his car.

Her eyelids fluttered open for a moment. She was delirious. 'Where . . . am . . . I? Where's my baby? He'll be all covered in mud, and the grave will float away.'

He laid her down on the back seat of the car, stripping off her wet clothes and wrapping her in his shirt and jacket.

She was shivering uncontrollably, teeth chattering, lips and eyelids blue with cold.

'Don't worry, little Brigette,' he said, remembering her when she was a child. 'Stay with it, we're getting help.'

'I lost the baby,' she sobbed hysterically. 'I lost my baby.'

'It's okay,' he said, running around and jumping into the driver's seat bare-chested. 'We're getting you to a hospital, honey. Hang in there, it won't be long.'

☆

Carlo had noticed the car behind him, and it bothered him. What would a car be doing out here at this time of night in the pounding rain?

He had no intention of stopping to find out. He had an uneasy feeling that maybe somehow Brigette had been able to summon help, and someone was coming to get her.

If that happened . . .

He wasn't too far from the house when his Maserati hit something in the middle of the road and veered over to the other side. Fortunately this forced the car behind him to stop, and checking out his rear-view mirror, Carlo roared away. They'd never find the hunting lodge – nobody would unless they knew exactly where they were going.

A few miles on he took a sharp left turn, then two more rights, and finally he was there.

The house was in total darkness since there was no electricity. He'd left Brigette a few candles and some matches, but obviously she wasn't using them. Grabbing a flashlight from the glove box, he jumped out of the car, threw open the front door, and ran into the house.

'Brigette!' he shouted. 'Brigette – where are you?'

No answer. He hurried into the living room, the flashlight making shadows on the wall. Then he saw the dried blood all over the floor. Oh, Christ! What had happened here? Had she killed herself? Was he about to find her dead body somewhere?

He hoped not, for he was under enough suspicion as it was concerning the death of Isabella's husband. If Brigette's body was discovered at the hunting lodge, he'd be the first person at whom they'd point an accusing finger.

Quickly he set about searching the house. Upstairs. Downstairs. All around.

She was not there.

He searched again, shouting out her name.

No Brigette.

How could she escape from this place? She had no phone, no car, no means of communication. It was impossible for her to get away.

And yet . . . she was gone.

He searched one more time, and then he ran out to the Maserati.

He would find his wife. And when he did, she would be very sorry indeed.

92

Lucky pulled up at a stop light. She was on her way to see Lennie, which made her feel good. She'd enjoyed her short meeting with Alex, he was still her best friend, but she couldn't believe he'd said that if she got back with Lennie, he was marrying Pia. What was *that* all about? Was he trying to piss her off?

Too bad, Alex. It doesn't piss me off at all. I'm simply worried that you're settling for less than you deserve.

Although who was she to interfere? Maybe Pia was the right one. She'd certainly been with him longer than any of the others, so she obviously made him happy.

Hey – it wasn't Lucky's problem. Right now all she had on her mind was seeing Lennie and working things out. She called Venus on her cellphone.

'Wasn't I right?' Venus crowed, picking up on her private line.

'You were *absolutely* right,' Lucky agreed. 'Billy is great. Between you and Alex, you'll get him doing everything you both want.'

'Let's not forget *you*,' Venus said. '*You*'ll have him running around with his *dick* hanging out. We all know how you like equal nudity on the screen.'

'Quite right too,' Lucky said succinctly, remembering how when she'd taken over Panther, that had been one of her edicts. If the actress takes it off, so must the guy. Boy, there'd been some screaming about *that* one.

'Wait till Cooper gets a look at him,' Venus said. 'He'll throw a jealous fit!'

'Why are you always trying to break Cooper's balls?'

''Cause that's our shtick,' Venus explained, laughing. 'We have fun doing it.'

'So here's the latest,' Lucky said, moving away from the light, which was now green. 'It's juicy stuff.'

'What?' Venus said. 'Tell me immediately.'

'Okay, okay.' A beat. 'Steven has found himself a new girlfriend.'

'I think that's great!' Venus exclaimed. 'Is she nice?'

'Well . . . nice isn't exactly the word I'd use to describe her.'

'Is she *pretty*?'

'Staggeringly gorgeous.'

'Staggeringly gorgeous?' Venus repeated. 'Hmm . . . who is she?'

'Lina.'

'Lina? You mean *the* Lina from the fashion mags and the runway shows, and every gossip column in the world? Isn't she in bed with Charlie Dollar?'

'She sure as hell ain't in bed with him now,' Lucky said. 'She's sharing living quarters with Steven, and from what she says, they've settled into domestic bliss.'

'You've *gotta* be kidding me!' Venus said.

'*I* think it's great,' Lucky said. 'I mean, if you think about it, who's he going to find? Some little bimbo who'll be in Mary Lou's shadow for the rest of her life? Lina has it going for her. She's her own woman.'

'Good for him,' Venus said enthusiastically. 'Does Charlie know?'

'What does he care? He's engaged.'

'Yes, for seven years!'

'Anyway, I gotta go,' Lucky said, pulling up at another red light. 'I'll keep you informed, and I'll see you at lunch tomorrow.'

She caught the guy in the car next to her staring. Oh, God, she hoped he wasn't a journalist. Lately they'd been following her.

As soon as the light changed, she took a few sharp turns at high speed and soon lost him.

Then she set off up Loma Vista to the address Lennie had given her.

☆

'Good evening,' Duke said politely.

It was dusk and, since the sun was just beginning to set, he considered it a most appropriate greeting.

Claudia was exploring the bedroom when Lennie saw him. A medium height white man with a baby face. But it wasn't the face Lennie noticed first, it was the gun.

'You really should learn to lock the door behind you,' Duke said mildly, standing in the doorway. 'This *is* Los Angeles. Shit happens.'

Lennie stared at the gun and the baby-faced gunman, and every bad memory of the night with Mary Lou came back. 'Don't hurt anybody,' he said, very slowly. 'We'll do what you want, just don't hurt anybody. I've got a watch, a few hundred dollars, credit cards, and you can take my car. It's parked right outside.'

'That's what I like,' Duke said cheerfully. 'A sensible man. Now, both of you continue being sensible and take your clothes off.'

'What?' Lennie said.

'First throw your money and watch over here, and *then* remove your clothes,' Duke instructed, savouring every moment.

Claudia was petrified. She gazed at Lennie, seeking protection.

Christ! What was *he* supposed to do? This was a nightmare. The second time in months he'd had a gun in his face. Fuck! No more Mr Nice Guy Liberal. From now on he was carrying a gun at all times, and shooting back just the way Lucky would.

Oh, God, Lucky! She was going to be here soon. If she walked in on this . . . It didn't bear thinking about.

'Listen, man,' Lennie said urgently, throwing over his money, credit cards and watch. 'Take the stuff and go. We're expecting other people.'

'Really?' Duke said, like he couldn't care less. 'Are you going to do as I tell you?' he added, waving the gun in Claudia's direction. 'Or perhaps I should shoot her. What do *you* think, Mr Golden?'

'Take off your dress, Claudia,' Lennie said, in a strained voice, trying to figure out how the gunman knew his name.

She looked at him questioningly. 'What?'

'Take it off,' he repeated. 'He doesn't want us running for help, that's why.'

'Good,' Duke said expansively, as Lennie started removing his shirt. 'You understand me. Sometimes people don't. And then it can get most unfortunate.'

Tentatively Claudia began unbuttoning her dress.

'Step out of it, that's the way,' Duke said encouragingly.

Once again she looked at Lennie. He nodded. She stepped out of her dress.

'Pants off,' Duke said to Lennie.

'You've got what you came for,' Lennie said, wanting to kill him. 'It's not necessary to humiliate us this way.'

'Brave man without a gun,' Duke said. 'I have to admire that, but you'd better watch the way you speak to me because I'm in charge here. Now get your pants off, and tell her to lose her underwear.'

'Do as he says, Claudia,' Lennie said, his voice even more strained.

'But, Lennie—' she began.

'Do it!' he repeated, remembering saying the same words to Mary Lou, who'd ignored him, and look where it had got her. 'Quickly, Claudia.'

She unhooked her bra and her breasts came tumbling out.

Duke stared at them, licking his lips. 'Nice,' he said. 'Very nice. And all real, huh? You're not one of those silicone whores.' She put her hands up to cover herself. 'Now the panties,' Duke said.

'Lennie . . . I – I don't understand,' she whimpered, almost in tears. 'Why he do this to us?'

'Because I can,' Duke said. 'Now hurry up!'

She stepped out of her panties, vulnerable and exposed.

'You see that bed over there?' he said. 'I want you to take off the sheets and tear them into strips, then I want you to tie your boyfriend up. Got it?'

'Why don't you just take the goddamn money and go?' Lennie said. 'You'll get caught if you stay. People will be here any minute.'

'I'm really scared,' Duke jeered.

Claudia tore up the bed sheets, and Duke instructed her how to tie Lennie up. When she'd completed the task and Lennie was immobilized, Duke ripped the remains of the sheets and strung Lennie with his arms above him to a low ceiling beam so that he was almost suspended, although his feet just about touched the floor.

While he was doing this, Claudia made a vain attempt to attack him. He slapped her away, telling her to sit down and be quiet, or he'd kill her boyfriend.

She did as he asked, fear written all over her face.

When he was sure that Lennie was secure and could not move, he turned his attention back to Claudia. She was definitely a beauty: he planned on taking his time with this one.

He looked around, discovering a sound system built into the wall. He tuned the radio to classical music and turned the volume up loud. Then he sat in a chair and instructed Claudia to dance for him.

She was scared. He could see the fear all over her face and he liked it.

Reluctantly Claudia began to dance.

Duke watched her, soon becoming aroused. She was not skinny, she was rounded and womanly, with large breasts and long legs. He anticipated what he was going to do to her and smiled.

Lennie was watching her too. He had no choice.

'I thought you were a *married* man,' Duke said. 'Is this your piece on the side? Is she a good lay? Does she come easily? Tell me about her, 'cause I plan to fuck her later. And *you*'re going to watch.'

'You're a sick bastard,' Lennie muttered. 'A sick sick bastard.'

'Thank you,' Duke said. 'I'll take that as a compliment.'

93

Arriving at the house on Loma Vista, Lucky pulled up and parked behind Lennie's car. She was glad he was here first. They'd take a quick walk through the house, she'd give it her approval, then the two of them would go out somewhere to talk. She really needed to be with him, living apart was pointless. She knew now that they could work this out.

She got out of her car and walked over to the front door. It was locked. She tried the bell, but it didn't seem to be working, so after a few minutes she made her way around to the back.

It was almost dark, and she was startled to see the young boy out there by himself. Why was Leonardo here? She was not pleased.

As soon as he saw her, he ran up to her, trying to say something.

'Hi,' she said coolly. 'Is your mom around?'

The boy shook his head frantically, pulling at her jacket.

'What *is* it?' she said, irritated.

He began dragging her down the side of the pool towards the back of the house, where lights blazed from the bedroom and loud classical music blared. As they approached, she could see everything through the big glass windows.

She could see Claudia, naked and dancing.

'Oh, my God!' she gasped.

You bastard! Lennie Golden. This is it! I've had it with you.

Without thinking, she turned quickly to leave.

The boy hung on to her jacket, trying to drag her back, making guttural noises in his throat, pointing, desperately attempting to make himself understood.

She turned around, about to tell the stupid kid to leave her alone, when she saw Lennie, almost hanging from a beam, his arms and legs tightly bound.

And she saw the man sitting in a chair, a gun balanced on his knee.

And then she understood.

And she was scared.

And she knew what she had to do.

Grabbing the boy, gesturing for him to be silent, she pulled him along with her as they edged back the way they'd come. At the other end of the pool she pushed him into the bushes. 'Hide!' she whispered vehemently. 'Stay quiet. *Muto! Muto!*'

The boy crouched down, understanding what she was telling him to do.

Adrenalin pumping, Lucky made it to the front of the house and her car. Reaching for her cellphone, she called 911, summoning help, then reached into the glove compartment and took out her gun.

Her mind was racing, a million thoughts. Should she wait for the cops?

No. What if by waiting something happened to Lennie? She had to act now.

Fumbling in her purse she found a credit card and approached the front door. Boogie had taught her, long ago, how to break in to anywhere. Within seconds she'd sprung the lock and was inside the house, entering stealthily, although nobody could possibly have heard her because of the music blasting away.

Her heart was in her throat. This was not the kind of deal she cared to get involved in – not with three kids at home and responsibilities. But, fuck it, Lennie was in trouble, he needed her. And goddamnit, she was there.

☆

Duke was getting bored with the girl's dancing. She was clumsy, not graceful as he had hoped. His sister was graceful. Quick on her feet and light as air. He felt sorry for Maybelline, locked in a jail cell with the girl with the pointed face and mean expression. He couldn't wait for her to get out so they could do things together. And once he'd taken care of step-grandma Renee, they could move back into their house and be a real family again.

'Stop dancing,' he said to the girl. She stopped, frozen with fear. 'Go bend over that stool,' he said, pointing to a chair with no back.

This was the best part, getting them to do whatever he wanted. And today it was even better because he had a reluctant voyeur, trussed up like a Christmas turkey, forced to watch what he didn't want to see.

'For God's sake,' Lennie yelled, 'leave her alone.'

'Why?' Duke said, quite enjoying the fact that Lennie Golden wasn't scared to speak up. 'You saving her for yourself?'

'You son-of-a-bitch motherfucking coward,' Lennie shouted.

'Don't listen to your boyfriend, dear,' Duke said, unfazed. 'Bend over that chair. AND DO IT NOW!'

Claudia jumped to obey him.

'Jesus Christ!' Lennie groaned, anticipating what was to come. 'Don't do this.'

Duke stood up, unzipped his pants, and took out his erect penis. It was small, but capable of doing what he planned.

Slowly he walked towards the chair and a passive Claudia.

☆

Lucky moved like a cat along the corridor leading to the bedroom, holding her gun in front of her. The music was still blaring, blurring her concentration. Fuck it. She was going to nail this perverted bastard, whoever he was.

She reached the bedroom door, which was slightly ajar, and with one fast fluid movement, kicked it open.

Lucky saw Claudia first. Claudia was naked, bent over a stool facing the door. Duke was positioned behind her, about to mount her. Lennie was hanging helplessly by his wrists.

As if in slow motion, Duke jumped off Claudia and reached for his gun, lying on the floor beside him.

'Drop it!' Lucky commanded.

'Who? *Me?*' Duke said, up for the challenge.

'Yes, you.'

'Sorry. No can do.'

She took a long deep breath. Dealing with homicidal

maniacs was never her favourite way to spend a day. 'Do it!' she said. 'Or I'll blow your dumb brains all over this goddamn room.'

He turned his gun towards Lennie. 'If you're fast enough,' he said, his finger tightening on the trigger.

And she knew she had to shoot, because if she hesitated, all would be lost.

She let blast, and so did he.

His bullet, meant for Lennie, connected with Claudia, who threw herself in front of Lennie just as Duke fired.

Lucky's bullet penetrated Duke's heart.

He slumped to the ground, a slack smile on his baby face.

It was over.

94

It was past ten when Maybelline was called from her cell to see the warden.

'What's going on?' Mila asked, waking up.

'Dunno,' Maybelline said. She'd decided she hated Mila, they'd been arguing all night.

'Shit!' Mila muttered. 'I hope it's not about me. You'd better be careful what you say.'

Maybelline stalked off without a word. She returned twenty minutes later.

Mila could see something was wrong. 'What's the matter?' she demanded. '*Was* it about me? You didn't tell them anything, did you? 'Cause if you did, I'll fucking kill you!'

'No,' Maybelline said. 'It wasn't about you.'

'Then what was it?' Mila asked. 'They don't pull you out of your cell at night to tell you nothing.'

'It's my brother,' Maybelline said flatly. 'It's Duke.'

'What about him? Did he get Lennie Golden for me today? Is that what happened? Did he hit Lennie and get his sorry ass caught?'

Maybelline looked at her with dead eyes. 'He got killed – that's what happened.'

'Killed?' Mila said blankly. 'How could he get killed?'

'He was in a house. Lennie Golden was there. And someone shot Duke.'

'Was it the cops?'

'I feel like my heart has been ripped from my body,' Maybelline said, as if speaking to herself. 'Duke was everything good.' She turned on Mila, her expression fierce. 'If it wasn't for you, he'd never have been there.'

'Don't blame me,' Mila said.

'Ever since you came into this cell I've had nothing but trouble,' Maybelline said. 'And now you've taken away my only reason for living.'

'What did he do with my gun?'

'Your gun?' Maybelline said. 'My *brother* is dead, and you're asking about your *gun*.'

'I'm going to sleep,' Mila said. 'I have to be in court again in the morning. I have to sit there while those dumb lawyers go, "We will prove to you that Mila Kopistani planned this crime, and set out to murder Mary Lou stupid fucking Berkeley."'

'You're the dregs,' Maybelline said. 'If Duke was here now, he'd punish you for your sins.'

'I'm sorry about your brother, but he's left me in the shit. How am I going to get my gun now?'

'If Duke can't punish you, then God surely can,' Maybelline said, her voice rising. 'You are a bitch from hell. My brother is dead because of you!' And with that she reached under her bunk, and produced her one prized possession: a lethal shard of glass.

Maybelline struck out, slitting Mila's throat with one fell swoop.

Mila didn't even see it coming. She fell on to the floor of the cell with a horrifying gurgling sound.

'See how *you* like it,' Maybelline said. 'See how concerned *I* am about *you*.'

She got into her bunk and tried to sleep, while Mila bled to death on the cell floor.

☆

Price was reading the *LA Times* in the living room when Irena came in and asked if she might talk to him for a moment.

'Does it have to be now?' he said. 'I'm not feelin' great.'

'I'm sorry,' she said, 'but I must explain something to you. You see, I feel that everything that's happened over these last few months is my fault.'

Christ! He wasn't in the mood. 'Huh?' he said.

'I never treated Mila in the way she expected a mother to treat a daughter,' Irena said. 'I was always cold towards her.'

'What're you talking about?' he said, frowning.

'I resented her from the moment I gave birth,' Irena said, rambling on. 'She – she changed things for me. She came between you and me.'

'Came between us?' His eyebrows rose in surprise. 'Hey, Irena, I know we've had our moments, but I never led you on, never told you anythin' was gonna happen between us.'

'There's something I must tell you.'

'What now?' he said impatiently. The last thing he needed was true confessions from Irena.

'Well, you see, this is the way it happened—'

And just as she was about to tell him the real truth, the phone rang.

Relieved, he grabbed it. 'Yeah? Uh-huh.' He listened carefully for a few minutes. 'Oh, *shit*! Well, what's gonna happen? I – I'll tell her myself. Yeah, I will.' He put the phone down, stood up and held out his arms. 'Come here,' he said.

She walked over to him. 'What?'

He enclosed her in a tight embrace. 'I have kind of . . . shocking news.'

'What *is* it?'

'It's Mila. She was attacked by another inmate. I'm sorry to tell you this, Irena, she's . . . dead.'

EPILOGUE

Six Months Later

'**Good morning,**' Lucky said, as Lennie, accompanied by little Gino, Maria and Leonardo, came bounding up the wooden steps from the beach, all four of them wet and sandy, their faces covered in smiles.

She had breakfast laid out on the deck overlooking the ocean. Muffins, fresh fruit, yogurt, French toast and bacon. 'Who's hungry?'

'Me, please!' said Leonardo. Since the successful operation to restore his hearing, he was learning to speak at an alarming rate, picking up all kinds of expressions from little Gino and Maria.

'Then *you* can sit at the head of the table,' she said, giving him a big hug.

Leonardo and she had bonded. Totally inconsolable after the death of his mother, Lucky had been the one he'd clung to. And she had looked after him as if he was her own – which, in a way, he was, because he had Lennie's blood flowing through his veins, and that was enough to make her love him unconditionally.

They'd given Claudia a very moving and special funeral. The service was read in both English and Italian.

After the tragedy, Lucky had expected Lennie to go into another slump. But he hadn't. Instead he'd faced life with a new attitude, brushing up on his shooting skills at the firing range and taking up karate.

She applauded his way of handling it. Action gave him back his power and strength, it made him feel good about himself again.

'*I* wanna sit at the head of the table,' Maria said, pouting.

'Well, *you*'re not going to,' Lucky replied. 'Maybe tomorrow – if you're very, very, *very* good.'

'I can be that!' Maria said, with a cheeky grin.

'I thought so,' Lucky said.

Lennie came up behind her, giving her a warm, sandy hug. 'How's my wife today?' he asked.

'Your wife is fine. How's my husband?'

'All the better for seeing you,' he said, nuzzling her neck.

'Honey?' she said.

'What?'

'We have to leave at noon today, everybody dressed and ready. So don't be clinging to your computer when I say it's time to go.'

'Now would I do that?'

'Yes.'

He grinned and hugged her again. 'Noon. Washed and brushed. No problem.'

'Good. It's not every day we get to go to a wedding.'

☆

'You're wearing it!' Brigette insisted.

'I am *not*!' Lina replied.

'Oh, yes, you are.'

Lina took the frilly blue garter and tossed it in the air. It landed in a champagne bucket full of ice.

'*Ooops*, sorry,' she said guiltily. 'Can't wear it now, it's all wet.'

'So are you,' said Brigette, frowning. 'Haven't you ever heard of something borrowed, something blue?'

'Yeah, but not that skank bit of tat thankyouverymuch.'

'You're impossible!'

'That's what Steven says.'

They'd taken over a suite at the Bel Air Hotel and were having fun. The night before they'd hit the town with Kyra, Suzi and Annik, Lina's bridesmaids-to-be. It had been a double celebration. One, Lina's bachelor party. And two, she'd finally made the cover of *Sports World International* and was ecstatic. She was also happy to see Brigette in such good shape. Brigette had cut her blonde hair very short, put on weight and developed a healthy tan.

She seemed at peace with herself, and perfectly content to do nothing for a while, even though her New York agent was begging her to return to work. She'd suffered a terrifying ordeal, and she was taking her time getting over it.

For a while it had been pretty scary. She'd languished in an Italian hospital with pneumonia for almost three weeks before Lucky was allowed to bring her back to America. Boogie had arranged twenty-four-hour guards at the hospital, to make sure that Carlo did not gain access.

Count Vitti had screamed and carried on, until an Italian police official had visited him at the palace and warned him to stay away. 'Miz Santangelo has important friends,' the man said. 'For your own health, do not bother the American girl again.'

Carlo was incensed. The 'American girl' was his wife. He would bother her as much as he wanted. In fact, through his lawyers, he would bother her for ten million dollars. Only then would he go away.

It was not to be. Lucky Santangelo flew in and arranged to see him. They met for drinks in the bar of the Excelsior Hotel. He thought she had come to settle. He was arrogant, prepared to go away for nothing less than the ten million. After all, Brigette was one of the richest women in the world.

Lucky drank champagne, made innocuous small-talk, and finally laid ten crisp one-dollar bills on the table. 'Payment in full,' she said briskly.

'What?' he said, confused.

'And if you value your precious Italian cock, you will *never* attempt to contact Brigette again. The marriage will be annulled.'

He'd stared into her dangerous black eyes and known that she was telling the truth.

'Ask anyone, Carlo. I do not make idle threats.'

He didn't care to fuck with Lucky Santangelo.

He fled to Sardinia to be comforted by his one true love, Isabella.

Too late. She had married a seventy-year-old industrial billionaire and gone to live in Buenos Aires with her new husband.

Carlo was destroyed.

☆

Maybelline Browning reported to the authorities everything she knew about Mila Kopistani. She told them how Mila had boasted about shooting Mary Lou Berkeley, and how she'd tricked Teddy Washington into putting his prints on the murder weapon.

She also told them Mila had been threatening her, and that she'd been forced to kill her in self-defence. The result was that by the time she got to court she received only a ten-year sentence.

She didn't care. She had nothing to live for now that Duke was gone.

☆

Teddy Washington ended up with eighteen months' probation, which delighted his dad, whose movie had finally come through. To celebrate, Price planned a trip to the Bahamas for him and Teddy – *anything* to get away from Ginee, who was constantly turning up on TV, basking in her own personal fifteen minutes of very dubious fame.

At the last moment Price invited Irena to come along. He felt sorry for her. After all, she'd suffered a devastating loss and he could see how depressed and miserable she was.

Teddy was pissed, but so what? Price knew he could do exactly what he wanted, and right now he wanted the company of a woman who put him before anything and didn't drive him crazy.

☆

The children walked down the aisle first. Maria, Carioca and Chyna, the three girls in simple pink dresses with daisies in their hair. Then came the boys, little Gino and Leonardo, resplendent in white shirts and black velvet pants.

The assembled guests oohed and aahed in an appropriate fashion.

'Isn't Chyna the most adorable little girl in the universe?' Venus whispered to Cooper, proud as only a mother could be.

'She needs a sister or a brother,' Cooper said.

'Really?' Venus said, smiling provocatively. 'Well . . . since I'm between movies, we'll have to see what we can do about that!'

Sitting behind them, Pia said to Alex, 'Do you *like* children?'

'From afar,' he answered, glancing over at Lucky, who looked particularly sensational in a red dress. They'd had quite an experience making the movie. Lucky was a hell of a producer, and he hoped, with Lennie's blessing, they would get to work together again soon.

Pia reached for his hand. He still hadn't asked her to marry him, but he was definitely thinking about it.

Gino nudged Paige. 'Get a load of my grandchildren,' he boasted. 'Not bad, huh? A bunch of tough little Santangelos. I love it!'

Next came the bridesmaids, Annik, Kyra and Suzi, three gorgeous supermodels who had every man in the place drooling. They sashayed down the aisle in their deep pink dresses, all long legs, delectable cleavage and, for a change, demure smiles.

The maid of honour, Brigette, was right behind them. So glowingly beautiful that it brought tears to Lucky's eyes. She thought of all her goddaughter had gone through in the last year – the drugs, the miscarriage, her escape from Carlo. It was a miracle that she'd recovered in every way.

Bobby, sitting next to Lucky, his hormones raging, said, 'Wow, Mom! Brig looks *hot*!'

'Calm down, Bobby, she's family,' Lucky admonished. 'You're her uncle!'

'Don't get spaced, Mom, just *looking*. Hey—' he added cheekily, 'd'you think I'm too young for one of the bridesmaids?'

Lucky couldn't help laughing. She was going to have to watch Bobby. He was a womanizer in progress.

Lennie stood next to Steven at the front of the church. He was Steven's best man and proud of it.

Steven couldn't keep still. He was nervous and apprehensive. All the time he kept wondering if somewhere, somehow Mary Lou was watching him. And, if she was, did she approve?

Lina appeared, and a gasp went up. She was a vision in a Valentino wedding gown created especially for her, and on her head was a Harry Winston diamond tiara.

Steven stared down the aisle at his bride-to-be and had no doubt he'd made the right decision.

☆

And so Lina and Steven were married, and the assembled guests cheered, and Lennie went to find his wife and when he did, he said, 'I love you, babe. *And* I've had this amazing idea.'

'What idea?' Lucky said, thinking how much she loved him.

'Let's do it again.'

'Let's do *what* again?' she asked, putting her hand up to stroke the back of his neck.

'Have another wedding.'

And she smiled and said, 'Yes,' and knew that as long as there was life, she and Lennie would be together.

DISCOUNT OFFER

Purchase any of these four paperbacks from www.panmacmillan.com for just £4.99 each.

£1 postage and packaging costs to UK addresses, £2 for overseas.

Lady Boss   **Lucky**   **Chances**   **The Love Killers**

To buy the books with this special discount

1 visit our website, www.panmacmillan.com

2 search by author or book title

3 add to your shopping basket

4 use the discount code **JC** when you check out

Closing date is 01 April 2010.
Full terms and conditions can be found at www.panmacmillan.com.
Registration is required to purchase books from the website.
The offer is subject to availability of stock and applies to the paperback edition only.